CROWNED: A MAFIA REVERSE HAREM ROMANCE

PAGEANT, 2

LILITH VINCENT

A twisted game gone too far. A woman on the run. Three men who won't stop hunting.

The pageant has ended, but for us, the game has only just begun.

Konstantin, Elyah, and Kirill made my life a living hell during the pageant, and now I'm going to return the favor.

They want me and the secret I'm carrying, but they'll have to prove they're worthy before I let them call me their queen. It won't be easy when their pasts come back to haunt us. Pasts that are soaked in blood.

The chase is on, and this time, the prize is more precious than diamonds.

The prize is my heart.

Author's note: Crowned (Pageant, 2) is the final book in a mafia reverse harem duet. The heroes only have hearts, eyes, and dicks for the heroine. It contains dark themes, violence, and a Why Choose romance with ruthlessly possessive men. The story is potentially triggering, so please read responsibly.

CROWNED: A MAFIA REVERSE HAREM ROMANCE (PAGEANT, 2) by LILITH VINCENT

Copyright © 2022 Lilith Vincent

| All Rights Reserved |

Cover design by Untold Designs
Editing by Fox Proof Editing
Proofreading by Rumi Khan

No part of this book may be used or reproduced in any manner whatsoever without written permission from the publisher, except brief quotations for reviews. Thank you for respecting the author's work.

This book is a work of fiction. All characters, places, incidents, and dialogue are drawn from the author's imagination and are not to be construed as real. Any similarities between persons living or dead are purely coincidental.

❦ Created with Vellum

A NOTE TO READERS

If you're here, congratulations for making it through *Pageant*. That was a wild ride, and the ride continues now. There are dark themes in *Crowned*, but they're different than the ones in *Pageant*, so please read carefully.

This book contains attempted starts-with-r-and-ends-with-ape (not by the heroes) and flashbacks of child loss, child physical abuse, and suicide. It also contains scenes of a violent and sexual nature that some readers may find upsetting, disturbing, or triggering.

This is a reverse harem romance. There are group scenes with the heroine and all the heroes, and she never has to choose just one. The heroes only have hearts, eyes, and dicks for the heroine. There is no cheating or sex outside the harem.

1

Elyah

My hungry eyes scan the face of every blonde in the dive bar. It's Saturday night and the room is packed with tattooed men in ripped jeans and women wearing skin-tight dresses and eyeliner. The crowd is young, single, broke, and horny, and they don't give a damn that the carpet is threadbare and sticky and half the lightbulbs over the bar are dead.

My kind of place.

Or it was when I was Ivan Kalashnik's driver. I would sit in bars like this, moodily stripping the labels from beer bottles as my mind lingered on his beautiful young wife. Ignoring every pair of tits that were thrust hopefully in my face as I relived the precious moments I'd spent in Lilia's company that morning. Feeling that fierce ache in my chest if I managed to make my angel smile. Sometimes it would only be a matter of seconds before Ivan stomped heavily down the stairs from the master bedroom and dragged me away from her, but what glorious seconds they were. The spill of Lilia's dark gold hair down her back. The curve of her lips as she flashed me looks from beneath the lashes of her sea-green eyes. She wanted me, and that terrified her. It should have terrified me, too, because if he found us together, Ivan would have made me watch while he slit my belly open, dragged out my intestines, and fed them to the dogs.

I didn't care. No woman could compare to Lilia Aranova, and one kiss from her was worth a thousand deaths. The first time I fell in love with her, she was filled with sweetness and vulnerability. She needed me to save her from all the cruelty that life had thrown at her and hold her close against my chest. Protect her. Adore her.

The handful of days we spent with her during the pageant showed me that the idea I had of Lilia was bullshit. Lilia Aranova doesn't need me. She's not some vulnerable little flower who must be sheltered from the storms. She's a treacherous bitch who tore my *Pakhan's* dreams apart, stole from him, and humiliated three ruthless killers.

She's deceitful.

Dangerous.

She's all I fucking want.

Lilia could walk up my body in stiletto heels and hold a knife to my throat, and I'd lift my chin and bare it for her. Watching her run from me with the winner's tiara in her hands, I realized how she played us all. She showed me who she really was that night.

That was the second time I fell in love with Lilia Aranova.

I'm a lost man until I find her again. I want to put a

weapon in her hands, hold it to my heart, and tell her, "*Either kill me or let me spend every waking moment for the rest of my life begging for your forgiveness.*"

There's no chance that she'll step foot in this dive bar one state over from where she used to live with Ivan Kalashnik, but I stare into the face of every blonde woman just the same. Some perk up hopefully and smile as their gazes linger on my body, but I turn away as soon as I realize it's not her. I'm not here for them. I'm not even here for Lilia.

I'm here for blood.

A drunk man in skinny jeans blunders into my shoulder, and I slam him into the wall without looking at him. His nasal voice whines distantly as I step past him, deeper into the bar.

As I scan the room for the person I'm looking for, my focus, my frustration, and my rage combine into one blazing thought. I'm going to commit murder tonight, and my victim's screams of agony will soothe the turmoil that has savaged my days and nights ever since we left Italy.

"Nice seat. Now, fuck off." Kirill has appeared at my side and he's standing over two probably underaged boys seated in a booth. The pair take a long look at his prison tattoos, muscles, and the glittering expression in his dark eyes, and scramble to vacate their seats.

"Fuck this music," Konstantin growls through his teeth as he sinks into one of the seats. He pinches the bridge of his nose, his brows drawn together in pain as sweat shines on his forehead. Shiny scar tissue scores the left side of his face, from his cheek, through his eyebrow, across his temple, and up into his hair. Ever since the bullet sliced across his skull, loud noises and stress cause our *Pakhan* debilitating migraines.

Kirill and I exchange dark looks. We both know it's not the music that's causing his agony. Konstantin has had perpetual pains stabbing through his skull ever since Lilia Aranova dove headfirst into the waters of Lake Como five weeks ago, ruining his pageant and taking fourteen million dollars' worth of pink diamonds with her.

"You want vodka?" Kirill asks us.

Konstantin falls back against the shabby booth seat, glaring at the dark-haired man. "I want Lilia Aranova bound and gagged, sitting at my feet."

"I'll go pull her out of my ass, shall I?" Kirill mutters, getting to his feet.

I shoot him a warning look. We're all frustrated, but the last thing we need to do is turn on each other. Kirill stalks toward the bar, a string of Russian expletives swallowed up by the pounding music.

I drape an arm along the back of the booth, trying to look like someone out for a good time with my crew on a Saturday night. On the inside, I'm reliving the moment I put the noose around Lilia's neck in the judging room. Even when her life was hanging by a thread, she didn't beg or cry when I confronted her with the proof of what I was so certain she'd done.

"*I saw the photos of you sitting in the car with the federal agent. There is not a chance in hell that you are innocent.*"

"*I don't know what you're talking about. I never sat in a federal agent's car. I have never spoken to a federal agent in my life.*"

"*But I saw you!*"

"Believe me or not, but I'm not going to fight with you about it, Elyah."

She held her chin up like a queen and wouldn't even look at me. Either Lilia was lying to me, or someone else was. Just hours later, she dove off a cliff into the waters of Lake Como with Konstantin's tiara on her head.

And now? I have a suspicion about those photos. A dark, nasty suspicion.

My gaze sweeps across the crowd, filled with malevolence, until it comes to rest on Konstantin. My *Pakhan* is staring at me.

"What?" I ask.

Konstantin gives a mirthless laugh and shakes his head slowly. "The day before the pageant begun, I felt sorry for you."

I don't reply. I was in a dark place the day before the pageant, consumed with blood-soaked revenge fantasies. The same fantasies I'd been having every day since I stood in the master bedroom at Ivan Kalashnik's home and realized Lilia's things were gone.

Konstantin rubs a hand over his jaw. "I thought to myself, Elyah just needs to get his mind off things. How stupid he is, getting hung up on a woman." His eyes glitter with malice. "But she is not merely a woman, this Lilia Aranova. You tried to warn me, but I wouldn't listen. She is a fucking viper."

My jaw clenches. Everything I've said to Konstantin about Lilia being a treacherous bitch was based on a lie, and yet the things she said and did during the time we held her prisoner proves that he is right. "If she is snake, then we are the ones who made her bare her fangs."

Konstantin puts his head on one side, regarding me. "You still want her, don't you?"

I feel like I'm being torn in two directions. I want Lilia Aranova, and my *Pakhan* wants her dead. "I will know what I want after tonight."

Konstantin laughs, a short, humorless sound. His eyes are haunted, and his temper is stretched as tight as a bowstring. "Don't fucking lie to me, Elyah. That woman could slit your mother's throat right in front of you and you would fall at her feet."

Kirill returns, three glasses held between his cupped hands. He passes them out and slides into the booth, muttering, "*Vashe zdorov'ye.*"

Konstantin gazes dispassionately at his drink. A warm glass, room temperature vodka and ice. A disgusting way to serve vodka. "Is it Russian?"

Kirill slams his drink down, his eyes sparking. "In this shithole? Of course it's not fucking Russian."

"Kirill," I mutter, kicking him under the table. He's been just as moody, just as bad-tempered as Konstantin since the pageant fell apart. He snarls, he snaps, he picks fights. My body is covered in bruises from our sparring matches. I'm bigger and stronger but Kirill is fucking fast, and his rage that Lilia slipped through our fingers has him pulling no punches.

I take a swig of vodka. The three of us are a fucking mess. When we locked Lilia inside her cage, I believed that I would finally be cured of the obsession that plagued me for two years. Instead, Lilia Aranova has infected all three of us, and we think of nothing else but her.

Konstantin fishes the ice cubes and a sad piece of lemon out of his drink and tosses them onto the carpet. It's so dark that no one notices or cares. Then he knocks back the cheap vodka and grimaces. "Disgusting. I hate this fucking country."

I remember how little I thought of American food and drink when I first arrived. I craved the flavors of my motherland, but I had to make do with beer, bourbon, and fried chicken. Unless I was around at Ivan Kalashnik's house, drinking proper, ice-cold Russian vodka, and eating *borscht*, *pirozhki,* and *solyanka*, the beef and sausage stew that was my *babushka's* specialty. Lilia's was even more delicious. Everything tasted better when Lilia made it.

"You want Number Eleven?" Kirill snarls at Konstantin. "Then shut up and drink your shitty vodka."

Any other *Pakhan* would backhand one of his men for talking to him that way, but Konstantin's never expected us to behave like his underlings. He owes us his life and he treats us like equals. Besides, he knows he's being a bad-tempered shit.

My hackles rise as they always do when Kirill or Konstantin refer to Lilia as Number Eleven, but I throw back my vodka and swallow it down, along with the angry words I want to say. I have to focus.

And I'm glad that I do because someone walks through the door into the bar, and recognition slams through me. I almost jump to my feet right then, every nerve screaming at me to grab him and slaughter him right here among a hundred witnesses. I have one chance at this, and I can't fuck it up, for Lilia's sake.

I make myself take a deep breath.

And then I turn to Kirill and jerk my chin at the new arrival.

The dark-haired man turns to look and smiles a slow, malicious smile. He gets to his feet and disappears into the half-inebriated crowd.

Konstantin doesn't turn to look, but he's suddenly radiating interest and attention. Slowly, gazing at the heavy rings on his fingers, he cracks one knuckle after the next. Violence. He craves it as much as I do.

The man we're all here for makes his way toward the bar. I stand up and collect our empty glasses as if I'm going to take them back and get us another round. Out of the corner of my eye, I see the shorter, mousy-haired man with a gold chain around his neck suddenly freeze, and all the hairs stand up on the back of my neck. I take my time, pretending that I'm in relaxed conversation with Konstantin. It takes all my willpower not to reach out and grab him by the throat.

My mark turns on his heel and walks quickly toward the exit. Before he can get there, Kirill steps into his path carrying three more glasses of vodka. They collide, and Kirill snarls in annoyance as vodka spills over his hand. "Watch where you are going, *korotyshka*." Runt.

The shorter man tries to sidestep him while Kirill deliberately gets in the way, moving left and right, laughing nastily each time he "accidentally" cuts him off.

"Vasily?"

He freezes at the sound of my voice. The music and voices in the bar are loud, and he pretends not to hear me, trying twice as hard to get around Kirill, but Kirill doesn't let him.

Kirill jerks his chin at me standing by our table. "My friend is calling to you."

Vasily stares and has no choice but to turn around.

I put down the empty glasses I'm holding and spread my

arms, smiling broadly. "What the fuck are you doing here? Kirill, Konstantin, this is my friend, Vasily. I have not seen him since I left my last job."

Vasily, the lowliest of Ivan Kalashnik's men. The one who cleaned the scene after I beat a man to death on the first night I joined their crew. The one Ivan never invited to dinner. The man who told me that Lilia had been the one to betray Ivan to the feds and showed me the photos that apparently proved it.

Vasily's eyes fill with fear as he forces a smile. He waves and tries once more to head for the exit, but Kirill uses his shoulder to shove him toward our table.

I reach out and grab his hand, pulling him toward me and clapping him on the back. "My old friend. I cannot fucking believe this. You must have a drink with us."

As I grin, I study every terrified emotion flickering on his rat-like face.

Sweat has broken out on his brow. "Elyah, sorry I have to—"

Kirill puts the glasses on the table and forces Vasily into the booth. "Sit, *korotyshka*. You're being invited to drink. Do not insult our *Pakhan*. I will get a bottle and another glass." He heads for the bar once more.

I get into the booth after Vasily and trap him against the wall. Konstantin gazes with heavy-lidded eyes at Vasily and cracks another knuckle. Vasily turns even paler.

I'm the only one who's smiling. "We have got so much to catch up on. *Vashe zdorov'ye*." I hold up my glass of vodka and press another into Vasily's hand.

"*Vashe zdorov'ye*," he mutters, toasting me and automatically taking a drink.

"This man," I say to Konstantin, clenching Vasily's shoulder so hard that he winces, "saved my life."

Konstantin's expression doesn't change. "Is that so?"

Vasily gives him a weak smile. "It was nothing. A long time ago."

I scoff at that. "A long time? Barely two years. What have you been up to since that bitch betrayed us?"

Vasily relaxes a little at my words. "Oh, you know. This and that. I heard you left the country."

"*Da*. I fell in with these two." I point at Konstantin, and then at Kirill as he sits down with a full bottle of vodka and pours himself a glass. "You are drinking with the *Pakhan* of the London Vanavora Bratva, Konstantin Zhukov."

Vasily doesn't seem to know if he should be impressed or not, and I doubt he knows anything about the Bratva anywhere else in the world but here, but he nods respectfully. "I'm honored to meet you, Konstantin Zhukov."

I jerk my chin at Kirill. "Him, I was in prison with back in Russia. I served fucking years, while this asshole was in and out in a matter of months."

Kirill rolls his vodka around his mouth and then swallows. "You ever been to prison?"

Vasily shakes his head and takes another drink.

"You should smell the inside of a Russian prison. Piss, blood, and fear." He lifts his T-shirt and twists in his seat to reveal his broad, muscled back. There is a Russian palace floating in the clouds inked across his shoulders, and five towers crowned with cupolas. "Five kills on the inside." He nods at me. "Three of them I shared with Pushka. This man is a machine."

"Pushka?" Vasily asks, his eyes shining like a little boy

hearing tales of cowboys and Indians. I never shared my prison nickname with my new crew.

Kirill turns back and toasts me with his glass. "Pushka the living weapon. I still breathe because of him."

It's inked across my ribs, but I hate that nickname. I was barely human in that place, and with each kill I felt closer and closer to a feral animal. I killed because I had to, so I would survive, but I know what my fellow inmates thought of me. That I was a cold-blooded psycho.

Vasily nods eagerly, his earlier wariness evaporating as he's excited to share stories of his own with the table. "This guy. You are so fucking lucky to have this guy with you now. First night I met him, this fucker barely speaks a word of English, but he doesn't have to. He let a baseball bat do the talking." Vasily mimes swinging a bat, and laughs.

"His English seems good to me," Konstantin observes.

Vasily affects a cheesy Russian accent. *"I am Elyah. I am new driver."*

I force myself to laugh when I really want to smash my fist through his skull. This was why no one liked drinking with Vasily. One vodka and he would act like a clown. "It is better now. I have learned."

Vasily is already talking over me. "Ivan Kalashnik never appreciated Elyah. This guy is fresh from the gulags of Siberia or whatever, knew nothing about America, but he could make people do whatever Ivan wanted just by standing over them and glaring." He shakes his head and takes another drink. "But Ivan never appreciated any of us. Useless fuck."

Kirill's eyes narrow almost imperceptibly. A man who

drags his *Pakhan's* name through the mud, even a former, dead *Pakhan*, is a piece of shit.

"Anyway, what brings you all to the land of the free?" Vasily asks.

I glance at Konstantin and tap my glass with a forefinger. Pretending to hesitate, I say, "We are involved in something big. Very big."

Vasily immediately brightens. "Oh? I know these streets like the back of my hand. There's no one better than me if you need an insider. For a cut," he adds quickly.

I want to laugh. What happened to the "this and that" he's got going on? I pretend to consult my friends, exchanging silent looks with them, before turning back to Vasily and leaning closer. "I can trust you?"

Vasily leans forward as well. "Of course you can trust me."

"Then you have come along at the right time. We have hit wall, and you could unstick us."

"Of course I could," Vasily says. He seems so delighted that I wonder if he's been spinning his wheels since Ivan's death, no money and no crew.

I drain my glass and get to my feet. "Not here. Come back to Konstantin's suite and we will talk."

The four of us head out of the bar together, Kirill, Vasily, and I talking and laughing while Konstantin leads the way. Vasily always became overexcited when he was around the crew. So grateful to feel included, like a stray puppy. The man would not last five seconds in a Russian prison.

Konstantin's suite is the penthouse at a hotel several blocks away. Vasily gives a low whistle as he strolls through the door, taking in the acres of thick carpet, the white sofas, the vista of the city beyond the floor-to-ceiling windows. "Quality place. I've seen better, though."

Konstantin and I exchange looks behind Vasily's back. His expression tells me that if I'm able to confirm my suspicions tonight, he'll happily murder this idiot alongside me.

Kirill is on the room phone, ordering up drinks. A few minutes later, there's a knock at the door and a server comes into the sitting room with a bottle of Stolichnaya Elit over ice and four glasses. Premium Russian vodka. Kirill gives him a tip and tells him to go, and cracks open the bottle himself.

"Finally, a proper fucking drink," he says, passing the glasses out as we make ourselves comfortable on the sofas.

Vasily throws an arm along the cushions as he accepts his drink. "You know something else about that asshole?" he asks, turning to me. "Ivan was always leaving me out of shit. I was never invited to the house. It was always Dima and Bogdan and never us."

Vasily is enjoying his whining too much to notice that Konstantin is gazing at him like he wants to hurl him out of the floor-to-ceiling windows and watch him fall ten floors to the ground.

"I was invited to the house," I tell him, and I'm immersed in the memory of Lilia in tight dresses and gold jewelry, pouring glasses of vodka with a blank expression on her face. She must have been so lonely. So trapped between Ivan and her father. If only I'd taken her and run.

Vasily screws up his face in annoyance. "You? For fuck's sake, I'm glad that fucker's dead. He never fucking appreciated me."

"You are appreciated now, my friend," I say, toasting him with my glass and smiling.

"I always did like you best, Elyah. Did you ever hear from Ivan's wife again?"

The smile dies on my lips, but I force it back. "That bitch? If I had she would be dead."

Vasily casts me a sly look. "But you didn't always want her dead, did you?"

Kirill sits up and pours more vodka into Vasily's glass. "What do you mean?"

"I mean that Elyah was a lovesick puppy every time Lilia Kalashnik was in the room. Fuck me, what a stunner she was. Ass like a peach. Tits to make you weep. Turns out, she had it bad for Elyah, too. Can you believe it? Married to a *Pakhan* and getting her pussy wet over his driver."

My thin smile feels like it's going to shatter my face. I grip my glass while fantasizing about smashing it into Vasily's stupid grin.

Get my woman's name out of your fucking mouth.

"I can believe it," Kirill says, patting my cheek. "This asshole is too good-looking for his own good."

"Tell me about it," Vasily moans. "We used to go to this strip club and the strippers would practically be paying *him* to dance in his lap."

"All of you, shut up," I say, shaking my head like I'm embarrassed.

"It's true." Vasily turns to the other two. "Get this. I go around to Elyah's apartment one afternoon. He's half naked and all hot and flustered. Tells me he's been *sleeping*." He elbows Kirill in the chest. "Behind him on the carpet, what do I see? A red Versace handbag. The same red handbag that Lilia Kalashnik was always carrying around. I knew right then what was up, and I couldn't fucking believe it.

Elyah's lucky I'm not the sort of man to rat on him to our boss."

Silence falls around the table. Vasily is still chuckling, and he doesn't notice the chill wind that has swept through the room.

I tap my finger on my glass. "But that is not right, Vasily. That is not what you told me the day Lilia disappeared."

"Hm?" Vasily looks up at me, and his face drains of color. "I—what?"

I stare at him as he scrambles to straighten out his lies from the truth, and all the while my heart is swelling with rage. "You told me that you already knew that there was something up between me and Lilia."

There are three seconds of brutal silence before Vasily gabbles, "I mean, yes! I already knew, which was why I knocked on your door. To stop you from making a mistake. But it was just so funny seeing her purse lying on your floor for anyone to see."

"For anyone to see," I repeat. I play the memory in my mind. Answering my front door to Vasily. Him looking past me and seeing the red purse lying on the carpet. Me turning to stare at it.

I must have looked so fucking guilty.

Vasily must have come up with the whole plan in that moment. He would pin everything on the cheating wife.

Vasily puts down his vodka. "Anyway, I should get going. I forgot that I was supposed to be meeting someone."

As he gets to his feet, Kirill stands up and forces him down. "But we are about to talk business, *korotyshka*."

"Another time," Vasily stammers, but can do nothing as Kirill shoves his glass back into his hand and pours vodka into it. Kirill keeps pouring as he moves the bottle up Vasily's arm and above his head, still pouring. The vodka runs through his hair and spatters in his lap and on the couch.

"Please, I've got to go," Vasily whines.

His voice sets my teeth on edge. He thinks that if he whimpers like a wounded animal I will take pity on him. I can feel the ropes in my hands, the ones I wound around Lilia's neck. I tortured the woman I love. I nearly killed her because of this *blyat*.

"I lied. I have seen Lilia Aranova."

Kirill stops pouring vodka on Vasily's head and he blinks to clear his eyes. "You—you have?"

"I locked her in cage. I starved her. I tortured her. I hanged her with noose."

His face goes blank with shock. Then hope bleeds into his expression. "She's dead? It's what she deserved, that treacherous bitch."

A muscle tics in my jaw and the room has narrowed into a point. The *pushka* tattoo on my ribs burns for blood. I killed for my sisters. If any man hurt them, I broke all the bones in their bodies and feasted on their screams, but I'm the one who hurt Lilia. Her agony is all because of me, and all because I put my faith in the filthy rat that sits before me now instead of trusting the woman I loved.

I get up and walk slowly over to Vasily, taking off my leather jacket and then pulling my T-shirt over my head. He knows what this means. I did this the first night we met, and Ivan Kalashnik put a baseball bat in my hands.

I'm going to beat a man to death.

"No, no, no," Vasily moans, turning white.

I take the empty bottle of vodka from Kirill, smash it over

the edge of the coffee table, and hold the jagged edges to Vasily's throat. "I was not fucking my boss's wife," I seethe. "I loved my boss's wife. She loved me. She was so close to falling into my arms forever. With her husband dead, she could have been mine. I would have found out where her father took her, and I would have gone to her."

My shout echoes around the room. Neither Kirill nor Konstantin move.

"But she betrayed us, Elyah," Vasily whimpers.

What burns the most after the memory of the way I tortured Lilia is the fact that I was tricked by a sniveling little runt. This lowlife piece of shit made me believe that Lilia betrayed me.

Vasily.

Vasily made me hate her.

Vasily made me put my hands on her in anger. Threaten to kill her. *Nearly* kill her.

"Go to the fucking bathroom," I seethe.

I can't kill him here with these white sofas and all this white carpet. Vasily protests and tries to flee for the door, but Kirill twists his arm behind his back and marches him across the suite and into the bathroom. I follow and slam the door behind us.

Vasily cries like a bitch, backing away as I close in on him. "Elyah—no—the photos. Remember the photos."

Fuck those fucking photos. How he got those, by trickery or photoshopping, I don't care. I don't believe in them.

I believe in Lilia.

I brandish the broken bottle. "I am going to torture you just like I tortured Lilia. I am going to make you feel every inch of the agony I put her through. A thousand deaths are not enough for you."

The pain I put my woman through is unspeakable. I told her she was going to die and forced her to relive the darkest days of her life. I want to excise those deeds from my soul, but I can't, so I'll settle for rending Vasily's worthless flesh.

"What was I supposed to do, Elyah?" Vasily wheedles, his big, stupid puppy dog eyes making me want to rip them from his skull. "The cops found drugs on me. If I didn't give them information about Ivan, they were going to send me to prison."

"Then you should have gone to prison!" I roar. He stands in front of men who have done hard time and complains about a few years for drug possession in a low-security hotel? If he had done his time and kept his mouth shut, he would have returned to his *Pakhan* a trusted man. No matter who you are or what you've done, you take the fall. You don't bring your fucking friends down with you. The cops can't touch us if we all give them the finger and turn our backs. Men like us, we are nothing without our crews and our loyalty to each other. *Nothing.*

I grab Vasily by the throat and shove him against the wall. "I went to prison. Kirill went to prison. We shut our mouths and we did our time like men. We did not rat on our friends to save our own skins."

Kirill has stepped up to my side and he's glaring at Vasily. He hates a snitch just as much as I do.

"All right, I'll tell the truth!" Vasily screams.

I hold the broken bottle close to his face, but I wait. "What is the truth?"

Vasily takes a gulping breath. "I needed someone to seem

like the informant in case someone became suspicious of me. I didn't think anyone would hurt Lilia. Ivan loved Lilia."

That's a lie and Vasily knows it. If a *Pakhan* learned that someone sold him out, even a beloved wife, he would kill her. Ivan did not love Lilia. Ivan beat her for having a fucking miscarriage.

"Listening to this idiot snivel is making me sick," Kirill says.

I bring the bottle closer to Vasily's face. "I agree."

"Just listen to me! I told the federal agent that Lilia Kalashnik wished to inform on her husband. I sent an anonymous text message to Lilia that her father needed to speak to her urgently, but he was sending one of his men. I gave them both the same date and time. Lilia got into his car, and I took some photos. I don't think she knew she was in the car with a cop, but she seemed to realize right away that something was strange and got right out again."

Of course she would realize something was strange. Lilia is too clever to linger where there's danger, but it only took a few seconds, and the damage was done. I believed those fucking photos, an empty bedroom, and a lowlife piece of shit who would throw a woman under a bus to save his own skin.

Vasily must see the rage on my face, because he stammers, "It was just a few photos and I only showed them to you, Elyah. No one else."

As if that makes any fucking difference.

I bare my teeth at him. Kirill looms over from the other side. Vasily darts looks between us and realizes he's heading down the wrong path, thinks fast, and turns down an even worse one. "If you hurt Lilia then that's on you, Elyah.

That's not my fault. You're the one who believed what I said about her. If you turned on her that fast you didn't really love her."

The world turns a lurid shade of red. Isn't that what I tell myself every night when I wake up in the dark? My heart is too black, too twisted, to love anyone. I've killed too many men. Done too many despicable things. I'm not capable of love. Only violence.

I don't deserve to love someone as pure and good as Lilia.

I've heard that from myself over and over, but to hear it echoed back to me by this piece of shit makes my rage go nuclear. I pull back my arm and drive the broken bottle into Vasily's guts. It makes a sick, wet sound, and I yank it out and thrust it back in.

Grinding and twisting the bottle while Vasily screams in pain, I growl through my teeth, "You feel that, you piece of shit? I am going to tear your guts out and shove them down your throat. When I am finished with you, I will lay your corpse at my woman's feet so she can look into the face of the man who betrayed her."

The fantasy is so sweet—dragging Vasily's worthless body before Lilia and throwing it down as a tribute. Except I have no idea where in the fucking world Lilia is, and in my rage, that's all Vasily's fault, too.

The smaller man is beyond words. All he does is scream, and Kirill jams a face cloth into the man's mouth so I don't have to listen to him.

I go on stabbing as blood flows over my hand, and Vasily's belly turns into a pulpy mess. "You are fucking nothing. You will burn in hell for what you have done." My howl of fury ends as I thrust the jagged bottle into Vasily's throat. He makes a gurgling sound, and his eyes are wide and staring in his gray, clammy face.

Kirill and I step back, and Vasily falls in a heap onto the tiles, blood pumping from his stomach and his throat. It takes him a full minute to die, and I stand over him holding the broken bottle and breathing hard, savoring every fucking second. I wait for triumph and vindication to wash over me. I've exacted revenge for my woman by killing the man who wronged her.

Only nothing happens. No sweet sense of retribution. No absolution from the horrors that I subjected Lilia to.

It wasn't Vasily who tortured Lilia.

It was me.

I hurl the bloodied, broken bottle into the bath with a roar of pain, and it smashes into a thousand pieces.

The door opens and Konstantin casts his gaze over the blood-streaked bathroom and our blood-spattered faces and bodies. Kirill's face looks like a horror film. I can barely see the tattoos on my arms beneath all the gore.

"The hotel manager has been at the door. He reminds us to keep it down for the comfort of the other guests." Konstantin takes in Vasily's mangled corpse and the puddle of crimson that's flowing toward the drain. "So, we are sure that he was the informant and Lilia was telling the truth?"

I swipe my forearm over my bloody face, my gaze burning. "I swear it on my life. Lilia Aranova is innocent."

Thoughts are flickering behind my *Pakhan's* eyes. Dark, angry thoughts.

"We will get your diamonds back, Kostya," Kirill assures him. "She can't hide from us forever, and she can't sell pink diamonds. Not on her own, and she has no one to help her."

My insides twist at the thought of those diamonds. Konstantin doesn't forgive and forget, and if he doesn't get that tiara back, he will want Lilia dead. It doesn't matter that I'm in love with her. He will insist she pay for her crime in blood.

Konstantin braces a forearm against the doorway, still staring at Vasily's mangled corpse. Finally, he says, so low it's more to himself than to us, "She can't sell them? I wouldn't be so sure about that. After all she's done, I'll put nothing past Contestant Number Eleven. I wonder who made her this way."

Kirill and I exchange glances, but he looks as perplexed as I feel.

"Kostya?" Kirill prompts, frowning.

Our boss rouses himself and meets our eyes. "Get yourselves cleaned up and let's get rid of this corpse. I need to meet Aran Brazhensky."

2

Konstantin

It takes us two grisly hours to process Vasily's corpse. We snip his fingers off with bolt cutters, pull his teeth with pliers, and pare the tattoos from his flesh with a knife. After wrapping the body in black plastic bags, Elyah and I load it into a spare suitcase while Kirill uses the showerhead to chase every drop of blood down the bathroom drain.

The whole business is messy and bloody, but we're professionals, and there's not a visible spot of blood left anywhere in the suite when we're done. The bathroom wouldn't pass a luminol test, but as long as no detectives are called in to investigate a crime, no one will ever find out what happened here.

At four in the morning, we're all dressed in fresh suits and we're wheeling our luggage through the lobby, three foreign businessmen on our way to catch an early flight. Harder and meaner than any Americans who are staying in this hotel and too scarred and tattooed for any legitimate business, but money gives us all the respectability we need. I hand over my platinum credit card to the hotel desk clerk and he falls over himself to say that he hopes we had a pleasant stay.

The valet brings us our rental car and helps us with our luggage. When he takes Elyah's case from him, his muscles strain as he lifts it into the trunk of the car.

"What have you got in here, dead bodies?"

We all laugh, and Kirill grins as he passes him a twenty. "Only one."

"I will drive," Elyah says, and catches the keys when I throw them to him.

I sit in the back seat, the upper left part of my face throbbing. The scarred part. It used to be that I was barely aware of my injury, but ever since the pageant came undone, the scar tissue aches like a fresh wound.

As always, the moment I stop doing anything, my mind returns to Contestant Number Eleven. I see her again just as she was the first time I laid eyes on her, unconscious in the passenger seat of Kirill's black Ferrari. Pale. Helpless. Unintimidating. A woman with morals so loose that she would sneak around her husband's back with his driver and then sell him out to the cops.

How I despised her. Women like her should be dragged outside and shot in the back of the head before they can wreak chaos on your existence.

But I was magnanimous. I allowed her a few extra days of her worthless life, for Elyah's sake. He needed to understand why she had betrayed him or he would never move on. Elyah is a brutal killing machine, but at his core, he's not like Kirill or me. He's ruled by his heart, not his mind. It's not a weakness. It's Elyah's strength. He senses things that Kirill and I don't because we look with our eyes and listen with our ears and believe what they tell us. Elyah is attuned to something beyond his five senses, and I brushed aside his warnings at my peril. He saved my life eight months ago. He warned me that Lilia Aranova was as dangerous as a viper, and yet I still believed I had bested her when I had her at my feet.

Now I'm paying for my foolishness.

She's not innocent, as Elyah claims.

She's far from fucking innocent.

A woman like Lilia doesn't happen by chance. She is made, forged in brutality and pain. Was it her father who made her this way? Her mother or a sibling? Someone broke her down completely and she managed to build herself up again into something so powerful that she overwhelmed three dangerous men and turned their plans upside down.

I will burn like acid in your heart every time you think of me.

My blood boils as Lilia Aranova's memory scorches me afresh. One question has plagued me since she dove from the cliffs into the waters of Lake Como.

What made Lilia Aranova similar to me?

No.

Better than me?

The sun is coming up over the horizon and trees and houses flash by the window. My nails dig into the leather armrest as my head throbs with pain. Lilia beat me at my own game, and I don't know what I crave more. To take her in my arms and choke the life out of her or make her mine forever.

Aran Brazhensky lives in a city the next state over, and

there are hundreds of miles and many hours between us and our destination. We stop for food and Kirill and Elyah eat, but my stomach is churning. Coffee is enough for me, and it keeps my mind sharp through the pain of my oncoming migraine. I fantasize about Lilia's cool, slender fingers stroking across my brow. She's a warm weight in my lap once more, only this time, she's curled against me, and my arms are wrapped protectively around her. The feeling it evokes is so sweet that my headache ebbs away and I even manage to drift off to sleep.

"Konstantin?"

I sit up and realize that the car has stopped, and Elyah is peering through the open passenger door at me.

"We've arrived?"

"*Da*. That is the Brazhensky house." He straightens and steps back, nodding at a large, white house with columns out front.

My eyes sweep over the prominent façade as I get out of the car and do up my suit jacket. Lilia was raised in wealth and comfort, an easier start in life than if she grew up in poverty and squalor, but comfortable houses and manicured gardens don't always mean happy childhoods. I wonder what sort of man Aran Brazhensky is. If he beat his wife or terrorized his daughter. A man who thinks himself above the law can justify almost anything.

It's late in the afternoon and golden sunshine is slanting over us as we stand on the doorstep and I ring the doorbell. A housekeeper answers, and she takes one appraising look at us and recognition sparks in her wary eyes. We're like her boss, which means we could very well be enemies.

"Yes? Can I help you?"

I give her my most charming smile. "Good afternoon. We wish to speak with Aran Brazhensky. Is he at home?"

Strangers, and we're Russian. Elyah and Kirill stand on either side of me, menacing and wintry-eyed. If we were friends of her boss, he'd be expecting us. The housekeeper turns pale and tries to slam the door in our faces.

Elyah lazily sticks his foot out and jams it in the door, hands still deep in his pockets. The woman half turns to scream over her shoulder.

"Do not," Kirill orders, opening his jacket to reveal the gun holstered beneath his arm.

The housekeeper's knuckles turn white on the doorframe. "What do you want?"

"We wish to speak to Aran Brazhensky," I say again.

"He's not here." She seems to realize her mistake as she quickly adds, "But many of his men are."

"We are not here for trouble or violence." I hold out several bills between my forefinger and middle finger, but she shakes her head. A Russian would know that I'm not asking her to take a bribe. It seems I have to spell things out for this American. I nod at Kirill. "Take it, or my friend here will make sure you never walk again."

The woman takes the money and holds it gingerly between fingers.

"Where is your boss?" I ask again.

The woman swallows. "Italy."

Italy? He's in fucking Italy, the country we just left? From either side of me, I feel shock radiating from Elyah and Kirill as well.

"Where in Italy?" Elyah demands, looming closer.

She shrinks away from the much bigger man. "I don't

know. He left in a hurry. Please, I don't know anything. I can't help you."

Is he looking for Lilia? Why would Aran Brazhensky leave for Italy in a hurry if not to find his daughter?

"Where is Lilia Aranova?" Kirill demands.

"Aran's daughter? She hasn't stepped foot in this house for two..." She cuts herself off, realizing she's saying too much.

For two years. So, Lilia did come here after Ivan was killed, just as she told Elyah. According to her, she was forced to come here and then she escaped. "Does Lilia have any other family?"

"The Brazhensky family is all over this city. Go talk to them." The housekeeper grasps the front door and tries to shove it closed, but Elyah keeps his foot stubbornly jammed against it.

"What about her mother's side?" I ask.

The woman thinks for a moment. "A grandmother. That's all."

"Give me her address. Then we will leave."

The housekeeper is delighted to hand over the old woman's address and get rid of us.

Elyah stalks down the path toward the car, both of his fists clenched. When he reaches the sidewalk, he rounds on us. "He is in fucking Italy? Why is he in Italy? Lilia would not ask that man for help."

"Who else is she going to ask? You?" Kirill replies.

Elyah's response is a murderous glare. I feel my blood pressure rising at the thought of Lilia turning to any other man—even her father—for help. Some son of a bitch who can hide her away and put walls between us.

"I'll email Khaos and confirm where exactly Aran

Brazhensky is," Kirill says, pulling out his phone. Khaos is a hacker who can slip into all kinds of official databases and find secrets. At a price, of course, but he's worth his weight in gold.

"Good idea. I'll drive this time," I say to Elyah, reaching for the keys. Doing something will keep my mind off the pain boring into my skull. "Did Lilia ever mention her *babushka*?"

Elyah gets into the passenger seat and slams the door. "Never. The only family she talked about was her father."

It doesn't take long to reach the address we've been given, and we pull up on a suburban street outside a small residence. The house is old and worn, white paint peeling around the door and the light above the front step hanging askew. We're a world away from Aran Brazhensky's luxurious mansion.

When I ring the doorbell, there's a moment of silence before we hear footsteps shuffling over carpet.

The door opens, and a tiny woman with white hair and dressed in black peers up at me. We gaze wordlessly back at her as her severe, watery eyes sweep over us. This old woman is not surprised to find three hard men standing on her doorstep.

I don't bother with English and speak in Russian. "*Dobryy vecher, Babushka*. May we come in?"

She raps out, "I have nothing to do with Aran Brazhensky or the Brazhensky family. I washed my hands of them long ago. You have wasted your time coming here."

"We're not here about Aran. We're looking for your granddaughter, Lilia Aranova."

Her face flushes with anger. "Who do you work for? Aran?

Or the Kalashniks? I want nothing to do with those *ublyudki*." *Bastards*.

A smile touches my lips. "I work for my own interests, and my name is not important."

"Then neither are you."

My eyebrows creep up my forehead. No one has dared speak to me like this in ten years.

"Like grandmother, like granddaughter," Kirill mutters.

"*Dama*, please," Elyah says, using the respectful term for an older woman. "I just need to find Lilia. It is important and I will not rest until I do." His expression is filled with heartfelt desperation.

The woman stares at him for a moment, and then she shakes her head and turns away from the open door, muttering, "You're going to come in whether I invite you or not. Walk all over a poor old woman with your big, dirty feet if you must."

In the kitchen she starts to make tea, but Kirill brushes her aside and reaches for the samovar. "Sit down, *Babushka*."

For a moment she actually fights him for the box of tea leaves. Finally, Lilia's grandmother throws up her hands, shuffles over to the kitchen table, and takes a seat. She makes a grudging motion, telling us to sit down as well, and Elyah and I do as we're told.

A few minutes later, she's regarding three strange men at her kitchen table with steaming glasses of tea sat before each of us.

"Where is Lilia?" I ask.

"Why do men like you want to know where my *kroshka* is? She has had enough pain in her life already. When my Lilia was five, she lost her poor, abused mama to a terrible illness.

Her *papa* raised his hand to his little girl. A tiny, innocent child. Again and again, he beat her until he threw her away like a piece of trash."

"That piece of shit," Elyah growls.

The old woman isn't impressed by his outburst. "And you? Can you sit in her *babushka's* kitchen and swear that you never laid a hand on my Lilia?"

Elyah drops his eyes to the tablecloth. "I made a mistake."

The old woman sneers at him. "The lie that every man tells himself, and that every woman knows better than to believe. *It was a mistake. I will not do it again.*"

"I will not," Elyah insists. "I would sooner cut off my own hands."

The old woman gets to her feet, pulls a large knife from the block, and slaps it down in front of him. "Here. Get started."

Kirill grins from ear to ear, his knees spread wide as he lounges in his chair. "You are feisty for an old woman."

"And you are a scruffy young man," she bites back, poking him in the stomach with a bony forefinger. "Look at you. Slouching. Messy. Sit up straight at my table."

Kirill winces at her jab and does as he's told, rubbing his belly as he sits up.

"Lilia Aranova has got herself into trouble," I say, ignoring my tea. My scar throbs. My impatience burns. "We wish to help her out of it."

"You have helped no one but yourself in all your life," the old woman replies. "Break all my fingers. Tear out my fingernails. I will never speak a word about Lilia to men like you."

Kirill glances at me. "Now we see where Lilia gets it."

The woman smiles a little and lifts her chin, as if proud to have a mouthy, troublemaking granddaughter just like her.

I cocked my head to one side, watching her closely. "Why has Aran Brazhensky gone to Italy?"

Her wrinkled face drains of color and her hands tremble ever so slightly in her lap. "Has he? I don't know. What that *mudak* does has nothing to do with me."

A nasty smile spreads over my face. She knows exactly why Aran Brazhensky went to Italy. Five weeks have passed since the pageant ended, and I would never have dreamed that Lilia could still be there after all this time. It's the perfect place to hide from me.

"*Spacibo, dama,*" I say, getting up from the table. "That's all I wanted to know. We will leave you in peace."

Lilia's grandmother grabs my arm, panic glistening in her watery old eyes. "Why do you even want to find Lilia? Can't you leave her in peace?"

When I pull my wrist from her grasp and straighten my cuffs, she turns to Elyah, who's getting to his feet, his expression determined.

"And you?" the old woman asks. "Why can't you leave her alone?"

"Because I need her. I love her."

She gives him a scornful look and turns to Kirill with a questioning expression.

He gives her a wicked, pointed grin. "Your *kroshka* is the most fun I've ever had. Do you know how rare a woman like her is? I haven't had my fill yet."

"What will be left of her when you have?"

Kirill runs his tongue over his teeth and smirks at her. "I haven't decided."

Finally, the old woman turns to me. "Why must you hunt her down like an animal? Why can't you just leave my granddaughter alone?"

"I have unfinished business with Lilia Aranova," I tell her. "Fourteen million dollars' worth of unfinished business. I will get my money back, or I will drain every drop of blood from her body."

"We will get the diamonds back," Elyah insists. "It will not come to that."

"You won't find her," the old woman tells us. "If she has made a fool of you once, she will make a fool of you again. Lilia will slip through your fingers like sand, and you will be left with nothing. Whatever you did to Lilia, she probably deserves your diamonds."

Anger races through me as I glare down at Lilia's *babushka*, and I see Lilia herself gazing back at me. Defiant. Beautiful. Proud.

My diamonds? Lilia deserves my diamonds? They're *my* fucking diamonds. She had her victory, but I'll die before I let that woman take everything from me.

Kirill's phone buzzes and he reads the message that he's just received. "It's Khaos. Aran Brazhensky is in Trieste."

Elyah pushes his hands through his hair, exclaiming, "Are you fucking kidding me? Lilia was few hundred miles from us all along?"

Trieste. Northeastern Italy. We've traveled halfway around the world looking for Lilia while she's only taken a drive down the road.

Lilia's *babushka* suddenly looks very small and scared sitting in her chair at her worn kitchen table. I can't wait to see Lilia looking at me just like that.

Caught.

In my trap.

I lean over the kitchen table and place my hands on the wood. "I guess that means we're going back to Italy. If you talk to your *vnuchka* before we do, please give her our regards, and tell her that we will see her soon."

Quick as a snake, the old woman raises her hand and strikes me across the face. It doesn't hurt. It doesn't even sting. There's little strength in her withered limbs, but I feel Lilia's disgust behind it. Lilia's hatred for me. I close my eyes for a moment, my jaw clenching. Tense silence fills the room.

I turn back to the old woman and open my eyes. "Lilia Aranova will pay for that, too."

3

Lilia

My heartbeat thunders in my ears. All my muscles are locked tight with fear as my nerve endings scream *danger*.

The muscular, suited man contemplates me from the other side of my hotel room from beneath hard, half-lidded eyes. Though his body is relaxed back in an armchair, anger radiates from every pore, from his hands gripping the armrests to the set of his jaw. This man hates me from the top of my head right down to my toes. He loathes the air I breathe and the ground I walk on. From this moment to my last, he wishes me nothing but suffering.

Though I'm frozen to the spot, I realize my hand is cupping my belly. I was overcome with dizziness and nausea when I stood up too quickly from a café table. The dizziness turned to horror as I realized my period is four weeks late. I purchased a pregnancy test on my way home and it's burning a hole in my handbag right now. Am I carrying the child of a *Pakhan* or his cruelest enforcer who has wanted me dead for the last two years?

Maybe.

Possibly.

Oh, God, what if I am?

The man in the armchair tilts his head to the side, and one clear thought blares in my mind. He can't know I might be pregnant. It's too dangerous for the child.

I let my hand fall away, surprised at how strong the feelings are to protect my maybe-baby.

"Nothing to say to me, Lilia?"

I take a deep breath and let it out slowly. If I go to pieces now, the next thing I know, I'll be on a plane with this man's hand manacle-tight around my wrist. Fear is what he wants. I can see him hunting for it in my face, those cruel eyes narrowed. Fear is how he has always controlled me.

I take another deep breath and open my mouth to greet him. "Hello, Dad. How are you?"

Aran Brazhensky smirks at my faux-casual tone. He's not fooled even one tiny bit. His two tattooed goons stand on either side of me, ready to grab me in case I lunge for the door. One of them cracks his knuckles menacingly, malice glinting in his eyes as if he really hopes I try.

"You never call, you never write. I'm starting to think you don't love me anymore." Dad settles comfortably back in his seat, his arms along the armrests, one long leg crossed over the other. The cut of his suit is tailored and expensive and his leather shoes gleam. I'm reminded of another proud, smirking Russian man who enjoys fine suits and tormenting women. For a few seconds before my eyes focused on Dad, I thought it was Konstantin sitting in the armchair, and Elyah and Kirill were flanking me. It's not much of a relief to find that it's Dad instead. If anything, my heart sank even further. Dad kept me prisoner for years through marriage and emotional blackmail. Konstantin only managed a few days.

"Whatever gave you that impression?" I ask with a shrug, glancing toward the window. I'm four floors up and the window doesn't open. There's no way out of here except through the door behind me.

Dad's eyes flash. "Don't bother looking for an escape. You should never have run. It was only a matter of time before I found you."

"How did you find me?"

Dad affects a woman's high-pitched voice. "*Babulya, I am in Trieste.*"

I groan and close my eyes. He had *Babulya's* phone tapped. What a stupid mistake to make.

"Trieste is an interesting place for a young woman on the run. Why come here? Where have you been all this time?"

Where have I *been*. How long has he got?

To buy myself some time to think, I put my handbag down on the side table and grab a bottle of water. After a long drink, I screw the cap back on.

After my husband was killed by the feds, Dad plucked me from my life as Mrs. Lilia Kalashnik and forced me back into his home. I was reeling from the shock of losing my husband. Rumors were spreading that I had been the one to sell him out to the cops. All of Ivan's friends, family, and men were turning on me.

But surely not Elyah.

Elyah, the man who claimed to love me, who cherished me above all things. He held me in his arms as I sobbed after losing my baby. Elyah would never believe that I gave the cops one shred of help after what they had taken away from me.

I fled my father's home, and the first thing I did was go looking for him. His apartment was abandoned. My former home with Ivan stood empty and no handsome, tattooed man with ice-blue eyes and proud cheekbones stepped into the driveway and swept me into his arms. *Solnyshko, I have been waiting here night and day hoping you would return.*

Upstairs in the master bedroom, I realized he never would. Someone had smashed in the mirror on my wardrobe. He'd broken every picture of me. I could feel his rage and betrayal boiling in the empty room.

If Elyah ever saw me again, it would be to wrap his powerful hands around my throat and choke the life out of me.

So, I changed my name and slipped away.

The universe must have been holding its sides in hysterical laughter the night I crossed paths with Kirill in Milan, a dangerous, psychotic killer with the face of a beautiful devil. He hunted me down for sport and delivered me unconscious into the hands of his *Pakhan,* who was about to embark on a dark and twisted imitation of a beauty pageant. If that wasn't terrifying enough, there was my former lover, vowing to kill me as soon as I was eliminated from the competition.

I eye my father warily. Summed up like that, it sounds preposterous, but I have one of the few fathers on this earth who would actually believe the tale. He's in the Russian mafia in America. He knows how these men think, how they work, their convoluted plans and schemes. I haven't cried since I escaped the villa at Lake Como. I haven't had the energy. Maybe if he were some other Russian mafia father, I could cry all my tears of terror and heartache out on his shoulder while he promised that I was safe and that he would hunt down the men who took me prisoner and personally execute them.

But my father has never loved me or treated me like his daughter. He's only ever been interested in what I can do for him.

I shrug and play with the water bottle cap, making my tone one of nonchalance. "I was working in Milan. I wasn't sure what to do next and Trieste seemed as good a place as any to hide from you."

"You didn't call your *babulya* for days and days, and then you told her where you were. You have never done that before. Something has happened."

I keep my face carefully blank. It's not that the pageant is a shameful secret I have to keep, or that Konstantin, Elyah, and Kirill must be protected. Far fucking from it. But my father is the last person who needs to know about my trauma and vulnerabilities.

"What's different is that you're here in my hotel room, uninvited. Go back to America, Dad. I don't want anything from you and I'm not coming home."

He gives me a thin smile. "Yes, you are, Lilia. You're going to do exactly what I say."

The two muscle-bound assholes Dad brought with him close in on me.

Shit.

I need two things if I'm going to get out of this predicament. Time and money. Real money, enough to disappear so completely that Dad will never find me again.

"You and I are getting on a plane, and—"

"Wait." A plan is forming in my mind. It's risky as hell, and it might blow up in my face and leave me in an even worse position than the one I'm in right now, but it's the best idea I have. "I'm not going anywhere with you until we've discussed what my future will look like. I want to have a say in what happens to me next. Let's go have coffee and talk about it. Just the two of us. Not them." I jerk my chin at his men.

Dad taps his fingers on the armrests, regarding me in silence. "What a silly plan, Lilia. Do you really think I'm going to take you somewhere alone just so you can escape?"

"It's not a plan." Not all of it, anyway. "This is my private business, and I don't want your muscle-bound idiots listening in on what we talk about. I'm tired of everyone spreading lies and rumors about me."

"They'll keep their distance, but my men are coming with us."

"Fine, but it had better be a good distance. Shall we?" I pick up my handbag and pull it over my shoulder.

As Dad and I walk along the streets of Trieste together, his men are half a dozen steps behind us. We make our way through the sunshine, past shoppers and tourists, feeling Dad's sharp gaze on the side of my neck and knowing that he's ready to grab me at any moment if I try to run.

Just five weeks ago I was filthy, hungry, and hiding in barns, an escapee from Konstantin's crazy pageant. Now I'm walking quietly at my father's side while my stomach churns, once again a prisoner of a dominating, controlling man.

Out of the frying pan. Into the fire.

We sit at a café table very close to the one I was sitting at this morning. Dad opens his mouth, but I interrupt him and get straight to the point. "I'm not getting married again."

His lip curls as the waiter arrives at our table and he sits in hostile silence while I order espressos and glasses of water.

"You must marry. What else are you good for?"

Even after all these years, Dad's cruel barb finds its mark in my heart. "You seem to believe that I'm still yours to order around."

"Who else do you belong to you?" he asks, eyes narrowing as if searching for dirty male handprints all over my body. They're there if only he looks close enough. Three sets of them.

I lean forward as if I'm about to tell Dad a secret. "I have some surprising news for you. I belong to me."

Dad brushes that aside with a flick of his hand. When our espressos are set before us, he stirs a spoonful of sugar into his hot coffee. "What could you even manage alone? You don't know how to do anything."

"I'm working as a runway model. I'm carving out a life for myself. I won't be forced into another loveless marriage with a man of your choosing."

The gentle clinking of the spoon in his coffee cup becomes a rattle. "You will do what you're told, or your precious *babulya* will be thrown out onto the street to die in the gutter."

This is the threat that he's held over my head since I was eighteen. *Babulya's* home and the money that pays for her food and insulin all comes from my father, and he could cut her off in a heartbeat, but I shake my head. "That won't work anymore."

"Why? Do you not love your precious grandmother anymore?"

I blink, tears pricking my eyes as I remember what she told me two years ago when I escaped my father's house. It was the last time I saw her. "*Babulya* said she will step into traffic if I disobey her by walking down the aisle with another man of your choosing."

Dad's face turns mottled red with barely suppressed rage. "You're lying."

I wish I were. "*Babulya* hardened her heart to her granddaughter for years in order to trick you into handing me over to her. You think she wouldn't take her own life to keep me from marrying another man like you?"

"That vicious old bitch," he seethes.

Clever old bitch, actually. A clever woman who taught me all I know.

I pick up my espresso and take a sip. "I don't want us to fight, Dad. If it's so shameful that your daughter is out in the world all by herself, then I'll come and live at home. But I won't give up my job."

It's the right thing to say. Defiant enough to seem believable, but not so disobedient that I'm capsizing the boat.

Dad sits back and glares at me, a muscle in his jaw pulsing. "Is there a man that I don't know about?"

I burst out laughing. Genuine laughter. "I assure you that there isn't. Not one man. Not two men, or even three."

"You can have six months working at your little job, and then you will marry."

I take another sip and think about this. "You seem very

confident that any man in your circle will want to marry me after my last husband had his brains splattered all over the street because of me."

Dad slams his palm on the table, and our cups and saucers rattle. "Do not repeat those filthy lies, even as a joke. Once you are home I will be able to present my obedient daughter to the world and clear your name."

Maybe he can, or maybe he can bully enough people into taking his side, but anyone desperate enough to marry me under those circumstances would probably treat me worse than Ivan did.

"Twelve months working as a model," I counter.

"You will be twenty-one," Dad seethes, as if it's disgusting that a woman can be such an age and unmarried.

"Exactly. So old that the modeling industry will be ready to spit me out. I'll have no choice then but to take whichever bully you decide should wed me."

Tension crackles between us. A woman is daring to negotiate with the great Aran Brazhensky.

"Fine. Have your twelve months," Dad finally growls. "We will call it a mourning period, but we are flying home today."

I sigh and gaze around the square, pretending to think. "All right. But I have one more condition."

His eyes bulge. "Another condition? What is it?"

"Can I please borrow three hundred euros?"

Dad seems almost offended by such a small amount. "Why do you need three hundred euros?"

I nod at the pawnshop across the piazza. "I sold some jewelry there last week when I was running out of money. I'd like to buy it back before we leave."

Dad digs out his wallet, muttering to himself about "that

old hag" while he counts out the money and slaps it in front of me. He grabs my wrist as I take it and get to my feet. "Don't try anything stupid. Mikhail and Dmitry will be right outside the door."

I struggle in his grip for a moment and enjoyment flashes through his eyes. Finally, I wrench myself out of his grip. "I wouldn't dream of it."

Mikhail and Dmitry close in on me as I approach the pawnshop. I can feel Dad's beady eyes lasering into my back, and my skin crawls.

The man inside the shop is in his late forties and beams at me from behind a glass counter filled with second-hand watches, earrings, and chunky gold pinkie rings. I have been watching this shop and the owner for weeks. Nothing about the place seems out of the ordinary, but I have a strong suspicion that this jeweler is involved with the local Venetian mafia, which controls this northern part of Italy.

I only have a few minutes. I give the man a cursory smile and get straight to the point. "*Lei parla inglese?*"

"Of course."

"My name is Lilia Brazhensky. My father is Aran Brazhensky. He has jewels to sell. Jewels that I believe your friends will be interested in."

The man gives me an ingratiating smile. "*Signorina*, I am more than happy to do business with you. I buy any quality gold by weight for a very good price."

He thinks I'm a tourist with a few necklaces to sell. I slip a hand into my bag and find the small compartment I sewed into the lining. When I draw it out, there's a pink diamond glistening on my palm.

As soon as I place it on the counter, the man's mouth

drops open. He reaches for the stone along with his magnifying eyepiece and inspects it without a word. Every second that ticks by makes me want to shout at him to hurry up, but it's vital that I appear calm and confident.

When he finally looks up, the man's eyes are gleaming. "A diamond such as this is very rare, *signorina*."

Of course it is. Konstantin sourced only the best stones to crown his queen.

"My father understands...sorry, I didn't catch your name."

"Marco Bartoli."

"Mr. Bartoli. My father understands that you are in a unique position to find a buyer for diamonds such as these."

"There are more?" He goggles at me.

"Of course," I say with a careless shrug.

Bartoli licks his lips and glances around the empty shop, before dropping his voice, "How many diamonds?"

Cha-ching. "Sixteen."

His eyes widen. Sixteen pink diamonds. A delectable collection for anyone who appreciates good stones. "All as perfect as this one?"

"Of course, and worth fourteen million dollars. My father is in a hurry, so he'll accept six million in equivalent cryptocurrency. Will your friends be interested?"

"*Si, signorina*. I think they will be interested."

Of course they will. At this price, these diamonds are a steal. Konstantin would probably weep if he knew how I was practically giving them away.

"Papa and I are having coffee in the square, but he is not to be approached by anyone. He can't be seen with people like you." It grates on my nerves to say *Papa*, like I hold a shred of affection for the man, but I'm playing the role of a doting daughter.

Bartoli frowns. "You think you are too good for us, *Americana*?"

"*Russa*," I correct him with a smile. "My accent is one thing. My roots are another. And please don't be offended as this is nothing personal. Papa needs this done quickly and quietly without any of his Russian friends finding out about it. These are the account details, and my email address." I slide a piece of paper across the counter, upon which is written the number of a cryptocurrency account I set up two weeks ago and the email address associated with it.

"As soon as I receive a notification that the funds are in escrow, I will forward you and the buyers the name of a hotel, room number, and safe code here in Trieste. After you've examined the jewels, you will release the funds, and you'll never hear from us again." My tone is casual, almost bored, but the back of my neck is prickling. Any moment now Dad is going to send his men in here to drag me out. If he finds out about the diamonds...

I remind myself how careful I've been. No one knows where the diamonds are but me.

Bartoli gives me a doubtful look. "And my buyers are meant to take your word that there are fifteen more diamonds just like this one?"

I push the solitary pink diamond across the counter with my forefinger. "Hold on to that. Show your friends."

"You are very bold, *signorina*," he tells, me, pocketing the diamond.

What he really means is trusting. I open my mouth but hesitate. I know how Dad would play this. *How could I not trust a family man with two beautiful little girls. About two and five, aren't they? Very sweet.*

I picture Mr. Bartoli waking up in a cold sweat every night for the next month and checking on his daughters. Worrying whenever they're out of his sight for even a moment.

I give him a smile. "I'm not bold. I've done my research. This deal benefits both us and your buyers. And it benefits you, *signor*. Enjoy your finder's fee."

Reminding him that he will receive a tasty cut of six million dollars seems to settle things. "I will contact my buyers about the diamonds."

"*Grazie.*" I take a quick look around at the display cases, and then hand over the euros that Dad gave me. "I'll take the locket. Don't bother with a box."

With a baffled expression, Mr. Bartoli unlocks the display case and hands over an old-fashioned gold locket, a piece that's about as far from a sleek pink diamond as you could possibly imagine.

I stroll back across the square with the locket in my hand and I'm doing it up around my neck as I take my seat opposite Dad, who's scowling at the length of time I took.

"The jeweler tried to screw me, but I wasn't having it," I explain, settling the necklace carefully into place. "Let's order some food."

I'm already signaling for a waiter, my heart doing somersaults in my chest.

As we eat pasta in silence, I notice several dangerous-looking men in suits enter the square and consult with each other in low voices as they stare at me and Dad. One of them is on his phone and he shows the screen to his companions. I imagine it's images of Dad on the steps of various courthouses as he's yet again found not guilty or the charges are dropped. They're verifying that he really is Aran Brazhensky, a *Pakhan* in the Bratva.

One of the men steps forward to approach us, and I nearly drop my pasta in my lap, but another man grabs him and shakes his head, and they all walk out of the square.

I breathe a silent sigh of relief. Step one of my escape plan, tick.

The next steps, though? My stomach is in knots when we finish our meal and I get to my feet. All I have to do now is accomplish the tasks of secretly selling Konstantin's diamonds, escaping Dad, and hiding from my captors for the rest of my life.

And take a pregnancy test.

When can I take the pregnancy test?

Back in my hotel room, Dad turns to me, buttoning up his suit jacket. "All right. Pack your things. You are returning with me to America, we are going to clear your name. I have information that it was one of Ivan Kalashnik's men who was informing on him to the feds."

Dad goes on ranting about what he'd like to do to people who accuse his flesh and blood of working with the feds. He turns to the mirror and starts fixing his tie. "It's always worth having a dirty cop on your side in our business. It should be easy enough to find the real rat. You're lucky you have me."

That's taking things way too far. I throw my handbag on the bed and sink into a chair. "Lucky? Every time some muscle-bound Russian asshole hopped up on testosterone comes anywhere near me, my life crashes and burns once again."

Dad catches my gaze in the mirror. "Who are you talking about?"

"I'm talking about all of you," I seethe. "You, Ivan, your friends, anyone you might want me to marry. I wish you would all just leave me alone."

"Boss, look at this."

One of Dad's men has picked up my handbag and started going through it. He throws Dad a small white box, who catches it and turns it over in his hands.

I sit up and clutch the arms of the chair. "How dare you go through my things."

"Lilia. What is this?"

I stand up and snatch the pregnancy test out of his hands. "I bought it by mistake. It's nothing."

Dad's eyes bulge and a vein throbs in his temple. There's so much hatred and disgust in his face as he stares at me. Even more than the day I had my first period all over his white carpet and he threw me out of his home and life for seven years.

"Are you pregnant?" he spits.

A scared little girl's voice cries in the back of my mind, *No, Dad, please don't be angry. I didn't do anything wrong. I didn't mean it.*

As if I had any choice but to have sex with Konstantin and Elyah, but Dad wouldn't understand that. I grab my handbag, shove the test back into it, and stand up straight. "That's none of your business."

Nothing ratchets Dad's temper up faster than open defiance. "You're pregnant? I'm supposed to get you married, and you're carrying some other man's bastard?"

"I don't know. I haven't taken the test yet."

Dad points at the bathroom door. "Do it. Now."

Fear makes my belly swoop. What if I'm not ready to know yet? This isn't how I imagined becoming a mother. I thought I'd have a roof over our heads and a husband to protect us, but there's just me and my horrible circumstances.

I shake my head and clutch my handbag strap tighter. "I will take the test when I'm ready."

Dad is clenching and unclenching his fists in a way that tells me he's dangerously close to hitting me, pregnant or not. "Take that test, or I will tie you to a chair until you piss yourself."

Angry tears gather in my eyes as his men advance on me. One of them grabs a chair while the other pulls a length of fine rope out of his pocket. They put their hands on my shoulders and force me into the chair.

I hold up my hands. "Wait."

A vision comes to me of a tiny baby swaddled in a white blanket and cradled in muscular, tattooed arms. The handsome face that gazes down at the child with love is Elyah's, and my stomach twists. Then the picture changes and it's Konstantin's arms holding the bundle, and his normally malicious eyes are soft. Silver rings glint on Konstantin's fingers as he cradles the baby's head in his large hand. He leans down to press a gentle kiss to the baby's brow and a tiny hand splays against his scarred cheek.

I take a shuddering breath. What a ridiculous fantasy.

"Fine. I'll take the test."

Dad flings the bathroom door open. "Get in there."

I dig the test out of my purse, and to my horror, Dad follows me into the small room. "What the hell are you doing?"

His expression is granite as he folds his arms. "I'm watching you piss on it. I don't trust you to not to just run it under the faucet."

My mouth falls open. "Are you crazy? No, you're not."

"Mikhail, Dmitry!" Dad shouts, not breaking eye contact with me.

Before his goons can crowd into the bathroom and get their disgusting hands all over me, I slam the door in their faces. Cheeks burning with humiliation and fury, I reach under my dress to pull my underwear down and sit on the toilet.

Several minutes pass while Dad and I glare at each other. I can't relax. I can't pee.

"Hurry up," Dad growls.

"I'm trying," I reply through gritted teeth. I want this over even more than he does. I close my eyes and think of rushing rivers. Waterfalls. The sound of rain dripping off a roof.

Just as I'm about to give up and try drinking a gallon of water, my muscles relax, and I can finally pee. A moment later, I brandish the test in the air where Dad can see it, and he grunts and leaves the room, slamming the bathroom door behind him.

"Come out when you have the results," he calls through the wood.

I lay the test on the sink and wash my shaking hands. In a few minutes, I'll know whether my life as I know it is over. I'm broke, desperate, and there's nowhere to run. If I can't escape Dad, I'll end up back in his house waiting for Konstantin to appear and tear me apart. Dad might think he's strong, but he can't protect me from a man like Konstantin.

As my heel bounces nervously on the tiles, an even worse

thought occurs to me. Dad takes me home, Konstantin appears, and the two of them decide that the solution to both their problems is to force me to marry him.

I push my fingers through my hair and moan. Married to Konstantin? That would be even worse than being married to Ivan. My husband could torture me whenever he felt like it and use our child to force me to do whatever he asks. He'll let Elyah and Kirill screw me and torment me, and when he's finally bored with me, he'll slit my throat.

I open my eyes to try and dispel the horrible images that are dancing through my mind, and my eyes land on my worst nightmare.

Two lines.

Pregnant.

I clamp my hand over a sob that rises up my throat and sink down onto the bathroom mat. Tears run over my fingers. I had to fight for my freedom with my bare hands, but it hasn't been enough. I'm trapped all over again, and now I've trapped a child with me.

I grapple on the vanity for the test and hold it up before my eyes, hoping I saw it wrong the first time, but I didn't. There won't be any tender moments of Konstantin or Elyah cradling this baby. There'll only be terror, pain, and sorrow.

There's a sharp rap on the door and Dad calls, "Well? What does it say?"

That my life is over. Really and truly over. I can't protect this child. I can't even keep myself safe.

I stand up, open the door, and show him the test. "I'm pregnant."

Dad stares at me in shock. He takes the test from me and stares at it while he turns a mottled shade of red.

"Who is the father?" he roars, throwing the test onto the carpet and cursing in Russian.

I shake my head, and realize he thinks I'm refusing to tell him. "I don't know."

"You don't *know*? You disgusting woman. How many weeks?"

"Five."

"We'll take care of it back in America. Come on."

He grabs my wrist and pulls me toward the door, but I resist him. "What do you mean, take care of it?"

"Get rid of it, of course."

Get rid of my baby.

Kill my baby.

I yank my wrist from his grasp. "You want me to get an abortion?"

"Of course get an abortion. You can't even name the father and you want to bring this brat into the world? What happened to your precious career? What about my plans to clear your name and find you a husband? No man will want you if you keep this child."

My hands splay over my belly. I can't predict what's going to happen next. This child could live a life of fear and suffering at the hands of a father who is far crueler than my own. That man could be Elyah, Konstantin, or another man of Dad's choosing.

I can't feel anything beneath the flesh of my flat stomach, but I know that this baby is in there, snug and protected. Fierce protectiveness flares through me, and I know I would sooner throw myself off a cliff again than hurt this child. If Dad, Konstantin, or Elyah try to take it from me, I will fight them until there's no strength left in my limbs.

This is my baby, not theirs.

Get rid of it? As terrified as I am, that's not going to happen.

Dad reaches for me again, but I pull away. "Go to hell. You're not deciding the fate of another person like they're an inconvenience to be dealt with."

"You've made an unholy fucking mess of your life, Lilia. I'll decide what's right from now on. Now, get downstairs and get into the car. We're going to the airport and taking the next flight back to the States. As soon as we land, I'm taking you to a doctor and we're getting rid of this brat."

My blood turns cold hearing him talk about an unborn baby in such callous terms. "This is your grandchild you're talking about."

"This is not my grandchild! My grandchildren are the sons and daughters that you will bear with your husband, not some foul little offspring of a nobody. I could've already been a grandfather if you hadn't been a careless and selfish bitch like always. Ivan told me how you lost his baby. The one thing you're good for and you couldn't even do that right."

It's one thing to hear the nasty voices in your own mind tell you that you're damaged goods. It's another to hear their words blasted in your face by your own father.

I'm hit suddenly by a powerful recollection of the longing in Elyah's face when I offered to let him touch my belly when I was carrying Ivan's child. I could be carrying Elyah's baby right now and it would fill him with agony and rage to know that another man was ordering me to kill it. My hand cupping my belly feels like his hand, large and warm, his caress filled with love. I can picture his lips curving and his eyes brightening as he touches me.

He'd smile like that even if it wasn't his baby. As long as I was his, that would be enough for Elyah.

Tears fill my eyes and I quickly blink them away. How long would he be gentle before he turned violent again? I can't trust Elyah, and I'm not going to let this pregnancy soften my heart to a dangerous murderer.

"I'll get on the plane, but you're not treating this child like you treated me. This is my baby."

Dad sneers. "This...*impostor* is the whelp of some Italian peasant. I can't think of it as a child, and I won't."

My heart beats in a panicked rhythm and my breathing comes faster. I have to calm down because this can't be good for the baby. I had a miscarriage once before because of stress.

Dad watches me in frosty silence as I turn to my suitcase and start packing the few personal effects I've purchased the past five weeks. Open and constant defiance is going to ratchet up his temper and make him turn violent. *Babulya* taught me all I need to know about dealing with men like him. Pretend to be obedient and wait for your chance.

Play the long game.

When my clothes, shoes, shampoo, and toothbrush are packed away, one of Dad's men takes my bag from me and marches toward the door. Dad takes hold of my upper arm, and we follow, the final man bringing up the rear.

After checking out, we get into the waiting car outside and take off through the city. My thoughts are consumed with my baby. What if this is my only chance to be a mother? What if something happens to me? To them?

A jet is refueling on the tarmac when we reach the small, private airport. As we step on board the luxury plane, a smiling flight attendant greets us, offering a tray of champagne and orange juice.

Dad forces me into a plush leather chair and sits down opposite me, nostrils flaring and watching me like a hawk for any sign that I might be about to run. His attention is snared by the gold locket I bought in the jeweler's to excuse why I spent so long in the shop.

"That's your mother's locket. You sold your mother's locket?"

I stare at him in surprise. He remembers that Mom gave me a locket? I actually lost the real necklace when my school bully threw it down the drain. I never got the locket back, though I doubt Dad remembers seeing as he spent that night shouting at me and hitting me for getting blood all over his white carpet.

I clasp my hand around the locket and hold on tight. "Only temporarily. I was always going to buy it back."

Dad nods absentmindedly and looks away to where Mikhail and Dmitry are boarding the plane. In the cockpit, the pilot is adjusting switches.

"How long until we're in the air?" Dad calls.

"We're cleared for takeoff, Mr. Brazhensky," comes the pilot's reply. "Once you're settled in and the aircraft is secure, we'll be on our way."

I shake my head when the flight attendant tries to offer me a drink, and Dad waves her away angrily.

"Just shut the fucking door and let's get going."

"Of course, Mr. Brazhensky."

Outside, a brisk male voice calls, "This is airport security. There's been a problem with your documents, Mr. Brazhensky. Will you please step outside for a moment?"

Dad glances at his men and jerks his head at the door. "Go and tell them that there's no problem with my documents."

Mikhail and Dmitry get to their feet and head down the steps, muscled shoulders bunching with menace. Dad and I sit in silence with nothing to look at but each other. I realize with a thread of apprehension that he's staring at my necklace again, eyes narrowed with puzzlement.

"Didn't you lose that locket years ago?"

Any moment now, Dad's going to realize that the story I told him doesn't add up. If I've lied about what I was doing in the jeweler's he's going to insist on knowing why. One phone call to the jeweler or a threat to punch me in the stomach until I miscarry, and the whole story about the diamonds is going to come out.

He can't find out. Those diamonds are my only chance for freedom.

"*Babulya* helped me get it back," I tell him, but my voice shakes.

"You're lying to me, Lilia," Dad says through his teeth. "Why are you lying to me?"

"It wouldn't be the first time. All Lilia Aranova does is tell lies."

Dad and I both look up at the sound of the strange voice, sleek and accented with notes of black velvet. There's no sign of Mikhail and Dmitry. Three men have stepped into the aircraft. Tall, strong men with hard eyes and tattoos.

At the front of the pack is a man in a gray suit that matches the color of his eyes. A proud smile just touches his lips as he gazes at me. His crisp white shirt is open at the neck to reveal the edges of the tattoos on his chest; tattoos I've never seen despite the fact that we've had sex.

On his left is a man with high cheekbones and cold blue eyes, his fair hair pushed back from his face and his muscular shoulders taut beneath a tight black T-shirt. Ink decorates his throat, arms, and fingers. Prison tattoos. Words and symbols that document his brutal life. The moment he lays eyes on me, he seems to stop breathing.

On his right stands a lean, muscular figure with dark hair, menace and mischief dancing like twin flames within his even darker eyes. He jams his thumbs into the waistband of his black jeans, his expression almost flirtatious as he tilts his head in greeting, black curls falling across his forehead.

All three men are watching me, their hungry eyes filled with delight and victory. Konstantin, Elyah, and Kirill. Men who took me prisoner along with fifteen other women. Men who tortured and tormented me. Men who swore to murder me at the end of a twisted week.

Dad unbuckles his seat belt and tries to get to his feet, but Elyah pulls out a gun, and Kirill produces his telescoping baton, extending it with a vicious downward flick and pushing Dad back into his seat.

"Who the fuck do you think you all are? Get off my plane," Dad growls. "Mikhail, Dmitry!"

Everyone ignores him. Mikhail and Dmitry are either out cold or dead.

Elyah's gaze runs over me, and when he seems satisfied that I'm safe and in one piece, he walks confidently into the cockpit and jabs the barrel of a gun into the pilot's neck. In his deep, clipped Russian accent, he intones, "In the air. Now."

The pilot gabbles in panic, turning in his seat to cast a desperate look at Dad, but Dad's too busy glaring at Konstantin to give a damn about anyone else.

Whistling like he's having the most wonderful day, Kirill grabs the shaking and whimpering flight attendant, marches her down the aisle, and locks her in a bathroom. Then he strides back to the front of the jet, pulls up the steps, and expertly closes the door like he's done this a hundred times before. Seeming to notice that I'm staring at him, he glances over his shoulder, pins me with a heated look, and winks.

A shiver goes through me, and I quickly look away.

Elyah cuts off the pilot's protests by grabbing a fist of the man's hair and giving him a shake. "Get this plane in the air or I will blow your fucking brains out." He speaks in a deep, unflustered monotone as if he's doing nothing more remarkable than ordering a latte.

The pilot grabs for the controls, and a moment later, the engines roar as we start down the runway. He suggests timidly, "Everyone should be seated for takeoff."

Elyah makes himself comfortable in the doorway, leaning one big shoulder against the frame with the gun still pressed against the pilot's neck. "I will be fine," he replies, staring directly at me.

I can't fathom the expression in his eyes. Fury? Hatred? It's only when the plane lifts off and his mouth curves up at the corners that I realize what he's feeling.

Elyah Morozov is hijacking a plane, but he barely notices because he's so fucking happy to see me.

Konstantin takes the seat across the aisle from mine and lounges comfortably in the cream leather, a smile playing around his lips. "How wonderful to see you again, Lilia."

I regard him in cold silence. He can't fool me. I saw the victory blazing in his eyes as he stepped aboard the jet. The real Konstantin runs hot, not cold.

"Stop pretending, Konstantin. We both know this cool, detached attitude isn't the real you."

Konstantin arches his scarred eyebrow. "Own up to who I really am? You first, *milaya*."

"Oh, you met her. The real me looks beautiful in diamonds, don't you think?" I say with a smile.

Anger burns in his eyes. There's the man I know.

"I think some introductions are in order," I say lightly. "Konstantin, this is my father, Aran Brazhensky, a *Pakhan* in the American Bratva. Dad, Konstantin is in the Russian mafia, too. I'm sorry, I don't know what his last name is and where he conducts his illegal activities, but I'm sure you have a lot in common. These are his right-hand men. Enforcers, bootlickers, whatever you want to call them. Their names are Elyah and Kirill. Fun fact, Elyah used to work for Ivan."

Dad glares from one man to the next, and then his accusing eyes swing back to me and land on the locket resting on my T-shirt. "I knew that thing was a lie."

I frown down at the necklace, confused why Dad's distracted by a piece of old jewelry when his plane is being hijacked. "Sorry?"

"You lost your mother's locket down a drain when you were eleven. I know what you were really doing in the jeweler's. Calling these men to rescue you, you vicious little bitch."

Konstantin's eyes narrow. "Lilia was in a jeweler's?"

My stomach clenches. It's been less than five minutes and Dad is already spilling my secrets to my enemies. Any second now he's going to tell them I'm pregnant.

"Like you don't know," Dad growls at the other man.

The plane turns and gains speed, and the engines roar as we hurtle down the runway. The wheels lift off and we soar into the air, the ground falling away beneath us.

At the front of the plane, Elyah says to the pilot, "If you use that radio to call for help, I will take you apart while you are still alive, along with that woman we locked in the bathroom, and you will both be carried off this plane in pieces. *Da?*"

The pilot, now pale and sweating, nods vigorously.

"Good." Elyah turns to me, tucking his gun into the back of his jeans, the coldness in his expression melting into tenderness. "Are you all right, *solnyshko*? Did anyone hurt you?"

Solnyshko. Like I'm his precious sunshine again, as I was on the floor of the judging room when he held me in his arms. I angle my chin up. "I'm great. As you can see, even the rope burn around my neck has faded."

He has the decency to look ashamed.

I turn back to Konstantin. "I was in a jeweler's because I was repurchasing some pawned jewelry. Nothing valuable. Only sentimental value. Dad gave me the euros himself." I turn to Dad. "This is Mom's locket. *Babulya* and I called the local council and they got it back for me. You'd know that if you hadn't thrown me out of your life."

Dad glances at my stomach. "Was it one of these men who—"

Oh, hell no. I speak over him as fast as I can. "I have some diamonds, Dad. Konstantin says I stole them, but I earned them, every last gemstone. They're rightfully mine."

A vein throbs in Konstantin's forehead and his expression

turns murderous. "They're not your diamonds, Lilia. Where are you hiding them?"

I tap my chin, pretending to think. "Oh, um—go fuck yourself."

Kirill grins down at me from where he's standing next to Konstantin's chair. He has his arms folded and his bicep muscles bulge beneath his T-shirt. "Sounds like our favorite girl needs some persuading."

Konstantin seems to agree. "Take her into the back of the plane. Search her, and don't bother being gentle."

4

Kirill

Lilia Aranova glares at me as I move down the plane toward her. How I've dreamed about this moment nonstop for five fucking weeks. A beautiful woman totally at my mercy, and one as clever and unpredictable as Lilia? I'm obsessed.

I reach out for her, pull her to her feet and into my arms. With her jaw in my hand, I lick slowly up her cheek, tasting the woman I've beat off to every night and morning since she escaped.

My tongue moves against the roof of my mouth as I savor her. "Mmm. I've missed you, *detka*." *Baby girl.*

"I bet you say that to all the girls," she says, jerking her head away from me.

"No. Just you. Will you be my *detka*?" I put my lips against her ear and whisper, "Until I flay your flesh from your bones and you bleed out at my feet."

Her sea-green eyes are filled with hatred. "If you carry on threatening me, I'll have to kill you when I escape this time instead of just humiliating you."

A laugh rises up my throat, and I wrap my arms even tighter around this slender, beautiful woman. One of my hands slides up the nape of her neck and my fingers plunge into her silky hair. As I tuck her into my shoulder, my head bows to breathe her in. Her hair smells like flowers and I inhale deeply. "Fuck, I missed you, you treacherous bitch. How many fingers do you want in your pussy when I check to see whether you stashed the diamonds up there? Pageant winner's choice."

"She didn't win the pageant," Konstantin interjects. "She ruined it."

"She won my pageant," I murmur, stroking her silky tresses. Lilia wriggles in my arms like an angry kitten, and I have to pin both of her hands behind her back with one of mine. "We searched for you all night. Konstantin swum laps of the lake. Elyah and I crossed the water back and forth, hunting for you in the darkness. You vanished into nothing. Where did you go?"

I watched Lilia like a hawk the entire pageant, delighting in the way she danced on the end of Konstantin's line. None of the other women could match her nerve, her beauty, her defiance. I was disappointed when Konstantin broke her. She had been made of steel but suddenly she was glass, shattered at his feet.

Or so we all thought.

I'm the trickster, yet I realized nothing when she took her

passport from Kostya and stole the key to her cage from Elyah. Then she disappeared into the night.

My favorite toy, suddenly gone.

Her short, angry breaths fan my neck. Her heart beats wildly against my chest. I have her back, and I'm not letting Lilia Aranova go.

I want to fuck her.

I want to kill her.

I don't know which I want first. I dip my head and run my tongue along her lower lip. There's a short, frustrated groan from the other side of the plane. With her arms pinned behind her back, her breasts are squashed against my chest and her neck is arched and bared to me. Elyah's eyes are fastened on Lilia's mouth, and his body is taut with desire and jealousy that I've kissed her before he got the chance.

It wasn't a kiss. It was a taste. I suck my lower lip and pull it through my teeth, grinning at my friend. "Honey sweet. Just how you like her."

She was his to kill, and then they fucked on the floor of the judging room and exchanged their bullshit *I love you*s. He has to know that she didn't mean a word of what she said. In his own words, this woman is a viper.

Elyah moves toward us, but I pull Lilia closer to me and step away from him. "Ah-ah-ah. It's not your turn."

"This is not game," he snarls.

Not a game? Then why is this so fun? It's even better now because instead of fifteen terrified women, I have Lilia's father as my audience. So far, Brazhensky hasn't made a move to help his daughter, but surely he'll come to his daughter's aid if I torment her hard enough.

Her golden tresses are curved against her cheek, and I

stroke them back with a forefinger. "We have hours and hours. Let's all fuck her in front of her daddy. I bet he's dying to watch." I toss a wink at Aran Brazhensky, who's turning an angry shade of purple. "He can even join in if he wants."

"You sick asshole," Lilia says. "I don't have the diamonds with me. Search my bag. Search me if you have to, but you're not going to find anything."

Konstantin crosses one leg over the other. "Kirill will do whatever he wants if he takes you to the back of the plane. No one will be there to stop him. If you want to sit back down in that chair, safe and sound next to your father, tell me where the diamonds are. We'll land, fetch the diamonds, and then the two of you can go back to America."

Like hell he'll let her go. Konstantin hasn't searched feverishly for Lilia just to put her on a plane and send her home.

Lilia gazes up at me. "I'm more than a match for one pervert, remember?"

I laugh and nip her neck with my teeth. "I was hoping you'd say that. Let's go."

With her arms still pinned behind her back, I spin her around and push her toward the back of the plane. There's a doorway to a bedroom and I shove her through it, slamming it behind me.

Lilia falls face forward onto the bed and puts out her hands to catch herself before whirling around to face me. Her glorious golden hair flies around her, and her hands clench on the bedclothes. She's trying to hide it, but she's afraid of me.

I advance on her slowly and reach out to cup her jaw. "We can do this the easy way, or the hard way. Please, let's do it the hard way. I've always wanted to hate-fuck on a private jet. Where are the diamonds?"

"Does it make you angry that I fooled you all and destroyed your boss's pageant? I bet your dicks shrivel up every time you think about me."

I grab a fistful of her hair and yank her face up to mine. "I love that my dick is on your mind. Did you stash the diamonds somewhere? Sell them?"

"They're hidden. You'll just have to murder me like you did the Lugovskayas. Those were good people you killed."

My insides convulse at the shock of hearing their names. The world turns red before my eyes. I grab Lilia by the throat, lift her up, and shove her against the wall. "Good people? You think they were good fucking people?"

I've known hatred in my life, but that word isn't strong enough for the all-consuming fury that burns through me every time I think about the Lugovskayas.

Lilia's eyes bulge as she struggles to breathe, and she scrabbles at my hand with her nails.

"I forgot you knew those pieces of fucking scum. Did you want to cry over their corpses after I killed them? I wish I could kill them every day in new ways for the rest of fucking eternity."

I realize she's trying to speak and loosen my grip.

"What did they do to you?" she gasps, dragging air into her lungs.

I slam my fist into the wall by her head and roar, "They took everything from me."

Lilia flinches. "What everything?"

The only thing that ever mattered to me or ever will. Now I just survive. Just fuck. Eat. Sleep. Protect Kostya.

"You think I'm going to spill my guts to a bitch like you? They're dead, and that's all you need to know. Now my life is Kostya. My life is Elyah. And my life is making yours hell. Spread your fucking legs."

I reach beneath her dress, grab hold of her underwear, and pull. She's wearing a thong and it rends in my hands and falls to the ground in tatters. When I push my knee between hers, she goes for my eyes with her nails. I only just turn my face away in time. Then she tries to punch my balls, but I jerk my hips away.

She wants to fight dirty? I can fight dirty.

I pull off my belt and wrench her arms behind her back, binding them tight. With my body crowding hers against the wall, she's not going anywhere. The dress she's wearing is flimsy enough for me to rip it apart with my bare hands. The buttons pop open, and I stare down at her.

No bra. Her tits are perfect, curved and soft with dark pink nipples. I've seen them plenty of times by now but my mouth still waters at the sight. I spit on my middle and ring fingers, staring her right in the eyes.

"Last chance, *detka*. Or I'm going to have to get mean."

She looks down at herself and then up at me, her cheeks turning pink. "Be my guest."

I drag wet fingers down her breasts, over her belly to her cunt, and then shove them into her pussy. I meant it to punish, but as her hot flesh grips my fingers I groan and bow my head.

Don't fuck her. It's what she wants.

And yet I draw them out and slam them into her again, quick thrusts of my fingers that have my cock aching to replace them. She squirms in my grip, her cheeks flaming red and her mouth opening in a moan. Holy shit. She's enjoying this.

Lilia bites her lip and drags it through her teeth. "Nothing you can do to me will make me tell you where those diamonds are hidden. I hate you all too much to give you the satisfaction."

I lean closer to her until my lips are whispering against hers. "And I loathe you too much to give you quick a death. I promise you that killing you will never be a waste of my time."

I don't want her to come. She doesn't fucking deserve it. But as her eyes grow hazy, a mischievous smile curves her lips.

"Moan louder. I need them all to hear you." I want Kostya's envy. Elyah's burning jealousy and twisted longing to see his friends fuck his woman. I want her father to hear his daughter panting for me before she screams for mercy.

"You're supposed to be torturing the diamonds out of me, not making me come. You have your orders from your *Pakhan*, you trained dog."

Lilia is dying to piss me off. I pull my fingers out of her and smack her pussy, and she cries out. I thrust back into her, deeper this time. I can't help myself from bearing down on her G-spot.

"Come on my fingers, you twisted bitch."

Three breathy words fall from her lips as her head falls back. "Fuck you, Kirill."

Wetness surges around my fingers and her muscles ripple against me. I groan and bury my face in her neck. I need to be closer to her. I need fucking everything from her.

I wrap an arm around her waist and pull her tight against

my cock. My hips rock into her, mimicking thrusts as I sink my teeth into her shoulder. I want her so bad I could burst in my jeans. My jaw tightens in frustration as she screams in pain. Yes, oh fuck yes. I release her flesh from my teeth, move over an inch, and bite her again. Another whimper of pain.

"I need to fuck you, *detka*," I groan against her throat. It's been too long since I hammered her with my cock and saw her pussy glistening with my cum. She doesn't remember that moment, but I do. It's all I've been able to think about.

"If you screw me, I'll be guaranteed to escape. Don't you remember what happened when your friends thought they could use my body?"

I remember that she climaxed on their dicks while I was left on the fucking sidelines.

I grasp the nape of my T-shirt and pull it up over my head. Lilia's attention drops to my muscled chest. My flat stomach. The tattoos decorating my flesh. The swollen bulge pressing against my zipper.

I savor the way her eyes dilate at the sight of me. Maybe there are benefits in fucking a conscious woman, after all. I grasp her arm and turn her around, my teeth sinking into my lower lip at the sight of her plump little ass.

"Are you mad at Daddy?" I whisper into her ear.

"I hate him more than I hate you," she pants, her cheek pressed against the wall.

That won't do. I'll have to step it up a notch. "Then make sure you moan nice and loud as I screw you. Living well is the best revenge. People believe that bullshit, don't they?"

With a flick of my fingers, I undo my jeans, reach inside, and wrap my hand around my cock. "Five weeks of jerking off to the thought of you choking on my dick. That's a lot of cum

I've wasted on my sheets when it should have been on your face."

I kick her feet apart, tug her hips back against me, and the head of my cock finds her slippery core. With one thrust, I'm home. She cries out at the shock of my intrusion, the most delicious thing I've ever heard. Who knew a woman could sound so hot?

As I pull my hips back and drive up into her again, she closes her eyes and utters my name like a curse. I fuck her slowly, and there's barely any room to move with her body clasped so tightly in my arms. I have the whole bed to spread her out and fuck her on, but I can't make myself let go of her.

My lips whisper up the side of her neck. "Your pussy is slippery as fuck for my cock. I bet your clit is…" I reach for her, and smile against her skin as I find what I'm looking for. Her tight bundle of nerves is swollen to the touch, one stroke of my finger has her moaning even louder.

I find her ear with my mouth. "And I thought the way you came on Elyah's gun as I fucked you with it was messed up. The harder I push you, the wetter this pussy gets."

As I talk, I rub her with my fingers and her breathing grows heavier. She's desperate to cry out, but she keeps biting back her moans. If she wants to come—and Lilia wants to come—I'm going to hear her scream. Everyone on this plane is going to know what we're doing in here.

I pull out and shove her face-first onto the bed. "Ass up. Now."

Lilia lays on her belly, twisting her hands in my leather belt that's holding them behind her back. She wants to be fucked, and I plan on screwing her. "You want to come? Get that ass up and let me shove my cock hard and deep into that needy pussy."

"Kirill—" she begins, furious and flustered at the same time.

Lilia gathers her legs beneath her and gets on her knees, her cheek still pressed against the mattress. She even arches her back so her wet slit is bared to me. The physical expression of *please fuck me.*

My mouth falls open. This is a fucking trick.

Isn't it?

I look toward the door, and then back at her. She can't unlock anything and escape when we're thirty-five thousand feet in the air.

While I'm still hesitating, Lilia says, "I don't think my dad is mad enough yet, do you?"

I can't take my eyes off her glorious pussy, offered up on a platter. She's a Venus flytrap and I'm falling into her snare. I grasp the root of my cock and sink into her.

I groan, holding tight to her hips as I start to thrust. Deep, greedy thrusts. It shouldn't feel this amazing. But it does. Holy hell, it does.

Suddenly, the door is wrenched open, and Konstantin stands framed in the doorway. He takes in Lilia naked and ass up on the bed, her knees spread and back arched, behaving like the slut she is.

My rhythm doesn't stutter as I catch my boss's glare.

"The diamonds, Kirill," he reminds me.

"Well, they're not in her pussy." I'm checking fucking thoroughly.

I loosen the knot binding her wrists and pull the belt off.

"Rub your clit for me, *detka*. Give Kostya a good look at how his precious Number Eleven loves to be fucked."

Lilia reaches between her thighs and swirls her fingers on her clit. She moans, and the expression of ecstasy doubles on her face. She watches Kostya, lips parted, and her cheek pressed into the blankets.

Kostya keeps a straight face but his nostrils flare. He's dying to rip his clothes off and join us on this bed. "Isn't she too conscious for your tastes?"

"Horny and angry is just as much fun. Who knew?"

My *Pakhan* watches me screw Lilia for a few more moments. Over his shoulder, Elyah can see us, and I hope Brazhensky can, too. Kostya slams the door closed and leaves us alone.

I pull out of Lilia and flip her over onto her back, and she gazes up at me, panting and flushed. She hasn't come yet and neither have I. My gaze roams from her mouth to her tits to her pussy, wondering where I should blow my load.

But there's no contest. I grasp her hips and yank her down the bed toward me. Poised to sink into her, I take hold of my cock and growl through my teeth, "I nearly fucking lost it when Kostya nutted in you, and then Elyah. I thought for sure you'd make them pull out, but you're a greedy bitch. I bet you were panting for their cum."

Lilia's face is flushed, and she stares at my dick and then up at me. My mouth hooks into a smile. If only she knew that we've been here before.

"Watch," I order her. As soon as she lowers her eyes to my length, I push it slowly inside her. I take my time, fucking her with steady thrusts while my thumb swirls on her clit. I could get addicted to the expressions of pleasure flitting over her face. She bites her lip. Then her brows draw together and upward. For a moment she smiles. *Fuck.*

"Your pussy is so ripe I could breed you right now. You want my baby, *detka*?"

"You want me pregnant?" she replies in a strangled voice.

I slip my hand around her throat and squeeze, and her eyes fly open. How can I not when she looks so pretty like this? Just a little squeeze to make the blood rush to her head and make her come even harder for me. I admire my tattooed fingers around her delicate neck, squeezing and releasing. Playing with her until she's not certain whether she's going to come or die.

"Try and run from us with your belly full of my child. You won't be able to."

Lilia's eyes flash. "You think you'd own me if I were pregnant?"

I slide my hand around the nape of her neck and lift her head so she's staring at my cock plunging into her. "I own you now. You're mine until you're dead."

Lilia's eyes are glued to the sight. Her moans grow to a fever pitch, and then her whole body arches with her orgasm and she cries out, loud enough for Elyah to hear, Kostya to hear, Daddy to hear, the pilot to hear, the woman locked in the damn bathroom to hear.

Her rippling inner muscles clamp down on me and she sends me to fucking heaven. I pound her even harder, getting as deep as I can. I've fantasized about killing her a million times, but the thought of getting her pregnant is even hotter.

I drag my cock out of her, see how I'm shining with cum, and shove myself back into her. This is a trap even more dangerous than she is, but fuck, I want it anyway.

When I lift my gaze from her perfect pussy, Lila has pushed herself up on her elbows and she's glaring at me like I didn't just make her come so hard she saw past the universe.

"Lay back, *detka*. I'm not wasting a drop."

Her eyes widen as I pull out of her, only to slide two fingers deep into her pussy, needing to feel how coated she is. Groaning, I pump my fingers deeper into her. "You stay here, and I'll send in Kostya and Elyah for their turns. Between the three of us, we'll have you pregnant in no time."

I want the child to be mine, but it really doesn't matter who the father is because I'm never leaving Kostya and Elyah. As long as Lilia is pregnant and tied to the three of us, I'll have everything that I want.

"Their turns? Get the hell off me." Lilia shoves me away and gathers up her clothing, red-faced with anger and sex. Her dress is torn but she pulls it on anyway and ties it in a knot over her breasts to keep it closed.

Head held high, she opens the door and walks back down the plane to the others while I'm still pulling my jeans up. I follow her at a saunter, a lazy grin on my face as I tug my T-shirt back into place. Brazhensky is snorting like a bull and staring at my prison tattoos. In our world, I'm scum to him. Far too lowly to get my hands on a woman like Lilia. Kostya would be suitable as a husband, but Elyah and I aren't fit to be her bodyguards.

As he meets my gaze with his furious one, I smirk. "Your daughter just loves prison dick."

Lilia sits down and stares straight ahead.

"This is the way you have been behaving since you left my house?" Brazhensky seethes at his daughter. "Like a bitch in heat? Have you no shame?"

She finger-combs her long hair, neatening it back into place. "You always thought I was a whore. At least I have fun this way."

Brazhensky is spitting now. "Fun? Spreading your legs for this nobody?"

Lilia arches one brow and points to me. "This man? Just this man? No, Dad. I've fucked them all."

"If your mother knew she'd given birth to a slut she would have drowned you in the bath."

That wipes the smile off Lilia's face. Elyah steps forward, grabs the front of Brazhensky's shirt, and sinks his fist into the man's jaw.

Aran Brazhensky's head snaps to one side and he moans in pain, clutching his face. As soon as he's able to speak again, he turns back to Elyah and snarls, "You will regret that, you piece of shit."

"You will never speak to Lilia like that again. You will not even look at her or I will break your fucking face."

"How noble, defending your whore."

Elyah smashes his forehead into the bridge of Brazhensky's nose. The man howls in pain and blood spurts over his mouth and chin. His lips and teeth are coated in red, and he glares at Elyah with fire in his eyes. "You piece of fucking scum. Your life is over, you hear me? I'll kill you like the animal you are and feed you to my dogs."

These threats pass over Elyah like he hasn't even heard the man. He turns to Lilia. "This man beat you. He beat your mother, too?"

You only have to look at a man like Aran Brazhensky to know he's liberal with his fists. He's got the same mean look in his eye that my father did.

In the face of Elyah's ferocity, Lilia softens. His eyes are locked on her beautiful face, and she nods.

"I will kill him for you. He will never hurt you again."

Kostya holds up a hand. "Not yet. Not until I've got my diamonds."

Reluctantly, Elyah steps back from Brazhensky, but spits at his feet. He goes to stand behind Lilia's chair, his arms folded across his chest.

"Nothing?" Kostya asks me.

I reach for Lilia's handbag and rummage around in it before pawing at the lining for any telltale lumps. Then I drop it at her feet. "No diamonds."

"Then you and I have a problem, don't we, Lilia?"

I crack my knuckles. "I'm not finished with her. I'll take her to the back of the plane and finish the job."

Now that my craving for Lilia's pussy has been satisfied for now, I should be able to keep my mind on the job. I cast my eyes down her body, wondering where I should start first. Lilia is stubborn so she'll need some pain to motivate her. It would be a shame to ruin her beauty or scar that body of hers. A few broken fingers should do the job. I'll just have to gag her and break them quickly so that Elyah doesn't try and save his woman.

I take a step toward Lilia, but Kostya holds up a hand again and I stay where I am.

Kostya turns to Brazhensky. "I'm taking your daughter. You can have her back when I am once more in possession of sixteen pink diamonds."

"And if she never tells you where they are?"

"Then you can have her back in sixteen pieces."

Behind her chair, Elyah flinches.

"You can't have her. My daughter is arranged to be married. Or she was, until—"

Lilia exclaims, "Dad, enough! There's no way in hell I'm marrying one of your shitty friends again."

Kostya looks thoughtfully from father to daughter. "I'll marry Lilia."

Lilia splutters in anger. "I wouldn't marry you if you were the last—"

"For a dowry of fourteen million dollars."

"The cost of the diamonds?" Brazhensky guesses.

"Of course."

Brazhensky's lip curls. He was hoping to make money or earn favors by marrying his daughter off, not be out of pocket a sizable chunk of money. "I'm not paying you to take my daughter off my hands. You're going to pay in blood for hijacking my plane."

Elyah pulls his gun from the back of his jeans and jabs it against the man's head. "If you threaten my *Pakhan* one more time, I will put bullet in your head."

From the brutal expression in his eyes, nothing would make him happier than killing Lilia's father.

Kostya spreads his hands and smiles. "I have no quarrel with you. When we land, you can be on your way, but I'm taking your daughter with me. Find some way to convince her to do what I'm asking of her, or you'll never see her alive again."

"Who are you to threaten me? I'll have you all killed," Brazhensky shouts at the top of his lungs, his face turning red and a vein throbbing in his temple.

Kostya flinches and presses his fingers to his temple. Sweat has broken out on his brow, a sure sign that he's enduring one of his intense headaches. I grab a fistful of tissues and cram them into Brazhensky's mouth and bind his wrists with a length of twine that I fish out of my pocket. Elyah hauls the man to his feet, and together, we drag him down the aisle of the plane and lock him in the other bathroom.

Lilia is watching Kostya. "Migraine?" she guesses.

"Yes," he mutters, still rubbing his brow.

"It must be agony. I could help you with that." Then she turns away and gazes out of the window.

Kostya casts her a baleful look and then gets to his feet. Walking to the front of the plane, he addresses the pilot. "Tell air traffic control you're having engine trouble. Land at a small airport, as close to Paris as you can get."

A few minutes later, we begin our descent. No one speaks in the jet until houses and roads below come into view.

"Where are we going now? Moscow?" Lilia asks. All this talk of chopping her into pieces doesn't seem to concern her, or she's hiding it well.

"Russia is no longer my home, *milaya*. I'm taking you to London where I'll torture the location of the diamonds out of you myself. The longer you hold out on me, the less of you there will be for Elyah or one of your father's men to marry. Keep it up long enough and you'll be dead."

She smiles at him. "So not telling you where the diamonds are will get me out of another marriage I don't want. Wonderful."

Kostya glares at her. "You are the most infuriating woman I have ever met."

With one hand extended, she examines her nails. They're not the perfect glossy almond shapes they once were, but she gazes at them like they are. "Can't get enough of me, can you?"

"You will take this seriously soon enough," Kostya tells her.

The air pressure around us changes and I take a seat farther down the plane, one where I can watch Lilia. Elyah sits beside me with his jaw tight. How it must be tormenting him to hear so much talk of his beloved being torn apart. The only way he can save her is to persuade her to talk, but Lilia has never done as he's asked even once in her life.

Lilia recrosses her long legs, and we both stare at her slender calves.

I put my head on one side as I appreciate the memory of those legs around my hips. "Give it up. She doesn't love you."

"You do not know what you are talking about. Lilia is playing for time right now, but Konstantin will get his diamonds, and I will get Lilia."

I bristle at his words. "And what do I get?"

His expression darkens. "I listened to you fuck her. Since when did you want anything else from a woman?"

"I don't know. Maybe I do want something."

"Since when?"

Since we stood on that clifftop, staring down into the dark waters of Lake Como.

Since we crisscrossed the surface of the lake, hunting for her with a powerful light.

Since I told her she's mine until she's dead, and it made her pussy gush against my fingers.

"Maybe she wants me and not you."

Elyah stares at me and then smiles, showing his strong white teeth. Handsome Elyah who fucks her like she's a queen and whispers words of love into her ears. Anger races through me as he laughs and shakes his head.

"Sure. Okay."

"You fucked up two years ago. She'll never forgive you for doubting she loved her baby."

That wipes the smile off Elyah's face. "Fuck you. You do not even love her."

I never said anything about love. There's not one scrap of my soul that deserves a woman like Lilia, but I've never concerned myself with things like *deserve* and *earn*. Only *take* and *own*. Elyah desperately wants Lilia to love him, but I don't give a damn if I have to lock Lilia in a cage for the rest of her life to keep her.

"For a while there, I thought you were getting all hot over the idea of sharing her."

Elyah's frown deepens and he stares out the window.

"Go on, Elyah. Admit it. When I was fucking her just now, you didn't burst in and rip me off her because hearing her getting railed by me had you nearly blowing in your pants."

The three of us have been through too much together for us to be split apart by jealousy, and I think we all know that we have our hands full when it comes to Lilia. She's too much for just one of us to handle.

Elyah passes a hand over his face and shakes his head. "I do not think she will ever give a man what he really wants from her."

I smirk and draw a length of rope from my pocket and slide it through my fingers. "Don't worry, my friend. If she doesn't give it willingly, there's always plan B."

5

Lilia

"Choose."

Elyah grinds the gun into the side of Dad's head, his eyes sparking with anger. Dad is kneeling on the floor of the plane, his face a bloody mess from Elyah's handiwork earlier. We've landed somewhere outside Paris, but the cabin is still sealed.

I can see how badly Elyah wants to kill Dad, but Konstantin is giving me the chance to choose. I doubt that he's interested in whether or not I want to show Aran Brazhensky mercy, the man who made and continues to make my life hell. I think Konstantin just wants to see what I'll do.

If Dad dies, no one else on this planet will know that I'm pregnant except me. Letting Elyah kill him is probably the safest thing I can do for my child. The thought leaves a bitter taste in my mouth. Will this be my first act as a mother, to kill my own father?

I look at Elyah and give a tiny shake of my head. Elyah's eyes narrow. His stubborn jaw juts. Then he raises the gun and looks away, anger flashing through his eyes.

"Don't come after me," I tell Dad. "Don't try to find me. Don't allow my name to ever pass your lips again. And leave *Babulya* be."

Dad raises eyes so furious they're almost black to my face, and my heart skips, wondering if I've just made the wrong decision. I'll just have to make sure that I hide myself so well that Dad never finds me to take revenge for this humiliation.

When the four of us disembark, leaving Dad, the pilot, and flight attendant tied up on the floor of the plane to be discovered after we've gone, we're greeted by a freezing wind and a waiting car.

"I will drive," Elyah says, and takes the keys from the man who brought the car, a black Lexus with heavily tinted windows.

He gets into the front seat, and I'm corralled into the back between Kirill and Konstantin. His migraine seems to have eased and his eyes are bright and determined as we head out of the airport. Whatever he has in store for me next, it's going to be brutal. I recall with how much pleasure he ripped apart my composure and self-esteem in the judging room.

Were you a good daughter, Lilia Brazhensky? Were you a good lover, Lilia Aranova?

My hand passes briefly over my belly, a secret greeting to the tiny life inside me. If I can protect this child, then all the versions of myself who came before no longer matter. I stare at the road ahead, my mind racing. I can endure pain for myself. I would have let Elyah break my arms to save Hedda from the same fate. The night Kirill strung me up in the cellar, I suffered hours of agony with barely a whimper. If they want to torture the location of the diamonds out of me, I think I could endure their torment for hours, maybe even days, out of sheer stubbornness. But it's not just me anymore. If they hurt me, I'm going to have to tell them about the baby. It's their baby, Elyah's or Konstantin's. Couldn't they—wouldn't they—

Love it?

Elyah's eyes meet mine briefly in the rearview mirror and they're stormy with emotion. Konstantin slips a hand around my thigh, warm and possessive. On my left, Kirill's bare, muscular arm is pressed against mine, reminding me how I shattered beneath his brutal touch just hours ago. Now I'm going somewhere with these men, and I'm going to be truly alone. The memory of Elyah's large, strong hand on the nape of my neck while Kirill fucked me with a gun and Konstantin watched on flickers across my mind, and a hot, fluttering feeling fills my belly.

Jesus Christ, Lilia. They're planning on torturing you to death, not having a gangbang.

We drive for hours, and I think we're bypassing Paris and heading for the coast. The countryside around us is rural, but not so remote that there aren't cars on the road and occasional houses dotted around the field. All the while I'm silently arguing with myself. Tell them about the baby. Don't tell them about the baby. They have to know. They might hurt it without realizing.

Fuck.

"I need to pee," I announce.

Konstantin's jaw flexes, but he says nothing. A few minutes later, Elyah announces, "There's a gas station coming up."

I turn to Konstantin. "I *really* need to pee. Please."

The *Pakhan* says nothing, but Elyah turns off the highway anyway and into the garage. It's a tiny place with two pumps and no one around but an indistinct figure inside at the till. The sign for the bathrooms directs people around the back.

Konstantin jerks his head at the passenger door on Kirill's side of the car. "Go with Kirill and Elyah."

"Can you take me, please?" I ask him.

Elyah's eyes narrow, and I remember how he declared that I'm a viper and Konstantin shouldn't trust me. "I will come, too…"

I hold my handbag open for them to look into. "I'm not armed. Kirill checked me thoroughly. Konstantin has a weapon, don't you?"

"Why me?" Konstantin asks.

I shrug, tucking my hair behind my ear. "I thought we could have a talk while I pee. There's something I need to tell you."

Konstantin opens his jacket and shows me the gun holstered under his arm. "If you try to get away from me, I'll shoot you. If you ask anyone for help, I'll shoot them. A bleeding heart like you won't want that on her conscience, will she?"

He thinks I'm weak for letting Dad live. "I don't want innocent people to die, how sappy of me. Can we go? I'm going to wet myself back here."

When we're standing outside the car, he grasps my upper arm and holds me close as he steers me toward the women's restroom. Elyah and Kirill follow behind. It's a ramshackle, rusty kind of place with old cars and barrels stacked everywhere. There's buckled old shelving by the restroom door holding an array of oil tins and car parts.

I'm not surprised when Konstantin follows me inside the dank, smelly little restroom, and he puts his foot in the door when I try to close the cubicle.

"Can I lock this?"

"No. Leave it open."

There's no window in here. It's not like I can escape somehow. "You're really going to watch me pee?"

"Lilia, I'm counting to sixty, and whether you have peed or not, we are going back to the car."

I feel a jolt of surprise as he says my name in his deep, precise voice. That hits different to *Number Eleven* or even *milaya*. For the second time that day, I tug my underwear down in front of a man and sit on the toilet.

We stare at each other, and absolutely nothing happens.

"You're not going," he accuses.

"Give me a second, this is weird as hell," I mutter under my breath, wriggling around on the seat. I can't believe I have to pee in front of a man again. I open my mouth to say, *You're just like Dad*, before I realize Konstantin will wonder why the hell my dad was watching me pee.

I look around for something to distract myself and my eyes land on his scar. Whatever caused that wound, it must have been painful, and from what I've seen of his migraines, he's still suffering.

"What happens when you get a migraine?"

Konstantin regards me in silence.

"My *babulya* gets migraines and there are pressure points that can ease them. Ask me to help you next time."

His damaged eyebrow creeps up his forehead at the phrase *next time*. "The next time I have a migraine you will be dead or back in America."

Because I will have revealed where the diamonds are? If so, maybe I'll be dead, but I won't be in America. I don't believe for a second he's going to let me go. I've humiliated him too badly.

"High-pitched noises bring on your migraines, don't they? It's the same with *Babulya*. She can't stand noise and light when her headaches get bad. The whistle of the kettle is excruciating. Even the doorbell ringing she described like shards of glass stabbing through her skull."

"Just pee, Lilia."

"I'm trying. It's putting me off, having someone stare at me," I huff. I gaze around the bathroom stall, trying to read the French graffiti. "Did you really expect to find a loyal and loving wife through that messed-up pageant?"

"Lilia—" he growls in a warning tone.

"I need a distraction, Konstantin. Please."

His handsome face is suffused with annoyance, and he casts his eyes to the ceiling briefly. "The pageant was wicked and criminal, but my life is wicked and criminal. I needed to see who could survive in my world. Most of the contestants would fail, but I suspected there would be one or two who would realize what I was offering them and put their hearts into it, and I was right. The final half dozen women were promising."

"Which one did you want the most?"

He smiles his sleek, devilish smile. "She was exquisite.

Long, golden hair. A proud heart. Nerves like fucking iron and the face of an angel. Her beauty was perfection against those sparkling pink diamonds. All she had to do was reach out and take my hand." The smile drops from his face. "But she chose death instead of life by my side, so she wasn't the one, after all."

I remember the mixture of shock and delight on his face as the wind blew our hair around our faces on the edge of that cliff. He held out his hand to me, and I didn't know if he intended to kiss me or kill me. "You would have married me if I'd stepped away from that cliff edge and into your arms?"

Konstantin runs his tongue over his teeth, considering this. "After everything you did to the three of us, I would have been crazy to take you as my wife. So yes, I would have married you."

I burst out laughing. "Really? You're crazy, you know that?"

He returns my smile, leaning back against the wall. "I love a challenge, *milaya*. I always want the best of everything, and despite what I thought, the best woman isn't a tame dog." His gaze arrows into mine. "A pity you ruined everything by stealing from me."

My laughter dies away. "You ruined it by taking seventeen women prisoner and murdering one of them."

"But then I never would have met you. Elyah thought I was insane for putting my hands on you, considering what my last bride was. I ignored the warning signs when it came to her. I trusted her when I shouldn't have, and I never tried to earn her loyalty."

I'm still not peeing, but both of us seem to be enjoying

our conversation too much to care. "How would you earn mine?"

He puts his head on one side, gazing at me. For a long time, he doesn't say anything, and I realize he doesn't know what to offer me. Disappointment washes over me, but I quickly shove it aside. I don't want Konstantin to understand me inside and out. I want to run and never see him again.

"By giving you what no man ever has. His total and utter respect and devotion."

I swallow hard and force my face not to reveal anything as my heart thumps hard in my chest, every pound echoing with *yes, yes, yes*. "Respect and devotion? Please. How about, *Sorry for locking you in a cellar*?"

"We're well past sorries and explanations, *milaya*. I don't want that from you, and you can expect nothing of the kind from me."

"Elyah gave me his devotion and I never fell at his feet."

"Elyah saw a damsel, not a woman. He underestimated you, and I underestimated you, too." His eyes fill with challenge and...warmth? Shock slams into me as I realize that cold, cruel Konstantin is giving me what no man ever has.

Respect.

For my mind. For my abilities. For standing up to him at the peak of his power and brutality. What would it be like to have his devotion as well? I imagine taking my place at his side, not as his vessel or his subordinate, but as his equal. My gaze drops to his hands. I can picture them cupping my swollen belly and whispering that he will protect our child with his life.

I take a shaky breath and push a hand through my hair. Why can't I just freaking pee?

"What was it you wanted to tell me? Is it about the diamonds?"

I lick my top lip, thinking carefully. "My situation has changed since I escaped your pageant."

His gaze narrows. "How?"

I open my mouth and hesitate. Careful, Lilia. "Things are...complicated."

"How?"

"I won't go back to being someone's unthinking doll," I say quickly. "Being smacked around for having a miscarriage."

Konstantin's brows have drawn together but he says nothing.

"I don't want that and you..." I rub my forehead as if it pains me to say this. "You don't either. You want an equal, and we both know I'm it."

"There's just one problem, Lilia."

"I know. The diamonds. Well, I won't give them back. My pride won't allow it after everything you did to me and the other women. But...what if I keep them and you keep me?"

I fight with everything I have to keep a straight face. With my underwear around my ankles, sitting on the toilet in a freezing cold restroom, I'm giving the performance of my life.

Konstantin's eyes widen in shock. His lips part and he's about to say something, but then a wall slams down behind them. "Just fucking pee, Lilia."

I sigh and drop my head as if he's dashed my last hope. A few moments later, after managing to use the toilet, I stand to pull my underwear on and wash my hands in the tiny, cracked basin.

Konstantin is gazing at me with an unguarded expression,

something like regret tinging his features. I think he might be imagining something like I was painting for him a few moments ago.

I rummage around in my handbag, my movements casual like I'm hunting for lip gloss. My fingers close around a long, slim tube.

I turn to him and put my hand on his sleeve, my eyes huge and sorrowful. "Konstantin, what you said about earning my loyalty..."

He's too busy staring into my eyes and wondering what might have been to notice when I lift something to my lips. The object is just a few inches long and it's hollow and tapered at the end closest to my mouth. I bought this in Trieste. Just for Konstantin.

I blow through the tube. Hard.

A high-pitched shriek rends the air. It's not loud, but it's viciously sharp.

"Fuck!" Konstantin grabs his skull and doubles over, gasping in pain. The whistle is more powerful than the screaming of a woman in pain, a sound that Konstantin finds excruciating. His knees buckle beneath him, and he hits the floor.

I like him down there on his knees, sweating and swearing and clutching his head. "You really think you can ever earn my loyalty? You'll be groveling for a thousand years before I give you one little piece of my heart."

I run past him and burst out of the bathroom. My hair is flying around my head and my face is wretched with anguish as I come face to face with a startled Elyah and Kirill.

I point behind me and cry, "Something's wrong with Konstantin. It's his head."

Their boss. Their friend. They push past me to get to him—but both of them immediately realize their mistake and turn back.

I kick the shelving by the restroom door with all my strength. It's so old and rusted through that it immediately collapses, right across the doorway, barring Kirill and Elyah's way.

Elyah swears and immediately grasps the twisted metal, trying to push it away, but there's so much wreckage and it's jammed. "*Lilia.*"

Kirill meets my gaze through the jumble of broken shelving and cans. His black eyes flash with fury.

And then he smiles. It's the twisted smile of a villain who realizes the chase isn't over yet and there are many more miles to run. He jabs two fingers into his throat either side of his windpipe and then points at me.

You're dead.

Then he blows me a kiss, and I swear I can feel the ghost of his lips against mine. I don't linger over the sensation. My heart beating wildly, I turn and run.

A line of trees and thick hedges behind the gas station are the only obstacles between me and the three narrow roads tucked behind the greenery. A truck towing a tractor is trying to pass a car on one of the lanes. I race across a strip of grass, toward the tractor, and reach up and open the door, praying both of the drivers are too deep in their argument to notice me. I pull myself up and into the cab and close the door behind me, all while the two drivers are shouting at each other in French. The floor of the tractor is covered in mud and bits of straw and grass, and I lay down on it with my head pillowed on my handbag.

The truck driver guns the engine, and we move off. With my heart thundering in my ears, I strain for the sound of deep Russian voices shouting for the driver to stop.

∼

COFFEE, pastry, and scrambled eggs. Everything tastes more delicious when you're free. It's morning and I'm sitting in a tiny motel restaurant after an anxious night, trying to figure out what happens next.

Operation Hide from the Russian Mafia, version 3.0.

Back in Trieste, I pawned three of the plain diamonds from Konstantin's tiara. So after hiding inside the tractor yesterday, I disappeared into a small town and used some of the leftover cash at a nearby thrift store. I bought jeans, a thick sweater, a baseball cap, and a backpack.

This morning I went out and purchased a burner phone and a second-hand laptop. I boot the laptop up and check my email address, typing the login details with shaking fingers. Did my plan with the jeweler and the Mafia Veneta work?

I nearly punch the air as I see a bunch of email notifications telling me that six million dollars' worth of cryptocurrency has been deposited in an escrow account. Someone from the Mafia Veneta has contacted me to ask the location of the remaining fifteen diamonds.

Grinning from ear to ear, I type out a reply, telling them that the diamonds are located in the safe of a particular room in a Trieste hotel. They should ask for Tomas Szabo at the desk, and he will give them the room key.

For the next forty-five minutes, I drink coffee and chew my fingernail, checking my email every so often. If they disappear with my diamonds without releasing the funds, I'm screwed.

Finally, an email pops up. Six million dollars of cryptocurrency has been released into my account.

Six million dollars.

I've never had more than a few hundred under my personal control at any one time. This money is more than I ever dreamed of.

It's not just my money, though. The women who suffered with me in the cellar, they earned this money too. I do the math in my head. Split sixteen ways, six million dollars is nearly four hundred thousand dollars each, and that's enough for me if I can get a job as well. The money can in no way undo the terror of the days we were held as captives, but it's something to help the women get back on their feet. But how do I track all the women down when I only know their first names? Only a handful of them have come forward to the press, and how would I get the money to them?

But that's a problem for later.

Hugging my cup of coffee in one hand, I navigate to a map of Europe. Where to next? I don't want to return to the United States, and I don't want my passport scrutinized too closely at international borders. If I stay within the European Union where there are no hard borders and travel by road and train, I might be able to pass from country to country without anyone so much as glancing at my passport, let alone recording my movements.

My eyes rove over the mountain ranges and unfamiliar cities as I take a sip of coffee, wondering where might be safe for me and the baby. My other hand is cupping my stomach.

"What do you think, little bean?" I murmur, staring at the

screen. "You don't know? Me neither. So how about we let fate decide?"

I close my eyes, circle my pointer finger over the map, and jab it at the screen.

When I move my hand and read the name of the city, it says Prague, in Czechia.

I stare at the name for several minutes, trying to remember if I know anything about Prague, but I come up with nothing. I don't even know anyone who's been there.

An internet search shows me pictures of a beautiful old city overlooked by a castle. Cobblestone bridges cross a wide blue river. A gothic clock overlooks a place called Wenceslas Square.

As I scroll through the images of the ancient city, a sense of peace washes over me. Prague is a place of beauty far from everything I've ever known. When I look up the cost of living, I'm thrilled to find it's cheaper than home.

I stop scrolling and navigate back to the map, searching for a route to Prague via train. I'm currently in the countryside outside Reims, and I'll have to make my way to Dijon before crossing through southern Germany and then into Czechia. A grueling fifteen-hour journey to travel six hundred miles, but no rental company will let me drive a car out of France, and they'll require ID and a credit card. Better that I buy train tickets with cash and keep my baseball cap pulled low.

The following afternoon, I board a train in Dijon with my backpack containing a clean T-shirt, some underwear, a toothbrush, and holding a cup of coffee and a sandwich in a paper bag. The train is half empty and I settle into a seat by a sunny window. As soon as the carriage shudders and we start to pull out of the station, my shoulders unclench, but just a little.

As I watch the countryside flash past and sip my coffee, my heart starts to feel lighter.

I switch trains in Germany with a few furtive glances over my shoulder. The platform overflows with people walking this way and that, pulling small suitcases behind them. For a moment I catch sight of a tall, proud-looking man in a white shirt, and when he turns toward me, my stomach flips. Only his eyes are brown, not gray.

My eyes close, and sleep envelops me in a velvet blanket.

There's a warm weight in my arms and it's making soft, sleepy noises. I gaze down into her cherubic face and realize it's her. My daughter. She's only a few days old and her tiny hand is clenched on the blanket that swaddles her. I'm so full to the brim with love that I pay no attention to the presence behind me. Several presences.

One moves closer and a large hand squeezes my shoulder. He presses his lips to my temple and breathes in my ear, "She is beautiful, Lilia."

I come awake with a gasp, my eyes wide and staring around me. The dream was so vivid that, for a moment, I don't know where I am. The dimly lit train carriage rattles through the night.

I slide a hand over my belly. A girl. Will it be a girl? My heart aches at the thought that my daughter might grow up among dangerous men who will use her as the men in my life have used me.

Just past eight in the morning, the train pulls into Prague Hlavni, and I alight along with the other weary travelers. It's a morning filled with watery sunshine, and the crisp, dry air smells like pastry. The seasons will soon be turning, and as I make my way to the exit, I smile at the thought of watching the trees of this beautiful city turn red and gold.

The first thing I do in my new city is find an apartment to rent on the east side of the river, as close as I can get to the city center. It's small and the bed is narrow, but it's cheap and quiet and looks out onto a peaceful garden.

A few days later I manage to find a waitressing job in a restaurant by Wenceslas Square. They're short-staffed and she can offer me up to ten shifts a week. It's a thirty-minute walk from home, and the walk will get harder and harder the bigger my belly grows. Still, it's a start and a little bit of hope.

Czech food shares a great many similarities with Russian food, I'm pleased to find. The hearty stews, soups, and pickled vegetables remind me of *Babulya* and help me remember the orders. At the end of my first four-hour shift, my feet are aching, but the manager is smiling at me. I have the job.

Morning sickness comes and goes. Most of my shifts start at midday, and I feel better after my walk to the restaurant. Most of the food we serve smells heavenly, except for the cheeses. If someone wants to finish their meal with cheese, I have to hold my breath and avert my face.

On Halloween, I carve a pumpkin and light it, and set it in the living room window. The candle dances merrily within, casting spiky shadows all around the room. The wickedly grinning face seems friendly to me, like it's chasing away all my enemies.

On Christmas Day, I stand on Charles Bridge as flakes of snow flutter down. I'm thirteen weeks pregnant, and I think I can feel my baby with my hands for the first time. For weeks

I've stared at myself sideways in the mirror, wondering if my waist looks thicker, but today I'm sure of it.

"Hello, baby," I whisper, my vaporous breath curling around me. "Merry Christmas. Soon it will be New Year, and the year you will be born. I can't wait to meet you."

Will the baby have blue eyes, or gray eyes? Will I see one of my tormentor's faces looking back at me when we finally meet or only the innocence of a child?

"Whatever happens, baby, I'm going to protect you from everything bad in the world," I murmur, gazing out across the dark, frigid waters of the Vltava River. "I don't have much to give you except my love. I hope it will be enough."

I won't be able to lavish this child with the luxury I once knew, but plush white carpets and gold-edged dinner plates don't mean anything when a house is cold and cruel.

On my way home, I remember my resolution to track down the other pageant women and share the diamond money with them. As soon as I get in my front door, I boot up my laptop and start searching social media accounts. I know a few of their full names and find their Facebook and Instagram accounts. My hand hovers over the message button, but it doesn't feel right to pop up in their inboxes and possibly retraumatize them.

Instead, I switch to a search engine and start reading about how to anonymously transfer cryptocurrency to people who don't have a cryptocurrency account. I learn that it's possible, but you need their email address or phone number.

A few hours later, I close my laptop and head to bed. It will take a lot more research to find everyone and somehow verify their contact information, but at least I have a plan now, and a plan makes me hopeful.

By the end of February, I've sent out three payments, one to Hedda, one to Deja and one to Olivia. Every transfer is anonymous but comes with a message that only they will understand.

One-sixteenth, with love from eleven. And I add a diamond emoji. None of the women will have forgotten Konstantin's glittering tiara.

The day I log in and see that Hedda has transferred her portion of the money into a bank account, I stand up from my computer with a whoop of delight. My first win, and it sends a rush of happiness through me. I'm still a long way from tracking down everyone, but if I have to hire a private investigator to find some of the women, I will.

According to the internet, my baby is due on the tenth of June. A summer baby. I picture sitting on my tiny balcony, surrounded by potted plants, bathed in gentle sunshine, and nursing the little one in my arms. I still haven't seen a doctor for a checkup, but I know I have to, and soon. I'm putting it off as long as possible because I'm terrified of being deported if an official discovers I'm in this country illegally. I don't know how I'll obtain a birth certificate for this child without showing my own passport. I lie awake at night worrying about it.

I don't know what to do except keep putting one foot in front of the other, so that is what I do. I work at the restaurant and pay my rent. I eat nutritious food for the baby, and I scour second-hand markets to make a little nursery in the corner of my living room. A sturdy stroller. A yellow wooden crib. A mobile of elephants and tigers in yellow bowties to hang above. Baby clothes so tiny and adorable that they make me smile every time I look at them.

On my mornings off I'm so exhausted that I can do nothing but sit in cafés and watch the world go by, and I start to notice something about myself that makes me dig my nails into my palms.

I can't stop looking at the men.

Tall, handsome men in tight T-shirts and running shorts, jogging along the river. Sleek businessmen in tailored suits that show off their muscular shoulders. Tradesmen in overalls, sawdust lacing their muscular forearms and strong hands. It's infuriating to acknowledge it, but I'm hornier than I've ever been in my life.

The bar for my libido is pretty low. It wasn't until I came face to face with Elyah that I felt the first stirrings of interest in a man. I find myself staring into space remembering the soft way he used to say, "Good morning, Lilia," in his thick accent while gazing into my eyes. Every time I opened the front door to him, I wanted to reach out and touch him. Cup his neck. Feel the muscles of his shoulders. His belly. Watch him inhale roughly as I slide my hand down over the front of his trousers and feel the thick outline of his cock. Those brief weeks when Elyah was kissing me and touching me were filled with nervous energy and frustration so intense that I thought I might explode if he didn't make me his, but that was nothing compared to what I'm feeling now. What I wouldn't give to feel his heavy body on mine while my hands splay over his tattooed chest, aching and ready for him to thrust his thick cock—

Lilia. *No.*

I sit up straighter, pull my coat tighter around me in the freezing air, and take a mouthful of stone-cold coffee. I don't want that man. I don't want any men.

And yet not even two minutes pass before I'm staring again at the men in the street, my restless eyes moving over their bodies, hands, and faces. Some of them are handsome. Some have large, powerful bodies and beautiful eyes that sweep over me with interest. A handful of men have approached me in the past few months, picking up on the need I seem to be broadcasting with a fifty-foot aerial. *This woman needs to be fucked.* I shake my head at each one because I don't dare get involved with another man when my trust in their kind is at an all-time low. I tell myself that's the reason, but the truth is much darker.

None of these men are *them*.

If it were merely Elyah I lusted after, I could understand and forgive my body. Once, he was gentle with me. He held me like I was the most precious thing in the world. But it's not just Elyah. I recall the rough way that Kirill stripped me and screwed me in the jet with a whimper. I shouldn't have enjoyed that at the time, but it just felt so good to be bad with him.

I even relive the moment Konstantin shoved me to the floor after screwing me, gripping my jaw in his hand and growling, *"When I'm finished with you, wait for your orders. Don't take fucking liberties."* I don't recall it with revulsion. I recall it with a hot lick of desire. In my fantasy, I run my tongue over my top lip and whisper, *"Yes, ser."* His ferocious expression softens, and he slowly thrusts his thumb into my mouth for me to suck. All the while, Kirill and Elyah are watching me, dying to take their turns. I want all their hands on me at once as they lick, suck, bite, fuck.

Thrusting my coffee cup away from me, I get to my feet. I'm due at the restaurant for my shift, so I walk away quickly, trying to put that lurid, dangerous fantasy behind me.

The lunch shift is busy, and I lose myself in the work of taking orders and carrying steaming plates to tables. My section is full of fall tourists who have come to see the beautiful city of Prague under crisp blue skies and occasional showers. They have all the time in the world to order courses of food and bottles of peppery red wine. I'm carrying yet another armload of dirty dishes back into the kitchen when the new kitchenhand, a boy of seventeen and very little life experience, blunders into me while talking to the chef over his shoulder. I trip over his ankle and all the dishes go flying across the kitchen. I start to fall, and the floor rushes up, hard, and unforgiving.

The baby.

I grab my belly and cry out, putting a hand and leg out to protect the baby. Horrible images flash through my brain. Being hit by a drunk driver as I try to cross the street. Someone stealing my baby from its stroller because I'm trying to juggle ten things at once. Being so sleep-deprived as a single mother that I make a terrible mistake and hurt us. I'm all alone with this baby. Not just now, but always. There's no one to catch me when I fall.

I fall hard, and my palm and knee hit the tiles. I stay where I am for a moment, breathing hard while terror pounds through my veins. I'm fine. The baby's fine.

So why do I feel like I'm dangling over a precipice?

I grimace and sit up, wincing as the floor grinds against my bruised knee.

"Lilia! Are you all right? Jakub, watch where you are going." The chef, Pavel, puts his hand under my arm and helps me to my feet. I decided to use my real first name at the restaurant because it's so hard adjusting to a fake one, but no one knows my real last name.

My hand is still clamped over my stomach, and it's outlined through my apron. I must look like I've seen a ghost as Pavel looks from my belly to my face and asks, "You're pregnant?"

I wasn't ready to tell anyone, and this is not the moment. I start to shake my head to vehemently deny it. "I'm—"

Pavel breaks into a smile. "But that's wonderful. When are you due? Is it a boy or a girl? Who is the father?"

Every one of his questions hit me like a bullet. "Five and a half months. And I don't know if it's going to be a boy or a girl." I pretend not to hear the question about the father.

Pavel beams at me. "You want it to be a surprise? Old-fashioned. I like it."

So "old-fashioned." No scans. No doctors. Not even a midwife and a birthing plan. Panic grips me anew at how unprepared I am, and the chef gazes at me in concern.

"You are not in trouble, are you? Where is the father?"

I gaze up into Pavel's friendly, lined face. Someone worrying about me. Someone being concerned over me. I didn't know how much I was craving it until this moment, and tears well in my eyes.

I swipe quickly at my lashes and take a quick breath. "I… left him behind. He's not a good man."

Pavel's face creases with worry and he reaches out to touch my arm.

"I want to keep working here," I say quickly. "I'm fine. I just tripped, that's all. I've got plenty of time before I'm due."

The longer I can resist dipping into my sixteenth of the diamond money, the more secure I'll feel.

"Of course. My wife worked up until she was seven and a half months pregnant with all our children. But you must slow down if you are too tired. It's not good for you or the baby. Jakub, clean this up," he adds, pointing at all the dishes the kitchenhand made me drop. The boy gets to work with a brush and pan.

I give Pavel a quick smile, adjusting my apron so my belly doesn't show too much, and head back into the restaurant. I have a new table, but one of the waitresses is handing a menu to the solitary male diner for me, so I have a few minutes to check on the others. A young couple wants more glasses of beer, and on my way to tell the bartender, I sweep past my new table.

A large hand catches hold of my wrist and a Russian-accented voice says, "Lilia? What the hell?"

6

Lilia

For a second my brain refuses to believe I've heard anyone speaking English with a Russian accent. I'm only aware of a man holding on to me so I can't escape. His large hand grips me like a manacle and my gaze travels over his expensive watch, up the arm of his suit jacket, and into a tanned face with dark, slightly curly hair.

With a jolt, I recognize him. Maxim Vavilov, the son of Artem Vavilov, one of my father's closest friends. He's smiling at me, confused but pleased.

I tear my wrist from his grip and rub it as if he's burned me. I have to get out of here. I have to *run*. If it gets out among the Bratva that I've been seen in Prague, I'm screwed. I'm going to have to uproot my life all over again.

The warm smile dims on Maxim's face, and I feel a jolt as

I realize he's not chasing me. This is a coincidence, and maybe I can persuade him to keep his mouth shut.

I plaster a smile on my face and make my tone as friendly as possible. "Sorry, I just tripped over in the kitchen and it gave me a fright. Maxim. How wonderful to see you. What brings you to Prague?"

He relaxes once more and spreads his hands with a smile. "Work. Always work."

I suppose his father must have some contacts in this city. I shudder as I remember the Bratva are everywhere.

"I saw your father last summer. He's been missing you since you left America."

I let some sadness creep into my tone. "It's been difficult for me since Ivan passed. I'm not ready to be at home yet. Too many bad memories."

"Of course. But a waitress, Lilia? You're too good for this."

Irritation crackles up my spine. He's a criminal and he thinks people like us are too good to wait tables? This is honest work, and I'm proud of it. "I like it here. Now, what can I get you?"

I take his order to the kitchen, my mind racing, trying to come up with a plan. Maxim stares at me the whole time he eats, his eyes tracking me to and fro across the dining room.

When my shift finishes, he's waiting for me outside.

"Lilia, there you are. Have dinner with me tonight."

I'm bundled up tightly in my coat to hide my belly. My bruised knee is aching. "I really can't, I'm sorry. But could I ask a favor? Please don't tell my father or your father that you've seen me. Dad's getting impatient with me, but I still need more time before I go home."

"All right, but will you make it worth my while?" Suddenly, Maxim's smile is filled with innuendo.

The imploring expression drops from my face. I'm so sick of men. All they do is demand, manipulate, take. I turn away. "Fuck you, Maxim. I'm not going to sleep with you."

A hurt expression flashes over his face and he hurries to catch up with me. "I didn't mean that. I meant dinner. I always liked you, Lilia, and now that Ivan's dead, I thought we might have more to talk about."

What a lovely way to talk to a widow. "I'm sorry, I'm just not ready to date anyone right now."

"I want to ask your father for your hand," he blurts out.

My eyes widen. Another arranged marriage. I wonder how fast he'd run if I lifted my shirt and showed him my pregnant belly.

If I leave now, Maxim is going to pick up the phone this very night and my presence here will be blown wide open. I have an apartment here. I have a job. I have a *life*. This isn't fair.

All I can think to do is buy a little time, and I smile at Maxim. "I had no idea you felt that way about me. I'm flattered, though I have to warn you I'm going to take a lot of courting. It's not up to my father who I marry next. It's up to me."

His mouth hooks in a smile. "I'm a patient man."

Trying not to reveal how reluctant I am to ever lay eyes on him again, I tell him, "There's a bistro just off Wencelas Square called Nechci. Meet me there at eight."

At home, I pace up and down. Maybe I should just run, but my eyes land on the yellow crib in the corner, so bright and hopeful and ready to shelter my baby. My heart aches at the thought of leaving this precious refuge behind.

Maxim kisses my cheek when I arrive at the restaurant at eight, and I have to hold myself carefully away from him so that his arm doesn't brush my pregnant belly.

"Wine?"

"No, thanks. Just water for me."

"You can have one."

He tries to pour wine into my glass, but I cover it with my hand. "Honestly, I'm not drinking these days."

"Probably a good idea. You've filled out since I last saw you."

He laughs, and the smile drops from my face. Commenting on a woman's weight, what a charmer. We knew each other as children, and I remember how he once had a meltdown over losing a game of snap. He probably hasn't changed much.

Maxim does most of the talking over dinner, and he doesn't seem to notice or care that I'm giving monosyllabic responses to everything he's saying. When I do manage to slip in a question or two to try and steer him in a useful direction, he either gives me a vague response or ignores me completely.

Our evening finishes and I've discovered no leverage over Maxim or thought of any way to persuade him to keep my presence here a secret.

"I'll drive you home," he offers, and leads me down a narrow side street. I get into his car with the vague hope that I might still discover something useful.

Instead of starting the engine, though, he leans over the handbrake and his mouth lands clumsily on mine. I wince and try to turn my head away, but he clamps his hand on the back of my neck. Despite my endless fantasies about Russian men, I feel no attraction to Maxim. Negative attraction to Maxim. The thought of sleeping with him makes me want to rip my flesh off with my nails.

I tear my lips from his, unable to hide my disgust. "Never mind. Goodnight."

But as I reach for the door handle, he grabs me and pulls me back. "Come on, Lilia. We're miles from your father and mine. We can have a little fun."

How stupid does a man have to be to imagine there is any chemistry between us? As he tugs at my dress, I realize Maxim either doesn't believe I couldn't be attracted to him, or he just doesn't care.

Before I know what's happening, Maxim's found the lever on my seat and it jolts backward, laying me flat with it. My eyes open wide in panic as memories cascade through my mind. Ivan pawing at me. Screwing me while I gritted my teeth and cried. Discarding me on the sheets without a word.

"Stop it. Don't." But my cries fall on deaf ears as I fight to push him off me.

Maxim grabs my waist to pull him closer and he feels my swollen stomach. "What the fuck? Are you pregnant?"

Suddenly, the pressure of his body looming over me is gone, and I breathe a sigh of relief. All I want now is to go home, so I reach for the door handle once more.

But Maxim grabs hold of my wrist. "What the hell is this, Lilia? Did you think you could trap me into marriage while I raise another man's bastard?"

My eyes open wide with surprise. "I'm five and a half

months pregnant. How stupid would you have to be to believe this child is yours?"

But Maxim isn't listening to me. He's staring at my body with utter revulsion, as if he's seeing all his dearest plans go up in smoke. He must have become attached to the idea of marrying into the Brazhensky family, and now I've ruined it.

His furious gaze snaps to mine. "Did you just call me stupid, you fucking whore?"

Without waiting for my answer, he grabs me again, pushing me down against the seat and tearing at my clothes. I fight him with everything I have, clawing at his hands and trying to knee him in the balls. I'm not winning. Maxim is. He reaches beneath my dress and rips my underwear off with a tearing sound. He reaches down and fumbles with his pants and the sight of his ugly, angry-looking penis makes my blood turn cold.

Oh, no.

Oh, *fuck*.

Every time that Ivan shoved himself painfully, cruelly inside me comes flooding back. His elbow jabs my belly and fierce anger and self-protection rise up in my chest. My baby. This man will not harm my unborn child. I won't lose another one. I fumble around by the door for my handbag, desperately trying to hold Maxim off as I shriek, "Don't fucking touch me! I'm warning you."

Maxim's face is clenched in fury. He grabs hold of my legs and forces them open just as I find what I'm looking for.

A weapon.

These days I'm never without a weapon, and my fingers close on cold steel. I lift my fist and a long, thin dagger flashes in the dim light.

"*I said get off me, Ivan.*" I plunge the stiletto into the side of his neck, and his eyes go wide. He gasps, and it turns into a gurgle as I yank the dagger out again. Blood sprays all over me, the interior of the car, the windshield.

He scrabbles at the side of his neck, fear and confusion making his eyes comically wide. Nothing about this situation is funny, but hysterical laughter bubbles up my throat as I watch him topple onto me in slow motion. I'm shaking with laughter as he collapses over me, blood trickling down my face.

I just killed a man.

Maxim is an unresponsive weight on me, and suddenly everything is as still as a grave. Blood trickles from his throat and down over my chest. My laugh turns into a sob.

I shove Maxim off. Without stopping to look back, I scramble out of the car, clutching my bag for dear life.

I just want to go home. I keep away from main streets and streetlamps. The darkness and my black dress hides most of the blood, but I can feel it drying on my face.

Somehow I make it home and up to my apartment without anyone spotting me. I don't reach for the light switch by the front door, afraid of what I'll see in the mirror that hangs in the living room.

A deep, purring voice speaks out of the darkness. "Lilia."

I think I stop breathing altogether. I turn around slowly.

I can sense one man sitting on the sofa in front of me, another by the sink, and a third by the doorway into the bedroom. On any other night, fear might have clutched at my throat, but I looked fear in the face tonight and stabbed it in the throat. I'm coated in death.

They think they're the ones making the grand entrance.

"Someone turn on a light," I call.

There's a click, and a warm yellow glow bathes the living room. Three sets of cold, triumphant eyes widen in shock as they stare at my face, my chest, arms, and hair.

"Lilia!" Elyah exclaims in panic and steps toward me. He thinks it's my blood. I hold up a hand to fend him off and we both realize at the same time that I'm clutching a bloodied stiletto dagger. I turn it slowly in the light, fascinated and horrified by the fact that I'm still holding it.

Kirill steps forward and twists the dagger out of my fist, dropping it into the sink with a clatter. "Been having fun without us, *detka*?"

My legs start to shake and my teeth chatter. I've never felt less like anyone's baby girl. "Oh, loads. You should have been there."

Konstantin is watching me from the sofa, his expression baleful and his shoulders clenched. I've ruined his dramatic entrance.

"Are they dead? Who was it?" Elyah asks.

"A friend of my father's, and yes, he's dead. Very dead." I can still see Maxim's wide, dead eyes staring into mine as his bleeding body crushed me into the seat.

Elyah takes my face in his hands. "It will be all right, *solnyshko*. Kirill and I will get rid of the body. Where is it?"

Another bubble of hysterical laughter threatens to escape my throat. What's the right thing to say when the potential father of the baby I'm secretly carrying offers to cover up the murder I just committed? Thank you?

"Wait." Konstantin gets to his feet and crosses the room toward me. "This is the end of the road, and no one is leaving this apartment until I have what I want. Where are my diamonds?"

I've rehearsed this moment in the shower, imagining how I'd keep a cold silence and tell Konstantin nothing if I ever came face to face with him again. After the night I've had and the things I've done, I don't care what he knows or what he does. He can kill me if he wants. If he doesn't, Maxim Vavilov's father will.

I'm not afraid of the wrath of this deadly man.

"Fine. I'll tell you where they are. Long gone, that's where."

Konstantin examines me closely, staring past the blood that's covering me to the woman underneath. Trying to fathom whether I'm telling the truth. "What have you done with my diamonds?" he growls.

"They're not your diamonds. They belong to the women you tortured and tormented for a week in a cellar in Italy."

Konstantin grabs my dress and hauls me closer until we're nose to nose. "Don't play with me, Lilia."

I struggle in his grip, trying to wrench myself free. The dagger is laying in the sink, glinting, inviting me to snatch it up, but it's too far away. "Get your hands off me, you asshole."

"Konstantin, stop," Elyah calls out.

Konstantin ignores him. His gray eyes are sparking with fury. The trick I pulled with the whistle, using his weakness against him, totally humiliated him.

"I have thought of nothing but choking the life out of you these past few months. The only thing that's going to keep you alive is if you start talking."

"Konstantin!" Elyah shouts. He grabs hold of his *Pakhan* and tries to pry his fingers from my dress.

Konstantin rounds on him with a snarl. "I warned you not to get in my way."

"Look," Elyah insists, pointing. His face is blank with shock.

Konstantin's gaze follows Elyah's, and so does Kirill's. Everyone's eyes fasten on the fabric pulled tight over my stomach.

My swollen, pregnant stomach. I stare at it myself, shocked that it's given me away. Suddenly, I look a lot more pregnant than I did this morning.

I look huge.

A shocked whisper falls from Konstantin's lips. "*Blyat.*"

He lets me go, one finger at a time releasing my dress. I smooth it down and step away from them, my heart racing frantically.

"Get out. All of you."

No one moves. All three men are staring at me like I've suddenly sprouted tentacles. I can see them making the calculations in their minds, counting back the days and weeks.

"Lilia," Elyah breathes, and reaches for me with both hands, but I pull away from him.

"*I said get out.*"

"How many weeks? Whose is it?" Elyah demands.

"Bugs Bunny's. Whose do you think it is? What was happening to me twenty-two weeks ago?"

His pale blue eyes are stormy as he stares at my belly. "Look at you. I have imagined you this way ever since you first told me you were pregnant. You are beautiful."

Beautiful? I'm covered in blood.

My stomach lurches as I see the wonder and adoration in

his eyes. It's just how I imagined the man I love would look when I told him I'm pregnant. A look that apparently I've been secretly longing for because it goes straight to my heart.

"You are even more beautiful because the child is mine," Elyah breathes.

Konstantin looks at him sharply.

I try to step back but I've run out of apartment and my back hits the wall. Elyah puts his hands on me, cupping my swollen belly, gazing at me in adoration as he strokes across the firm, curved planes of my stomach. This is exactly what I daydreamed about when I was married to Ivan, Elyah bestowing looks of love on me while touching me like my belly is a miracle.

"Please, don't," I whisper helplessly, unable to tear my eyes away from his face.

Another hand reaches out to touch me, this one hesitant at first, but then it's placed firmly on my belly. I look up and see naked shock on Konstantin's face. His silver rings are glinting on my belly as he touches me with devastating tenderness.

"Get your hands off me." But my words are a whimper, not a demand. Konstantin lifts his eyes to mine and shakes his head.

He won't.

He utterly refuses.

A third set of hands joins the others on my belly. Strong fingers, tattooed like Elyah's but not as calloused. Sweat has broken out on Kirill's brow, and his face is blank with astonishment.

Elyah swats Kirill's hands away, but Kirill puts them back. I meet the tall, dark-haired man's gaze and discover that he's just as rocked to the core by this sudden revelation as the other two.

Except there's no chance it's Kirill's.

"What are you doing? It's not yours."

"It could be," he retorts.

"I was pregnant for weeks before we had sex on the plane."

He glares at me, something dark flickering behind his eyes. "I was there at the pageant. It could just as easily have been me."

"That is not how this works," Elyah mutters.

I stare at the three men reverently touching my belly like I'm a living saint. A moment ago, Konstantin was threatening to choke the life out of me.

The *Pakhan* lifts his eyes to mine. "It's mine. I was first."

What the hell is happening?

"But the diamonds," I choke out, but Konstantin doesn't seem to hear me. I almost want to get down on my knees and beg him to be furious with me again.

Elyah shakes his head. "It does not matter who was first, the baby could still be mine."

"I'm not going to—" I start to protest, but Konstantin and Elyah speak over me, their hands gentle on my stomach but their voices raised in fury.

"You have no right to claim Lilia and this child," Konstantin growls. "She was part of my pageant, and she is in my debt. I decide what happens next."

"It is my baby because Lilia is mine. She is going to marry me."

The two men stand off against each other, nostrils flaring, ready to tear each other apart.

7

Konstantin

Of all the tricks and surprises I thought this woman would have in store for us, I never anticipated anything like this.

Lilia.

Having *my* baby.

I remember her spread on her back on the judging table, my cock buried deep inside her as I thought I was putting her firmly in her place, this woman who thought she could outsmart me. The woman who *did* outsmart me.

That's when I got her pregnant. That wild moment.

"I'm not waiting around here while you two have a fist fight over a baby that doesn't belong to you." Lilia ducks under our arms and retrieves her handbag that she dropped on the floor.

Elyah follows her. "Not ours? Of course it is ours. Whose else could it be but mine or Konstantin's?"

"My baby belongs to me and no one else. I absolve you all of the responsibilities of fatherhood. No father's name will be listed on the birth certificate." She changes into some sneakers, grabs a coat from a hook, and reaches for the front door.

I brace my hand against the wood and slam it closed. "Where do you think you're going?"

Lilia gazes up at me with burning, sea-green eyes and a blood-streaked face. "Anywhere but here."

I thought I'd walk in here to find the Lilia I saw every day at the pageant. Tense, scared, wearing terrible clothes. Here she is in a fashionable black dress with her long, golden hair in curls and makeup on her face. Smokey, dark eyes. Dusky rose lipstick. Like she's been on a date.

Jealousy spreads through my chest. Carrying my baby, and Lilia has been dressing up for another man?

"You're not going anywhere. What happened to you tonight? Who were you with?" She's pregnant and she's covered in blood. I need answers before I decide what happens next.

"Some man tried to put his hands on me and the baby without my permission. You're next if you don't back off."

"He *what*?" There are red marks and bloody handprints all over her neck and arms, and now that I look closer, I see that Lilia's dress is torn. She's been shaking slightly this whole time, but I thought that was because she was shocked to see us.

"What man? Where?" Elyah asks.

Lilia passes a forearm over her brow to wipe her face, but

all she does is smear the blood. "I dealt with him myself. He's dead."

If I weren't so fucking angry, I'd be proud of her.

I take her shoulders in my hands and pull her closer. "What happened tonight?"

Lilia flinches and looks away. "I don't want to talk about it."

"*Detka*," Kirill drawls lazily, but with a dangerous inflection to his voice. "Whoever you killed probably has friends. Maybe they followed you. Perhaps they have found the body. What will they do to you and that baby if they find you?"

Lilia swallows hard. She needs our help, and she knows it.

"I was working today. I'm a waitress near Wenceslas Square, and a man came in at lunchtime. Someone who knew me from my old life."

"Who was it?" Elyah asks, stepping forward.

"Maxim Vavilov, the son of a friend of my father's."

A member of the Bratva, I presume. Someone who is going to be missed by powerful people. "He tracked you down here?"

She shakes his head. "He was in Prague on business, and he came into the restaurant where I was working. After my shift he insisted on taking me to dinner, and then after..." She trails off with a shudder.

I feel that shudder through my fingers as I'm still holding on to her shoulders. I've thought of no woman but Lilia since I first laid eyes on her. Curious about her. Suspicious of her. Dedicated to outwitting her. Hating her. *Wanting* her. She became my obsession with every passing day, and now I find out another man got to her while I was mere hours away and put his filthy fucking hands on my pregnant woman?

Through clenched teeth I grind out, "Let me get this straight. You ran into an old friend, and even though you're pregnant, he forced you?"

The world turns red before my eyes. I'll kill his entire fucking family for what he did to Lilia. Elyah and Kirill close in on Lilia from either side, their expressions incandescent with fury.

"He tried, but I had a knife in my purse."

Elyah's shoulder's slump with relief and he reaches out and touches Lilia's cheek, murmuring words of relief and gratitude. Kirill's body relaxes, but only a little.

From the looks of Lilia, she fought with everything she had to protect herself and the baby. My woman and child, out there in the streets, vulnerable and unguarded. I won't stand for it a moment longer. She's never leaving our sight again while she carries this child.

"Konstantin?" she asks, and I realize I'm digging my fingers into her shoulders.

I release her immediately. She wasn't forced. He tried, but she stopped him, just as I would expect a wife of mine to do.

The blood streaking her face and arms looks suddenly beautiful.

I reach out and caress her cheek. "You did well, *milaya*. You were perfect."

Just as she did when I praised her during the pageant, calling her perfect, my angel, Lilia looks as if I've pulled the ground out from beneath her. Her lower lip trembles and her face creases like she's about to cry.

"I shouldn't have got into his car. I shouldn't have even gone to meet him. He could have hurt the baby. I wanted to pack up and run far away, but I made a home for us here, and—"

Elyah looks pained and motions for me to move aside so he can take her in his arms.

Like hell I will. He's not the only one who wants to protect Lilia.

I draw her against me, maybe a little hard because she gasps when her cheek hits my chest. With her folded in my arms, I can feel how she's trembling with cold and shock. Her belly is pressed against mine, curved and solid. Five and a half months she's been carrying my child. She's big enough to notice that she's pregnant, but she'll get much bigger.

For a moment, Lilia is tense, and then she burrows her face into my shoulder, still shaking.

"Where is the body?" I murmur into her hair.

"In his car behind a restaurant called Nechci. I just walked away and left him there. I was in a daze. I've never killed—" She shudders and falls silent.

I look at Elyah and Kirill over the top of her head. "Can you both go and sort that out? I'll stay here with Lilia."

Kirill nods, his expression set and determined. Elyah seems more reluctant to leave, but the longer that corpse sits out there, the more chance there is that someone is going to find it.

"We will be back soon," Elyah promises her, brushing his knuckles across her cheek.

I keep her tight against my chest, but Lilia gazes at us in confusion. "You'll help me?"

Elyah gives her a look like she's crazy. "*Solnyshko*, of course. We cannot leave bodies lying around. We are professionals."

Kirill steps closer and slides his hand over her belly and leans close to murmur in her ear. "Be a good girl while we're gone and tell Kostya everything about this Vavilov shit, so we know how much damage control we have to do. *Da?*" He pats her. "Good girl."

Whatever they find in that car, Elyah and Kirill will make it disappear without a trace. No one will be coming after Lilia if we can help it.

I watch the pair of them heading out the door. They'll be gone for hours, which means for now, I've got Lilia all to myself.

I take a step back, and my gaze lands on her swollen belly.

Fuck, she's pregnant.

Pregnant.

I'm hit hard with the realization every time I look at her. She must have already been expecting when we had her on the plane, and she didn't say a damn thing. She should have told us. For one thing, I ordered Kirill to get information out of her however he liked. He chose to fuck her rather than torture her, but it could have so easily been the other way. He could have hurt the baby because of me.

For another thing, I have a right to fucking know she's having my baby.

"You're glaring at me," Lilia says.

"That's because I'm furious with you. Does your father know about this?"

She nods. "He caught me with a pregnancy test in my handbag and he watched as he made me take it. He was taking me back to America for an abortion."

Hatred burns in my heart. Aran Brazhensky, I should

have murdered you when I had the chance. "Is that what you wanted?"

It's Lilia's turn to look furious and hurt as well. "You think I fled halfway across Europe, bought baby things, and I'm working my ass off because I don't want this child?"

I put my hands on her shoulders and just look at her. I've seen pregnant women before, but never one who looks as beautiful as Lilia, even covered in blood. After the pageant, I planned to get my new wife pregnant. Have strong sons so I can pass onto them everything I am building. Lilia ruined my ambitions, now here she is and everything's back on schedule.

If anyone could turn my world upside down and then put it back together again, it's her.

She has a wary expression in her eyes. "Now you're smiling. What's going on in your mind?"

"I was just thinking that you're more dangerous and unpredictable than the three of us put together."

The sink isn't far from the front door in this tiny apartment. I cross to it and run a cloth under the faucet, but when I approach her, she jerks her cheek away from me.

"Leave me alone."

"Let me help you. You're still shaking."

"I was managing fine by myself."

Over her shoulder is a yellow wooden crib with a mobile of animals dancing over it. They both look second-hand, and this room is tiny, but she placed these objects with so much care. So much love.

Suddenly, vividly, I can picture my child. It has Lilia's golden hair and her delicate features. A tiny hand with even tinier fingernails that grips my finger as it gazes up at me.

"Konstantin?" Lilia turns her head to see what I'm gazing at. "Oh. I know it's not much, a second-hand crib in the living room. You're thinking how much better you could do this than me."

I shake my head. "I wasn't thinking that at all."

Our eyes meet, and her beautiful ones grow troubled. "Stop looking at me like that."

I cup her jaw and begin to wipe away the blood. The makeup. The mascara stains on her cheeks. "Like what?"

"Like there's something for you here."

There's everything here for me. Lilia commands my attention, and she's going to have every last drop. She can't do anything to stop me.

The diamonds... I don't know what to do about the diamonds. She offered to trade herself for them once. As long as she does what I say from now on, I might consider the debt repaid.

"What happened tonight? Tell me everything," I murmur, wiping her throat and arms. See, Lilia? I know how to be a husband. I can protect you. Cherish you.

I run the cloth down between her breasts. Desire you.

"Why?"

I want to get her under the shower and wash all this blood away, but she'll close that door and shut me out. "Because I have to know, or I'll lose my goddamn mind."

"I stole from you. Don't you want to rip my flesh from my body?"

"Where did he touch you? What did he do to you?"

"But the diamonds—"

"Shut up about the fucking diamonds!"

Lilia's eyes widen as I breathe hard through my nose,

struggling to control my temper. "I need to know what happened to you tonight, and you are going to tell me every. Single. Thing."

Lilia purses her lips. "I don't get you, Konstantin. For months you've been obsessing over those diamonds and chasing me all over the world to get them back. Now that I'm offering to tell you exactly what I did with them, you won't listen to me."

I throw the cloth down in the sink. "I haven't decided what to do about the diamonds, but I have decided what to do about you. The child makes it obvious. You're going to marry me."

"But what if the baby is Elyah's?"

I think on this for a moment. "Elyah is strong. I have no objection to raising his child as my own."

Her mouth falls open. "You would just take his child from him?"

"Not take. Elyah isn't going anywhere."

Her eyebrows shoot up. "So, you'd be what? Co-fathers?"

I don't have all the answers right now, and all these details are getting on my nerves. She doesn't understand the main point.

I take her face between my hands, lower my head, and kiss her. I feel her sharp inhalation before my mouth seals hers, and her lips are softly crushed beneath mine.

She tastes even better than I anticipated. As I move my mouth over hers, I realize how vividly I've been imagining this between my darker fantasies of choking the goddamn life out of her.

Lilia moans against my mouth, sounding like a protest, but her slender fingers curl into the muscles of my shoulders.

Sometime over these past few months, this became the fantasy.

Lilia.

All mine.

I break the kiss and slant my head the other way, claiming her mouth again. I can't remember the last time I kissed a woman. I can't remember it ever feeling like this.

"No one's going to lay a finger on you from this moment on. You're safe. You're mine." I feel drunk as I kiss her over and over again and her mouth opens beneath mine.

"The dagger in my handbag was for you," she says breathlessly in between receiving my kisses. "I was going to drive it into your throat the next time I saw you."

I taste her violent words with my tongue. My fingers thread through her heavy golden hair, which is tangled with blood. I always wanted a woman who would look good covered in blood.

"Whenever you're near, you make me lose sight of everything but you," I murmur, biting into her lower lip. "You're dangerous and devious."

"You're worse. I don't understand anything that you're doing." Lilia reaches up and touches my cheek. Her fingers brush my scarred flesh, and if it were any other woman, I'd jerk my head away and growl at her not to fucking touch me there.

But her touch feels like adoration.

"Then we're a good match, you and I." With my fist still tight in her hair, I sink my mouth down over hers in another brutal kiss. Every drop of anger, every impulse to murder Lilia with my bare hands, is now driving me to possess her with my entire body. I crave her taste after months of aching for her. To prove she's mine, along with this baby.

"I need to see you," I breathe, feeling for the buttons on her dress. I want to tear it open, but the memory of what she's been through tonight makes me pause, and I look up at her.

She stares at my fingers and realizes I'm asking for permission.

That realization seems to daze her more than walking in here and finding us in her home. Slowly, she nods.

I pop the buttons open one by one, the fabric rustling. The sound is loud in her silent apartment as we stare at each other. There's fear in her eyes, but longing, too. No one's ever looked at me like that, and I feel like I'm drowning in her eyes.

I peel the blood-soaked dress back from her shoulders and toss it aside, revealing Lilia's body in a black-lace bra. Her dusky nipples are tightened into points, just glimpsed through the rose-patterned fabric. There are smudges of red adorning her flesh.

No panties.

"Did he rip them off you?" I ask through my teeth.

She nods slowly, and I feel my blood boil.

Reaching behind her, I unhook her bra and, with my forefinger, drag it down her arms and let it fall to the floor. Lilia takes a breath, her body trembling, and her eyes huge.

I let my gaze travel down her body. She stands before me like Aphrodite, dressed only in blood, blonde hair cascading over her luminous shoulder, and her breasts full and heavy.

But it's her belly that draws my attention, rounded and perfect. I can't stop staring at her.

Every man craves to see the woman he's obsessed with full of his child.

Our heads are bowed together and our breaths mingle. My heart is lodged in my throat. I've never seen anything more beautiful in my life.

Lilia squeezes her eyes shut. "Don't look at me like that, please."

"I'll look at you how I choose. You're my everything."

I scoop her up in my arms and carry her into the bedroom. Gooseflesh has broken out on her body. I feel like I'm burning up, and I clasp her tightly, sharing my heat with her. Her bed is narrow and the space in here is scant, but there's room enough in here for the two of us as I lay her down.

With her blonde hair gleaming on the pillow, she gazes up at me with wide eyes, her hands pressed against my chest. For the moment, all the anger and poison in my life melts away, and there's just us.

Her and me.

She strokes her fingers down my cheek. "This doesn't feel real. Where did you even come from? How did you get here?"

As if that matters right now as I stroke my fingers down her bare legs.

Lilia closes her eyes. "I've compared every man I've met these past few months to you. To all of you."

"What, ordinary men? Nothing men? Why did you even bother?"

"Their hearts are ten times your hearts. Their honor is a hundred times your honor."

My lips curve into a smile as I push her knees apart. "My

wicked heart is what you crave. My twisted honor is all you ache for."

"No," she cries softly, closing her eyes but arching her back.

She can protest that I'm wrong all she wants. I move down the bed and swipe her sex with my tongue. *Fuck.* Her flavor bursts in my mouth, making my cock stand to attention.

"*Milaya*, you make me lose my goddamn mind." I run my tongue over her again and again, and she cries out in pleasure.

I remember how I felt about Lilia all those months ago when I pushed her to her knees and humiliated her in front of my men and all the women of the pageant. *If you behave around a woman like she's a flawless, bewitching goddess, then she's going to start thinking that she is one.*

I thought I taught her a lesson that day, but she was teaching me one.

Lilia's nails dig into my shoulders through my shirt. She smells like blood and flowers, a combination that drives all thoughts from my mind except thrusting my cock into her tight, wet heat. I go on licking her, listening to her moan, and feeling her getting wetter and wetter against my tongue. She's been without a man for over four months in this state. She must be losing her mind.

"Konstantin," she cries out, and I can't bear it any longer. I sit up, and with her breath fanning my chest, I pull my shirt over my head, undo my pants, and push them down. Taking my heavy cock in my hand, I survey her, wondering how best to leave my mark on my woman. Make her suck me. Fuck her tits. Fill that sweet pussy with my cum.

A spasm goes through my balls. No contest. I didn't savor

it when I was getting her pregnant. I need to relive that moment and burst deep inside her.

I line myself up at her wet and swollen entrance and thrust into her. I curse at the delicious grip on my cock and stop to capture her mouth with mine.

"We shouldn't—" she starts to say against my lips, but I draw back and pound into her again, making her moan.

"You want those other men now?" I brace one hand by her head and push her knees up to her shoulders so my dick drives deeper into her pussy. How vulnerable she looks with her swollen belly. "Are you wishing some lesser *mudak* was here with you, with his tiny dick and pathetic heart?"

Lilia holds tight to my muscular shoulders as she gazes up at me breathlessly. I can tell she's wondering if this is some strange dream.

I'll just have to prove to her how real I am.

Every few thrusts she moans louder, breathes harder, looks a little more desperate. Her cheeks are flushed pink and her mouth is parted. My desire for her is molten lava.

"Konstantin," she whimpers again.

"That's right, fucking moan my name. I want it on your tongue when you come for me."

"This is wrong. We shouldn't be doing this. It's making everything worse."

But she clenches my shoulders tighter, and she wouldn't let me stop fucking her even if I tried. Her pussy is gripping my cock like a vise, full of what she needs.

"What will Elyah and Kirill think if they come back from doing my dirty work and find us like this?" she asks between moans.

I love seeing her like this. Bent to my will and more beautiful than ever. "They will be picturing it this very second, full of envy that I'm the one who has you pinned to the bed with my cock."

"You mean jealousy."

"*Envy*," I say again. "I was full of envy watching Kirill screw you on the plane. When you came for him, I felt you on my dick as vividly as I did the first time. Now it's my turn, and Elyah and Kirill will smell the sex all over us when they return, and they will crave to know every detail about what we've done and wish they were in my place."

I pin her to the bed with as much weight as I dare and smile wickedly. "Will you fuck them, too, *milaya*? They won't want you to wash me off before they take their turn with you. When you come for them, I'll feel that, too."

"Turn?" she says in a strangled voice.

I've never wanted to share a woman before, but talking like this to Lilia makes me feral with desire. I want them to fuck her. I need them to make her ours. Leave their mark on her and keep all the other worthless men away. "Maybe we won't bother to take turns and I'll fuck your mouth while they take your pussy. We've got months of frustrations to take out on you."

"In your dreams," she gasps, her hands pressed against my chest, but it sounds like an invitation, not a refusal.

I sit up and slide my hand beneath her head, cradling it so she can watch me fuck her. "This is no dream. Look at me claiming you."

Lilia's hands clench on the sheets. She shudders with shock and desire, forcing me deeper. And then she comes with a long, ragged cry. Her inner muscles ripple so hard that I feel like I'm riding a bucking horse. I thrust deeper and harder, and suddenly my own climax rushes up, fierce and overwhelming. I feel myself burst inside of her in four long, hard thrusts.

I rest on my fists, my head bowed over her as I catch my breath. Then I slowly draw out of her, aching to go but longing to see her pussy filled with my glistening cum. I rub her inner lips until it finally wells up against my thumb.

I murmur, "That's perfect, *milaya*. That's what I've been missing."

It should have been like this the first time. My heart feels a little lighter knowing that I've set things right.

Lilia looks dazed from the sex, but she slowly sits up and shakes her head. "Konstantin, this isn't right. We shouldn't have done that."

I sit back on my haunches and flex my head from side to side, feeling a delicious stretch in my shoulder muscles. I feel better than I have in months. "Shouldn't we have?"

"Are you even sorry for what you did?"

I crack one eye open and look at her. "Why would I be sorry for having sex with you?"

"No, sorry for the *pageant*," she seethes.

Oh. That. "All that's in the past. What matters is what's here in front of us. You, me, and this baby." A great rush of emotion fills me from head to toe as I realize I will get to meet this child in less than four months' time. I will hold it in my arms and vow to protect it from every terrible thing in this world. It doesn't matter who fathered the baby in a literal sense, I will be its father and Lilia will be my wife. Elyah and Kirill will be co-fathers, uncles, whatever they like. But they will stay close, and no one will stand in our way.

I think about it, rubbing the back of my neck and smiling.

Lilia will realize how perfect this is too, soon enough.

I brace my hands by her head to kiss her, but she turns her face away from me.

"You're not sorry at all," she says, and her voice is choked. "Even now that you know you're possibly going to be a father, nothing has changed."

"Nothing has changed?" I growl. "The whole fucking universe has changed. Am I punishing the woman who stole from me, or am I holding her in my arms and swearing to cherish and protect her and our baby for the rest of their lives?"

"You mean cage and humiliate us." Lilia pushes me off her and sits up. "Say you're sorry for what you did to me and the other contestants."

"Why? What would be the point?"

"So I can have one tiny grain of hope that you might become a better man."

A better man? I am the best fucking man. She said it herself. She's only craved us. "I can't go back and change anything that I've done. This is the man I am and always will be."

She purses her lips and regards me in angry silence. "Do you know why I hated my first husband? He treated me like an object and a vessel, not a person."

"I would kill him if he weren't already dead."

"I don't want your jealousy and your anger." Lilia's expression is filled with anguish. "I want to know that you see how wrong it is to treat people that way. You can't take someone's freedom and crush it to dust."

I rub my fingers across my forehead and my suddenly aching scar. "What do you want from me, Lilia?"

"Just say you're sorry. Start there. Admit that you shouldn't have done what you did."

A muscle tics in my jaw. This is one of Lilia's tricks. If I tell her that I'm sorry about the pageant, then she will use it against me somehow. "Stop trying to trap me into something."

"What kind of trap is it to ask you to speak one word of sympathy or regret? Are you so proud? So inhuman?"

Why should I apologize for what I did when it worked? I found the perfect woman for me.

"Konstantin," she whispers sadly. "How can you expect your wife to love you if you're never able to say the words *I'm sorry*."

I stand up and reach for my clothes without looking at her, "That's enough talking. Go and take a shower and get the rest of that blood off you."

"You are unbelievable."

What I am is practical. I found the woman who is worthy of my name and to bear my children. She's already pregnant, so now all that needs to be done is marry her. "Elyah and Kirill will be back soon, and as soon as they are, we're all leaving for London."

"What's in London?"

"My home. Which is going to be your home now, and where we will raise our children."

She swings her legs over the edge of the bed and holds on to the mattress. "You speak of marriage and a home and children when your barbaric pageant stands between us?"

"My pageant worked. Here is my bride, Contestant Number Eleven."

Lilia flinches and starts breathing faster and faster. "You

can't say one word to make up for the mountains of pain that you heaped on my head and the heads of the other women in your pageant? Not one word, Konstantin? How could it hurt you? Just say you're sorry."

I glare at her in defiance. I can sense what's waiting for me on the other side if I speak that word. Remorse delivers nothing but pain, and I have too many other things that need my attention.

Lilia gets to her feet and paces. She's naked and her belly is swollen, but she doesn't seem to be aware of either. "You're all the same. My father. Ivan. Maxim. When will I be free of men like you?" She whimpers and cups her belly. "Now I'm carrying your baby. How can I ever hope to be free?"

I don't like the way she's turned pale so fast when her cheeks were flushed not long ago. "You need to sit down. You're going to make yourself sick."

"You're the one who is sick," she seethes. She whimpers again, shock flickering over her face. Then she staggers.

"Lilia?" Panic slices through me, and I cross the room and grab her arms. Her skin feels cold and clammy and there's sweat on her brow.

"I feel... I feel..."

Alarm blares in my skull. Elyah described to us how she collapsed when she had her miscarriage. The police invaded her home. Lilia's safe little world that she'd built for her baby was encroached upon and she couldn't bear it.

The three of us have done the same thing by coming here tonight.

Lilia collapses in my arms, her face chalk white and slack, and her eyes closed.

"Lilia!"

8

Elyah

The car is exactly where Lilia said it would be, abandoned in an alleyway behind the restaurant. It's so dark that we have to cup our fingers around our eyes and peer through the windows to see if it's the right one. When I open the passenger door, the top half of Maxim's dead body flops out of the vehicle. He's wearing a dark suit and tie and his white shirt is soaked in blood that's poured from a wound in the side of his neck.

Kirill sticks his finger in the bloody hole and wiggles it. "Damn. Lilia got him good."

I grin at the grisly sight. She sure did. One clean stab of the slender blade and this piece of shit was done for. "Where are his keys?"

Now that we have Lilia back, I don't think I'll ever stop smiling.

Once they're fished out of his pocket and we've stashed his body in the trunk, we head north out of the city, me driving Maxim's car and Kirill following in our rental.

We don't have to travel far from Prague before we're in the dark, deserted countryside, downriver from the city. Kirill gets to work mangling the man's fingertips and knocking out his teeth with a rock. While undressing the body, I gather his ID and credit cards, then point out tattoos to flay from his flesh. Using the man's shirt, tie, and pants, we lash heavy stones to the body and hurl him into the river.

Another mile downstream, I spot a hill above the river where we can roll the car into the water. With the handbrake off, Kirill and I push it over the precipice and watch it race down the slope and sink beneath the surface.

Kirill brushes his hands together. "Nice work. Hungry? I wonder if Lilia has any food."

Food is the last thing on my mind as we head back into the city. We stink of blood, but I barely notice that when all my thoughts are of Lilia.

She's having my baby.

My baby, as it should have been from the beginning. I'm being given a chance to put things right for her. There's a warm weight in my chest and a smile touches my lips again.

Beside me, Kirill is running his fingers through his hair, his knees spread wide as he lounges in the bloodied passenger seat. "I don't know what you're smiling about. It's my baby."

I roll my eyes and ignore his nonsense. "Your timing is all off, my friend. Be careful she does not stab you in the throat for sticking a gun in her pussy. That is what should be on your mind right now."

"Will that be before or after she slits your throat for threatening to break her arms, or promising to kill her, or nearly killing her by putting a noose around her neck?"

I grind my teeth together and glare at the road ahead. "We are lovers. We have been lovers for more than two years and the world has been against us. Of course, there have been misunderstandings. I will make everything up to the woman I love now that I know the truth and we are going to be a family."

"Fuck your family. I want that baby."

An ominous feeling rolls down my spine. I know everything about what landed Kirill in prison all those years ago. He told me the whole story between us beating our enemies to death and adding new ink to our bodies. We've been closer than brothers ever since, but if he's set his twisted heart on making Lilia and that baby his, then he and I are going to have a big fucking problem.

Both of our phones chime at the same time. Kirill reaches for his and reads the screen.

"It's from Konstantin. He says get back there now."

I grip the steering wheel. "What? Call him. Find out what is wrong."

Kirill does, but he lowers the phone a moment later. "No answer. Do you think it's Lilia and the baby?"

"Do not even say that," I growl, putting my foot on the gas and tearing along the road.

Before we even turn onto Lilia's street, I see the flashing of emergency lights. My throat feels tight, and I can't feel my fingers as I park haphazardly in a squeal of rubber and get out of the car.

Lilia is strapped to a gurney with an oxygen mask on her face. Her eyes are closed.

What is happening? Did we do this to her? *What the fuck is happening?*

The EMTs load her into the ambulance and get in behind her. One of them starts to close the doors, but I grab them and pull myself up and inside.

"I will ride with her," I say in both Russian and English, hoping that they will understand me.

"Are you her husband?" the EMT replies in English, and glances over his shoulder at Konstantin. "I thought—"

"I am the father," I say, pushing past him to crouch by Lilia's head. I can barely force the terrible words out. "Is she losing this baby, too?"

"She's had a miscarriage before?" the EMT asks, getting to work on her with a stethoscope and other things that I don't recognize. The doors slam shut, and we drive off down the street.

Lilia's face is pale, and the circles are dark beneath her eyes, just as they were last time. I remember every horrible detail of her first miscarriage, and it's repeating before my fucking eyes. This time, the baby is right there for me to see, swelling her belly, and this one is mine. Oh God, it's mine. I can't fucking bear it. "Two, three years ago. She was only a few weeks along."

I clasp her hand in mine and press it to my forehead, bowing over it and whispering a frantic prayer. We did this to her. We invaded her life and her home when she thought she was safe, and the shock was too much for her.

Those fucking diamonds.

That fucking pageant.

I have ruined my happiness and hers because I am proud, vicious, and stupid.

At the hospital, I follow helplessly behind Lilia and the EMTs as they wheel her into the ER. I'm made to stand in a corner while a doctor examines her and a nurse takes her vitals.

They manage to wake her up, but she's confused and so ill-looking, I want to put my fist through the wall.

Konstantin and Kirill hurry into the room just as the doctor finishes examining her and walks over to me.

"This woman is your wife, girlfriend?"

I swallow, hard, terrified of what I'm about to hear. "My fiancée, Lilia."

"Your fiancée has low blood pressure, but she is doing fine and so is the baby. The fetal heartbeat is strong."

I let out a groan of gratitude and close my eyes. Either side of me, I feel Konstantin and Kirill sag with relief.

"Your fiancée should see her obstetrician first thing in the morning. Meanwhile, she needs rest, and she's not to be placed under any stress."

I could get down on my knees and thank this doctor all night. Instead, I round on Konstantin and growl in Russian, "What were you doing to her when she collapsed? Were you torturing a pregnant woman over some fucking diamonds?"

He shoves me away from him, his eyes glittering. "I would not harm the mother of my child. We were talking about our future."

To my surprise, Kirill is seething with just as much anger as I am. He's never angry with Konstantin, but he reaches out and grabs a fistful of his shirt. "What the fuck were you talking about to make her so sick?"

"I don't know what happened. She was fine. We even had sex."

I grit my teeth, hard. She was attacked tonight, and the first thing he did was fuck her?

"Then I told her we would be leaving for London, but she kept talking about the pageant."

I shove his shoulder. "Why were you talking about the pageant at a time like this? What the fuck is wrong with you?"

"I didn't bring it up, she did. She kept insisting I apologize."

We're practically shouting and we're drawing stares from the medical staff. We're probably a hairsbreadth from being thrown out, and worse, we're adding to Lilia's stress during a time when she absolutely doesn't need any more.

"You should have said sorry," I seethe, lowering my voice. "The pageant, the diamonds, they do not matter anymore. Why can you not see past the end of your proud fucking nose?"

"You think I am not worried about Lilia when it is my child she is carrying?"

His child? I could fucking punch him.

I turn away from him and stalk over to Lilia, the fury melting from my face as I reach out and gently take her hand. "*Solnyshko*. How are you feeling? Did they tell you the baby is just fine?"

"Yes. But, Elyah—"

I place a gentle hand on her stomach. A moment later, it's joined by Konstantin's, and then Kirill's. I wonder if I should push their hands away and snarl that this baby is mine, but I haven't got the heart. Something about all our hands on her belly makes my temper cool, and I don't think I want to.

"This is insane," Lilia whispers, staring at our hands. She lifts her gaze to mine, and then to Konstantin and Kirill. "What are we going to do?"

I stroke her hair back from her brow. There are threads of dried blood among the gold strands. "We will figure it out. Do not worry about it right now."

"A moment ago, you were all fighting. You're going to keep fighting over this child, and we will be caught in the middle of you. I can't—"

Kirill takes her chin in his hand and draws her face up to his, his expression fierce. "*Detka*. Stop. We three fight sometimes. We are hotheaded idiots. It is nothing." He raises his eyebrows, waiting for her response.

Slowly, she nods.

"Him," he says, nodding at Konstantin. "He will do whatever you want. You just tell us if he won't, Elyah and I will punch his stupid fucking face until he does."

Lilia's mouth twitches.

He pats her cheek. "You see? Simple, not hard."

Kirill glares at me and Konstantin, waiting for us to agree. I nod, but Konstantin doesn't say anything. I flash him a look to tell my *Pakhan* that if he upsets Lilia again, we really will punch his stupid fucking face.

"Who is your obstetrician?" I ask Lilia. "I will call them in the morning and make an appointment for you."

Lilia shakes her head. "I don't have one."

"Then which doctor have you been seeing?" Kirill asks.

She purses her lips and doesn't answer.

He stares at her in astonishment. "No one? No one has done a checkup on you and the baby? Your blood pressure? Nothing?"

She glares up at him. "You think it's that easy? You think I could have walked into a doctor's office while I'm in hiding from the three of you and working illegally in this country?"

I want to tell her that she above all people should know how important it is that she gets proper medical attention when she's pregnant, but I swallow it down. Under normal circumstances, Lilia would be lavishing everything on this baby that she could. It's our fault that she's not. "Of course. We are sorry."

Lilia shoots a ferocious glare at Konstantin. "At least one of you can say it."

He glares back at her.

I scoop Lilia against my chest and hold her, pressing a kiss against the top of her head. "Do not worry. We will find you doctor in Prague, and you will have all the scans and tests you need. Nothing is going to happen to you and the baby, I swear it."

For a moment I feel her melt against me. This is all I want. To comfort my woman when she needs me. To know she relies on me to protect her and the vulnerable child inside her.

Her fingers trail down my chest as she draws away from me and my arms feel empty without her. She turns to Konstantin and regards him coolly.

"If you're going to lose your temper, I suppose the best place is here where there are security guards. I have something to tell you."

All the hairs stand up on the back of my neck.

"Something to tell all of us?" Kirill asks. "Or just Kostya?"

"Just Konstantin," she replies, gazing at our *Pakhan*.

He glowers back at her, his jaw set.

"There's no point in pretending you want this child just so you can get the diamonds back. There are no diamonds. There's no money, either. I broke the tiara into pieces and sold the diamonds months ago. The money is being sent to various accounts and you'll never be able to touch it." Her beautiful eyes flare with anger. "Now you know everything, so you can just get out."

9

Lilia

I stare at the grainy image on the ultrasound screen. My baby.

That's my *baby*.

I'm seeing them for the first time, and I can't tear my eyes away. I trail my fingers over the shapes of light and dark that are their head, their body, their little limbs, every single part of them precious. A miracle, so tiny and vulnerable and nestled within me.

"Do you want to know if it's a boy or a girl?" the obstetrician asks, moving the scanner over the jelly on my stomach.

"No," I whisper, still gazing at the screen.

"You want it to be a surprise?" she replies.

"I don't care if it's a boy or a girl. I just want it to be safe in my arms."

A hand reaches for mine and squeezes it, and I know

without looking that it's Elyah. Still enraptured by the monitor, I squeeze back without thinking because it's what eighteen-year-old me wants, that innocent girl who loved him with all her heart.

"Boy or girl," he murmurs, his voice husky with emotion. "It does not matter."

I don't want to see his face, but a force stronger than I am impels me to look up. Elyah is staring at the monitor with an enraptured expression on his face. Feeling my stare, he smiles down at me, his bright blue eyes gentle and filled with love.

"They are beautiful, Lilia."

For a moment, I can't breathe.

Down by my feet, Kirill is staring at the screen with folded arms, his curls falling into his eyes and hiding his expression. I'm used to seeing him swaggering around, not a care in the world. Now, he's rigid and so intent on the monitor that he doesn't seem to be aware of anything else in the room. I don't understand his outburst at the hospital last night, threatening to beat Konstantin if he kept stressing me out. Maybe he's worried that if Konstantin and Elyah fight over the baby, it will tear his crew apart.

Konstantin is standing back against the wall and glaring at me, his gaze burning into mine. He hasn't moved since the four of us entered the room with the obstetrician. After the bombshell I dropped on him at the hospital, I think he's secretly planning my demise. A way to punish me using this baby.

A chill creeps over me as I wonder if he'll try to rip the child from my arms the moment it's born.

"You must come to all your appointments," the obstetrician tells me, putting down her equipment and wiping the jelly from my stomach with a smile. "Especially now you know I don't bite."

We made up a story about me being terrified of doctors to explain why I avoided having a checkup and scan for so long.

"I—"

But Kirill is the one who answers. "She will."

I give him a strange look. Neither Elyah nor Konstantin seem to think Kirill's behavior is weird.

But it's *weird*.

The obstetrician tells me I can get dressed. Elyah's firm grip is on my hand and my waist, and then he's handing me my underwear and leggings. I think he would dress me himself if I let him, and I have to be insistent about dragging the Lycra up my own legs. Before I can stop him, he settles the waistband over my bump. I stare at his tattooed fingers moving so gently against my skin.

"I can do it," I say, feeling flustered, knowing everyone's eyes are on me.

"I know. I just want to," Elyah tells me, a smile playing around his lips. He adjusts my T-shirt into place around my shoulders, and then his forefinger slowly brushes my throat, and his smile dies.

For a long time, I bore the brutal red mark of the rope he placed around my throat. His gaze locks on mine, and I can tell we're both remembering the same thing.

You have to go on believing I'm a liar. Otherwise, you'll have to face up to all the cruel things you've done to the woman you love for no good reason.

The last time he was standing so close to me, he was putting a hangman's noose around my neck. I nearly strangled to death, but Elyah brought me back, and the rope lay on the floor next to us while we made love.

I needed that key in his pocket.

It wasn't about sex.

But I still wanted him.

It's so fucking messed up. I suck in a frightened breath and reach for my handbag.

With his hands gently on my shoulders, he dips his head so he can murmur in my ear, "I will not hurt you. I am not going anywhere. I am sorry, Lilia."

His touch and voice never fail to send golden sparks winging through me, but then they cluster in my throat as unshed tears. Why does loving Elyah have to be so painful?

He turns away and addresses the obstetrician. "Lilia really is well? She will not collapse again?"

"As long as she follows my directions about keeping her checkups, eating properly, and resting, she will be fine," the woman assures him with a smile.

"Can she have sex?" Kirill is still standing as still as stone with his arms crossed.

The obstetrician frowns at Kirill. "Well, she… I thought this man was the father?" she says, gesturing toward Elyah.

Kirill smiles broadly at her, wickedness glinting off every white tooth.

My face burns.

"Yes, intercourse is perfectly safe." She hesitates, looking from one man to the next, at their tattoos, their hard eyes, their muscles, and I can tell she's thinking that there's nothing safe about these three men.

"Sex isn't on the table," I say quickly. "These men aren't

my partners, and you don't need to pay any attention to them."

The obstetrician gives me a quick, tight smile, as if to say, *It's none of my business*, and leaves the room.

I glare at Kirill. "Why did you have to ask her that? I have to see this woman until my baby is born. She probably thinks we're in some kind of weird sex cult now."

His demonic smile grows even wider. "You'll be thanking me for asking that question when you're climbing the walls, begging for all of us to fuck you."

All of them.

"You wish," I reply, but I don't sound defiant. I sound breathy.

All the love and excitement from seeing the ultrasound is cycling through me. I'm in a confined space with three men I haven't been able to stop thinking about. I crave to feel their hands on me. Their lips on me. Hell, I need to be touched so badly that I'm this close to begging all three of them to press in on me from all sides and just squeeze me tight. My face full of their chests. Their heavy breathing in my ear. My gaze grows unfocused as I vividly imagine it, and there's a fierce pounding between my legs.

Kirill smirks and holds out his hand to the door. "Let's get you home before you start taking your clothes off again."

I snap back into myself and push past him with a glare. Just because my body is craving something, doesn't mean I want to give in to it.

Back at my apartment, everything feels far too small with three huge men taking up all the space. Elyah takes the obstetrician's instructions deeply to heart and corrals me into the bedroom. When he tries to help me undress, I swat his hands away. I'm not so helpless that I can't put my own pajamas on.

Before I can stop him, Elyah presses a kiss to my forehead, and my stomach swoops. "Rest here. I will cook."

I don't need to be told to get into bed because after the night I've had, I'm exhausted. Tucked up in my bed, I can hear Konstantin in the living room speaking on his phone in Russian. Working, I presume.

The moment I start to drift off, I sit up with a gasp and cry out, "My shift."

Kirill pokes his head through the door. "Your what?"

I explain to him about the restaurant and how I'm supposed to be working today. How am I supposed to carry plates around a restaurant for hours if I also need to rest? Perhaps another waitress can take my shifts for a week.

"I will take care of it," Kirill says, and disappears, closing the door behind him.

With an uneasy feeling, I lay back down.

When I wake, the sun has shifted in the sky and hours must have passed. Someone is standing over me, and I realize it's Elyah, holding a bowl. He crouches down next to my bed, and I realize he's offering soup. It smells wonderful, and my stomach growls.

I want to tell him to get out and that I can look after myself, but once he settles the bowl in my lap and hands me the spoon, my willpower vanishes. Just one meal. I need strength if I'm going to tell them to leave.

To my surprise, it tastes wonderful. I didn't think Elyah was the cooking type. "You made this?"

He clears his throat. "I bought it. I am not good cook. But I will get better," he adds quickly.

I don't know what to say to that. *Don't bother* sounds churlish, seeing as I'm eating what he's given me.

When I finish, Elyah takes the bowl from me. "Please do not collapse again. I cannot bear it."

It's on the tip of my tongue to snap back that I didn't enjoy my trip in the ambulance either, but he looks so crushed already. He must have been terrified and reliving the day I miscarried. "You looked as scared as I felt at the hospital."

"I was, *solnyshko*," he says, cupping my face. "No one is going to hurt you. Not your father. Not that man's family. You do not have to worry."

I presume he means Maxim's family, and I remember all over again that I killed a man last night. Then these three showed up. No wonder I fainted.

"I found out who betrayed Ivan to the feds," Elyah says, and his expression is suddenly stormy.

"You did? Who?"

"Vasily," he says through clenched teeth. "The police caught him with drugs, and instead of holding his hands up to what he did, he started informing on all of us."

Vasily? The name doesn't mean anything to me. "Who?"

Elyah stares at me. Then he laughs, but it's a tired, sad laugh. "It is not funny, but somehow it is. Our lives were ruined by someone who was so far beneath your notice."

I don't like it when Elyah talks about me like I'm some lofty princess. I'm just me, pregnant and terrified. "He wasn't beneath me. I just don't remember anyone called Vasily ever coming to the house. As far as I've known all this time, Vasily didn't do anything to hurt me. You did."

Elyah's expression flickers with pain and he reaches for me.

I put a hand on Elyah's chest to fend him off. "Where is Vasily now?"

He drops his hands with a sigh, but his eyes are burning with hatred and defiance. "I killed him."

Another man dead. I realize that Vasily probably died months ago, but the body count around us is really stacking up. One of Ivan's own men betrayed him, and for such a stupid, careless reason. I wait to feel shocked, or even surprised, but the first word out of my mouth is, "Good."

A smile spreads over his face. "Really? It is not the sort of thing that usually pleases a woman."

Vasily tore Elyah and I apart over some drugs that he might not have even gone to prison over. He was the reason the police came into my home and I lost my baby. Laying here in this bed worrying over this new pregnancy seems to have given me a taste for blood and vengeance. "How did he die?"

Elyah flicks a dark look at me. "With a broken bottle in his guts while I screamed in his face that I was avenging you." He stares at my stomach, covered by the blanket, and reaches out tentatively to touch me. "But you are right. It was not him who hurt you. It was me. I am sorry, Lilia. *Prosti menya.*"

Forgive me.

I stare at his hand on my belly. Elyah leans closer, reaching up to cup my jaw as his lips brush over mine. A soft question.

Do you still want me, solnyshko?

My eyes close and I just breathe, my lips parted. Elyah presses his mouth over mine with a soft groan and gathers me closer. His fingers skim my throat, and though it's long healed, I feel the burn of the rope.

Panic slams through me. He's trapping me in a cage again, after all I went through to free myself of him and his friends last year.

I turn my face away from his. "I don't forgive you. I can never forgive you."

It doesn't matter how good his kisses feel. It doesn't matter what my body wants. I can't allow myself to love him after everything he's done.

Elyah doesn't move. "I will never stop trying. I will not give up."

As I stare into his frost-laced blue eyes, I believe him, but it changes nothing. "You do what you have to do, Elyah. I will do what I have to do. This baby is what's important. Not us."

I put my hands against his chest and push him away, and he goes, but his expression is crushed as he stands up and moves toward the door.

With all the strength I have, I harden my heart to him.

His love turned to hate in a moment when someone told him I betrayed him. He doesn't trust me. He doesn't believe in me.

Elyah casts me one last look, and then he's gone. I pull the blankets into my arms, hugging them, holding on tight and wishing they were his body.

As I'm lying there, I feel my belly shift all on its own. It's a strange sensation, and for a second I don't know what it is, until I realize with a gasp of delight that it's the baby moving.

I jump out of bed and reach for the door so I can call for Elyah to come and feel, too. Then my fingers fall from the door handle.

What am I thinking?

Sharing that moment with him would be as good as

telling him that I want him to be the child's father. A hollow feeling opens up inside me as I remember a fantasy I had a long, long time ago. So long ago that it feels like it belongs to another woman. Lilia Kalashnik daydreamed about her husband's big, strong driver holding her in his arms while his hands cupped her belly and he smiled in wonder.

An impossible dream, but she longed for it with all her heart.

"Foolish little girl," I whisper, sitting back down on the bed, tears slipping down my face as my lonely heart is full of tender thoughts about Elyah.

∞

My small apartment feels even smaller with three massive men living alongside me, and I'm hyperaware of them at all times. Breathing. Flexing. The deep rumble of their voices. I try to block them out and do the things that need to be done, but I can't get so much as a cup of yogurt from the fridge without one of them getting in my way.

They're sitting on my sofa. Using my towels. There are vodka bottles in my trash and shaving foam in the bathroom sink. They're too big for this place. I can see them. I can smell them. I can practically taste them, and it's driving me up the wall.

"Why can't you all go to a hotel?" I shout at them one afternoon, snatching one of my bras from Konstantin. I left it hanging over the back of a chair last week to dry. That doesn't mean he can get his dirty hands all over it. "Why do you have to live in my apartment? Better yet, leave the country."

"Lilia. The baby," Elyah reminds me. He's just come back

from somewhere, the supermarket I presume, and he places bags of groceries on the counter. I only have one tiny square of counter to prepare food, and I wanted to make myself some lunch, but now there's no space.

"I'll worry about my baby, thank you," I snap at him. "Did it occur to you that you're adding to my stress by being here?"

The bathroom door opens, and Kirill steps out in a cloud of steam, stark naked. Water droplets cling to his muscles and drip from his dark curls. His cock isn't standing to attention, but it's thickened, as if he's been in there thinking about sex.

He *looks* like sex.

I can vividly imagine what his chest would feel like against my tongue and the way his shoulder muscle would feel between my teeth.

"What is all this fuss?" Kirill asks with a frown, walking over to me. "We are following your doctor's orders. How can we take care of you and the baby if we are somewhere else?"

I can't take my eyes off the way his semi-hard cock swings as he moves. The orgasm that Konstantin gave me feels like it was eons ago.

A smirk passes over his lips. "Keep giving me those sex eyes, *detka*. See what happens to you."

Oh, Jesus Christ. I turn away and hurry into my room.

Kirill follows me, his dick still out and swaying. I throw a towel at him, and he catches it but doesn't wrap it around his waist.

"The three of us decided that when your blood pressure is normal, we are leaving for London. It's not safe here in the city where you murdered a man."

Maxim's father won't know it was me. As far as anyone

else is concerned, Maxim has disappeared without a trace. "I'm not going anywhere with you."

Kirill places a finger over my lips and his eyes travel down my body. "You are tense because you need to come. How about a game of Russian roulette? We don't need the gun this time. We don't even need the roulette. Just the Russian."

He reaches for the waistband of my leggings and the world disappears in a horny pink haze. His dick is getting harder and harder. I stare at the thick vein at the root of his cock and imagine what it would look like disappearing inside me, over and over again. "I would be insane to have sex with you."

"Good, because I'm crazy, remember? Tell me you will not come. I will enjoy proving you wrong."

He gets my waistband down to my hips before I come to my senses and push him away. "Stop that. If you're so worried about me and the baby, get out of my apartment. We will be so much happier."

Kirill pushes a hand through his damp curls and smiles lazily at me. A water droplet runs down his chest and over his washboard stomach, and a moan nearly escapes my lips.

"Come find me when you're ready to be fucked. Meanwhile, rest, and let us take care of everything. It's what we do best."

I watch his muscular ass as he swaggers off in search of clothing, lost in a fantasy of being licked, stroked, and fingerfucked to orgasm over and over again, all the while denying them their own release. That would teach them.

I put my hands over my face and shake my head. That would teach them nothing, and the next thing I'd know, one or more of them would be dicking me down while telling me they've definitely learned their lesson.

Elyah cooks something with beans and smoked sausage for dinner. I can't tell if it's soup or stew when he puts it down in front of us, and some of the vegetables looked burned. As much as I resent his presence in my apartment, I know how hard it is to cook when you have no idea what you're doing. I lift my spoon and have a taste, reasoning that it probably isn't as bad as it looks.

It is.

Konstantin is gazing at his dinner like he wants to put a bullet in it.

Kirill takes a mouthful and grimaces like it's poison. Then he throws his spoon down. "If I were the judge at your trial, I would sentence you to another ten years for this crime."

Elyah is standing by the stove, dishing out his own bowl. "It is not good? It is what my *babushka* cooks when someone is pregnant." He frowns. "Maybe I did not do it right."

I force myself to swallow a mouthful. Elyah has put in too much seasoning and overcooked it, but it's got everything I need. Vegetables. Protein. I wince as I take another bite into something crunchy. Whole cloves of raw garlic. Did he add those at the end? I'm pretty sure Elyah's *babushka* would have minced them.

Kirill fishes one out and holds it up. "At least the baby will not be a vampire."

Elyah drops the serving spoon into the pan with a clatter and advances on Kirill. "Does this say world-class cook?" he asks, lifting his T-shirt to reveal the Russian word inked across his ribs. "Does this say Michelin star fucking chef?"

Kirill holds up both hands, leaning back in his chair. "Whoa, Elyah—"

"It says what I am good for. *All* I am good for. I am a weapon. I know how to kill, but I cannot make you fucking cordon bleu."

I stand up and put a hand on his chest. "You're not a weapon, Elyah. Don't talk about yourself that way."

His expression softens as he gazes down at me, and the longing in his eyes broadcasts exactly what he's thinking. That I'm the only one who can make him believe that he has more to offer than violence and death. Slowly, he reaches for me, sliding his hands around my waist. As he dips his head and his lips brush mine, his palm cups my swollen belly. Every taut line of his body softens.

For me.

Only for me.

As he touches me, it feels like they're all touching me. He groans, crushing his lips over mine and holding me tight against his chest.

My eyes fly open, and I struggle in his arms. How did we get here? We were having dinner just a moment ago.

"Lilia, please," Elyah murmurs huskily, letting me go, but slowly, hoping I'll change my mind. Disappointment and frustration wash over him.

As I glance around at the other men, there's irritation on Kirill's face and stony resignation on Konstantin's. I push my hands through my hair and groan. Having them here is making me crazy.

I head for my bedroom. A moment later, Elyah appears in the doorway.

"I will go get something else for dinner. What do you want?"

His fine blond hair is rumpled and there are red stains on his T-shirt. "You've got sauce on you."

Elyah glances down at himself and plucks his T-shirt away from his chest. Then he pulls it off. "Do you want pizza? You should not have pizza all the time, but you must be hungry, and pizza is quick."

I should be immune to the sight of Elyah's naked torso, but all that warm, tattooed flesh makes my mouth water.

Fuck the pizza. I want you.

He must see the need in my eyes as his expression changes and he steps closer. Moving slowly this time. Carefully. Like he used to do when he was Ivan's driver edging closer and closer to his boss's wife.

"You shouldn't be alone with me," I murmur, backing away, but not very fast. "What if I plunge a knife into your heart?"

"I would say thank you for the gift of this precious knife, *solnyshko*. And then I would die happy in your arms."

With a casual hand, he reaches up and rubs the back of his neck, muscles rippling, and I'm reminded of the day he fixed things so that I would come upon him half naked in the laundry room. He took my hands and pressed them to his chest, stopping just short of kissing me, though all I could think about at the time was him pulling me into his arms and taking whatever he wanted.

"You're doing it again," I say, folding my arms and trying to feel annoyed. My pussy has got other ideas and they all involve forgiving Elyah right this second and pulling him down on top of me.

"Doing what?" he asks, with a faux-innocent lift of his eyebrows.

He's getting closer and closer. My flesh is burning up. "Pulling off your T-shirt and posing."

He glances down at himself with a smile and then back up at me. "I am not posing. I am just standing here."

He's standing there flexing, every muscle of his chest and abdomen defined. "You're peacocking."

A smile breaks over his face and he laughs. My heart twists. He looks so handsome when he laughs. "I am what?"

I gesture vaguely at his beautiful body, but it's a mistake because now I'm staring at him again and heat flushes through my body. "Strutting about to get my attention."

Still pretending to be casual, he saunters closer, the muscles of his shoulders catching the light. How many times have I pictured my hands right there as he fucks me, my nails digging in to urge him to thrust deeper, harder? To use all that strength he was given to make me shatter.

"I am not strutting," he murmurs.

"Yes, you are," I say absentmindedly, my gaze dropping to the hard line of muscle on either side of his narrow hips. There's a rose tattoo inked on one side, the petals disappearing into his black jeans. Making me think of his cock. I can see his cock through the denim as he gets harder and harder.

Elyah reaches for me. I skitter away from him, shaking my head. "Stop that. I'm not falling for your tricks."

"Tricks? I do not have any tricks. I am too fucking stupid to trick anyone."

I'm surprised at the bitterness in his voice. When I gaze

into his face, I can see he's caught between seducing me and berating himself. "You're not stupid, Elyah."

"I thought you betrayed me because I am so fucking clever?" he growls. "I put you in a cage and tortured you because I am *smart*?"

I swallow, hard. There's so much pain on his proud features.

"Maybe your mind was clouded by anger and heartbreak, but you are not stupid," I tell him. "You knew what you were doing to me, and you did it anyway."

"Yes," he seethes. "I did it anyway, and keeping you prisoner brought me no pleasure at all. I do not call myself stupid because I think it will excuse what I did. I say it because it is true. I have been stupid all my life. In school I did not know what the fuck any of my teachers were talking about. I cannot even cook a meal. Do you know what I would give for my brain to work like yours or Konstantin's? I am fucking stupid." He raps his fist on his skull like he's knocking on a piece of wood.

I grab his hand and pull it down. "Don't do that. You're not stupid. You were the only one who knew that I was up to something at the pageant. You tried to warn Konstantin, but he wouldn't listen to you."

He flings his arms out. "So what? Did it help anyone that I felt something and could not explain it? No, I just saw fucking crows in the garden and bad omens. I was no use to anyone." Elyah's eyes fill with desire and longing, and his voice is roughened with emotion when he speaks. "I should have known that you would never have done anything to help the people who killed your baby. I will never forgive myself."

I wrap my arms around myself, feeling hollow. If only I

had been at the house after Ivan was killed when Elyah came for me to take me away. Everything would have been so different. "You're not the only one who is stupid. I shouldn't have gone anywhere with my father. If I'd put my foot down and waited, you would have found me."

Elyah carefully reaches out to take my shoulders in his hands, and I let him.

"The day Ivan was killed, the moment I pulled into the street where his office was, I just stopped," he murmurs.

"That probably saved your life," I point out.

"But not Ivan's."

"I'm glad." My voice is low and filled with venom. "A wife isn't supposed to think it, but I'm glad he's dead."

Elyah's gaze burns with malice. "I should have killed him the first time he laid his hands on you in anger."

I shake my head, not sure if I'm pitying myself or pitying him. "In the hospital? Oh, Elyah. That wasn't the first time."

He clamps his hands to his skull and squeezes his eyes shut. "Fuck. *Fuck*."

"He made my life a misery, and he would have made my child miserable if I'd—if it—" Even now with another baby strong and kicking in my belly, my heart still aches for the child I lost.

"I would have loved that child," Elyah whispers.

I know. My mouth fills with the words, but I can't say them. This man has done terrible things to my heart and soul, and I shouldn't *want* to say them.

His large hand cups my cheek. "I will love this child. This is all I have to offer you both. Will you accept me, Lilia? Will you let me protect you both? It is all I want."

Elyah takes both my hands and presses them to his chest.

He's burning hot, vital, and delicious. When I don't immediately push him away, he takes his chance and captures my mouth with his.

"I don't forgive you," I whisper between kisses. "You're dangerous. You're cruel."

"I am," he says, his mouth melting over mine. "But this world is dangerous and cruel, and I will hold it back from you and the baby."

I have to get away from Elyah before I succumb to what his body is offering. I don't trust myself not to open my heart to him if I let him so sweetly devastate me with orgasms yet again.

But Elyah has other ideas.

He picks me up and carries me over to the bed. "I deserve to be dragged down to hell. I will fight every demon that comes for me because I will never leave your side, and, Lilia, you are meant for heaven."

How can a man who professes to be stupid say such devastating things? I don't feel angelic right at this moment, not when I'm craving Elyah so much I can't think.

"Am I going to have to be good for the both of us so you can reach heaven, too?" I ask him.

"You will teach me to be good." He unbuttons his jeans and pushes them down his legs, and his cock is thick and erect. Next he goes for my leggings, stripping them down my legs with a wicked gleam in his eye. "And I will teach you to be bad."

I expect him to pin me to the mattress, but he rolls over onto his back and holds out his hands to me. His stiffened cock stands proudly to attention, thick and glorious. I can't believe I'm thinking of a man's cock as thick and glorious—I feel so stupid, I feel so cringe, but he *is*. I ache to raise my hips over him and slide down his length.

"Please, *solnyshko*. We both need it."

Proud Elyah is saying please.

Begging *me*.

My cheeks heat with anger and frustration. "I won't."

"You will, Lilia. Come here and scratch your nails down my chest while you fuck me. Hurt me. Make me pay. Tell me you hate me and that it will be long, long time before you will believe I am truly sorry. Whatever you need, but just come here."

10

Elyah

Lilia still hesitates, so I take hold of her wrist and tug her toward me, and she falls across my chest. Her beautiful hair tumbles against my cheek.

"You want to hurt me? Go on. Attack me. Hit me. Punch me. But you have to do it while riding my cock."

"Go to hell," she seethes, but she doesn't fight me. She doesn't even try to pull away. She's breathing hard, her belly pressed against my stomach. A spasm goes through my cock and my balls ache. I want my woman like this. She's so fucking sexy I can barely breathe.

"I will get there eventually. Come on, *solnyshko*. Show me how angry you really are. Shred my chest. Make me bleed."

Lilia gazes down at my tattoos and then digs all of her fingernails into my chest. Her lips parted and panting, she drags them viciously down with all her strength. I groan and clench my muscles against the pain.

But I can't help the smile on my lips.

The second time she does it over my already flayed skin, I'm still smiling, but it fucking *hurts*.

I deserve every blaze of pain.

Her expression is feverish, and she straddles me, squeezing me with her thighs.

"You need me, Lilia. Your life will not be the same without me."

She reaches between her legs and wraps her hand around my girth. "I don't need you. I just need this."

I rock my hips beneath her, loving the way her body lifts and falls on mine.

"You have always wanted me." I break off with a groan as her hand massages up and down the length of my cock.

"I don't want you. It's just the pregnancy hormones."

"Was it pregnancy hormones when we were in the pantry at your husband's house? I thrust my fingers into you and you clenched so needily around me."

"Shut *up*." Lilia keeps one hand around my cock and rakes the nails of her other hand down my chest, and I groan in pleasure and pain.

"I like the tattoos you are giving me. They tell a new story on top of the old." The reaper I earned after my tenth kill. The cross that marks the occasion I nearly died. The bright red score marks from Lilia's nails tell a tale of fury, desire, and love.

I reach between her splayed thighs and find her clit. I stroke my thumb in slow circles over her, and her head falls back as her face flushes. I listen to the increasing pitch of her moans, but it's not enough. I want more.

"I never get to lick you. Come up here and give me your pussy." She doesn't seem to know what I'm asking for and stares down at me in confusion. "Sit on my face, *solnyshko*."

"But I'm—I'm too heavy."

I just laugh and pull her up toward me. Lilia walks her knees up my chest and straddles my shoulders, and I get a good look at her glistening wet pussy. She's still too far away, so I wrap my arms tighter around her and plant my lips on her clit. Then I give her a slow, sensuous lick. Lilia gasps aloud and grasps the headboard.

"Can you breathe like that?" she asks uncertainly, trying to edge away.

I pull her firmly back against my mouth. Who fucking cares. I'll manage somehow. With some encouraging strokes of my hands, Lilia arches her back and rides my face like it's my cock.

The other two can definitely hear us, and I have the feeling someone's watching us. He'll wait until Lilia is too far gone before he makes his presence known. He better, or I'll fucking kill him.

Lilia's moans increase in pitch, and she's teetering on the brink when I push her away from my face. I can see her now, her swollen belly, and her hands gripping the headboard. Her cheeks flush and her eyes are dark and needy.

She gives a cry of dismay. "Why did you stop?"

"Ask me to make you come. You know I love to hear you say my name."

My name. I want it on her lips as she comes. This isn't

about her hormones or the fact that we're all trapped in here together. She needs me and I'm going to hear her say it.

Annoyance flashes over her beautiful face. "What makes you think I'm going to give you anything you want?"

Lilia wriggles back down my body and grasps my cock. She lines me up at her entrance and then sinks down my entire length. The anger melts from her face as she cries out.

I hold on to her hips and tip my head back with a groan of ecstasy. She's gripping my cock like a vise.

Oh, yes, Lilia.

You are showing me.

Teach me that fucking lesson.

When she tires and starts to pant, I grasp her hips and drive up harder into her. A pregnant woman is so fucking beautiful. I've never imagined making love to a woman in this state, but Lilia is so feminine. So rounded.

"Was it hormones when you showed up at my apartment behind your husband's back? Was it hormones when I fucked you in Konstantin's chair and you came so hard you milked the cum from my cock?"

"I was only—"

"Shh, *solnyshko*, now is not the time for lies." I reach up and grasp her jaw, making her look at me. "You think I am the stubborn one? I said I am sorry. Can you not say my name?"

Lilia grabs hold of my wrist and gazes down at me desperately. All I want for the rest of my life is to be needed by her. She craves to be loved as fiercely as I love her.

"Please make me come, Elyah. Please."

I keep hold of her jaw, my fingers wrapped around her throat. Not squeezing, just holding her there while she holds on to me.

I've got you, *solnyshko*.

I can see everything you are, and you are glorious.

With my thumb grinding against her clit, I thrust up into her and drink in the pleasure on her face.

There's a sound from the hallway, half groan, half growl. The door is ajar. I'm not the only one addicted to the sound of her desire.

"Kirill is watching us."

"What a surprise," Lilia moans, but she doesn't stop. If anything, she thrusts her tits out and grinds even harder on my cock.

A wicked smile curves my lips. "You are showing off for him? You are very bad girl."

I pound up into her, loving the knowledge that Kirill is watching us, envious, panting, and probably with his cock in his hand. Listening to him fuck Lilia on the plane was equal parts torture and bliss.

"I am going to invite him in here to fuck this tender pussy after me, all full of my cum."

"You wouldn't dare," she gasps.

"I do dare, *solnyshko*. One man is not enough for you. I am going hold you tight against me while Kirill does whatever is in his twisted head that makes you so wet and weak for him."

Lilia whimpers and I feel her flesh heat beneath my fingers. She likes that idea. She's so close and she's about to burst all over me.

"Kirill!" I shout. "Get in here and watch our woman come."

"Stop with that our woman stuff," she gasps desperately.

Kirill pushes the door open, already stripping off his

clothes, his hungry eyes on Lilia. "That's cute. She thinks she's not ours."

"Not ours? When she looks so pretty waiting to be fucked by my friend?" I make a *tsk* noise as I gaze up at her. "Do not be little liar."

Once he's naked, Kirill sits behind Lilia and straddles my legs. He wraps an arm around her waist and replaces my fingers on her clit with his own. Held between us, Lilia gives up completely to the assault on her senses, her eyes closing and her head tipping back against Kirill's shoulder.

Our eyes meet across her, and I know Kirill's victorious smirk is mirrored on my own face. How much better this is with both of us. He moves her up and down on my cock while his fingers keep stroking her.

"*Detka*, I have been watching you enjoy Elyah, and now I am going to feel you come for him."

I'm struggling to hold on. The sight of her helpless in Kirill's arms while she moves up and down my length, clenching tighter and tighter, is making me lose my mind.

Lilia cries out and her body arches. Kirill wraps his arms tighter around her and drives her down on my cock, growling in her ear, "Good fucking girl. Get him nice and deep. Elyah is going to burst inside you."

Lilia is riding high on her orgasm and hasn't got a choice in the matter. My powerful climax rushes up, and I buck beneath her, pulsing my cum deep inside her.

I fall back with a gasp, breathing hard, my hands on Lilia's belly. I can't remember ever feeling such an intense release.

I sit up, pull Lilia off my cock, and turn her around. She's weak and pliable after coming, and with her lying back in my arms, I spread her legs open.

Kirill kneels between our thighs, pumping his cock in his fist with a devilish grin on his face.

I put my lips against Lilia's ear, her soft tits in my hands. "You have three seconds to close your legs and get up off this bed, or Kirill is going to fuck you. One. Two." I pause, and my lips curve into a smile as she doesn't move. "Three."

Kirill takes hold of Lilia's hip, positions himself over her, and sinks into her pussy with a long, loud groan. "*Detka*. You feel so good after you have been fucked."

He moves his hips back and forth in slow, deliberate thrusts, hungry for the drag of her pussy on his cock. I can't tear my eyes away from the sight of her swallowing him whole.

"Beg him not to stop," I whisper, pulling her legs wider.

"Stop making me beg," she whimpers.

I jerk my chin at Kirill, and he not only stops, he pulls out of her.

"No!" Lilia tries to grab hold of Kirill, but I lovingly restrain her, hugging my arms around her and planting kisses on her throat.

"You are bad girl who will not do as she is told. I said beg him not to stop. If you ask him for what you want, Kirill will give it to you."

Kirill pumps his hand along his length, which is now glistening with her wetness and my cum. Fuck, that's an incredible sight.

"*Detka*, I am suddenly obsessed with hearing you beg me. I'm not going to give you want you want until you ask for it."

My lips caress the shell of her ear. "Go on, *solnyshko*. Tell him that his cock feels like heaven, and you will die if you do not feel him inside you."

Lilia's hands flex and clench on my thighs. She doesn't want to, but the words burst from her lips. "Please, Kirill."

I moan and cup her inner thighs, watching Kirill thrust inside her once more and claim her. It's almost as good as fucking her myself.

"Harder, please," she begs him.

"I can fuck you harder, but you have to keep begging me. If you stop, I stop."

She nods rapidly as he gives her what she wants. "Please, please, please."

I wonder if Konstantin is listening to this. He isn't the only one who can turn this bewitching goddess of a woman into a needy, hungry girl who will do anything she's told.

"Your clit is so plump and pretty," I breathe in her ear. "Do you want me to play with you?"

"Please, Elyah."

I think I could become addicted to that sound and the feel of Lilia in my arms. Her clit is slippery and hot to the touch as I work her in slow circles to the rhythm of Kirill's thrusts. Lilia was made to be fucked like this. She must feel it, too, because she won't stop moaning our names. She comes again, one hand squeezing Kirill's shoulder, the other reaching behind our heads to clasp the nape of my neck.

Kirill stares into her face, and suddenly his thrusts stutter and he curses in Russian.

A moment later, Kirill draws himself out of her with delicious slowness. Lilia has opened her eyes and her fingers run woozily down his chest.

I reach out and grasp the base of Kirill's cock, clench it tightly and pull down his length, gathering his seed and mine in my hand. When it's coating my fingers, I push them into her. "Not wasting a drop."

Lilia pushes her hair out of her sweaty face and puts a hand on her swollen belly. "I'm already pregnant, if you haven't noticed."

"Does not matter. That is where we belong."

The spell cast by sex is evaporating and Lilia tries to cover herself with a blanket. Kirill and I don't let her. We want her right where she is.

"You both got what you wanted. Now let me up."

"You are what I want. You always will be," I tell her.

Lilia looks away quickly and shakes her head. She still doesn't believe that I have anything real to offer her.

I put my lips against her ear. "What do you want me to do, reach into my chest, rip out my bleeding heart and show it to you? If that is what it takes, I will do it."

11

Kirill

"Don't. Please let me up." Lilia plants her hands against my chest. She's crowded between my body and Elyah's.

I'm the only thing keeping her here, and I don't move. "You sound so beautiful when you beg, *detka*. It is not just Konstantin who can turn you into a sweet little kitten. You do it for us, too."

"Being pregnant is making me do crazy things. Can you please move?"

My gaze sweeps down her body, admiring the swell of her stomach, the dusky pink of her nipples. Her body is fascinating, and how pretty she looks resting against all of Elyah's muscles and tattoos. I didn't think anything would beat screwing her while she was so sweetly asleep, but the airplane hate-sex came close. This is even better.

"Why? Have you got somewhere to be?" I taunt her. She should stay right where she is in Elyah's arms. This man won't be satisfied with just fucking Lilia.

"It was just sex. Just scratching an inch. It won't happen again."

Hurt flashes across Elyah's face. "There is no shame in needing someone or loving them."

Lilia makes a strangled, panicked noise. She pushes me off her, grabs a cotton robe from the back of the door and hurries out of the room. A moment later we hear the bathroom door slam. Elyah and I stare at each other in frustration.

I get up and yank on my jeans. "What more do you need to say to that woman? She is impossible."

Elyah lays back with a defeated sigh. "It is my fault. Not hers."

"Crazy shit happens in our world," I growl. "She's had her revenge. She sold the diamonds. Now it's time for her to get over it."

I go and wait by the bathroom door, leaning against the doorframe with my hands in my pockets. As soon as Lilia opens the door, she gazes up at me in surprise.

"Why can't you give Elyah one scrap of kindness, you cold-hearted bitch?"

Elyah is one of the reasons I'm still breathing and every wound she gives him is my fucking wound.

Lilia's lips press together in annoyance. "Why do you think?"

I wave my hand. "Kidnapping you, terrifying you, nearly killing you, yeah, yeah."

"Don't *yeah, yeah* over everything that's happened. What

sort of crazy person would fall into any of your arms after the things you've done?"

I can still feel her against me as her orgasm tore through her. Lilia's exactly that sort of crazy person, and she needs to accept it. "That man has sincere fucking feelings for you, and he always has."

Lilia makes a disgusted face and tries to move past me. "Who are you to talk about feelings when you haven't got any?"

I slam my hand into the wall by her head, blocking her way, and snarl through my teeth, "You don't know anything about me."

"What is there to know? You're a weirdo, a pervert, and a killer. The first time I saw you, you were murdering some of my father's friends for no reason."

For no reason.

Is that what she thinks?

For no fucking reason.

"I'm glad you brought them up," I say through my teeth. "If anyone tries to take you from us, I will murder them just like I did the Lugovskayas. Painful, terrifying deaths."

"Why did you hate them so much? They were ordinary people. As ordinary as you can get in the Bratva."

"Don't be so fucking naïve," I spit at her.

"Then tell me! What did they do to poor Kirill? Tell me what gives you the right to act the way you do."

"They took everything from me," I shout, hitting the wall with my fist, and she flinches. She's going to fucking make me say it.

I take her belly in my hands. "This baby? I'm keeping this

baby, and you with it. This time, I will rip the throat out of anyone who tries to take either of you from me."

"This time?" She blinks up at me in surprise. "You had a child?"

Could she sound more scathing? "You can say whatever you want. Anyone can say what they want, but it counts. It still fucking counts."

"Why wouldn't it..." She trails off. "Oh."

She's remembering her miscarriage.

If only it was a fucking miscarriage.

Behind me, I feel Elyah come into the room. Konstantin is watching us from the sofa.

My hands find Lilia's swollen belly and I hold her tight. I don't want to speak a word of this, but it's driving me out of my goddamn mind.

In a softer tone, Lilia says, "If you want to tell me, I'll listen."

~

Eight years earlier

Hot sunshine melts my ice-cream cone all over my hand into a pink, glorious mess. Belkal Park is hot and dusty in the midsummer heat. Just about everyone from high school has congregated on the limp grass or is splashing about in the fountain. An ice-cream truck is parked beneath a tree, and people wait for lemonade and soft serve.

I'm staring so hard at Kristina among her pack of squawking, flapping friends that I barely notice as ice cream runs over my hand. When her gaze flits over me, I smile hesitantly at her.

Kristina takes in my frayed, hand-me-down jeans, the lurid black eye decorating my cheek, and the ice cream melting all over my hand, then turns away with a disgusted sneer. I watch as she talks animatedly to the other girls and points over her shoulder. All Kristina's friends turn to look at me, and one by one, they laugh and jeer at me.

Kirill, the class weirdo.

Loser, loser.

Where are your friends, Kirill? Don't you have any?

As a pack, they move off with a final, *Go drown yourself, Kirill* floating back to me.

They think they can make a fool of me and then walk away?

I throw my ice cream to the ground and follow them. It takes them a good five minutes to realize I'm walking behind them. When one of them nudges the others and they turn around to look at me, I put my forefinger and middle finger on either side of my mouth and lick the air.

The girls scream in outrage and cuss me out. My blood sparkles through my veins.

I can't make them like me, but I can make them hate me.

After a while it gets boring wandering after the girls, and I walk the long way around the village. Anything to delay the moment when I have to go home.

As soon as I walk in, I know it's going to be another shitty evening. There's an empty vodka bottle laying on the floor by my father's chair and a fresh one open by his elbow.

Dad glances up with yellow eyes, sees it's me, and his face transforms with hatred. "Where have you been? Lazy shit. Good for nothing."

He's still furious with me for barricading myself in the

attic last night, denying him the pleasure of beating the shit out of me. He got his workout every other night this week. Bruises have bloomed all over my body.

Mom is washing the dishes and she looks into my blackened eyes, but her gaze quickly slides off me as if I'm not there.

I don't even feel angry with her anymore. It's more like a dull, festering ache. When I was ten years old, and my dad had me on the floor, kicking me in the stomach while Mom washed the dishes, I quickly learned not to expect any help.

"Better than being a farting old man," I throw back at him.

Rage transforms Dad's face and he lurches to his feet. I realize with a swoop of alarm that I misjudged how drunk he was. Not nearly drunk enough yet for me to be safely talking back.

He grabs me by the front of my T-shirt and drives his fist into my face. My lip grinds against my teeth, slicing it open. Blood fills my mouth and spills down my chin.

I wrench myself out of his grip and run through the house. Soon I'll be bigger than him and I'll fight back, then he'll be fucking sorry. Blinded by pain, I lurch toward the window. My fingers are wet with blood, and they fumble on the catch as I hear Dad's bellowing getting closer and closer. The lock springs open, and I half dive, half tumble out of the window, landing in the weedy flower beds.

A second later I'm up and running into the trees.

I swipe my forearm across my mouth and wipe away the blood, but it keeps flowing. It's so dark outside now that I can barely see where I'm going. I stumble against the corner of a pale blue building with white roses growing in the flower beds.

Kristina's house.

I bet she's tucked up in bed, dreaming bitchy little dreams.

I make my way around the house, peering in all the windows. Her parents are up watching TV in the living room. A younger brother is asleep with his thumb in his mouth.

I find Kristina's room, and she's between the sheets with her head on the pillow.

All alone.

I'm out here watching her, and she can't stop me. Is she naked in that bed? Has she been touching herself? I bet she has, the dirty bitch.

I peer behind me, and there's no one there. Kristina thinks she can run from me, but she's got nowhere left to run. I can jerk off right here and it's almost as good as being in there with her.

A grin spreads over my face and pain sears my lip. I let out a gasp and Kristina suddenly sits up in bed.

I duck down out of sight, a hand clamped over my mouth. I want to laugh, and I don't know if it's because of the pain or because I've discovered something wonderful. Girls act brave when they're in packs, but how vulnerable they are when they're all alone in their beds.

I push away from the window, leaving a bloody smear behind. I hope she sees it and wonders who's been creeping outside her room.

As I continue walking down the street, I see another figure up ahead, walking with purpose through the darkness.

I follow him silently, wondering who it is. When he turns his head, I think I recognize his profile.

Artem?

I change direction and follow my older brother along the street, keeping to the shadows. He heads for the biggest house in town. It's a palace compared to our hovel, with huge windows, columns, and ornamental trees dotted around a sweeping lawn. The driveway is made of neat white stones, each one raked perfectly into place. Artem has no purpose here, and neither do I. Perhaps he's going to rob the place. That would be interesting, and I wouldn't mind giving him a helping hand. The rich people in this town look down on us like we're scum.

Artem climbs a trellis to a bedroom window, but instead of forcing it open, he taps on the glass and waits. A moment later, the window opens, and he climbs in.

I'm so surprised that the pain in my lip fades to nothing. Two girls live in this house, and one of them is the beautiful, eighteen-year-old Yelena. She's always been so fucking haughty whenever I've passed her in the street. My brother is just as much of a nobody as I am.

Proud, high-and-mighty Yelena has a taste for trash like us? This I have to see.

As silently as I can, I climb up the trellis and creep across the roof toward the window. There's a yellow glow coming from inside. As I peer inside, I expect to see beautiful, blonde, long-legged Yelena in a canopied bed, but the girl my brother is undressing is short and her hair is a muddy brown. Ekaterina. Katya for short. A mousy little thing in my class who's almost as much of a loser as me. She has a handful of friends but has her nose buried in a book most lunchtimes. I've barely noticed her, but I'm staring now as Artem kisses her roughly, squeezes her breasts with both hands and motions her back onto her bed.

After a few kisses here and there on her shoulders, he pushes his pants down and starts screwing her. I can't tear my eyes away from the sight. It's not particularly hot, but there's something animalistic and entrancing about it. Artem's finished surprisingly quickly and then he's getting off Katya, who seems unmoved by the experience, but she does want to hold Artem's hand. He lets her for a moment, but then he's pulling his clothes back into place and turning to go.

Toward the window where I'm watching them.

I duck out of sight and crouch-walk toward the trellis and scramble down. Then I'm running back to the road. My heart is beating so wildly that I was nearly caught again, and I'm grinning despite the pain in my lip. Blood is filling my mouth again, but I've never felt more alive.

Every night after that, I wander the streets, peeking in windows and spying on unsuspecting victims. I've discovered a secret world and it's all mine. I watch couples fighting. Screwing. Girls furtively touching themselves beneath the blankets. Trying on clothes their mothers wouldn't let them wear. I jerk off multiple times a night, turned on to crazy extremes by the fact that they can't see me or stop me.

I feel powerful for the first time in my life.

Without my father's nightly beatings, my body starts to feel like my own. I grow stronger, hauling myself over walls and climbing trees to get a better view into windows. Sometimes I can't get up to where I need to be, and I start doing push-ups out of sheer frustration. I have to get stronger. Climb higher. Get my fix. I'm fucking addicted.

I pick my victims at school. All the girls who sneered at me, made fun of me, looked down on me. I follow them home and find out where they live, then I watch them in the dark.

Months pass before I notice Katya again. She's too small and insignificant to look down on anyone, so I've been ignoring her, until one day I notice her crying behind a tree. She looks so wretched that I stare at her for a long time, wondering what could be wrong in her world. She's rich and lives in that big house, so what has she got to cry about?

Then I realize what the problem must be. She seemed to like Artem, but Artem doesn't like anyone but himself. He doesn't even like me.

Katya notices me watching her and quickly wipes her face.

I turn to go, but find myself turning back to her to say, "Just get over it. He's not worth crying over."

Katya replies in a shaky, tear-filled voice, "How am I supposed to get over it when he won't even admit that it's his?"

I stare at her in confusion. "What?"

Katya slowly turns red, before stammering, "The—the baby. He must have told..."

Though we live in the same house, I haven't talked to my older brother in weeks. "The *what?*"

Katya moans in horror before hurrying away from me.

That afternoon, instead of following any girls, I head straight to my own house and wait for Artem to come home from work. He comes in from the car mechanic where he's an assistant at a quarter past six with greasy hands and clothes, and I follow him into the laundry.

"Katya's pregnant?"

"Who?" Artem replies with a jerk of surprise, but I can tell from his shifty expression that he knows exactly who I'm talking about.

I punch him in the shoulder. "Don't pretend. I saw you with her. Why are you acting like it's got nothing to do with you?"

"You saw me?"

"I followed you."

Artem scowls and shrugs. "It was just a couple of times. That slut has probably been screwing everyone."

I burst out laughing. "Katya?" I almost add, *You think boys are lining up to screw Katya?* but she looked so sad today that I let the cruel words die on my lips. "Katya isn't like that."

"Yeah, she is. You know why? Because if she let me fuck her, she's letting this whole town fuck her. Now piss off." Artem shoves me aside and heads for his bedroom.

Katya's not at school the next day. Or the next. I tell myself it doesn't matter what happens to her and whether Artem got her pregnant or not. I've got my life and she's got hers, and it's not like anything bad can happen to her in that big, perfect house.

She doesn't come to school all week and it gets under my skin. On Friday night, I find myself heading across town to her house and climbing the trellis to her window. She's awake when I peer inside. I have zero interest in secretly watching Katya, so I tap on the glass.

She stares at me in surprise and opens the window a crack. "Kirill? What are you doing here?"

"Let me in."

She frowns at me. "I don't let boys into my room."

"Don't be stupid," I tell her. Not because I know for a fact that she does let boys into her room, but because I have zero interest in her that way. She's a nice girl. I only creep on the bitches in this town.

I wave her back from the window and clamber into her room. Looking around, I see it's a huge, lavish bedroom. No expense spared, like she's a fucking princess. "You've got your own bathroom, too," I mutter.

"What?"

I turn to her, my hands jammed into the back pockets of my jeans. I'll say what I came to say, and then I'll leave. "Artem's not going to help you. You should tell your parents."

"I told them already," she mutters, and hangs her head.

Something about her attitude makes me narrow my eyes. "What's wrong?"

"Nothing," she mumbles, and rubs her arm. There are bruises peeking beneath her sleeve.

"Did they hit you?"

"Not hard. Just a few slaps because I made them mad."

Anger blazes in my chest. "They hit you while you're pregnant?"

"Your parents hit you. Or someone does."

I'm a boy and my dad is an asshole. This sort of thing isn't supposed to happen in nice houses and to people like Katya who read books and never bother anyone.

"Artem says it's not his."

Tears spring into Katya's eyes. "I'm not lying! I never did it with anyone but him. I thought he liked me. No one believes—"

"I believe you."

She stares at me. "What?"

"I know it's his baby. But he doesn't want it."

Her face crumples and she sits down on her bed, defeated, one hand on her belly. I realize with a jolt that she has a bump. She's been pregnant for weeks. Months, probably. I saw them together ages ago. She's been alone with this all this time, and no one's said one nice thing to her?

"Um. Congratulations," I mutter.

"Screw you," she whispers through her tears.

"I didn't mean—I just think it's cool. Someone nice having a baby." I push my hand through my curls and shake my head. She's miserable and I sound like a prick. But nice people should have babies. Not assholes like my father and broken dolls like my mother.

"I'm so scared. I've never seen Mom and Dad so angry with me before. They kept saying that I've ruined my life and the family's reputation, and now I'll never get married."

Standing there with tears running down her face, she looks like the last puppy at the pet store that no one wants. If that's all they're worried about then I can fix that. "I'll marry you."

Katya stares at me. "What? You're sixteen. I'm sixteen. We can't get married."

I shrug. "Why not? We'll be seventeen when the baby arrives. I'm working. I'm earning money."

Marriage never seemed like such a big deal to me, but if it means that much to Katya's parents, I'll marry her if it means they will stop hitting her. She shouldn't be crying so much when she's going to have a baby.

She twists her hands together apologetically. "Sorry but... my parents won't have anything to do with your family. It's not what I think," she adds hastily. "It's just what they think."

I wave that off. I know all about what most people in this town think of my family, and I don't really care. If they're that worried about Katya's reputation, they'll get over it. "I'll talk to your parents. Artem didn't do that, did he?"

She shakes her head, her eyes filled with doubt. "No, but... Why would you do that?" she blurts out. "Marry me."

I stare at her for a long time. "You're different to the other people in this town. You're nice. You don't deserve to be all alone."

Katya offers me a tentative smile. "You, too."

I smile back at her. Look at us. The two town misfits, getting married.

For a moment, I wonder if I should get down on one knee and propose properly, but it doesn't feel right, and I doubt Katya wants that either.

Instead, I jump out of Katya's window, slide down the trellis, and walk around to the front of the house. There's a huge brass knocker in the shape of a lion and I beat it against the metal plate.

The door opens, and the house within is lit with golden light that reflects off the polished floors, huge mirrors, and sparkling chandeliers. I've never seen anything so beautiful.

A woman my mother's age peers at me with a frown on her face. Her hair is brushed and neat and dyed golden, so different to my mother's faded and untidy bun. She wears jewelry and her back is straight and proud.

"Can I help you?"

A man comes into view down the hall and approaches me with that same suspicious expression on his face.

"Hello, Mr. and Mrs. Lugovskaya. My name's Kirill."

The short, neat woman and the stocky man survey me

with unfriendly eyes. Mrs. Lugovskaya announces, "We aren't hiring any gardeners or grounds staff at this time."

"I'm not looking for work. I want—"

But a suspicious gleam has come into Mr. Lugovskaya's eyes. "What's your family name, boy."

The *boy* is a cold slap to the face. "Angelov."

His nostrils flare in outrage. "It was you who interfered with our daughter. Leave, immediately."

"No, listen—"

But Mr. Lugovskaya has turned a mottled shade of red and is advancing on me. He grabs me by the lapels and shoves me off his doorstep.

"That was my brother. I'm Kirill. Get your fucking hands off me."

For the past few months, I've been doing as many push-ups as I can manage as soon as I wake up. This week I've made it to two hundred, and I thought I noticed some muscle tone developing across my arms and chest.

But Mr. Lugovskaya is shouting at me, threatening to have me beaten. Cussing me out with all the names that have been heaped on my head over the years. He reaches for the umbrella stand by the door and brandishes a walking stick over his head.

I throw a punch at him that my father would have dodged, no matter how drunk he was, but Mr. Lugovskaya lives in a perfect house with a perfect life, and he isn't used to fighting. My fist smashes into his face and he goes staggering off to the side.

Mrs. Lugovskaya screeches at the top of her lungs. "How dare you attack my husband! Get out of our house!"

There's the sound of running footsteps from within the

house and Katya appears at the top of the stairs. She stares at the scene by the front door, wringing her hands with a wretched expression on her face.

With his hand over his bloodied nose, Mr. Lugovskaya points a finger at his daughter and bellows, "You, go back to your room."

Just before he slams the door in my face, he snarls. "I'll have you shot if you ever show your face around here again."

I turn away, flicking my aching hand. That probably could have gone better, but it doesn't matter. I'll marry Katya anyway. Permission is the last thing I need, and I was only asking because I thought it's what Katya wanted.

But first I have to fix something. I was lying to Katya about having money and a job, but I think I know what to do about that. I heard a rumor about some interesting work that pays well. The person who told me the rumor was arrested last week, but that's probably because he's stupid and careless.

I make my way across town in the dark. There are some warehouses down by the train tracks and a few guards scattered around, but it's easy to creep past them. I'm standing in a pool of light by some closed doors, wondering whether I should knock, when an angry voice calls out, "What the fuck? How did you get there?"

Before I can answer, a huge man grabs me by my collar and is half strangling me with my T-shirt.

"I know Stepan," I choke out. "I'm here for work."

"That prick," the man grumbles, but he opens a door and marches me through it, roaring, "Boss! Someone to see you about work."

The inside of the warehouse is poorly lit and filled with

stacked crates. The boxes are spray-painted with familiar food logos but inside one are guns nestled in straw.

The man holding me gives me a shove, and I stumble forward into a pool of light.

A tall figure with dark hair is checking the contents of a crate against a manifest on a clipboard. His indifferent gray eyes give me a once-over. He doesn't introduce himself, but I know who he is. Everyone does.

Konstantin Zhukov, the man who's replacing the disorganized criminals in this town with organized ones.

He's young, maybe mid-twenties, and I can imagine him with a beautiful woman like Yelena Lugovskaya on his arm. Everything about this man is sleek and expensive, but there's a hard and bitter expression in his eyes.

"How did you get past my guard?" Konstantin asks, turning back to his notes.

"I walked. It wasn't hard."

The man glances up at me, taking in my face, my ripped clothes. "Shouldn't you be in school? Why do you want work?"

"Fuck school. I'm going to be a father."

Konstantin stares at me. "At your age. Who's the woman?"

"Ekaterina Lugovskaya."

The man standing behind me bursts out laughing, but Konstantin watches me with a serious expression. "I haven't got enough money to keep the Lugovskayas happy. How do you expect to win them over working as a petty criminal for me?"

I stuff my bruised knuckles into my pocket. "That's my problem."

Konstantin thinks about this and then nods. "All right. If

you want work and you think you're tough enough and clever enough, I've got work for you. Welcome to the team."

"*Spacibo, Pakhan.*"

An amused smile touches Konstantin's lips. "No need to call me that. I'm not a *Pakhan*. Yet."

Thirty minutes later, I leave the warehouse with a spring in my step and my orders from Konstantin. He listened when I told him what I'm good at, which is sneaking around at night. He also cautioned me not to be an idiot like Stepan and tell anyone what I'm doing, even Katya. Women don't understand this sort of thing.

"She'll be happy about the money and that's all she needs to know. Women don't belong in our world. They're not strong enough," Konstantin said as he patted my cheek and sent me on my way.

My new work keeps me out until dawn most days. At first, Mom and Dad don't remark when I stop going to school and start sleeping all day. After a few weeks, Dad starts giving me suspicious looks, like he knows there's something different about me. It's not just the muscle I'm putting on. Konstantin treats me like a man, and I've started feeling like one.

Nights when I'm not working, I secretly visit Katya in her bedroom.

"My parents are so angry with you," she says in a harsh whisper, but there's a mischievous smile dancing around her lips.

I don't want to talk about her parents. I'm staring at her belly, which is getting huge. I hover my hand over the bump. "Can I?"

Katya rolls her eyes, smiling, and then nods. "If you want to."

I lay my hand on her stomach. She feels...great. Weird, but knowing there's a baby in there is kind of amazing.

"Wow," I breathe.

Katya peers up at me. "You really think it's so wonderful?"

"You don't?"

"I don't know. This baby has caused me nothing but tears." Her face softens as she gazes down at herself. "I guess it's not her fault. Or his fault. Maybe it is pretty cool."

Katya lets me lie next to her on the bed with my hand on her belly. She seems tense at first, like she's worried I'm going to try something, but I don't, and I don't want to. Eventually she relaxes.

"I don't love you," Katya suddenly announces. "I'm not going to fall for you or anything."

I shrug this off. "I don't love you, either."

Her mouth twists with amusement. "I already knew that. You haven't even tried to kiss me. Why are you even doing this?"

"It's a baby. What's it going to do without a father? And it's my flesh and blood."

Her eyebrows draw up and together, like she's pitying me. "You're really lonely, aren't you? I get that. I'm lonely, too."

My hand moves over her belly, and I find myself smiling. "I guess we won't be alone now."

When I arrive home, Dad is in one of his drunken moods and he's dying for a fight. I can tell by the way he keeps clenching and unclenching his fists.

"Where have you been? You come and go, treating this place like a hotel."

I'm not a scared little boy anymore. I'm a man, and I owe this asshole nothing.

Instead of cowering or running away, I step toward him. I'm surprised to find that I'm taller than he is now. So is he by the way his eyes widen.

Just try me. Fucking try me.

Dad sidesteps me and swipes a bottle of vodka off the counter like it was his intention all along. "You're not a man yet."

"As long as I don't end up like you," I mutter as I head for my bed.

The next time I see Katya, she's sobbing like her heart is breaking. Her stomach is huge now. There are just a few weeks until the baby is born.

"My parents have told me I have to give up the baby for adoption as soon as it's born," she chokes out. "I don't know what to do. They're so ashamed of me."

Adoption. Take her baby away from her. Away from me.

Anger races through me. Those two assholes downstairs think they're so perfect, but they're monsters.

I take her shoulders in my hands. "Let's run, now. Let's just go."

"I can't go now," she wails, both hands on her enormous belly. "Look at me, I'm huge. What am I going to do? I'm so scared. What if it hurts too much to have a baby? What if I die?"

"Nothing's going to happen to you. When the baby comes, I'll be right here. Whatever you do, don't sign the adoption papers."

She shakes her head, her teary eyes hardening. "I won't. I already told them that. They were so angry with me, but if I don't sign, they can't do anything."

I sigh in relief and pull her against my chest. Her stomach

bumps against mine. "It's going to be all—*shit*."

There are footsteps outside Katya's door and a key turns in the lock. I dive for the window and scramble through it just as the door opens.

An imperious female voice asks, "What's going on in here? Who are you talking to?"

I'm away in the dark before anyone sticks their head out the window.

Three days later I'm heading to the west side of town to look at an apartment that's advertised for rent when Artem's blue sedan pulls up next to me. "It's Katya. She's having the baby."

I stare at him in shock. Artem hasn't acknowledged the baby since I first talked about it with him. I wonder if he's started to wake up to the idea that this baby is real.

Fine. As long as he doesn't start thinking it's his. I already decided it's my fucking baby.

"She's not due for two weeks," I reply.

"She went into labor an hour ago. Get in."

I jump into the car and slam the door closed, and Artem roars off down the street.

"Where are you going? Her house is the other way."

"She's already been taken to the hospital. I was driving past the house as she was being loaded into the ambulance. Katya called out to me to tell you."

Ah, fuck, poor Katya. She must be terrified. "Why an ambulance? Was anything wrong? How did she look?"

Artem shrugs, looking bored. "How should I know? She looked like a woman having a baby."

Your fucking baby, I want to shout at him. My heart is racing. How can he act like this is nothing?

Ten or fifteen minutes must go by before I realize that we've headed out of town and we're driving through the countryside. "Which hospital did they take Katya to?"

"City Clinical No. 45."

The big one to the west. That makes sense, only we're traveling northeast. "But this isn't the way to—"

There's movement out of the corner of my eye and I realize someone's sat up behind me from the floor of the car. Ropes come around me and bind me to the seat, fast and tight.

I twist around and see it's Simeon, one of Artem's friends. "What the f—"

Simeon uses a bandana to gag me and ties it tight around my head. I really start to struggle and panic now and try to wrench myself free.

Artem just keeps driving. "Calm down, Kirill. This is for your own good. That girl was going to ruin your life."

I make an angry buzzing noise in the back of my throat. My arms are pinned to my sides, otherwise I'd grab the steering wheel and wrench us off the road.

Simeon pats me on the shoulder. "We'll split the money with you. You're not going to miss out."

Money? Someone is paying Artem to get me out of town, and I can guess who it is. The Lugovskayas. Katya must be having the baby right now, and they want me out of the way so they can force her to sign the adoption papers.

I keep trying to fight myself free but it's no use. Artem drives us miles and miles away, and then he and Simeon drag me out of the car and tie me to a tree out of view of the road.

Artem checks the ropes binding me and steps back. "If you don't manage to get yourself free and walk home, we'll be back for you in…" He waves a vague hand. "Twenty, thirty hours. By that time, everything will be fixed with Katya and the baby. You don't have to worry anymore, and you can just get on with your life."

Fuck you, I buzz at him through the gag, but he gets the message.

His face transforms into a glower. "Stay out of it, Kirill. They don't need you, and you sure as fuck don't need them."

I buzz harder and harder and kick my legs.

Artem and Simeon exchange a dark look and shake their heads, like I'm a pathetic waste of space. They rip my shoes from my feet, and then they turn and walk away, heading for the car and disappearing among the trees.

I rub my cheek against my shoulder and manage to spit out the gag.

"*Artem*." I scream myself hoarse, but a moment later I hear the car doors slam and the roar of the engine. They drive off, leaving me behind.

I thrash side to side in my bonds, the rope burning my arms and chest. My own fucking brother betraying me. He's just going to let the Lugovskayas give his kid away and he doesn't even care who gets it. The baby could end up with some asshole who beats it and tortures it. It could end up with someone like our own father. There are too many monsters out there.

I can't loosen the ropes, but I can try to edge them down my body and the tree trunk. It takes a long time, but I finally free myself. Without shoes on my feet, I head back to the road and start walking back toward town.

I walk for hours, trying to hitch a lift, but everyone ignores me. Finally, a farmer picks me up in the middle of the night and lets me ride in the back of his truck. I'll steal Artem's car and drive to the hospital.

But as I pass the Lugovskayas' house, something makes me hesitate. I go and check Katya's bedroom. Just in case they let her out already.

It must be nearly dawn when I limp across the Lugovskayas' lawn and painfully climb the trellis. When I peer in the window I see Katya, huddled on the bed.

But something's wrong.

Her belly looks smaller, but she's not holding the baby. There's no crib in the room, either. It's silent and empty.

I wrench open the window and tumble inside.

Katya gazes up at me, her eyes red and hollow. "Where were you?"

Her words are arrows in my chest. I pant at her, "I didn't—I couldn't—"

"I had to do it all by myself," she whispers.

"But you were at the hospital. The doctors and nurses helped you."

She shakes her head listlessly. "I was here. They locked me in. I banged on the door and screamed for hours, but they wouldn't let me out. They said...they said it was my fault because I am bad and disobedient, and it was in God's hands what happened to me."

Horror sweeps over me at her words. I get down on my knees next to her bed and reach for her hand. "But the baby. Where's the baby?"

Katya's voice is a cracked whisper. "It was dead. The cord was wrapped around its neck and it was blue. I didn't know what to do." Her face crumples and she sobs pitifully. "I'm so sorry, Kirill."

Dead. The baby's dead? But that's not possible.

I picture Katya locked in here, alone and screaming for help while everyone in this big, fucking expensive house ignores her. I thought the worst monsters were poor, dirty, and live in squalor, like my family, but they have nice carpets and polished furniture too. They dine on lobster as they listen to their daughter scream for help.

"What was it?" I ask, my voice hollow.

"A boy," she whispers, too tired and wretched to even wipe the tears from her face. They drip from her chin into her lap. "I think they buried him in the garden."

A boy. Artem had a son. *I* had a son. That baby was mine and it was Katya's. We wanted it, and Mr. and Mrs. Lugovskaya made sure it died.

I turn and walk blindly to the window, barely registering how I manage to climb out and make it to the ground.

How is the world so fucking cruel to a child that didn't even get a chance to live? I thought the world only sucked for assholes like me.

I stagger away into the darkness. Rocks prick my bleeding feet, and the moon follows me with her accusing silver eye. Everything I touch turns to shit.

I wander long into the night before finally coming to my senses when I'm confronted with my own front door. I don't want to go inside. If I lay eyes on Artem, I'll smash his fucking face in. I'll kill my father for what he's made us. Katya's parents would rather murder their own grandchild than be associated with us.

There's nothing keeping me here. I'll steal Artem's car, take Katya, and we'll drive away. Far fucking away from the families who hate our guts. I'll work, she'll get better, and she can find a decent man to marry. We'll tell everyone I'm her brother or something.

Rage simmers in my heart as I return to the Lugovskayas' house and climb the trellis to Katya's room. I can't wait to tell her I'm taking her away from all this.

Her bedroom is dark when I land on silent feet on the floor.

"Katya?" I whisper, gazing around at her unmade bed, the soft toys, and paperbacks on the bookshelves. Poor girl. She lost a baby, and she wasn't much more than a kid herself.

The bathroom door is ajar, and I push it open. The room is dark, but a shaft of moonlight falls across the bathtub. It's filled with water, and I can just make out Katya's outline in the gloom.

"Katya? What are you doing there in the dark?"

I reach for the light and flick it on, and I'm greeted by a nightmare. The water is bright red and fills the tub to the brim. More red water decorates the walls and floor. I don't understand what I'm looking at, until I catch sight of Katya's arm floating in the water, a jagged wound up her inner forearm.

"*No.*" I cry out and run over to the tub. When I grab hold of her, the water is freezing cold and so is she. She flops lifelessly in my grip, her flesh as pale as marble and her eyes dead and staring.

I slowly let her go and stand up. Bloody water drips from my fingers.

This didn't have to happen.

None of this had to fucking happen, and yet it happened around me while I was helpless to change even one tiny fucking part of this. I couldn't save Katya. I couldn't save the baby. They're both fucking dead. I'm standing here in the aftermath, useless and broken.

I wait for myself to feel sick or revolted as I stare at Katya's dead face. Even though she's gone, she's still so beautiful. More beautiful, really. All the pain she's worn for the last few months is gone and she resembles an angel in a painting. I close her eyes, and it's like she's asleep.

I kneel down on the bloody floor and take her face in my hands like she can still hear me. "Shall I kill them for you? For you and the baby? I want to see them suffer. I want to see them burn in hell."

Her cold cheek lolls against my hand, and it's like she's nodding.

"All right. I'll fucking kill them all," I growl through my teeth.

Even blinded with fury, I'm able to open Katya's door silently and sneak through the house, evading the Lugovskayas and hunting for what I need.

Gasoline.

Matches.

Katya's parents are tucked up safe in bed when the entire downstairs goes up in flames.

I watch the house burn from the road. The fire engines arrive and men with ladders help Mr. and Mrs. Lugovskaya safely away from the flames.

I swear and beat my fists against a tree trunk, fury raging inside me hotter than any fire.

They're not dead.

But one day, they'll be bleeding out and struggling for their last breath, and I'll show them as much mercy as they showed Katya and the baby.

I turn away, and with cut and bloodied feet, I walk out of town and don't look back.

∼

I MANAGE to avoid the police for two years, but they catch me just before my nineteenth birthday and throw me in prison for arson. The Lugovskayas were at my sentencing, victory and self-righteousness lacing their expressions.

I glare at them the whole time, even when the judge is addressing me. At one point, I'm reprimanded for "intimidating the victims" but I still don't look away.

I'm not trying to intimidate them.

I'm vividly imagining their blood and screams as I kill them.

They must realize what my expression means because, as I'm led past them on my way to serve sixteen years, they both turn pale. It doesn't matter if I have to dig my way out of prison with my fingernails, I will find them before they die, and I will make them wish they'd never been born.

Sixteen fucking years for burning a mansion down, and they are free while Katya and the baby are dead because of them. This world isn't fair.

From now on, if I ever see something I want, I'll make it mine.

After five weeks in prison, the rage is still burning within me. There are too many dark hours, cruel thoughts, and nightmares. I can hear a baby screaming all the time. I heard once that they break enemy soldiers by putting headphones on them and playing the sound of infants screaming for hours on end. I'm beginning to believe that it works.

I can see Katya bleeding slowly to death. I have dreams about unconscious women. The girls from my high school in their beds. I'm watching them and creeping closer and closer, not sure if they're asleep or dead. If it's Katya, she's always dead, blood dripping from her fingers and maggots crawling over her flesh.

Sometimes I wake up in a cold sweat.

Sometimes I open my eyes and my dick is hard.

The best dreams are when I know the women are asleep. There's no blood until I shove my cock in them and draw it out and it's smeared with red. I fuck their unresponsive bodies until I'm right on the brink. Then they wake up and catch me, but it's too late for them to stop me. I've got what I wanted from them, and I slip away into the dark.

During the day I distract myself by watching the other inmates. Most of them look like they couldn't count to ten. One man is different, though. He's taller than me, blond, well built. There are already several tattoos decorating his arms and chest, some that look like prison tattoos and others he must have got on the outside. He was in a gang. If he's in here, he probably took the fall for them.

Every other day it seems like someone is trying to kill him. I start following him around and watching him because seeing him in action is fucking glorious. His expression is always bored and stony, as if he's not thinking about anything in particular and he doesn't notice the one or two guys lurking in the shadows whispering to each other.

They close in, and at the last second the blond man parries some poor attempt to stab him in the kidneys. He takes the weapon from his attackers, slashes their clothing or faces, or if they've attacked him before, he drives the weapon into their necks and kills them. Then breaks the makeshift blade with his bare hands and throws the pieces to the ground.

I walk away grinning and shaking my head. He's fucking magnificent.

I hear the other men talking about him. They call him Pushka.

One day while I'm watching Pushka, it's not just one or two guys after him. It's five. He seems to know it as well because I see him swallow, the only outward sign of emotion I've ever seen from him.

He's not scared. But he is worried.

Three guys jump him at once, and if it were just three, Pushka could hold his own. But two more are closing in. They pass right by my hiding spot. It's none of my business who lives or dies in here, and the code of this place tells me I should keep out of it. But fuck those rules. I told myself I'd take what I want from now on and I want this man to live.

I trip up one of the men, take his blade—a toothbrush sharpened to a point on the concrete floor—and stab the throat of the other man. Nothing much happens except that his eyes go wide and he makes a choking sound. Then I pull the blade out.

Suddenly, there's so much blood.

Gushing from the man's neck. Pouring over my hand.

I fall on the second man at my feet and stab him in the guts, over and over again, my other hand covers his mouth so his screams don't draw the guards.

Strong hands grab my shoulders and yank me off him, and I fall onto my back. I presume it's the guards, and I anticipate the blows of their batons as they beat me into submission.

Instead, I wipe the blood from my eyes and find myself gazing up at Pushka's cold face. He offers a hand to help me to my feet and I take it.

Without needing to discuss it, we walk quickly away from the five bodies before any of the guards can find the scene.

"Why do you keep following me?" he asks.

"Who wants you dead so badly?"

Pushka takes his T-shirt off and wipes away the blood on his hands and face. I do the same thing.

"Everyone," Pushka replies.

If I hadn't been watching him all this time, I'd think he was bragging. "Then why don't you just let them kill you?"

Death at the end of a blade. If I didn't burn for revenge, I might let that happen to me.

Pushka's pale blue eyes are burning. "All my life I have lived for someone else. I am not going to die for someone else. When I get out of here, I am going to live for me. These scum are not taking that from me, too."

I see something in him that I've never felt before. Pride. This Pushka is a proud and stubborn man, and he's being crushed to death in this fucking hellhole.

"I'll make you a deal, Pushka. I'll watch your back in here. From now on, your enemies are my enemies."

Pushka considers me. "You are a good fighter. But what do you get out of this?"

I turn my hands over, staring at the blood under my fingernails. For the last hour, I haven't heard one painful scream or baby's cry echoing through my mind.

I get the sweet release of fucking forgetting.

12

Lilia

Monsters.

They come in every shape and size. Rich and poor. Pretty and ugly. I learned this lesson long ago, but it's still a shock to discover that the respectable, well-spoken people who have complimented your dress and eaten the food you cooked them are really demons straight out of hell.

For all these months, I felt sorry for the terrifying way Mr. and Mrs. Lugovskaya died. Kirill hunted them through their apartment and stabbed them to death. Mrs. Lugovskaya heard her husband's dying screams, and I remember thinking that it was probably the worst sound she'd ever heard in her life.

But this woman listened to her daughter scream for help

in the agony of labor, knowing that Katya could die or the baby could die, and she did nothing.

Nothing.

I don't realize I'm shaking with anger until someone touches my shoulder. It's Elyah, his expression creased with concern.

"Perhaps you should not have told her that story," he murmurs to Kirill.

I brush him away because I'm sitting down on the sofa. I'm not going to faint again, though my heart aches for Katya. I glance down at my belly, my baby, and hug it tight. Angry tears plop onto the fabric of my T-shirt.

"Are you crying for me, Lilia Aranova?"

I'm crying for Katya and the child, innocent people who deserved to live a full life instead of die at the hands of a couple of cold-hearted monsters. I'm crying for sixteen-year-old Kirill, who might have turned out so differently if he'd been given the chance to protect Katya and the baby. Instead, he was sent to prison and emerged a killer.

Kirill's voice has been flat and unemotional throughout his whole tale. He walks slowly toward me, his eyes dark and gleaming beneath his curls.

I wipe my face and gaze up at him. "I'm crying for everyone who deserves my tears, and yes, that means you, too."

His mouth hooks into a smile. "Don't. You may not feel sorry for me when the rest of my story is told."

I look up in surprise. "There's more?"

Kirill muses on this, tilting his head from side to side as if he's relishing a secret and deciding whether this is the time to tell it. "Or should I say, our story."

"You and me?" I ask, not understanding.

Over his shoulder, Konstantin raises his head and frowns. He didn't say a word or move a muscle this past hour, even during the parts of the story that included him. Elyah casts a curious look at Kirill, and it's clear they don't know what he's talking about either.

Kirill hunkers down on his heels before me and puts his hands on my belly. My heart rate picks up as I stare into his brutally handsome face. There's just something about a cold-blooded killer touching me so gently, so sweetly, that makes my body go haywire.

He raises those dark eyes to mine. "This is my baby, Lilia."

The finality in his voice surprises me. I can understand Elyah's need to claim this child as his own. To protect us with his body and prove he can love us as no other man can. I can even understand why Konstantin wants it to be his. A wife and a baby are the next phase of his life.

But Kirill? When I look into his face, I see nothing of the soft and almost innocent sixteen-year-old boy who craved to be kind to a fellow misfit. All that kindness was burned away the night he torched the Lugovskaya mansion. His only loyalty is to Konstantin and Elyah, and to the mayhem and chaos he thrives in.

I shake my head and push his hands away. "Don't start with that again. You can't just decide that this is your child. I'm not Katya and we don't need you."

"No, Lilia." His voice is dark and possessive. "It's my baby. You still don't remember?"

"Remember what?"

A sharp smile curves his lips, and his eyes glitter. That expression sends ice skittering down my spine.

"You really are a deep sleeper," he murmurs, caressing my throat.

I haven't heard those words in so long, but suddenly I'm strapped to a lie detector that gives me electric shocks while Kirill purrs, *Are you a deep sleeper?*

Konstantin and Elyah are staring at Kirill.

Kirill just laughs.

I stand up quickly, backing away from him. "You didn't."

He strolls closer, that hateful smirk on his lips. "You needed a little help to stay under, but it was just as good as I hoped."

I remember his body on mine, that first slow thrust of his cock. His kisses. His mouth on my body. My pussy. It was the most intense dream of my life, and I woke up with my heart racing, horrified that I was thinking about one of my captors that way.

"But it was a dream," I blurt out.

"Oh, *detka*. You do remember." Kirill strokes his fingers lovingly and possessively through my hair. "You were so delicious I couldn't help myself. And when I was finished, I tucked you so sweetly back into bed, full of my cum."

I shake my head. I would have noticed that. I would have realized the next morning that I was damp and sticky.

But mornings were so chaotic at the pageant, and I was always in a hurry to wash myself and get dressed. Could I have missed what happened to me while I was distracted thinking about other things?

I wrap my arms around my stomach and stare at my baby. This pregnancy was a shock, but I came to terms with it these past few months. Elyah or Konstantin gave me a baby because I gave myself to them in order to buy my freedom. That seems right to me.

Kirill, delighting over the way he deceived me and then getting me pregnant? I ram up against a brick wall in my mind and shake my head. "I don't believe you. I *won't* believe you."

Kirill wears a proud smile on his lips. "It was the third night of the pageant. Before Kostya. Before Elyah. I was with Lilia first. This is my baby."

White noise roars in my ears as Kirill reaches out and takes hold of me once more, sliding his hands around my waist.

I try to push him away, but he won't let me go. He laughs at my attempts, and I feel the vibrations against the palms of my hands.

"I had you on the floor of the Lugovskayas, passed out cold," he whispers. "You fought for your life and you nearly killed me. I was never so fucking turned on in my life. I had to have you, Lilia."

"But why would you do that?"

His smile is sharp and victorious, his lips just inches from mine. "You were just so proud, so high and mighty."

Just like the girls at school that he hated so much. "Is that what you think of me now? You need to put me in my place by screwing me while I can't fight back?"

He takes my chin between his forefinger and thumb and examines me with a puzzled frown on his face. "No. I don't. It's strange and I don't understand it." The smile spreads over his face once more. "But all the ways I've fucked you since have been even better than that first time. Watching you willingly take my cock, crave my cock, pant for me. I can't get enough of you, *detka*."

I wrench my jaw out of his grip. I don't want to be reminded of that right now. "Was any of what you told me about Katya even true? Or did you just want to soften me up before you dropped your bombshell?"

He lets go of me and spreads his arms, showing me his muscles, his tattoos, his hard eyes. "All of it's true. It made me the man I am today."

A man or a monster?

I turn away from him and come face to face with Elyah, who's glaring at his friend.

Kirill arches a brow and laughs. "Do you want to fight me for screwing the woman you told us all you were going to kill? Go on, take your best shot."

"You did not have to tell Lilia like that," Elyah seethes, his fists balling at his sides. "You are not sorry. You did not want to confess. You wanted to hurt her."

"Wrong," Kirill says, leaning comfortably against the wall and folding his arms. "I was staking my claim. I've had enough of you and Konstantin thinking this is all about you. It's my baby."

I can't stand breathing this man's air for another second. I point to my front door. "Get out of my apartment. All of you. I'm not spending another night with any of you under my roof."

"We're not going anywhere," Konstantin says, staring at his phone.

"He speaks," I snarl, with a sarcastic edge to my voice. Konstantin hasn't said a word to me in days. "Yes, you are. Get. Out."

He turns his phone around so I can see the screen. "Either we're staying, or you're leaving with us. They found Vavilov's body."

I snatch his phone from him and read an article that's been automatically translated from Czech. "Maxim's been found?"

The article relates how river workers found a body in the river, not far from a car that had been driven into the water. The man is unidentified, and I breathe a sigh of relief and pass the phone back to Konstantin.

"They don't know it's Maxim Vavilov. He's not from here so it's unlikely anyone will come forward saying they know who he is."

"True. And Elyah and Kirill will have done an excellent job removing Vavilov's fingers, teeth, and tattoos." Konstantin arches his scarred brow at me. "But when his frantic family hears that a body has been discovered in the Vltava River that matches their son's basic description, how soon will it be before they arrive in Prague and provide a DNA sample?"

My stomach plummets through the floor. Of course they will. They must be thinking of nothing but finding their missing son. They might already be in Prague. The sensible thing would be to leave.

But my *home*.

I go to the window but don't dare open it, worrying that someone might see my face and recognize me. I'm trapped in hiding. Trapped with three men and too many dark thoughts in my head. Kirill's tale took me on a roller coaster of emotions, and now Maxim's been found. I'm overwhelmed.

Without looking at any of them, I head for my bedroom. I don't know what to do, but I need to be alone right now.

"Don't follow me in here," I tell them, and close the door behind me.

I lay on my bed in the dark staring up at the ceiling.

I should be thinking about my own fate, but I picture Katya instead. The poor girl was so young to have a child. The pain she must have endured when she was locked in to have the baby on her own. The devastation of carrying her child for nine months, only for it to die before it could take its first breath.

I roll over on my side and hug my belly with one hand. As fraught as my own life is right now, I know that the three men in the next room want this baby to live, despite their dark and scheming hearts. Every time I've thought of the Lugovskayas, I've pitied them. Now when I remember the way Kirill stabbed them to death, I wish I'd helped him.

I fall asleep with screams echoing in my ears.

And I awaken to the sensation of my mattress sinking beside me.

I'm still half asleep, and too exhausted physically and emotionally to even open my eyes. It's probably Elyah, hurting because I'm hurting. I don't want to be comforted right now. I'm too angry to be comforted.

I feel him over me, breathing, and I lay still, hoping he gets the message that I'm asleep and leaves me alone. Then I feel the top layer of my blanket slowly being peeled back. So slowly. So carefully.

This isn't Elyah.

This is Kirill.

Rage blooms in my chest. It's only been hours since he confessed he drugged me and screwed me while I was locked in my cell, and he's trying to do the same thing again. Has he been doing this every night and I just haven't realized? What the hell *has* he been doing to me?

I want to sit up and punch him in the face, but the need to know burns in my soul. I wonder if it was like this at the pageant. Slow, furtive movements in the dark, so careful not to wake me up.

He pulls the blanket down to my knees, and then the sheet, deftly untangling it from my arms and legs.

Before I got into bed, I removed all my clothes except for my T-shirt and panties. Kirill skims his fingers down my bare thigh, stroking me lovingly, delighted by my bare skin. Then he edges my T-shirt up, exposing my underwear, then my belly, then my breasts.

He sucks in a faint breath, and I feel warmth radiating above my nipple before the slow lick of his tongue. I nearly breathe harder. Make noise. But I keep my expression smooth and unresponsive.

With excruciating slowness that's heightened by the fact that I can't see anything Kirill's doing, he edges down the bed until he's hovering above my panties. My legs are closed and he can't do much with me like this.

Using the sheet that's wrapped around my calf and a careful hand beneath my thigh, he rolls me onto my back and slides one of my legs open. He works so slowly and carefully that if I were asleep, I doubt I would wake up.

Kirill's breathing is rough and unsteady, as if every second that ticks by is heightening the pleasure for him. I bet he's hard. Kirill trims all the hair away from his cock, and his chest and stomach are smooth. I can picture his thick length jutting out in the darkness, maybe a pearl of precum at the tip.

With just one of my legs open, Kirill lowers his head and presses his mouth and nose into my pussy over my underwear. He inhales softy, swearing in Russian under his breath. Everything is to be savored. This man is in no hurry whatsoever, and he's taking pleasure in his favorite thing in the world.

He reaches up with his fingers and draws my underwear aside. His tongue worms between my folds and finds my clit, licking all around it. His tongue explores further, lavishing me from the base of my slit all the way to my clit, before pushing inside me.

I can't hold back any longer. I take in a shuddering breath and open my eyes, only to see my sleep demon grinning back at me, a malicious glint in his eyes.

"I knew you were awake. I love you for playing along."

My thighs are wrapped around his shoulders, and I glare at him. "I wasn't playing. I wanted to know the kind of tricks you pull."

"Tricks that make you wet, *detka*." He takes my hand and presses my fingers beneath my underwear and against my slit. I'm hot and slippery to the touch, and with the same devilish expression on his face, Kirill pushes both his and my fingers into my tight channel.

"I'd love to find you pleasuring yourself one day, knees spread, fingers working frantically. Lost in a fantasy world while I possess you in this one." He drives our fingers slowly in and out of me.

"You said that you only creep on bitches. Am I one of those nasty girls you hate?"

"Number Eleven was the queen of bitches," he murmurs, lapping at my clit. "I miss her. Let's play pageant. You pretend to be my untouchable ice queen and I'll fuck your pretty pussy while you sleep."

My head tips back with a moan. "You're so fucking messed up."

"And I know how to have fun with it." He pulls our fingers out and then shoves two of his own deeper inside me.

"Is this what you did to me at the pageant?"

"Until you started to wake up. I couldn't have you running to Kostya and Elyah about big bad Kirill secretly getting his dick in you and spoiling all my fun. I gave you a little help to keep you quiet and pliant like a good girl." He sucks slowly on my clit. "Then I fucked you, *detka*. Best time I've ever had, until that hate-fuck on the plane while Daddy listened to his angel come on criminal dick."

Kirill lifts himself up, and I see that he's naked and hard as he takes his thick cock in his hand. He massages the tip in his palm, his hungry eyes devouring me. "There are so many good ways to screw you. Close your eyes and let me play with you. Your huge belly is so fucking hot." He runs his tongue over my stomach. "I got you pregnant, *detka*. I need to fuck the mother of my child."

My pussy clenches on his fingers, and he moans as he feels it.

"You need it too," he murmurs, drawing his fingers out and my underwear down my legs. He hooks my thighs up over his shoulders and holds me tight against him. "Cross your ankles behind my head."

He's barely been speaking above a whisper this whole time. I don't think the other two know he's in here, and it feels illicit. His coaxing murmur does something to me, and I do what he says.

My pussy is gushing against the head of his cock as he rubs my aching flesh before pushing inside me. Filling me up. Stretching me around his invading cock. We both stifle moans of pleasure.

"Why didn't you tell the others what you did at the pageant? Elyah hated me then and Konstantin didn't care what happened to me."

"I cared," he snarls softly. "I needed you to be mine in the dark. Only mine."

It's twisted and messed up, but the way he's talking and what he's doing makes my heart beat faster and my core ripple around him. "Have you drugged me again? If you drug me while I'm pregnant I will actually kill you. You don't fuck with this baby."

"Why would I hurt my baby?" he murmurs, turning his head to run his tongue up my ankle, thrusting into me with a brutal rhythm.

His baby. It's too strange, too shocking to comprehend.

"I don't trust you. You do desperate things to get off. Your drugs could hurt it."

"*Detka*, you just don't get it," Kirill says, grasping my jaw. "Open your mouth."

He purrs the command like it's our dirty secret, and I obey him, parting my lips. He spits in my mouth.

"My mouth. Swallow."

His saliva is hot and lands on my lips. I lick it off and swallow it down.

Kirill pulls out and spits on my clit, saying, "My pussy," before turning me over and spreading my ass open. "My ass." He spits on my asshole and then slides his hand beneath me to palm my belly.

"My baby," he pants in my ear.

I'm lying on my side and he pulls my thigh up. The blunt head of his cock is right at my entrance once more. With a thrust of his hips, he impales me with every inch of his cock.

I groan at the shock of him filling me and let him envelop me with his body while he slams his cock into me. I reach back and hold the nape of his neck, turning my head so that our mouths are close.

Kirill kisses me, and his kiss owns me as much as his cock does.

"And if the blood test shows you're not the father?" I pant.

"Does this feel like I give a fuck what the blood test says?" With a hand holding my swollen stomach, he pumps into me. Deep, possessive thrusts. My inner muscles ripple against him as I moan in pleasure. I've been starving for this. For Kirill to not merely make me come, but to declare that this baby is his with his cock deep inside me and to fuck me like it is. I shouldn't want that, but I do.

Kirill sinks his teeth carefully into my throat and growls. "I want to steal you away while the others aren't looking. How fun that would be, fucking you in secret while Kostya and Elyah hunt us down."

"If you put me and this baby in danger, I'll cut your balls off with a rusty razor and you'll never see me again," I snarl over my shoulder.

Kirill groans and pulls back his hips, slamming into me. He does it over and over, his thrusts deep and luxurious. "Threaten me more. It makes me so fucking hot for you."

"Harder, please," I whimper.

He takes a fistful of my ass and squeezes, pulling me

open, before driving himself deeper into my pussy, growling, "Whatever you need, *detka*."

I edge my thighs wider and arch my back so he hits that sweet spot from a heavenly angle. I think I'm going to lose my mind I'm so desperate to come. With my cheek pressed into Kirill's bicep, I realize someone's watching us from the doorway.

Elyah, his hands in his pockets and leaning against the doorframe, but there's absolutely nothing casual about the expression on his face or the rigid set of his muscles.

I lick my lips, concentrating on the delicious drag and thrust of Kirill's cock as Elyah and I lock eyes. Being watched like this heightens the sensations. Heightens the danger. With Kirill panting in my ear and the short, sharp lifts of Elyah's chest as he breathes, I feel like they're both fucking me, and the thought drives me over the edge.

"Should I come on her ass or inside her?" Kirill asks, the pace of his thrusts growing faster and driving my orgasm higher and higher.

Elyah speaks in a voice that I've never heard from him, dark and velvety with need. "Come in her pussy. I want to fuck it into her."

"When did you get so fucking dirty, Elyah?" Kirill groans, echoing my own thoughts as he reaches his peak and thrusts once, twice more, and goes still.

Kirill slowly sits up, buried deep inside me, and notices Elyah still standing there. "What are you waiting for? She's in her sluttiest mood yet, aren't you, *detka*?" He squeezes the fleshy part of my ass and then spanks it.

I open my mouth to tell him to get fucked for calling me slutty, and then groan as the handprint on my ass tingles in the most delicious way. Right now, it feels so good to be slutty, one thick cock buried deep inside me with my legs spread open and another man surveying me like he's wondering where he'd like to get started.

Elyah prowls toward us and pulls his T-shirt off. "How many times did she come?"

"Just once."

"*Solnyshko*, that is not enough." He strips off his pants and underwear and his cock springs free, and I already know I want it. Need it. As soon as possible. I don't want to think. I just want to feel.

Kirill wraps his arms around me and turns us over so his back is against the pillows and I'm between his thighs. He spreads mine open for Elyah, and then my pussy, and the other man wastes no time in getting his mouth on my clit.

"I told myself that if I got my hands on you again, I would lick your glorious pussy every chance I got," Elyah says between lashes of his tongue. "I could have been doing this for fucking years. I will do this for fucking years."

The way he's making me feel, I have no complaints if he wants to carry on forever. "Don't you care that I've got another man's cum inside me?"

Elyah drives two fingers inside me, pumping them slowly in and out of me, admiring the shiny fluid that coats them. "Apparently, I do not care when it is him."

"What about if it's Kostya's?" Kirill asks.

Elyah mumbles something, too focused on me and what he's doing to me. But I feel Kirill inhale behind me and turn my head to see the mischievous glitter in his eyes.

He calls out, "Kostya, our woman needs you."

"He'll ignore you," I pant, pushing my fingers through Elyah's silky hair. "We're in a fight."

A moment later, Konstantin appears in the doorway, attempting to look casual, but failing. All the veins are standing out in his forearms like his blood pressure is through the roof.

He considers me, caught between his two men. I can't tell if he's angry with me. Disgusted with me. Judging me.

I lift my hand from Elyah's hair and give him the finger.

A smile quirks the corner of Konstantin's mouth. "How good is our *milaya* at sucking cock?"

"I bet she's wonderful," Kirill purrs, reaching up to finger-comb my tresses back from my face. "I'll hold her hair."

"Did she ever go down on you, Elyah?"

Elyah shakes his head, watching me as he pumps two fingers slowly in and out of me. "Not yet. Fuck, I want to see her suck cock."

Konstantin's gray eyes brighten as he moves toward us, and he unfastens his pants. The only person I've gone down on was my husband, and I hated every second of it. Elyah bears down on my G-spot and my legs shake in his grip.

I glance up at Konstantin, who's now towering over me with his hard cock in his hand. I want him to be angry with me. I want him worried that I will bite. "I only had sex with you in Italy because I was trying to get my passport."

"You don't have to remind me of what happened in Italy," he growls.

I smirk up at him. "Oh, I'll never forget either."

Rage sparks in his eyes. "You owe me, *milaya*. Fourteen million dollars' worth of pink diamonds. Now open your mouth."

"If I do this, are we square?" I taunt him.

Kirill is still holding on to my hair when he slides his thumb over my lower lip, encouraging me to open my mouth. There are too many men in my tiny bed, and they all want to see my face get fucked.

Konstantin strokes himself up and down in his fist, and I can see the inner fight going on behind his eyes.

Stay mad at me.

Or admit he doesn't actually care about those diamonds.

"Depends how well you suck me. Now open your fucking mouth."

He grasps the nape of my neck and thrusts his cock past my lips. My mouth closes around him, and I work my tongue against him. His thrusts are harsh and deep, and he feels so good every time he bottoms out at the back of my mouth.

Elyah groans and sits up, pulling his fingers out of me and positioning himself between my thighs. "She likes it. *Solnyshko*, I cannot fucking cope with how hot you look."

He sinks into me, staring at Konstantin's cock thrusting into my mouth and timing his own to match. The slow dual rhythm makes me moan around Konstantin's thick length.

"Look at you all filled up," Kirill murmurs in my ear, squeezing one of my breasts.

"She will not be filled up until one of us is in her ass, too," Elyah says, stroking hard with his cock.

I grasp the base of Konstantin's dick, choking a little, and not because he's fucking me too deep. Is that even possible?

"We could make it work," Elyah tells me as if reading my mind. There's a gleam in his eye, and I realize he's thought about it. A lot. And probably jerked off to it. "Nice and slow until you are all filled up and you finally feel you have enough."

When did my sweet driver learn to dirty talk like this?

Konstantin grabs my chin and forces himself deeper. "Until that baby is born, we are all the father, and you belong to all of us. You're our woman, and we're going to fuck you like our woman needs to be fucked. All three of us are very horny men, so it's up to you to satisfy us, and we are too impatient to take turns." He grips my throat, feeling himself moving inside of me. "And you're too horny to say no."

I moan, half furious, half falling apart from pleasure. Kirill moves his hand down to my clit and rubs me while Elyah pumps hard into me. I've never known what makes a blowjob good for a man, but I stroke the base of his cock and move my mouth by instinct.

"*Malyshka*," Konstantin hisses through his teeth, and I can hear how close he is to coming.

"Elyah, what would you think if Kostya blew all over her pretty tits?" Kirill asks.

Elyah has been watching himself screw me and Kirill rubbing my clit, but he runs his heated gaze up my body and stares at my mouth, his eyelids heavy with desire. "I think I will shoot my fucking load at the sight."

"Ladies first," Kirill breathes in my ear, and ups the pressure and speed of his fingers. Elyah is railing me so sweetly. I cry out around Konstantin's mouth as my climax rises up and breaks over me in a delicious wave.

As my body flexes, Konstantin shoves himself deeper and I don't even need breath. I just want him deeper in my throat. More of Elyah in my pussy. They both fuck me hard until suddenly they pull out of me, their breathing ragged.

Simultaneously, Elyah's cum splashes over my belly and up my ribs. Konstantin shoots over my breasts in hot, thick streams that drip down to mingle with Elyah's.

Kirill drags his fingers through the cum painting my body. "Look at you now, *detka*. Spent and panting. Covered in cum. Thoroughly used."

13

Lilia

Raw.
That's how I've felt since the four of us had sex two days ago. Raw, and stripped back to my most vulnerable layers.

Music is playing in the next room that sounds like Russian pop. Someone is frying bacon. I can feel the three of them out there, and their presence feels...different. Warm to the touch.

The bathroom is full of steam as I rinse the conditioner from my hair. The baby seems to be getting bigger and bigger with every passing day. When I look down, I can still see my feet, but only just.

Sex has wrapped me in a cozy, numbing cocoon, but one thought is clear in my mind. The men out in the living room want this baby to thrive just as much as I do. I've never had a man in my life whose needs and wants were aligned with my own, and now there are three of them.

I switch the water off and just stand there, running my hands over my stomach. My wet hair is pasted to my breasts.

The door opens and Konstantin appears, his brows drawn together in a frown.

"I couldn't hear anything in here and I wanted to check..." He trails off as he stares at me, the steam curling around my naked body.

I look up and meet those gray eyes, a strange sensation thrumming through me. He wanted to check that I'm okay?

A smile hooks the corner of his mouth as he sees me standing naked in the tub. We haven't spoken about what happened the other day. Our crazy foursome. No one has talked about it, but I know all three are thinking about it every time our eyes meet.

Kirill's dark expression is hungry and unapologetic. If he could go back and do it all again, the pageant included, he would. There will never be any kind of apology from a man like him.

Elyah is standing taller. Prouder. His smiles are tentative, but they're there. His crew is tight around him, just as he craves it, and I've been brought into their circle. I have never seen him happier.

And Konstantin? He seems as blindsided as I feel. He's fought so hard for everything to be the way he thought it should be, and yet here he is in a crummy Prague apartment with no diamonds and a woman who may or may not being carrying his child.

Yet wants her.

He wants nothing else.

"What are you doing?" Konstantin asks, but he sounds amused. Almost affectionate.

I run my hands over my belly, still standing in the tub, not one little bit shy that a man is staring at my naked body. "I feel beautiful for the first time in my life."

"You're always beautiful, Lilia."

I smile and cup my stomach. "Am I? I never feel that way. You probably don't believe me. I was a runway model. I've been a bride. I'm standing in a chipped old bathtub with a pregnant belly and no makeup on, but..."

Konstantin leans against the doorframe, watching me. Those gray eyes of his were so flinty and cold the first time I met him, but now they've softened. He said on that clifftop that he just wanted me, crowned with those diamonds. That's all he's ever needed.

But the diamonds are gone. Now there's just me.

"I feel like me," I whisper. "Just Lilia."

He holds out his hands to help me out of the tub, and I let him. With gentle fingers, he towels my hair dry, and from his touch I could almost believe he's never done one violent thing in his life.

My gaze fastens on the scar on his temple. "Why do you hate women so much?"

Konstantin stares at me in surprise. "You think I hate women?"

"Only a man filled with hate could come up with that pageant."

His fingers trail over the wet locks of my hair, pushing them back from my face. "I was very angry, *malyshka*. Angrier than I've ever been in my life."

"What—"

But he stops me with a finger over my lips. "We are not talking about that. We are never talking about that."

I push his hand away. "Did you know that trust grows from mutual respect?"

"Does it? I already trust you."

I frown up at him. "What?"

Konstantin steps closer to me, his fingers caressing the wet skin of my shoulders. "I can trust you to look after that baby. You will never let any harm come to my child. I believe in your desire for me, even when you're fighting me with every step of the way. All you have to do to be happy…"

His lips whisper over mine.

"…is stop fighting me."

Give in to this beautiful, powerful man and everything he wants. I swallow. "And why would I do that?"

"Because the three of us would burn the world down to make you ours." He cups my belly. "You and this baby."

Insanity.

It shouldn't feel so alluring to hear him say that.

"What if I didn't want you to burn the world? What if I wanted you to make it better? That would be a true test of your heart."

Konstantin talks right past my question. "Meanwhile, the four of us need to leave Prague. It's becoming more dangerous here with every passing minute."

Anguish fills my heart. These walls have become my security blanket. They feel even safer with the three of them in it. Here, we're just four people existing on toast and sex.

Out there, we're a *Pakhan*, his foot soldiers, and their pregnant captive.

"I'm so tired of running."

"Then don't run. One more journey, and you'll be home." He puts his lips against my ear. "What the four of us did the other day, we can do that in my house. My bed is bigger. We will treat you like our queen."

I remember all the things they said to me while we were having sex. "You talk so dirty to your queen."

His teasing smile grows heated. "That's because she loves every word."

I didn't know that anything like this was possible. I remember the scared, miserable eighteen-year-old girl who hated being naked with her husband. Sex with these men is incredible.

"So, are you going to do as you're told?" he murmurs.

I blink my lashes at him. "Who, me?"

Just because they've learned how to weaponize sex doesn't mean I forgive everything they've done. My body might give in to them, but my heart does not.

"No? We'll just have to keep fucking you like this until you're our good girl all the time, not just when you're full of cock."

I lean my cheek against his chest, wishing we could stay.

Konstantin wraps his arms around me as if he's sensing what I'm thinking. "I know you're frightened, but this baby is strong. It belongs to one of us, after all. One of us and you. An unstoppable combination."

"Even if the Vavilovs are looking for their son, they're not looking for me," I point out. "They won't find us. Prague is a big city."

Konstantin pulls away from me and shakes his head. "Not that big. I won't take the risk with this baby, and you shouldn't either."

I search for the right path, wondering which way to turn in this forest filled with thorns. There's light ahead, I can glimpse it, but I don't know how to reach it.

Konstantin wraps a bathrobe around me before we head out into the lounge. I'm greeted by a disarmingly domestic tableau. Kirill is buttering slices of bread. Konstantin pours coffee into mugs while he talks to Elyah, who is on the floor by the sofa doing crunches.

Kirill passes me a bacon sandwich on a plate and licks butter from his thumb at the same time. I feel that lick right down to my toes.

Elyah moves his legs so I can sit down on the sofa. He gives me a smile while he continues to work out, his eyes gleaming.

"Working out is fun?" I ask him, amused.

"It is when I am looking at you," he pants, still smiling.

I take a bite out of my sandwich and close my eyes. Damn, that's good. Soft bread. Crispy, salty bacon.

Kirill perches on the arm of the sofa next to me while Konstantin makes himself comfortable in a kitchen chair opposite, a mug of steaming coffee in his hands.

They discuss matters "back home," which I presume means London. I lose track of what they're saying as I eat, staring at the yellow wooden crib in the corner with the animal mobile. So many times, I've imagined placing my baby down to sleep while leaning over that crib.

When I've finished, Elyah takes my empty plate from me and places it on the kitchen table. He cups my cheek, his expression filled with sympathy.

"I know you want to stay, but you need to come with us.

We cannot protect you well enough here. That front door is weak. The window locks are not strong."

"Not to mention we are all living on top of one another here," Kirill points out, but there's a gleam in his dark eyes like he doesn't mind that part so much.

Konstantin gazes at me, his expression serious and his mind made up.

"Everything is sex and hormones now, but you could all turn back into the monsters you were last year," I point out.

"We had very different goals last year," Konstantin says. "That is not possible anymore."

Sure, he's probably not about to run another twisted pageant, but that doesn't mean he's father material. He still hasn't said sorry, and I doubt he ever will.

"You're still those men, and I remember what you did. You, hurting all those women," I tell Konstantin. "You, forcing me to the brink of death," I say, turning to Elyah. "And you, taking what isn't yours," I say to Kirill.

Elyah gets up without a word and goes to the window. Night has fallen and he pulls the curtain aside a crack and peers out into the darkness.

Kirill folds him arms and gazes down at me. "Just get on the plane. You have all the time in the world to forgive us later."

He reaches out and brushes crumbs from my lower lip, and his expression is as unapologetic as it was when he told me what he did to me at the pageant. "My baby is going to arrive in the best place, with the best people to take care of it. I won't let it be any other way, *detka*."

I rub my forehead, wishing I knew what to do next. I know they're right and we're not safe here. I rented this apartment because it was cheap, not secure. "Maxim Vavilov's father could know about the three of you from my father. He'll be able to find out where you live, Konstantin. If he somehow connects me with his son's death, how can you know we will be safe in your house?"

"We will be," Konstantin replies, without a millimeter of wiggle room for doubt. Kirill doesn't even bother replying. He's this close to scooping me up in his arms and carrying me out the door.

"Make the call," Kirill tells Konstantin.

The gray-eyed man takes out his phone, and I listen to him arranging an aircraft to fly us to London. "It will be ready in a few hours. This is for the best, *malyshka*."

"Elyah, do you think we will be safe in Konstantin's house? Elyah?"

He's still gazing out the window through a tiny gap in the curtains, and he puts up his hand and says quietly, "Hush, *solnyshko*."

"Why?"

"Because someone is watching the apartment."

All my muscles stiffen, and I freeze in place.

Without looking away from the window, Elyah picks up one of the guns that's on the counter. Kirill does the same thing, his expression instantly focusing. As they stand side by side, I can imagine them in prison jumpsuits. Pushka and Kirill, ready for anything.

Konstantin takes hold of my arm and starts backing me away from the window and the front door, shielding me with his body. His voice is low and calm as he says, "Stay close, *malyshka*."

"We can get out the window in the bedroom," I tell him.

There's a fire escape down to the first floor and an alleyway that leads around to the front of the building.

"We cannot. They will be out there, too."

He speaks these concerning words in that same soft tone, and I realize he's not speaking softly because he's not worried. He's trying to keep us all calm.

"Get down behind the sofa," Konstantin orders, pushing it away from the wall so I can crawl into the narrow space.

"But you—"

He pulls out his own gun and checks the clip, before slamming it back into place with the heel of his hand. "Don't worry about us. Protect yourself and your baby."

"Who has been outside or in front of an open window in the last twenty-four hours?" Elyah asks. His back muscles are tense, and he's got his finger on the trigger and his eye fastened to the gap in the curtains.

Kirill, Konstantin, and I glance at each other, shaking our heads.

"No one but you," Konstantin tells him.

"Then they think Lilia is in here alone, or with one man. They will—"

There's the sound of breaking glass from the bedroom. Footsteps thunder on the stairs up to my apartment. I dig my nails into the carpet behind the sofa, feeling terrified and helpless.

I can just see into the room, and my three men move as if they have choreographed this moment. Elyah turns toward the front door, aiming his weapon. Konstantin steps in front of the gap in the sofa, protecting me. Kirill darts across the lounge to the bedroom and braces his back against the wall by the doorway.

The front door bursts open, revealing a dangerous-looking man in black clothing and a tattoo beneath his eye. Elyah fires twice, kill shots to the head, and his expression glazes over. There's another man behind him, and he roars in fury, grabs the dead man by the shoulders to use as a shield, and propels himself into the room.

There are at least two more men in the doorway to the bedroom. Hard, dangerous-looking men in black leather jackets with aggressive-looking guns. Shots are fired, and the scent of gunpowder and blood fills the room. I wrap my arms protectively over my belly, my instincts telling me to run to him but knowing that it would be madness. I need a weapon. Someone should have given me a gun.

There's one laying in the middle of the room, dropped by one of the attackers. To get to it, I'd have to crawl out from behind the sofa and risk being struck with a bullet.

Elyah's attacker sweeps his legs out from beneath him and he goes crashing to the floor. The hitman lifts his boot and stomps on Elyah's arm. I think I hear a snap, and Elyah cries out in terrible pain.

The attacker lifts his boot again, this time over Elyah's head. He'll stomp on my lover's skull over and over again until he's dead.

"Elyah," I gasp in panic.

I scramble out from behind the sofa, grab the gun, raise it, and fire. I keep squeezing the trigger over and over, filled with panic.

I don't realize I'm screaming until the gun clicks in my hand.

Someone puts his hand on the gun, his breathing harsh in my ear. "He's dead. They're all dead."

When I don't move, Konstantin wrenches the weapon away from me.

"What the fuck did you think you were doing, Lilia? I told you to stay put."

I didn't think. I acted on instinct.

"I was saving Elyah," I pant. "I was saving all of you. If he went down, you all might have been killed."

Konstantin watches me with a narrowed, angry gaze. "We matter enough to save? I thought we were unforgivable."

That doesn't mean I want them to die.

It's...complicated.

There's blood on his shirt and I feel his arms and chest for injuries. "Are you hurt?"

"I'm fine," Konstantin growls, grabbing hold of my wrists. "Don't do anything like that again. One of us could have shot you."

"Elyah—"

"Elyah wanted you to protect the baby," Kirill seethes in my ear. He's come up on my other side with blood all over his face and chest, though from the looks of it, it's not his. "I had Elyah's back."

Even Elyah doesn't say anything grateful or reassuring. His expression is dark and troubled as he gets to his feet, his right wrist held close to his chest. "Let us do our jobs, Lilia. If I am shot or injured, it is part of this life."

"But if I can help—"

Elyah is either in too much pain or too angry with me, as he turns away and starts going through our attackers' pockets with his left hand.

I gaze around at the devastation in my tiny apartment. The broken front door. The furniture that was busted in the struggle. The bodies. The mess that the hitmen have made of everything.

Konstantin is still holding one of my wrists. "We are leaving this apartment. We should have left days ago."

I swallow hard and nod. We should leave quickly. One of my neighbors will have probably called the police by now.

Elyah comes toward us, cradling his right arm against his chest. His face is pale and sweaty as he holds something out to us. "Here."

It's a photograph.

Of me.

My golden hair is pinned up and there's a veil hanging down my back. I'm wearing a white dress with long lace sleeves, and there are diamonds in my ears. On my face is a closed-lip smile and my eyes are sad.

My wedding day with Ivan.

"Assassins," Elyah says. "Someone wants you dead. Either your father, or Vavilov."

Maybe it's both. Dad was furious with me last time I saw him. "I don't understand how they know I'm here."

Konstantin thinks about this. "In between Vavilov seeing you in the restaurant and going on a date with you, how much time passed?"

"Hours. He saw me at lunch, but we didn't meet until dinnertime."

He and Elyah exchange dark looks. "Plenty of time for Vavilov to contact his father and tell him that he had seen you in Prague."

"But I asked him—" I break off with a shake of my head. Of course Maxim would ignore my wishes. He was too excited by the idea of marrying me. When Maxim went missing, his father put two and two together and sent assassins after me.

Elyah pulls his wrist away from his chest and examines it. It's already swelling, the flesh turning an angry purple. There are bruises on his handsome face as well.

I go to him, my stomach in guilty knots. "You need to go to the hospital. I'll go with you."

Elyah shakes his head. "This is nothing. I will have doctor look at it in London."

Konstantin puts his hand on my shoulder and turns me toward the bedroom. "We're leaving for London now. Go pack. Don't argue with me."

I nod and do what he says, stepping over bodies to get to my room. Kirill stands guard by the broken front door, his gun in his hand.

Konstantin helps me pack, holding a bag open while I fill it with leggings, sweaters, and underwear. His forehead shines with sweat and his eyes are bloodshot.

"Have you got a headache?" He shakes his head, but I know he's lying. "I've got some—"

"Lilia. My headache is the last thing on my mind right now." He glances at my belly. "Are you feeling all right?"

There are questions in his expression. Am I going to faint? Is my heart racing? I fish a handful of underwear out of a drawer and stuff them in the bag. "I'm fine."

Kirill brings the car around to the front of the building and he and Elyah help me outside and into the vehicle. Konstantin emerges a moment later with my bags and stows them in the trunk.

Normally Elyah would drive, but he cradles his arm in the front passenger seat while Kirill drives us out of Prague.

"Get your head down," Konstantin tells me, pulling me over his lap. "We don't know if we're being followed."

There's a sheen of sweat on Elyah's brow as he cradles his wrist against his chest, and my heart twists. I've never seen him injured before. Despite all those fights in prison, I wonder if he's ever had a broken bone.

"How far is the airport?" I ask.

"A few hours, but this private airport is safer than the international one," Konstantin tells me, his eyes darting around the narrow streets as we drive.

My cheek is on Konstantin's thigh and my knees are curled up. There's silence in the car for a long time, until Kirill swears from the driver's seat.

He steps on the gas, and we lurch forward. "There's someone on our tail."

Elyah glances longingly at the steering wheel, and I can tell he's wishing his wrist wasn't broken. "If they get close, they are going to try and shoot out the tires or run us off the road."

Kirill breathes out fast as if he's coming to a decision. "Okay. Then they die first."

He puts his foot down and drives like a maniac. The car behind us accelerates as well.

I can't see much, but Kirill takes some turns at a high speed, and soon we're in the middle of farmland on an empty, narrow road.

"Kostya," he says through his teeth, and I don't know what he means.

But Konstantin does. He takes out his gun, rolls down the window, and turns in his seat.

Kirill rounds a bend, and then suddenly slows down. Konstantin takes careful aim, and fires two shots.

An engine races, tires squeal, and then there's a horrible crunching noise.

Kirill pulls over and he and Elyah get out of the vehicle.

I slowly sit up and see that the car following us has crashed into a tree. Konstantin blew out the tires.

"Stay here," Konstantin orders, before heading over to join the others. I peer over the back seat out the rear window to watch what's happening, my heart still pounding from the crazy ride.

Elyah drags a man who's still kicking out of the wreckage one-handed, and Kirill shoots him in the head. Another passenger appears to be dead already, and a third lays partly concealed in the twisted wreckage. Konstantin has his arms folded as his two friends pull the man the rest of the way out and prop him against the vehicle.

I see silver hair flash in the sunlight and my heart freezes over. It's Dad, wearing a tailored gray suit. His hair, threaded with silver, is spilling over his forehead and blood is running down the side of his face. He holds a gun in his hand, and he points it from one of my men to the next, trying to keep them back.

I fumble for the door handle and walk down the road toward the crash. If he's here, then I need to talk to him. We can't go on like this.

Konstantin notices me coming, and while he doesn't look happy, he doesn't say anything.

From Dad's expression as he watches me draw closer, he's beyond feeling anger or fury He glares at me like he wishes he could turn me to ice.

I stop a few feet away, and Elyah moves to shield me with his body. He has his own gun pointed at Dad.

"You sent assassins after me?" I ask him. "You're trying to kill me?"

"Vavilov is the one who wants you dead," Dad says through his teeth, not bothering to say hello either. "He had his chance, but I knew he would screw it up. The man can't do anything right."

"You gave him photos of me to give to his hitmen?"

"You killed his son, you stupid bitch. He wanted to marry you." Dad's face transforms in disgust, as if the idea of anyone wanting me is preposterous.

"I wouldn't have laid a finger on him if he hadn't tried to assault me."

"Bullshit," Dad seethes. "Stop playing the victim, Lilia. You killed him so he wouldn't blow your cover."

"Believe your daughter when she tells you something," Elyah growls. "She is no liar."

Blood trickles into Dad's left eye and he wipes it away, laughing. "You really believe that? You utter fool. Lilia speaks nothing but lies. She learned all her tricks from her bitch of a grandmother."

Dad grasps the car door and hauls himself to his feet. He's got a cut on his forehead and is favoring one leg, but other than that, he seems unscathed.

"I didn't come here to fight. I'm not here to talk to you either, Lilia." He turns to my men. "I have come for a discussion with you three. A deal."

Kirill gestures at the dead men. The wrecked car. "You are in no position to demand anything."

"I make no demands. I have an offer."

Konstantin, Elyah, and Kirill exchange glances. I wait for them to tell Dad to go to hell, that we have a plane to catch, but suddenly they don't seem to be in a hurry to get out of here.

"We're listening," Konstantin says.

"Don't listen to a word—" I begin, but Konstantin holds out his hand to silence me.

What the hell? I knock it away with a glare.

Dad smirks at me. "They're businessmen first, Lilia. Let the men do their business."

Revulsion crawls up my throat. If I didn't have the baby to worry about, I think I would try to punch him.

He turns to Konstantin. "I'll get straight to the point. I'm not a young man anymore. I don't have time to hold on to grudges when there are bigger, more important things on my mind."

What a lie. Dad is the king of holding grudges.

"I want my daughter back. From the looks of things, you three seem to have bonded with her. You might even believe you love her. But we all know women are easy to come by."

"Then why is she so important to you?" Kirill asks slowly, his eyes narrowed.

Dad gives him a cold smile. "I should say, women are easy to come by, unless you are a father. Lilia is the only daughter I have."

"I never had the impression that you loved her," Konstantin says slowly.

Dad meets my gaze and I see no love. No affection. Only a hint of the cruelty that's to come. "This is a matter of family pride. Lilia has defied me for too long."

My nails dig into my palms, and I shiver as a cold wind

cuts through my clothes. We humiliated him on the jet, but I'm the one who's going to be punished for it even though I spared his life. Dad's not above beating me. He's probably not above locking me up or starving and torturing me to death, either. I've outgrown my usefulness to him. He only wants revenge.

Dad turns back to Konstantin. "You mentioned diamonds. This is the deal. I'll recompense you for what she stole, and you give me back my daughter."

Konstantin doesn't immediately refuse, and all the hairs stand up on the back of my neck.

"Do not accept anything," Elyah urges his friend. "Money is not what is important here. Lilia and the baby are what is important."

"Are you three all going to play happy families with my daughter?" Dad sneers. "When I was with her in Trieste, she told me she was going to abort that baby. I suppose she changed her mind when she realized she could manipulate you all with it."

Elyah glares at him. "That is lie."

"I told you. My daughter is a master liar. Just like her *babushka*. How many times has she tricked you already?"

Konstantin and Kirill exchange glances, but I can't read their expressions. Elyah seems troubled, like he's wondering whether I would flip-flop between keeping and destroying this baby on a whim.

"Really, Elyah? You're going to believe a man over me again?" I say.

Dad casts his cold gaze over the bruises on Elyah's face and his swollen wrist. "Did you get hurt protecting her? Did she even say thank you? I doubt it. My daughter is a cold-hearted bitch, though she's excellent at using her body to get what she wants, I'm sure."

No one says anything, and my throat feels painfully tight.

"How much money did she swindle out of you?" Dad asks Konstantin.

"Fourteen million dollars," Konstantin says at once.

Dad is incredulous. "Fourteen million dollars' worth of diamonds?"

"They were very beautiful diamonds. Is she worth that much money to you?"

Dad glances around at the three of them. "I won't deny that the amount stings when she's already cost me so much over the years, but I lie awake at night thinking about how my own daughter has made a fool of me. This is a matter of personal pride."

The corner of Konstantin's mouth turns up. "Oh, I understand. Lilia has a way of making everything very fucking personal." He turns and flashes a vindictive glance at me. "Don't you, Lilia?"

His eyes are even more bloodshot than before. His head is pounding, one of his men is hurt, and he's out fourteen million dollars and a wife because of me, a woman who doesn't know her place. Suddenly he's wondering why he's bothering with me.

I feel like he's punched me in the guts.

He swore that he wanted me.

He promised to protect me.

His gaze fastens on my belly before turning back to Dad.

"But there's a difficulty. She's pregnant with my child," Konstantin points out. "I'm not giving up the child."

Dad rubs his jaw, thinking. "It delays things, but I suppose you can have the baby. I don't want it."

"No!" I give a strangled cry and step forward, but Kirill seizes my arm, though he's still staring at Dad. "Don't you dare take my baby from me. I won't let you take my baby."

Konstantin glances at Elyah and Kirill. "What do you think? We get the child and fourteen million dollars. Aran Brazhensky gets his troublemaking daughter back to punish how he chooses."

"I think it's a perfect deal," Kirill purrs. "The only other thing I would request is a recording of Lilia's punishment."

"That can be arranged," Dad says with a nasty smile.

Kirill bursts out laughing. "Then I say go for it."

Elyah says nothing. His silence is the coldest thing I've ever heard.

Konstantin turns to Dad. "Do not hurt Lilia until after she's given birth. If you do, I will kill you myself."

Dad holds up his hands. "I wouldn't dream of it. Children are the most important thing in the world. You can all join me in America until the child is born if you like."

I yank my arm from Kirill's grip, my chest heaving. "You can't do this. My baby is the only thing I can't live without."

Konstantin ignores me and turns to Elyah. "Are you sure about this? You're the reason we chased Lilia all over the world."

The blond man swallows, hard. He still won't meet my eyes. "I am tired of being pushed away by an ungrateful woman. Lilia Aranova has made it clear that she will never love me the way I love her. We should take what is ours and be done with this."

His expression closes and he steps away from me, cradling his broken arm against his chest.

I rejected him. I broke him. He has nothing left to say to me.

"Then it's a deal," Dad purrs.

"I have a plane refueling to take us to London," Konstantin says. "You're welcome to join us, and then we can fly to America from there."

Dad holsters his weapon and smiles at the men. "It would be a pleasure."

I sink to the ground, too shocked even to cry, both my arms wrapped around my belly. I was growing to trust these men. I was starting to love these men. They are going to throw me away over some diamonds because our love is difficult?

Since when has love been easy? When it's rare and hard won, you're supposed to hold on tighter than ever.

Konstantin hunkers down in front of me, his expression lit from within now he's getting everything he's ever wanted.

"I would have fought for us," I say, loud enough for the other two to hear. "I was going to try and make this work for all of us despite everything you've done, for the sake of this child, but you've thrown it all away."

"Ah, a sad day," Konstantin murmurs, brushing his knuckles over my cheek. "But it's not goodbye just yet, Lilia."

No, we have months together before he rips my baby from my arms and leaves me to die. That's all they've wanted all along, the three of them. The baby.

"We still have so much more ahead of us. Now, be a good girl for once and close your eyes."

"What?"

Konstantin takes my face in his hands and kisses me, his lips warm and soft. I'm so confused that my eyes are wide open as I watch Kirill and Elyah raise their weapons at Dad, whose smile is just beginning to fade into horror.

And they shoot.

Dad crumples to the ground, two crimson trails pouring from bullet wounds in his head and chest, puddling beneath his limp body, and running past my knees and into the gutter.

He's dead.

Konstantin draws back and smiles ruefully. "You never would do as you are told."

Kirill kicks Dad's body and spits on the corpse. "Good riddance, you piece of shit."

I stare at Konstantin. "You were pretending to make a deal with my father? Did you say all that just to mess with me?"

He smiles and shakes his head. "Of course not. We did it to make him put his gun away. He would have shot you if we'd turned his deal down. The three of us discussed this possibility weeks ago."

"And you didn't think to let me in on it?" I fume at him.

"A father might know when his daughter is faking her tears. We couldn't risk him firing his weapons. No one is taking you away from us. Not with money. And not with a bullet."

Elyah reaches out with his good hand and helps me to my feet. "Nothing anyone says about you matters to me, *solnyshko*. I believe Lilia."

I close my eyes and take a deep breath, trying to make my heart return to normal. The past few minutes were a nightmare.

I open my eyes and glare at them. "If it weren't for this baby, I would fight you all."

Kirill laughs. "We can have our fun and games on the plane, *detka*."

"The second you take your pants off, I'll twist your goddamn balls off," I snarl at him, and he smirks like the idea is interesting to him.

Elyah takes my face in his good hand. "I know I have made terrible mistakes. Will you believe me when I tell you that I have changed? That we have all changed together, and because of each other?"

I look from one man to the next. They're all different from the men they once were. I'm a different woman.

"I love you," Elyah murmurs, stroking my cheek. "I will not speak for the others, but Konstantin needs you. Kirill is obsessed with you."

Love. Need. Obsession.

The cornerstones of any sane relationship.

Are we really doing this?

Can I allow myself to belong to them even if part of me is still terrified of the things they're capable of? Konstantin and Kirill will never apologize for who they are. Elyah will never take my side against them.

Either I accept them, or I walk away.

I gasp and put my hand over my stomach.

"Is something wrong?" Elyah asks urgently, and I shake my head.

"The baby is kicking." I stand with my hands over my belly, next to the body of my dead father, his men, the wrecked car. The four of us are together in the empty road.

If not love, there's something between us that I can't explain, and I don't want to leave it behind.

I move Elyah's hand from my cheek to my belly and then take Kirill and Konstantin's hands and place their palms on my bump.

"I think the baby has something to say to its fathers."

Kirill's eyes are wide. "I have never felt this before. Our child is so strong."

Elyah strokes the place where the baby is kicking and Konstantin smiles as he gazes at me, his expression filled with amusement and self-satisfaction. *You are going to accept us, after all, Lilia?*

Damn his smugness.

I think I am.

We stand far too long on a road littered with bodies for four people who have a plane to catch.

14

Konstantin

I rise from the bed reluctantly at dawn, untangling myself from the limbs, arms, and twisted sheets. Large male bodies have invaded my bed. Elyah is hard in his sleep, and his cock is pressed into Lilia's ass. Kirill's face is against her breasts, and he has one of her thighs hooked over his hips. Lilia's belly is growing huge.

She fell asleep holding my hand, and while she's still stubbornly holding on tight in her sleep, I try to extricate myself from her. A man needs to work, not lie around all day sleeping and fucking.

But as soon as I'm free from all of them, I stand naked by my bed, rubbing the back of my neck and gazing at their sleeping forms. This is becoming a daily occurrence.

I need a bigger mattress.

It wasn't supposed to be like this. Elyah and Kirill moved

their bedrooms next door to mine, and at first Lilia was spending the night with each of us in turn. Not on any sort of roster but going to whichever man ready to sleep when she was. Her pregnancy has made her restless and her sleep schedule unpredictable. If she comes to bed with me, I often wake to discover Kirill or Elyah sleeping on Lilia's other side. Last week I awoke to the sound of her soft cries and saw that Kirill was going down on her while Elyah was thrusting into her mouth. In my bed. Three o'clock in the morning has never been the sexiest time of day for me, but right then it was.

A few days later, in the small hours of the morning, I got up to get a glass of water and found Lilia pacing the corridor with her hands on her belly. She muttered that she couldn't sleep, and then smiled and motioned me over to Kirill's bedroom. The door was open, and Kirill and Elyah had fallen asleep together. Elyah was on his back with one arm flung out, and Kirill had his head pillowed on his bicep.

Lilia smiled at them, and whispered, "They've been like that for hours. Like puppies. And they both complained about living on top of each other in my apartment."

They complained, but they weren't really bothered. In fact, I think they loved it.

I drew her into my arms and kissed her. "With you around, all of us are closer, *malyshka*."

And she kissed me back.

Without hesitation. Affectionate, but still reserved.

She has begun to tolerate me, perhaps even like me, but there's no love in the way she touches me, and that's starting to bother me.

Yesterday, I awoke to discover all three of them in my bed,

sound asleep. I had barely six inches of mattress. I opened my mouth to snap at Elyah or Kirill that we are not a wolf litter sharing a den, but Kirill sleepily murmured into Lilia's neck and squeezed her tight. Elyah reached out with his eyes closed to stroke her hair, breathe her in deep, and nuzzle her close.

I closed my eyes and went back to sleep. If this is what it takes for Lilia to bond with all of us, then this is what it takes. I have seen stranger; more sinister things happen in a bed.

Thanks to the last few months spent chasing Lilia back and forth across the globe, I'm behind with my work. I throw myself into what needs to be done, drinking too much coffee and vodka and not eating or sleeping enough. Two days in a row I skip my morning swim, and then it hits me.

The worst migraine I've had in years.

My vision refracts into stabbing white lights. Throbbing pain shoots up the back of my neck and hammers in my skull. I fumble in my desk for some of my stronger painkillers, but even as I swallow them down, I know they're not going to be enough.

Lilia finds me in the corridor on the way to my bedroom, one of my hands braced against the wall and cold sweat covering my body. She seems to understand what's happening as she takes me by the arm and compels me forward.

"This way. I've got you."

She helps me onto the bed in the darkened room and eases my head into her lap. My cheek bumps against her belly, and if she just stopped there, I think I'd be as happy as I could be with a splitting headache.

But Lilia doesn't stop there. She strokes my hair back and

her cool fingers press against my forehead, my brow, the nape of my neck. Her touch is firm but careful, and each time she eases off, my migraine lessens a little more.

I groan in relief and pleasure as her fingers dig carefully into the ropey muscles at the back of my neck, holds them, and then releases me. "You have a magic touch. I've never felt anything like it."

I remember her telling me once when I had a headache that she used to do this for her grandmother, implying she could do it for me, too, but stubbornly turning away. Telling me in no uncertain terms that I didn't deserve her care.

But I deserve it now?

We sit in sweet, comfortable silence for a long time, her with her back against the headboard and me laying crosswise on the bed with my eyes closed. I can breathe easier now that the throbbing in my skull has eased to a dull ache.

"Tell me about someone you have loved," she whispers.

"Your fingers," I murmur, not opening my eyes. She has magic fingers.

"Don't be flippant."

I run my hands over her belly. "Our baby."

"This little one isn't here yet. Someone who has made you laugh. Encouraged you. Frustrated you. Enraged you."

"Definitely you."

"You don't love me, Konstantin. Tell me more about yourself."

What a strange question. I know Lilia well enough by now that she doesn't ask idle questions. She's hunting for something, but I don't know what. Maybe she wants to know my softer side. Maybe she's looking for a reason to stay.

Too bad she won't find it like this. "No one, *malyshka*. You don't love your family and I don't love mine."

"I love my *babulya*," Lilia points out.

I smile against her stroking fingers. "Ah, yes. Your devious grandmother who taught her granddaughter all her tricks and made her into a slippery little devil."

"That's my *babulya*," Lilia says proudly. "Did you know your grandmother?"

"My family that is still alive are all in Russia, and half of them would kill me if they laid eyes on me. The other half are indifferent to my existence."

"Why is that?" she asks, her voice low and gentle.

She's prying into things I have never told anybody and don't fucking talk about. Kirill and Elyah know, but they were there, and I didn't have to speak the words. Or not many of them, anyway.

"Tell me how you feel today," I ask, changing the subject. "Have you noticed the baby move? I think I can feel them now." A little knee or foot is pressing against my cheek through Lilia's belly.

But she won't be sidetracked.

"I know so little about you." Her fingers trail across my suddenly tense neck and shoulders. "You get all clenched up when I mention the past. Are you worried about something?"

"It's not worry. It's bad memories."

Her hand sweeps across my brow. "Is it bad memories that give you these migraines?"

"A bullet that tore across my skull is what has given me these migraines."

She massages the pressure point between my brows, and the pain in my head slowly eases.

"I never told you what I did with your money. The money I got from the sale of your diamonds," she murmurs.

"How much did you get, by the way?"

"You won't like it if I tell you. I'll make your headache worse." Amusement lightens her voice.

"Tell me anyway."

"Six million."

I groan. "Fucking hell."

"I was in a hurry. There were mad Russians on my tail."

It's not nearly as much as she should have gotten for the diamonds, but as she says, she wasn't in a position to drive a hard bargain. The fact that she managed to sell stolen pink diamonds at all while in hiding is astonishing. "Is there anything you can't do?"

"Hide from you, apparently."

I reach up and caress the nape of her neck. "I'm glad you have this one weakness. Never lose it."

Lilia laughs. "While you're in such a good mood, shall I tell you what I've been doing with your money?" She decides for me. "I'll tell you."

She describes how she's been tracking down the women from the pageant, obtaining their email addresses and then sending them one-sixteenth of six million dollars.

"It's their money, not mine or yours. They deserve it after everything you put them through."

I don't know about that, but I keep my mouth closed. Barely any of them lifted a finger to help Lilia orchestrate their successful escape. Some of them were firmly against her. If I were Lilia, I'd feel no compulsion to give them anything, though we established some time ago that my conscience is pointed in a different direction than Lilia's.

Lilia sighs. "The thing is, I haven't been very successful, and I've stopped searching during the past months. I've barely found any of the women and sent them their money." Disappointment colors her voice.

The six million split up is less than four hundred thousand dollars each. It's not much money. It's barely anything, really. I wonder why she's beating herself up about it when it can't make that much difference in their lives.

Or maybe it would. My family was always wealthy. Poisonous, but wealthy.

"There," she finishes with a sigh. "Now you know everything."

With my eyes still closed, I murmur, "I know more than you think."

"Oh?"

"I know that you're beautiful, proud, and strong. I know that you are happy that your father is dead, though sometimes late at night you worry if this makes you bloodthirsty and callous. Do not bother wasting your time with those thoughts, *malyshka*."

After the lies he told about Lilia and the baby, Aran Brazhensky deserved to die like a dog in the street.

I reach up and caress her cheek. "And I know that you want to run from me once this baby is born."

I feel Lilia's expression stiffen. I wonder if she's going to lie to me and say it's not true. These past few weeks have been as close to bliss as I have ever known. Elyah is happy. Even though there hasn't been any bloodshed or mayhem, Kirill seems relaxed. The baby will arrive soon, but I'm not foolish enough to believe that we're all going to live happily ever after.

A moment later, Lilia resumes her stroking of my brow. "I haven't decided anything. Who betrayed you and made you hate women so much?"

Offering me a bargain, is she? Open yourself up to me and I might consider staying. I grind my teeth together in annoyance. "A woman."

"Did you love her?"

I laugh without humor. "I suppose I did. It's difficult to remember feeling anything but hate for that bitch."

I feel her flinch at my harsh words. "You loved this woman, and you can speak of her this way?"

"All this talk of love is irrelevant," I murmur. "Elyah loves you. Kirill does, too, in his strange way. But for me, there is power and there is us, and that is all that matters. I have the power to look after you and this child and that is all that should concern you."

"You're saying you won't love our child?"

A pang goes through my chest, and I find her hand and squeeze her fingers. "A child is different," I say softly. "Of course I will love our child, and when the baby is born, I want you to marry me."

"What about Elyah and Kirill?"

"Marry them, too, if you want. They are already in our bed. They will get you pregnant again soon enough, and they should be your husbands as well."

I stroke her belly as I think about it. I even like the idea. Elyah is hungry to get his child in Lilia, and so is Kirill. I smile to myself because maybe I'll beat them both. Again, if this baby is mine. A little healthy competition over our woman should be fun.

"You want me to marry you and wear your ring, and sleep with your friends? What kind of *Pakhan* are you?"

"A clever one. A strong one. I have not been beaten by a man since I was fifteen years old."

"And a woman?"

I hesitate. Just a few weeks ago, I would have told her to mind her own business, but in this darkened room with my head in her lap, my defenses are down. "Women have always been my blind spot. My weakness. And you're my greatest weakness of all."

"A woman shot you," she guesses, running her fingers down my scar.

"She did."

"Who was it?"

I sigh. "*Malyshka*, I was having happy thoughts about the three of us getting you pregnant again. Please don't spoil it by dredging up my past and giving me another headache."

"The past is important. It helps me understand you. There aren't many men who would be willing to share his bride with his friends."

"We're not like other men. We're your men." It doesn't feel like we are sharing Lilia. I don't have to remind myself to compromise or play fair with Elyah and Kirill. It just works because the three of us always have. First there was Kirill and me, all those years ago when I was starting out on my own and Kirill was sixteen. Then Kirill and Elyah in prison, and finally, the three of us. We have always worked so well together, and now we've found our woman.

"Some would call it perverted."

I laugh, and the sound is bitter. "Do you think so? Perhaps

my judgment is off. I have seen things in my life that are far more perverted."

"Like what?"

I open my eyes and gaze up at her. How the hell did she get me talking about this? Even now, the shame and disgust burns like it is my doing.

"I have never told anyone," I say stonily.

She waits, her expression expectant.

Suddenly, I laugh. "The irony is, I should not want to tell you because what you think of me actually matters. Yet, I can feel myself wanting to tell you anyway."

"That is why you want to tell me," she murmurs softly. "It's fighting to get out because you want to know that your secret won't change the way I see you."

What a clever thing she is.

"Can I show you something?" I ask her.

Her mouth quirks in a smile. "How perverted is it?"

"Oh, fiendish," I say, sitting up slowly. There's a dull ache in the back of my skull, but I can bear it.

I lead Lilia down the corridor by the hand to the room we've dedicated to the nursery. A crib is waiting in the corner with a folded yellow blanket, and there's a mobile hanging over the crib. Elephants and tigers in yellow bowties.

Lilia gives a cry of pleasure and reaches out to touch it, and all the animals go dancing around in a circle. "That's my mobile from Prague. I thought I had left it behind. You brought it with you. You remembered, despite all the fear and blood that day."

I put my hands on her shoulders and turn her to face me. "Lilia, I..."

But the words stick in my throat.

Say you're sorry, you fucking idiot.

But I don't feel it, and Lilia will know it's a lie. She'll hate me even more for lying than for staying silent.

I can't change what I've done.

The past is indelible, and I have to make her understand that.

Lilia understands Elyah. She knows what made Kirill into the man he is today, but she doesn't know what made me Konstantin, and she won't accept me until she does.

I brush her hair away from her neck and plant a kiss there. "Shall I bare my throat to you? Shall I give you every weapon you require to best me and lay all my vulnerabilities at your feet?"

I move my lips up her throat until I whisper against her mouth.

"Will you accept me then?"

∼

Nineteen years earlier

"I don't want the money. Keep your money." My voice is high with terror. I back away slowly through the water, the shallow waves lapping at my ankles and then my knees.

"Where are you going, Konstantin? Mother and I just want to talk."

My older brother advances on me slowly, a malicious smile on his face. It's a moonless night, and the surface of the water is black. A cold wind cuts through my clothes and chills my sweat-soaked skin. Pyotr is smiling but there's murder in his eyes. He's seventeen years old but as brawny as a full-grown man. When our father died three years ago, he stepped into his shoes as head of the family.

In every way that he could.

He and Mother have been whispering behind my back. Plotting. Scheming. I can taste their trickery in the air I breathe. The food I eat. Sometimes I wonder if Mother sprinkles the dinner she sets before me with poison. I check for shadows behind me on staircases. When I ride my horse, I check the saddle blankets twice over for prickles that could cause the stallion to throw me and break my neck.

In two years when I turn seventeen, I'll inherit my share of our father's fortune, a fortune that Pyotr and Mother are desperate to control themselves. Their greed is going to kill me.

But that's not why this is happening.

"Darling, why are you acting so strangely? Please come out of the water," Mother calls, her voice dripping with sweetness. She's beautiful, my mother. Long, dark hair, luminous skin and eyes, a proud, full mouth. Men have been falling over themselves to try and wed her, but she's not interested in men. To marry, at least. She's taken plenty to her bed. I've seen them in the kitchen or leaving by the back door, and they're getting younger and younger.

I stay where I am and don't take my eyes off Pyotr. Our enormous mansion rises behind us, all the windows dark and blank.

"Does she call you Grigor when you fuck her?" I seethe at Pyotr. Grigor was our father's name. "Was Father already dead when you started screwing our mother, or could you not even wait until he was cold?"

"How dare you!" Mother screeches.

She has enough shame to deny it, but what is the point? I turn on her, my chest lifting and falling sharply with disgust and anger. "Mother, I *saw* you."

And she knows I saw them. Our eyes locked when Pyotr was on top of her. She didn't even have the sense to screw her son under the sheets so she could pass off their sick relationship as "just cuddling."

I drag my eyes away from my mother, and I'll feel no sorrow if I never lay eyes on her again. She has treated me cruelly for as long as I can remember, and for no reason that I can fathom. She was cruel to Pyotr, too, but it always seemed as if he strangely enjoyed it.

I look only at Pyotr, my brother whom I have always loved and who has loved me. Deep down he must know he's making a terrible mistake. He's being coerced by an older and far more devious woman, and it's not his fault. "If you tell me she's forcing you, I'll believe you. Do you hear me, Pyotr? No question about it. I'm on your side."

Pyotr's handsome face, so like our father's, goes blank for a moment. I take a step forward.

"Pyotr, if this bitch got her claws into you, then I can help you get them out again. I will tear them out of your flesh."

He reaches out for me across the water. Our fingers touch.

And then he seizes my wrist, his eyes lighting up. "You always were too trusting, you little idiot."

Pyotr sweeps my knees out from beneath me, and I fall into the water with a splash. My back hits the rocks at the bottom of the lake and then Pyotr is on top of me, his knee on my chest and his hands around my throat, holding me under. I can see his face through the churning water and it's savage. Unrecognizable. Over his shoulder, Mother examines her nails, keeping herself out of the way of any splashes.

My vision goes spotty. My lungs start to burn. I want to take a breath, but I'll suck in water if I do. I need to fill my lungs. Though it's certain death, I have to fill my lungs. I can't override what my body craves, and it's terrifying.

With the last of my strength, I shove Pyotr's knee off my chest, and while he's off-balance, I throw him off and burst to the surface of the lake, flailing for air. I can't see through the water in my eyes, but Mother is shouting at Pyotr to grab me, so I blunder off to my left, away from them and away from the house. There are trees with low branches lining the water, and I scramble through them.

And then I run.

I run because my life depends on it, my lungs on fire now and my legs cramping from cold and effort. I don't look around. I don't check over my shoulder. I fix my eyes to the horizon where the moon is rising, and I book it out of there.

I outrun my fear.

I outrun my pain.

Pyotr and Mother can do whatever sick things they want with each other. As far as I'm concerned, my family is dead.

I'll make my own fucking family.

∽

THERE AREN'T many people I trust as I grow older. I've always been confident in my own cleverness, and I live to lead. I build up my own empire from scratch, and I'm not afraid to get my hands dirty. The only person I truly trust is myself.

When I meet Kirill, I'm impressed by his skills, but he's so young, so eager, that I don't think much about him. He'll probably die before his child makes it to school age.

Then I hear a strange tale about Kirill. His child was the one to die, killed in terrible circumstances by its own grandparents. Then the mother took her own life and Kirill was the one to find the body. He burned the mansion down in revenge, though the Lugovskayas escaped. A pity, that.

You can get people out of prison in Russia if you know the right people and have enough influence or money. I've never tried before, but as I think about the Lugovskayas, anger burns in my chest in a way it hasn't since my own family betrayed me.

So, I pull some strings, and Kirill emerges from prison to stand by my side, darker than he once was. Hardened, bloodthirsty, and as sharp as a honed blade. He has no one and nothing to care about, just as I have no one and nothing. Only money. Only power. His idea of power is the game he plays in the dark. He's more than happy to play while working alongside me. We're an excellent team, him and I.

One day we hear of a tall, blond man covered in prison tattoos asking around after Kirill. A friend, or an assassin? He finds us in our favorite bar in the city, drinking vodka in the early hours of the morning.

As soon as Kirill's eyes land on the man, he gets to his feet, a rare smile breaking over his face.

"Elyah fucking Morozov. What are you doing here?" Kirill greets the newcomer with an embrace like the man is his long-lost brother. "This is Konstantin Zhukov, my *Pakhan*. Kostya, Elyah and I met in prison."

Elyah nods respectfully, though he doesn't smile. There's something hard and bleak in his eyes, despite the fact that he seems to be glad to have found Kirill. "I am honored to meet you, *Pakhan*."

I nod politely, staying in my seat, though I'm curious about this man. I have never seen Kirill happy to see anyone except myself.

"You need work? We can give you work." Kirill turns to me. "This man is a fucking machine, and I would trust him with my life. I watched him take out three guys at once many times. Everyone was trying to kill Pushka, and no one could."

"I do need work," Elyah says, turning to me. His expression is proud, and his tone is even. "I was in prison and then I was in America. I need to start again."

When he finishes speaking, his cold blue eyes meet mine.

What a chatty fellow.

"What kind of work are you looking for?"

"Anything," is Elyah's reply. From his attitude and his myriad of tattoos, he seems like the sort of man who is capable of anything. "In America, I was working for Ivan Kalashnik. Driver. Bodyguard. I was with him almost every day for months."

"Why are you not with him now?" I ask.

"He was shot in the head."

The man's frosty bluntness has my eyebrows creeping up my forehead. "Wasn't it your job to make sure he wasn't shot in the head?"

I watch him closely, wondering if Elyah is going to become flustered or defensive. His deadpan tone or expression never wavers.

"My old *Pakhan* got himself killed by police. I was getting him out of there. He would be alive today if he had listened to me."

A smile spreads over my face. When Kirill came to me at the age of sixteen, he impressed me by his abilities and his blunt manner. Now, he calls me Kostya, and I should tell him not to be so overfamiliar, but I don't want to. I like how he carries himself through this world. I would have burned the fucking Lugovskayas' house down if I were him.

Kirill would never lie to me, and I sense that this Elyah is the brutally honest type as well.

"All right. I am getting married, and I need more protection. You seem capable enough."

Elyah shakes his head. "This is not the work for me. Send me to the streets. I will run drugs. Guns. It doesn't matter."

I frown at him. "This work is better. The pay is better. Why would you want that?"

"You do not want me near your wife. I nearly fucked Ivan's wife."

Kirill and I exchange glances, and I can see he's as shocked by this admission as I am. Holy fucking hell. His *Pakhan's* wife? "You're lucky your guts are inside your body. Why did you do this?"

Bitterness creeps into Elyah's expression. "She was beautiful, and he beat her. I lost my head over her."

It's difficult to imagine a man as icy as Elyah losing his head over anyone.

"Then she betrayed all of us and nearly got me killed."

"What would you do if you saw her again?" I ask.

Elyah's blue eyes turn even colder. "Wring her fucking neck. All women, they are not worth the hassle. I will not touch anyone for the rest of my life unless she is a whore I can fuck and send on her way."

I should send him away. With a record like his, anyone

would be forgiven for thinking that this man is bad luck. I turn my vodka glass in my hand, thinking.

"Come to the house tomorrow. Meet the other men. Meet my future wife."

Elyah frowns. "I didn't expect this. I only want enough money to eat and have a roof over my head. Why would you trust me in your home?"

"I don't trust a man who hasn't felt the burn of betrayal. It's a useful learning experience."

Elyah gives a snort of humorless laughter and shakes his head. "You are not fucking wrong. All right. I will see you tomorrow, *Pakhan*."

Kirill says his goodbyes to Elyah, gives him my address, and walks him out of the bar.

When he comes back, I tell him, "If he looks the wrong way at my fiancée even once, you will gut him from throat to balls, understood?"

Kirill doesn't even blink. "Understood."

∾

Elyah turns up at my house promptly, dressed neatly in black and wearing an expression of hostility that I imagine he perfected in prison. I leave him in Kirill's hands and see to my guests, a selection of my closest men who have gathered to celebrate our engagement.

The living room is filled with the sounds of people talking and glasses clinking. The double doors into the garden are open and warm, rose-scented air wafts inside. My fiancée is standing by the grand piano, her dark hair hanging in a waterfall down her back.

I've made it.

Not as far as I plan to go, but an excellent start for a self-made man who started from rock bottom. Or lake bottom, in my case. As I take a sip of champagne, I wonder what Pyotr is doing tonight. Mother died years ago, and I wonder—and then wish I hadn't—if he misses her as a mother or a lover.

"Why so serious, my love?" A hand slips into mine and squeezes. A canary diamond glitters on her ring finger.

My bride-to-be, Valeriya.

As I gaze into her beautiful face, I feel nothing, which is exactly what I wanted.

Over her shoulder and standing against the wall is a sober figure in black. I turn Valeriya around and draw her closer to the man.

"Elyah, this is Valeriya, my fiancée. Valeriya, Elyah has recently joined my crew. I believe I will make him my driver."

Valeriya always dresses to turn a man's head. Her cream dress is tight over her generous breasts and hips, and she beams at the man. "Hello, and welcome. I hope you're enjoying the party."

He eyes her coldly and then looks away as if he's bored. "Good evening."

Valeriya's smile falters and dims. She's used to being admired by one and all, and my men have a habit of behaving around her like she's a fairy queen. She's not. She's the illegitimate daughter of an arm's dealer who was working as a cocktail waitress in a high-end club until three months ago. None of her family acknowledge her existence and she gave up all her friends in Moscow to move here to marry me. She smiles and knows her place, which is what I like best about her.

Uncomplicated. Obedient. Demure. What all women should be.

I leave Valeriya with my men's wives and take a lap of the room, talking to my guests. An hour or so later, I'm coming back from talking to the caterer in the kitchen when I see Elyah watching Valeriya. They're both standing in an alcove, and it doesn't seem as if Valeriya knows he's there, watching her absorbed in the party.

He approaches her and asks in a hard and suspicious tone, "Who are you watching?"

Valeriya gives a guilty jump. Or perhaps she's startled. "I'm not watching anyone. I'm looking at my fiancé. My guests."

Elyah doesn't seem like he believes her. "It is my job to watch. When I see someone else so focused on what this person is saying and who that person is talking to, I wonder what she is planning."

"Why are you so suspicious?" Valeriya replies, trying to laugh but failing. "Practically paranoid."

Elyah doesn't reply. He simply stands there with his hands clasped in front of him, glaring until Valeriya walks away.

Several of my men have families and have brought their children and wives. Valeriya sits on the carpet with some of the toddlers and plays animatedly with them.

I draw closer to Elyah's side as we watch her together. "My fiancée is beautiful, isn't she? What do you think of her?"

Elyah says nothing for a long time, but his expression darkens. "She will be a good mother to your children."

I sense there's more he wants to say but he doesn't go on. A moment later he excuses himself and walks away.

At the end of the party, I send Valeriya back to her apartment. She's disappointed and protests she wants to stay, but I've had enough of people. I want to drink vodka and talk to Kirill.

The two of us sit at the kitchen table, a bottle of chilled vodka open between us and the remains of the party canapes spread out before us. Kirill makes a sandwich of grilled prawns, cabbage salad, and eggplant caviar. It looks terrible but he makes an appreciative sound as he bites into it.

"I thought you had good taste when it came to food."

Kirill shrugs and says around his mouthful, "I like to experiment. Enjoy your party?"

I tug on my tie and open the top button on my shirt. "I'll be glad when all this wedding bullshit is over, and I can focus on work again."

Kirill raises a sardonic brow. "You wife won't like hearing you say that. After you're married, she'll expect you to focus on her."

I give him my most sarcastic smile. "She can expect whatever she likes. What she gets is another matter. Besides, between shopping and raising my children, she'll have enough to do."

"It makes me wonder why you're bothering to get married." He takes another enormous bite of his sandwich.

"Stability. Duty. Lineage. I am going to do this family thing right. My own family was a nightmare." I don't need to spell it out to Kirill. He knows all about me just as I know all about him.

Kirill makes a dismissive noise and mutters, "So was mine, but you don't see me dragging myself up the aisle."

"What do you think of Elyah?" I ask, changing the subject.

Kirill wipes his mouth. "Interesting story. Elyah caught one of the waiters slipping a diamond earring into his pocket. One of your men's wives had dropped it on the buffet table and the waiter pretended he was clearing plates. I was standing right there, and I didn't notice a thing until Elyah handed the earring back and marched the waiter out of there, gripping the back of his neck. It was all over in a split second."

How fucking dare that waiter. And yet I didn't notice any fuss. Elyah managed to sort it out without upsetting the rest of my guests. Impressive.

"Should I hire him? He's not much fun."

Kirill grins and takes a swig of vodka. "I'm the fun around here. Hire Elyah if you want a good bodyguard."

True. "What does Elyah think of Valeriya?"

My friend laughs and wipes the corner of his mouth with his thumb. "That she is vain, stupid, and shallow." Kirill pauses, as if he's trying to decide whether to say something. "And possibly dangerous."

I frown. "Valeriya, dangerous?"

My friend shrugs and shakes his head. "I asked him what he meant, but all he could say was that he has a bad feeling about her. What are we supposed to do with that? After what happened to him, Elyah doesn't trust women. Any women."

Elyah put his neck on the line for his damsel in distress, and she kicked dirt in his face. I wouldn't soon forget a betrayal such as that either.

"Want me to have a word with him? Tell him to chill the fuck out?" Kirill asks.

Tell the man I hired to protect my life to back off? That would defeat the purpose of having him. "Leave him be. When he figures out that Valeriya is as threatening as a marshmallow mouse, he'll settle down."

Elyah turns out to be an excellent bodyguard and driver, focused, professional, and willing to use his fists when I need him to. Very good at using his fists, in fact. The three of us have fun together, and Elyah slowly learns to relax. I'm pleased to discover he has a dry sense of humor, and I understand why he and Kirill bonded so much in jail. If anyone is remotely threatening toward me, Elyah is on them like a guard dog.

The only time Elyah isn't fun to be around is when a woman is in the room. His hackles go up and he won't speak or relax until she's gone, and he seems particularly bothered by my fiancée.

One evening the two of us are sharing a drink at the end of a long day, and I ask him outright. "Elyah. What do you think of my bride-to-be? I want the truth this time."

The blond man was smiling a moment ago, and now he glares at his vodka like there's poison in it. "If you want the truth I will give it. She is hiding something. She is planning something."

"Is she?" I ask lightly.

Elyah's angry expression melts away and he squeezes the bridge of his nose. "*Govno.* I don't know. I used to like women. Now I just see lying mouths and scheming hearts."

I wait in silence, watching him carefully. I was the same all through my twenties. Kirill doesn't trust anyone, man or woman, and he was as highly strung as Elyah when he left prison and joined my side.

"How much do you know about your woman? What is her background?"

I describe meeting Valeriya by chance in a nightclub and the many background checks I ran on her. Over the course of many weeks, I have tried to trip her up on a lie, changing small details about the things she has told me and repeating them back to her to see if she notices. She always does and corrects me. Nothing about this venture has been careless.

"Valeriya has no unexplained connections. Nothing to hide. No one to interfere with our lives." Not having the bother of any in-laws is one of the things I like about her. "I have enemies, of course, but Valeriya is just Valeriya."

Elyah sighs. "You are probably right."

I pat him on the shoulder. "You just need to get your head straightened out. Take your time. I like your work. I like your company. I hope that you're not going anywhere."

Elyah nods and straightens his back. "Thank you, *Pakhan*. Do not worry, I am watching everyone, not just your fiancée."

∽

THE NIGHT BEFORE MY WEDDING, I throw a small dinner party for a dozen people. I'm keen for Valeriya to get to know my men's wives as she'll be easier to handle if she has a group of sensible women who can moderate her expectations. They understand what it means to marry into the Bratva, and I'm not certain that my bride does yet.

Valeriya arrives, as giddy as a schoolgirl in a Dolce & Gabbana dress, holding a gift bag with a big satin bow. "I can't stay too late. I need my beauty sleep for tomorrow."

"Of course you do," I murmur, kissing her on the cheek.

Kirill and Elyah join us for dinner, and I talk with them and my other men while Valeriya talks animatedly with the other women.

At the end of the evening, Valeriya lingers despite her determination to get an early night. She passes me a glass of whiskey, which I'm in the habit of drinking at the end of an evening. This is the sort of thoughtful gesture I hoped she'd pick up on.

"Can I sleep here tonight? I'll leave early in the morning to get ready." She gazes up at me imploringly.

I take a mouthful of whiskey. "But tomorrow is our wedding. Isn't that bad luck?"

"Only if you see me in my dress. Please let me stay the night. I haven't given you your present yet."

I'm exhausted and I want to be alone, but I don't have the energy to argue with her. "Fine. But let's go now. I want to get some sleep tonight."

I take the drink with me and finish it while she's brushing her teeth with my toothbrush. Our lives have been so separate that she doesn't have anything of her own here. That's all going to change tomorrow.

I'm lying on top of the blankets in my button-down shirt and pants when Valeriya emerges from the bathroom and straddles my hips. I wonder if I have a migraine coming on because the lights in the room are refracting strangely.

"Konstantin?"

"Hm?"

Valeriya smiles, and it's a strange smile. One I haven't seen from her before, and she runs her nails down my throat. "Do you know what it's like to drown?"

I frown at the incongruous question. "What?"

"Are you feeling all right, my love?" my bride asks, her tone perhaps a little too sweet now. I can't be sure. My head suddenly feels foggy and my limbs heavy.

"I'm fine," I slur. This is strange. I try to get up, but she holds me down with a light press of her fingers.

"We need to talk about something. Your brother."

"You now Pyotr?" But that's impossible. I checked up on all Valeriya's connections and she doesn't know my brother. I would never have been alone with her if she did. Even now, my brother probably wants me dead for what I know.

"Pyotr has been wondering if you've been spreading lies about him. Oh, I don't know him," she says with a shake of her head. "Not in any way that matters. This is a job, and I'm only interested in his money."

Valeriya's whole manner has changed. Instead of a simpering, stupid young woman, her expression is sharp, and her gaze is catlike.

Why does my body feel so *heavy?* "What lies? I haven't said a word to anyone about my brother."

Valeriya hesitates. "I told him that. I haven't heard one whisper about Pyotr the whole time we've been engaged." She shrugs. "But he told me it doesn't matter. He says the problem is that you *might*, and it would be terrible for his reputation. Did you know your brother is now a politician?"

"Pyotr thinks I'm going to tell people that he fucked our mother?" Suddenly everything seems funny, and I start to laugh. I'm dimly aware that my life is in danger, but I can't summon the energy to move. In my heart, I'm panicking, but the sensation feels very far away like it belongs to someone else.

"You shouldn't tell disgusting lies," Valeriya tuts. She reaches over, undoes the ribbon on the bag and opens it up.

The next moment, I'm staring down a gun and the barrel is a black, gaping hole.

"Sorry about this, Konstantin. You're a clever man. A handsome one, too. If I had one piece of advice for you, it's that you underestimate women. We're not as stupid as you think we are. Not all of us, anyway."

Everything turns white.

Blinding.

Screaming.

There's a roar of anger and then a feminine scream of pain. Elyah is pinning Valeriya to the wall by her throat, and Kirill is looming over me, his face chalk white as he rips off his T-shirt and holds it to my head. He's shouting at me, but I can't make out what he's saying.

The world fades away, and my last thought is that Elyah was right all along.

Not about Valeriya.

About everything.

~

THE STEADY BLEEPING OF A MACHINE. A dry mouth with a chemical taste coating my tongue. Grainy eyes. I fight through the strange sensations and open my eyes.

My gaze fastens on an unfamiliar, institutionally stark ceiling, and something's strange. Half my vision is black.

I clumsily reach up to my face, wondering where the fuck I am and what's happened. Wasn't my wedding day—

My fingers touch a bandage on my face, and I freeze.

Valeriya. She was sitting on top of me and holding a gun to my face. Did she blow my head off? Half my head? How am I still thinking if I'm dead?

I don't know what's happened to me, but I understand what Valeriya was now.

She was a fucking assassin.

My arm tangles in something, and I grab a plastic tube and rip it from my arm. Pain explodes in the back of my hand, but I don't care. I just want to find Valeriya and choke the life out of her.

"Konstantin. *Konstantin.* Lie still."

Someone tries to push me back into bed, but I don't let him. My head is throbbing, but I still have the use of my legs.

"What are you doing, you crazy asshole? Get back into bed."

"Where's Valeriya?"

"You're going to hurt yourself. We do not even know what you have. Ten concussions. Brain damage. You have been shot in the head."

"I said, *where's Valeriya*," I snarl.

Elyah keeps arguing with me, so I walk out of the room, straight down the corridor, and out of the hospital. Swearing at me and telling me I'm a fool, Elyah helps me into his car.

By the time we reach my home, I'm sweating and shaking, and my skull feels like it's going to split open. I have no choice but to let Elyah haul my arm over his shoulders and half walk, half carry me to bed.

"Kirill is with Valeriya in the basement. We'll know why this happened soon enough," Elyah assures me.

I must fall into a doze. I don't know how much time has

passed, but when I open my eyes, the light doesn't seem to have changed. Maybe a whole day has passed.

Kirill enters the room behind Elyah, covered in blood. It's spattered over his chest and throat and caked on his knuckles. "I have been talking to Valeriya."

"Looks like it was a good talk," I mutter.

"Her name is not Valeriya. It is Oksana. She was hired to spy on you and then assassinate you. She missed. If Elyah had not been standing outside the door when she shot you, she would have finished you off."

I close my eyes. No one told Elyah to stand outside my door. He should have been drinking vodka with Kirill and relaxing, but he listened to his suspicions, and I should have listened to him.

"He is not fucking paying attention," Kirill seethes.

Oh, I heard every word.

"Do you have orders for us, *Pakhan*?" Elyah asks. When I don't reply, he says through his teeth, "Give us the order."

"Get the hell out of my room. Both of you."

That's not the order they wanted. Both of them stay where they are. I can feel them glaring at me, but I'm not going to say what they want to hear.

Eventually, they walk out and close the door behind them.

Mother died years ago, and I thought the reason for Pyotr to hate me died with her. Now I'm faced with the realization that my brother didn't try to kill me to please her. He wanted to do it. He wanted his own brother to die, and he still does.

Strange how someone you haven't laid eyes on for nearly twenty years can gut you, burn you, lay waste to your soul and your will to live.

There's so much pain whenever I open my eye that I keep it closed. Sleep is my only relief. Kirill refuses to give me any drugs stronger than what you can get over the counter, saying he doesn't trust me with them in the state I'm in. I tell him to go fuck himself. He says it right back.

One of my other men stands guard over me for several days. Maybe longer. I start to wonder if my friends have abandoned their broken *Pakhan*. I might have done the same thing in their place.

Migraines hit me, one after the next, and have me groaning in agony. I was always prone to migraines, but now it feels like pain will be stabbing through my skull for all eternity. There's no beginning and no end. No time. No space.

Just pain.

I'm awoken a thousand years later to the sound of something being dragged across the floor of my bedroom. It's Elyah and Kirill, and they have their hands in the armpits of a bound and gagged man. His suit is torn and bloodied, and his gray eyes are gleaming with fury and fear.

They drop him to his knees at the end of my bed and Kirill pulls a hunting knife from inside his jacket. It's large and serrated with a wickedly pointed tip.

The man makes terrified protests in the back of his throat.

My brother, Pyotr, on his knees and whimpering in fear.

"We do not have your orders," Elyah begins.

"But we're doing it anyway," Kirill says. All the same, he waits, the knife flashing in his hand. I don't say anything. I have nothing left in me to feel rage, betrayal, or mercy.

With a growl, Kirill plunges the blade into the side of Pyotr's throat, and then tugs it out. My brother's eyes go wide as he makes a gurgling sound. Blood spurts everywhere. All over the floor. All over Kirill's legs.

The heavy metallic scent reaches me, and I slowly sit up.

Blood.

This is no migraine hallucination or fever dream. This is real.

I have no brother anymore.

My true brothers have avenged me.

As blood runs across the floor, I make a promise to myself. From now on, anyone who betrays me will bleed.

Without exception.

I push the blankets off me and struggle to get out of bed. My body is weak but at last my mind is determined.

"How are you feeling, Kostya?" Kirill asks as he cleans his knife on his jeans and puts it away.

"Better."

He frowns and touches my brow, and then lifts my bandage and winces. "You shouldn't be, you've got a raging fever and the edges of your wound are puffy. I'm calling a doctor before you die of blood poisoning."

First, they have to clean my dead brother off the floor.

The doctor changes my bandage and puts me on a course of antibiotics. If the swelling and fever don't go down, I'll have to be hospitalized because the wound is badly infected. Apparently, my skull didn't fracture from the bullet. It merely tore across my flesh, but I've made it worse by neglecting to take care of the wound.

Thankfully, the antibiotics do the trick, and ten days later I'm able to take the bandage off. The upper left quadrant of my face is an angry red mess.

I turn to Kirill and Elyah with a smile. Even smiling hurts, but I find I don't care. "How do I look?"

"You are going to have one hell of a scar," Elyah says, blunt as always.

"Elyah is the handsome one now," Kirill replies.

I pat Elyah's cheek. "He was always the handsome one. You were the scary one, Kirill. But now I beat you with this scar."

"Fuck off you beat me," Kirill laughs. "Now let's have a drink."

"I'll be right there," I tell them, and they head off while I finish getting dressed.

Someone has placed Valeriya's diamond engagement ring on the chest of drawers. I pick it up and gaze at it. I've always loved diamonds. Absolute perfection, frozen in place for all eternity. Diamonds never disappoint you. Diamonds never crumble. A woman with a heart of diamond who is only loyal to me, that's all I wanted.

Why can't I find her? Where is she hiding? I thought I had taken all precautions when I met Valeriya, but I allowed her to approach me when I should have selected her. I won't make that mistake again.

If only I had an assortment of beautiful women vying for the privilege of being crowned my wife. Like a competition, but one where the prize is diamonds.

A pageant.

I find Elyah and Kirill sitting at the kitchen table and the sight of them lifts my spirits even more. "Where were we before all these fucking assholes upended my life? Oh, yes. I remember." I smile at my most trusted men. My brothers. The only people I will ever trust in this world. "I need a wife."

Kirill shakes his head. "After what's just happened? I'll call you a fucking escort. You don't need a wife."

"No, I do, and not just any wife. The perfect wife. The strongest, most beautiful diamond in all the world, and totally obedient to me."

"She doesn't exist." Elyah's voice is granite hard with certainty.

"Oh, yes she does. And I know how to find her."

"How?" he asks, his heavy brows drawn together.

I pull out a seat and sit down. "Open the vodka and listen to me. I've just had the most wonderful idea."

15

Lilia

Of these three men, I think deep down that I've been afraid of Konstantin's past most of all. His scarred past is right there on his face, but the scars go deeper than that. All the way back to his childhood, as they do with mine.

My heart burns for his younger self, as it does for mine. What a sick, twisted beginning he had in life. No wonder he has looked on women with contempt if his own mother...

I shudder and try to get that mental image out of my head.

Konstantin takes my face between his hands. "And you know the rest, Lilia."

Yes, I know exactly where the story picks up. In a lakeside villa in Italy, with sixteen women locked in cages. His mother's incest and the woman who shot him help me see why he is the way that he is, but it doesn't excuse anything.

While he was talking, we sat down on the carpet together, my back resting against the wall. Konstantin is holding my hand.

And he's smiling at me, despite how much he hated telling the tale of his twisted family and the pain of his fiancée's betrayal. "Now you know everything, *malyshka*."

I drag my fingers from his. "I still don't understand why you won't say sorry for what you did in Italy."

"I won't. And I can't."

I thought telling me such a tale might have shaken something loose inside him, but even now he is utterly without remorse. "Why?"

He smiles at me, his sleek, winning smile. "Because the pageant brought me you, Lilia."

In a cage in his cellar, I relived the worst moments of my life with Dad in terrifying detail. Then I got up and busted out of there. I did that. I've proved what kind of woman I am to the only person who matters.

Me.

My hand is resting on my belly, and I realize how broken down I've felt ever since my miscarriage. I've always wanted a baby, and what a strange and twisted path led me here. "What you said about wanting the strongest, the most beautiful wife in the world, totally obedient to you. Is that still what you want?"

He gazes at me, amused. "Yes, where is my glass of whiskey?"

"Are you going to order me to bring it to you from now on?"

"*Malyshka*, if you did, I would hand you a gun, open my shirt, and ask you to put me out of my misery."

"Because you'd know that I was about to assassinate you like Oksana tried to do?"

He caresses my jaw with his large, warm hand. "No, because I would want to die knowing that my provoking, disobedient Lilia was no more." He shakes his head ruefully. "I'm such a fucking idiot."

"Why?"

"Because I love you."

I suck in a startled breath. "You're an idiot for loving me?"

"I'm an idiot for thinking that I wouldn't fall in love with you."

I stare at him, shock and—I don't want to believe it—pleasure rolling through me. "I thought love was off the table."

"So did I."

I won't let my heart be moved by this demon of a man.

I *won't*.

Too late.

I get to my feet, which takes some effort with this huge belly, and stare out the window at the thick, sinuous river. "You held the pageant on a lake. You make your home by a river. Strange, for a man who nearly drowned."

"I want everything that could kill me close to me at all times. Right where I can see it. Including you."

I turn to look at him, sitting on the floor with one long leg out in front of him and the other bent at the knee. "Do I frighten you?"

He smiles, revealing those pointed canines. "You terrify me, *malyshka*. I never want to let you go."

"I'm not going to do what I'm told. I'm not going to be the sort of wife you just described to me."

"Sometimes you will be," he murmurs, his gaze roving over me. "When the mood takes you."

Heat ripples between us, and I play along because playing with Konstantin is one of the best things I've ever known. I examine my nails. "If I say I want your heart on a platter, maybe I mean it literally."

Konstantin stands up, lifts me in his arms, and carries me out of the nursery. "I know how to make you stop talking back."

I wrap my arms around his neck. "I doubt it."

He carries me to my bedroom where Elyah is laying on my bed, frowning at a paperback. A crime novel in English. He's been working harder on his vocabulary, and gory thrillers seem to be his thing.

Konstantin lays me down on Elyah, who throws his book aside and accepts me in his arms.

"Hold her. Face down."

Elyah smiles lazily up at me as his hands encircle my wrists and he holds me tight. My belly presses against his stomach and my knees straddle his hips. "What are we doing with our *solnyshko*?"

I give him a pert look. What does he think is about to happen?

Elyah smiles even wider.

I can hear Konstantin undressing behind me. "Lilia has forgotten how good it feels to be put in her place. I'm going to remind her."

Elyah makes an interested noise deep in his chest and his

cock thickens against my pussy. "And I get a front-row seat. How wonderful."

I turn and frown at Konstantin. "You're going to punish a pregnant woman?"

His clothes are off and he's throwing them aside. Beautiful tattoos decorate his arms and chest. Konstantin must have visited the finest tattoo artist in Russia because the designs are works of art. An eagle. Coiled snakes. A lion. A forest scene. "I have my ways. The baby won't be harmed."

I turn back to Elyah. "And you? Are you just going to let him do whatever he wants with me?"

Elyah's blue eyes glimmer. "You love whatever Konstantin does to you. How are you going to put her in her place?" he asks him.

"I'm going to fuck her in the ass until she promises to stop talking back to me."

Alarm and desire zing through me. Ivan tried to screw my ass once, but I screamed and fought him so hard that he backed off, for once. I don't know if it's something to be feared or enjoyed.

Elyah groans, and I feel the vibrations in my stomach. "Perfect. I love watching you get fucked by my friends, *solnyshko*. You are so much sweeter afterward, and I have seen how beautifully you submit to Konstantin. You will enjoy this."

"But I—" I choke out.

Elyah loosens his grip on my wrists and softens his tone. "No one will force you. You can get up and leave if you want to. Konstantin will not hurt you. I will not hurt you. But you want to stay. I know you do."

Elyah always knows exactly what to say and do to make me trust him.

With a smile, his fingers tighten on my wrists again.

"You like when I hold you, *solnyshko*?" he murmurs huskily.

I gaze at his large hands wrapped around my wrists. Making me feel secure. Reminding me he loves me.

He lets go of me long enough to undress me and take his own T-shirt off. My palms are pressed against his bare chest, strong and warm as he wraps his tattooed fingers around my wrists once more.

We're alone for a moment, and then Konstantin is back, a tube of something in his hands. He rubs something icy cold and slippery up through my pussy to my ass. I shudder at the same time I feel my flesh heat.

Konstantin rubs the tip of his finger against the tight ring of my ass. It feels weird. It feels taboo. I don't know if I—

He pushes his finger inside me and I cry out. Not from pain, but shock. And maybe a little pleasure. It doesn't seem right that it should feel this intense.

"Good girl. You are just the sort of woman who needs to be fucked in the ass, deep and slow."

I close my eyes and groan as Konstantin's finger pushes deeper into my ass. "What sort of woman is that?"

"Ours," he tells me.

Every ounce of resistance and every smart reply melts away. I close my eyes and just feel. Konstantin finger-fucking my ass. Elyah breathing beneath me. The ache in my pussy because she's missing out on something so good.

"Aren't you our perfect girl," Konstantin murmurs, and his praise winds around me like a blanket made of stars.

In a moment, he's going to replace that finger with his much thicker, bigger cock. The thought makes my eyes pop open and the impulse to struggle and run away is strong.

But then he won't say what a good girl I am.

Elyah lets go of my wrists and plucks my nipples, his movements lazy and his expression delighted. "Lilia is so beautiful when she's about to be fucked."

I moan at the sensation in my tender nipples and the firmer thrust of Konstantin's finger. My whole body is turning to liquid.

"That's perfect, *malyshka*. You stay nice and supple for me. Elyah's got you."

They both have me. I'm surrounded by their heat and strength. The scent of them is making my body go haywire. I need them to prove what kind of men they are. I need to feel it deep inside me.

I glance over my shoulder at Konstantin as he puts one knee up on the bed. He has his cock in his hand, and a moment later, I feel the press of something blunt against my ass. Smooth. But thick.

My eyes go wide and I stop breathing.

Elyah is there to stroke my face and throat.

"Soft and melting, Lilia. Just relax," Konstantin murmurs.

When he talks at that pitch, his voice is both commanding and coaxing, and it works like magic on my body. Sex with these men is never hard. Everything else about them infuriates me.

But not the sex.

I moan and dip down onto my elbows as Konstantin's cock stretches me slowly open. He fucks me in short, slow thrusts, and I let go of every thought except for how it feels. I don't care about anything except for him getting deeper and deeper into my ass and giving me what I need.

"You are beautiful, Lilia. I wish you could see what I see."

"Fuck, so do I," Elyah groans. "How deep are you?"

"Five, six inches. She's being so good, aren't you, *malyshka*?"

I reach back and hold my ass with my hand, begging for more. Konstantin obliges by screwing me deeper. Every second of giving in feels like bliss, and my clit is pulsing even though no one is touching it.

"You will do as you're told from now on. Who's your master?"

"You are," I moan breathlessly.

No one has ever told me that I'm good, or precious, or beloved. In this moment, I'm beloved.

Craved.

Everything.

I'm everything to Konstantin, and he's everything to me as he fucks me, every ragged breath filled with desire. I'm everything to Elyah as he cradles me on his body. He works two fingers into my dripping pussy and thrusts them in and out of me.

"You need more, *solnyshko*."

I don't know what he means until I look down and see him unfastening his jeans, raising his hips to push them down. His cock is much thicker than two of his fingers and those already felt incredibly tight.

But I want him. I want the man who's loved me to the point of insanity and back again.

"Please," I breathe, my lips close to Elyah's. My belly is

pressed against his and there's not much room to maneuver. But there is enough.

"Anything for you," he murmurs, and Konstantin slows down his thrusts as Elyah finds my tight channel. In unison, they sink slowly into me.

I moan something incomprehensible that's lost among their groans. I've never felt so good in my life. Elyah and Konstantin match each other's paces, stretching me wider and deeper with every slow, delicious thrust of their hips.

"I've never felt anything so good before," Elyah groans, holding on to my hips as he pounds up into me.

I open my mouth with a cry of pleasure, and someone cups my cheek. There are already two sets of hands on my body, and I know without opening my eyes who this is.

But I do open them because I want to see him.

Kirill, standing naked by my head, his cock in his hand and a smirk on his lips. "You need more, *detka*. Open your mouth."

I refused to suck his cock during the pageant, and he's aching for me to do it now. "What did you call it? Sealed up tight?"

Kirill smiles his devilish grin. "I love our horny bitch."

He grasps my jaw and shoves his cock into my mouth. He's rough, but I'm expecting it, and my throat is relaxed enough I don't gag when he hits the back of my throat.

Elyah squeezes my breasts, growling, "I am going to lose my fucking mind. Look at her."

"Oh, I'm looking," Kirill says, a smirk in his voice. "Our *detka* can take three cocks so well."

"We are all fucking you hard, and you look like a queen."

I feel like I'm floating on air. I feel like a goddess. Elyah rolls his thumb against my clit, and a wave of pleasure passes through me. I don't want this to end, but I crave to come with all three of them inside me. I don't want them to stop.

Don't any of you stop.

They feel my need for them through my skin, and they can't stop bathing me with their adoration as they stroke my flesh, grip my body, hold tight to my hair.

The three of them thrust into me at the same time, and I shatter around them. The muscles of my body tighten up, and in response, they all start to fuck me harder, their breaths growing ragged.

"I'm going to shoot my cum straight down your throat," Kirill says through his teeth, pumping his cock faster. My orgasm goes on and on, and suddenly I hear his groan, and hot liquid floods my mouth. I struggle to swallow him down fast enough.

Elyah wraps his hand around my throat so he can feel it, and suddenly his fingers dig in and he ruthlessly pounds up into me, his beautiful body rippling with his orgasm.

"Don't pull out of her," Konstantin tells them, his fingers digging into the fleshy part of my hips. "I want you all right there while I fill her ass."

Elyah and Kirill lazily fuck me while they get their breaths back, both of them watching me get screwed by their *Pakhan*. Konstantin lands one hard spank across my ass and then he thrusts even deeper, groaning with his release.

I feel weightless. I feel boneless. The three of them slowly withdraw from me, and Elyah is the only thing holding me up.

Konstantin smooths my hair aside and kisses my back, and his lips move against my skin.

"You are incredible, *malyshka*. This baby will belong to all of us. We will protect this child with our lives. We will protect you with our lives. We swear it."

Kirill wipes my mouth with his thumb, gazing at my body. "As soon as you are able, the three of us will fuck you, one after the next, over and over, until you are pregnant again. We are all the fathers. We will love you, hard and strong."

"I can't tell if you are threatening me or adoring me."

He smirks. "Both, *detka*."

―

OVER THE FOLLOWING WEEKS, one or more of my men are always with me. Touching me. Holding me. Loving me. I know they go out and do violent things. Kirill and Elyah especially return covered in bruises or blood. The bruises are on their knuckles, but the blood is rarely theirs.

I clean them up myself, gently rubbing cream into the angry red marks on their hands and wiping away the blood. They are boyishly delighted by my care of them, especially Elyah, who thanks me with kisses and by lavishly going down on me whenever I clean the tiniest cut for him.

I grow so huge in the last month of my pregnancy that putting shoes on is awkward and exhausting, so I walk around barefoot. It's summer, and the house and garden are filled with sunshine. Konstantin's house is beautiful, and he has excellent taste. I feel comfortable and spoiled by everything he does for me. I feel a long way from any danger, and while I know that it's an illusion, it's one I want to cling to while I focus on my baby.

Our baby.

All of ours.

Konstantin has researched and ordered everything we'll need for the nursery, and deliveries arrive every other day. Kirill likes to sit with his head in my lap and his cheek against my stomach as I stroke his curls and he tells me what he's been doing, and I remember that sixteen-year-old boy who did the same thing with Katya. Then he says something that's more like the Kirill I know or gives me his dangerous smile, and I remember that he's not as innocent as he seems sometimes.

The three of them are often talking quietly together when I walk into a room. At first I thought they stopped because kissing me or asking me how I'm feeling was their way of reassuring themselves that all is fine with the baby, but it happens to often that I start to grow suspicious.

One day I'm so hot and cranky that I lose my temper with Konstantin. "I know you're up to something. What are you planning?"

He kisses my forehead. "*Malyshka*, we are always planning something."

I push him away and pick up a newspaper to fan myself with. "But why do I feel that this has got something to do with me? You're being so fucking furtive."

A smile spreads over his face as he gazes at me. "Ah, gentle motherhood."

I swat his arm with the paper and go back to fanning myself. "What's wrong with this country? Why isn't there any air conditioning here?"

"I'll buy you air conditioning."

"Stop changing the subject!"

Konstantin regards me seriously. "What are you really worried about?"

I shoot him a look. "The future. I'm always worried about the future. I don't think we've earned our happy ending."

"Look around. It's here. It's happening."

"But do we *deserve* it? I shouldn't be falling in love with my captors. We shouldn't all be loving this baby."

"Says who?"

The nameless pit of dread in my belly, that's who. I keep fanning myself with the paper. "All my life, men have only wanted me for what I can do for them. They see opportunity, money, holes to fuck. Now it's a baby."

"When we stood on that cliff and I held out my hand to you, I wasn't thinking about money or advantage. I wasn't craving your body or a baby. I was hungering for your soul."

I think about that night so often, replaying the moment I jumped from the cliff into the darkness. A leap of faith that I don't regret, even though I've ended up back here with the men I was running from.

"We don't want anything from you but who you are. Don't you understand, Lilia? Answer me, Lilia."

The sensation in my belly suddenly tightens until I'm being squeezed by an invisible hand. I bow my head and clench my fists. "I can't."

"Why, Lilia?"

I reach out and fumble for the edge of the desk, holding on for dear life, gasping, "Because I think the baby's coming."

16

Lilia

Despite all the drama of its conception, the baby arrives without fuss.

I spend hours of my labor walking up and down, breathing through the contractions. They seem to be building up to something dramatic, bloody, violent. Elyah walks with me, his arm around my waist.

Kirill watches us from the side of the room, his face in shadows and sweat on his upper lip. Konstantin stands to one side with his arms folded, firing questions at me until Elyah tells him to shut up. The midwife is the only one who's smiling, so I take my cue from her. If she's relaxed and happy, then everything must be fine.

I thought childbirth was supposed to be wall-to-wall drama and pain, but the baby is born with surprising ease.

I've barely had time to swear once before the midwife is placing my daughter's seconds-old body on my chest.

As soon as I lay eyes on her, I'm so shocked that I burst into tears.

All my men have crowded around me. I'm aware of their bodies and hands, but I can't see anything but the tiny, helpless thing laying on my chest.

"*Solnyshko*, what is wrong?"

"I wasn't ready," I sob, tears pouring down my cheeks. I don't think I would have ever been ready, but she's here anyway, insisting through her loud cries that we meet her, see her, love her.

The midwife cleans her up, swaddles her, and places her into my arms.

Get yourself together, Lilia.

You're a mother now.

I wipe my eyes and take my first good look at her, my heart pounding as I wonder which of my men's features I'll see in her face along with mine.

She looks like...a baby. A perfect little baby with blue eyes, a button nose, and tiny rosebud lips. Her hair is sparse and dark.

"She's perfect," Kirill breathes, and then glances to Konstantin and Elyah on his left and right. "Who will hold her first?"

Elyah is staring at the baby like he can't believe she's real. Then he pats his friend's shoulder. "You first."

My heart turns over and my eyes prickle with tears again. Of course Elyah would give this moment to one of the others. I glance at Konstantin.

"Go ahead, Kirill," Konstantin murmurs, leaning over to

press his lips against my cooling brow. "You're magnificent, *malyshka*."

Kirill smiles down at the baby, his curls falling into his eyes. If I hadn't heard about his past, I wouldn't be able to believe that a man like Kirill could be happy about a baby.

"You are loud, little baby," Kirill murmurs. "Good. Keep it up. You are strong like your fathers."

He kisses her forehead and then passes her carefully to Elyah.

Elyah can't seem to find any words. He just stares at her, touching her nose, her cheeks, her tiny fingers with the tip of his forefinger.

"What will we call her?" he asks softly.

"I would like to call her Viktoria. My *babulya's* name."

"So, you will teach her to run rings around her papas, just as her mother does?" Konstantin asks.

"You think there is any chance she won't learn how all by herself?" I say, amused.

Konstantin shakes his head, grinning. "She will be so spoiled, this little girl. God help us all."

"Baby Viktoria, you have three fierce papas to protect you and spoil you. Are you the luckiest little baby in the world?" Elyah asks her.

"She is," Konstantin says, holding out his arms as Elyah hands her his way. He meets my eyes. "Here is my diamond."

Exhausted, happy, I can't help but smile at him.

"She is perfect, *solnyshko*," Elyah murmurs, and presses his mouth to mine. "As beautiful as her mother."

∽

THE THREE OF them are keen to know how to look after the baby, but they're as clueless as me. We're all only children or the youngest in our families, and we have never so much as changed a diaper.

Thankfully, Konstantin thought to hire a nanny for the first month, and she patiently teaches all of us what the hell we're supposed to do with this tiny, adorably, shockingly loud little baby. Even with all the extra pairs of hands, I barely sleep because the sound of Viktoria crying can shock me out of slumber. Breastfeeding is hard. Pumping is hard. Trying to stick to any sort of schedule is hardest of all because Viktoria has her own ideas about that. She's extremely demanding, so she's taking after all her fathers at once.

I have no idea who put her inside of me, but at three in the morning when she's thrown up on me again, I blame them all.

At the same time, it's the most wonderful experience of my life. I stand over her crib and stare at her, twisting and turning the elephants and tigers in their bowties for her amusement.

At the end of the month, Konstantin tells me we can keep the nanny for as long as I want, but I insist that, with their help, I can do it myself.

So, the nanny leaves, and the same week, all those happy pregnancy and new mother hormones fade away. Everything seems twice as hard as usual, and the sleep deprivation is turning me into the walking dead.

Viktoria has decided sleep is for the weak, and so I pace the halls of the house with her in my arms, hoping she'll settle.

I worry about Konstantin's migraines and the baby's

screams, and so I avoid him while Viktoria is crying. Which is most of the time she's awake.

I finally get her settled and go in search of him. I miss him. I feel like we haven't seen each other this past week, but it could be a day. Time is only theoretical to me right now.

When I reach his open office door, I walk right in. Elyah and Kirill are here, but they stop talking immediately. That's normal, but I thought I heard my name before they saw me.

"What are the three of you up to?"

"Nothing, *malyshka*," Konstantin murmurs, turning to his laptop and starting to type.

Elyah kisses my cheek, but I'm gazing from him to Kirill to Konstantin, wondering what's up. From the gleam in Kirill's eyes, they're up to something, and it's not a nice sort of something.

I extricate myself from Elyah's arms and walk around behind Konstantin's desk, intending to talk to him.

Konstantin slams his laptop closed and glares at me. "*Lilia.*"

His voice cracks over me like a whip, and I reel back in shock. I haven't heard him sound like this since the days of the pageant. He's sweating. His eyes are bloodshot.

"You're hiding something," I accuse. "What are you hiding from me?"

"Nothing. Go get some sleep. I'll watch Viktoria."

"You can't, you have a migraine. I can tell just by looking at you. Viktoria is going to start screaming as soon as she wakes up." The sound will be torture for him.

"I will go. Come with me, Lilia." Elyah takes my hand.

I stare at Konstantin, but he won't meet my eyes. Suspicion and anxiety course through me, but I haven't got the energy or mental strength to figure out what the hell is going on here.

Elyah puts me to bed, murmuring that all is well and he will feed Viktoria when she wakes. I pass out, more than ready to fall asleep.

When I wake up and go to the nursery, it's nearly midnight. Elyah is there with a paperback in his hand as he watches Viktoria, though he doesn't seem to have been reading. I tell him to go to bed, and he gives me a sleepy kiss before he does as I suggest.

As I gaze down at my sleeping baby, all I see is Konstantin's closed, hard expression in his office. Shades of that expression were in Elyah's and Kirill's eyes, too. I thought that I would be content with Elyah's love, Kirill's protection, Konstantin's devotion. With the three of them flanking me, nothing in this world should frighten me any longer.

But the future frightens me when I don't know what to expect.

My words come back to haunt me.

We haven't earned our happy ending.

It's come at the expense of fifteen other women.

When I look into my baby's eyes, it's her that I worry for. It's she who could wind up with three tyrants for a father if I make the wrong move.

I push my hands through my hair, find it's in tangles, and rake it into a ponytail.

Pacing up and down the corridor, I keep going back and forth on whether I should be worried or not.

What if Konstantin talks to Viktoria in that tone one day? His migraines make him vicious. Kirill doesn't really know what it means to love someone, does he? Elyah can be the cruelest man in the world when his pride and heart are hurting. A daughter can so easily wound a man's pride.

Have I made a terrible mistake?

I thought I would feel better after a sleep, but my brain is suddenly rushing a mile a minute, presenting me with hundreds of shocking, heartbreaking scenarios for the future.

Wouldn't it be better to run, for Viktoria and me to take our chances on our own rather than risk this baby suffering at the whims of men, as I once had to?

I go into the nursery and clutch the sides of the cot.

She needs love, I think desperately, tears brimming in my eyes. Am I living in a home, or a trap? My heart feels like it's tearing itself to pieces.

Run.

Hide.

Don't ever trust anyone because they will betray you.

I'm a little girl bleeding on her father's white carpet, the wrath of a fire-breathing dragon being heaped upon my head. Before I realize what I'm doing, I'm picking Viktoria up, slipping my feet into shoes, and wrapping an oversized wool coat over us.

The house is silent as I walk quickly through the halls toward the back door. The door that leads onto the street. I push it open.

Holy shit. I'm outside.

I stand on the steps and stare around me at the path to the dark, deserted street.

Running. It's comfortable and familiar.

Standing still, that's the terrifying thing to do.

The cold wind outside hits me like a slap in the face. I

lean into it, bowing my head over the child and holding her tight against my chest beneath the layers of wool.

Keep moving forward.

Don't look back.

There is no friend I can go to. No refuge I can see. All is black and silent apart from the wind whistling in my ears. All is dark above and before me, the clouds so heavy that not a star can be seen. There is nothing—

Except for the neon glow of an official-looking sign. A train station? I've heard a train rattling in the distance on clear days when the windows are open. A station means somewhere to wait and gather my thoughts. A means to slip away.

This late at night, the ticket barriers are open.

As I step onto the platform, a programmed voice announces, *The next train to arrive on platform one...*

I don't have money for a ticket. I lean forward and peer down the tracks. A train is approaching that's heading toward the city. A place where I can throw myself on the mercy of a station worker and ask for directions to a women's refuge.

The train slows down while I wait behind the yellow line. The train glides to a halt before me. The doors open.

When they close and the train moves off again, I'm still standing on the platform.

I'm frozen in place, and it has nothing to do with the cold.

Viktoria stirs in my arms. Tears run down my face.

I've run so many times before and been just as badly prepared, so why does it hurt so much now?

Isn't it my duty as a mother who loves her child to run far, far away from these men?

Footsteps pound along the sidewalk out by the road.

A man rushes onto the platform, quickly peering up and down, and he's about to run out again when he spots me.

I wait for fear to slam through me.

But it's not fear I feel.

It's relief.

"*Lilia.*"

He races toward me, his frosty blue eyes alive with fear. When he's close enough to see inside my coat and the sleeping baby, he breaks into a stream of relieved Russian.

"I woke up and you were both gone," Elyah gasps, wrapping one arm around us and digging out his phone and making a call to the other. "I have found her. She is at the train station. We will wait here."

I blink more tears from my eyes, waiting for his recriminations, but all he does is rock me in his arms, murmuring his thanks that he found me. He helps me over to a bench and I sit down.

A few minutes later, I hear more running feet, so fast that it seems as though the person is running for his life.

When Kirill appears and skids to a halt, there is terror in his face. White flesh and wide, black eyes. His fear makes me sick at myself.

The world lurches beneath me.

I took his baby away from him.

Did I not think that these men would feel as I would feel if they tried to run with her?

Kirill kneels down next to me, his gaze intent on the sleeping child. His eyes are so dilated that there are almost no irises, and he's breathing so fast.

Tears spill down my cheeks. "I'm so sorry, Kirill," I whisper. It's all I can say, over and over. "I'm so sorry."

He touches Viktoria's cheek, and then mine. "You are all right. You and the baby. You're safe."

"You're not angry with me?"

He shakes his head dazedly and struggles to get his breathing under control. "Just tell me if you want to run. We will go anywhere, *detka*. All of us. We will run with you."

I nod rapidly, my throat locked up tight. "I will. I promise."

Konstantin comes running in, and the moment he sees me between Elyah and Kirill, his footsteps slow and he passes a hand over his face. It's not fury in his eyes when he finally meets my gaze.

It's relief. Or is it disappointment?

He stands there for a long time, drinking in the sight of me and the baby as if he's afraid we'll evaporate into thin air.

When he draws closer, he asks the question that I don't want to answer. "Why, *malyshka*?"

I take a shuddering breath. "I was so afraid that I'd made a mistake in trusting you all. I didn't think what losing her would mean to you all."

"No. Not why did you run. Why did you stay? Why didn't you get on a train?"

I blink up at him. "What?"

Konstantin reaches for my hands and squeezes them. "I want to believe it's because this time, at last, you couldn't leave us. Am I right?"

I gaze down at Viktoria. "I don't know. I told you, I don't know if we deserve our happy ending."

Konstantin hunkers down before me. "I have been hiding something from you, *malyshka*. We all have. I thought you wouldn't have to know, but…" He thinks hard and then looks at the other two. They both nod. "Tomorrow you will be going somewhere."

I frown at him. "You're sending me away?"

"Yes. You're going on a trip."

I hold Viktoria tighter against my chest, fear flashing through me that we might be separated. "I'm not going anywhere without my baby."

"The baby will never leave your side. She is always yours." Konstantin helps me to my feet. "But that is tomorrow. For now, you need to go to bed and rest. You and Viktoria."

∼

AT JUST AFTER nine in the morning, the baby and I are being driven along a narrow, country road through rolling hills. The driver of the Mercedes-Benz has left the city far behind us, and I have no idea where we are. Quaint village names appear on signs and vanish behind us.

My driver is a British woman, and she chatters away to me with a smile on her face, telling me how adorable Viktoria is and that she can't wait to have children of her own. Her name is Juliet, and I love her laugh, though it's hard for me to relax and chat with her when I have no idea what's going to happen today.

Konstantin, Elyah, and Kirill all sent me on my way with such somber expressions, but Elyah assured me that we would all see each other again very soon.

"We have arrived, Miss Aranova."

"Hmm?" I look up and realize that we're on a narrow country road outside a thatched cottage with roses lining the path to the door, and there are fields all around. "This place? Really?"

"Mr. Zhukov told me to tell you that Number Ten was waiting."

I feel like I've been kicked in the solar plexus.

Number Ten.

Olivia, who was in the cell next to mine during the pageant. Who always had my back and became my friend, and who I had to say goodbye to forever when she escaped with the other women.

Olivia Sparrow, who gave the press conference and spoke with such bravery and power that it brought tears to my eyes. Who told everyone about me and said that she'd never forget me.

I've never forgotten her, either.

I stare down at Viktoria in my arms. The baby of one of the men who took Olivia captive.

"Drive around the corner, please," I gasp suddenly, holding Viktoria to my heart.

I can't think until we're out of sight of the cottage. In a nearby lane, Juliet pulls the car over next to a field.

Juliet meets my eyes in the mirror, her brow wrinkled in concern. "You're not going in?"

"I...don't know if I should. An old friend lives there. So much has happened since we last saw each other."

"Did you part on good terms?"

"Yes. But it's complicated."

"If she's a true friend, she'll welcome you with open arms."

Olivia would do that, and I desperately need a friend. I

gaze down at Viktoria. "Could—could I ask you a favor, please? Would you mind holding the baby for me?"

Juliet breaks into a smile. "Mr. Zhukov said you might ask. I would love to look after the baby. I'm normally a nanny, you see. Not a driver."

I look up in surprise. Konstantin thought of everything.

With Viktoria cuddled in Juliet's capable arms, I take a deep breath and walk back down the lane and around the corner to Olivia's house.

What a beautiful place this is. A fresh breeze is blowing and there are wildflowers by the front gate. Olivia must be healing here. I pray that she's healing, anyway.

I walk down the path and raise my hand to knock on the front door.

I hear Olivia calling cheerfully to someone as she hurries down the passage. She opens the door, a smile on her face.

It freezes in shock.

We stare at each other, and my heart is racing a mile a minute. She hasn't changed. She's still the tall, beautiful woman with dark hair and coppery eyes, radiating strength and charisma.

Olivia's face crumples, and she bursts into tears. "Lilia. Oh, my God, Lilia."

She lunges forward and wraps her arms around me, and I start crying, too. Then we're laughing, touching each other's faces, and talking over each other.

"Olivia?"

A woman is standing in the hall, gazing at us uncertainly. She looks a lot like Olivia, but a few years older, and with a sadder look in her eyes. Her oversized sweater is over her hands, and she clutches the sleeves like a child.

Olivia wipes her face, beaming from ear to ear. "This is my sister, Beatrix. Beatrix, this is Lilia. The woman I told you about."

Beatrix lifts a brow in surprise. "This is Number Eleven?"

I stare at the older woman in shock. Olivia told me during the pageant that her sister had disappeared years ago. "Beatrix! But you're..."

Olivia is smiling so hard she can barely get the words out. "She escaped and came home. It's only been a few weeks. And now you're here! Everything is crazy right now, I can't cope. Come and have some tea."

I follow the two women through the cottage to the sunny kitchen that looks onto a beautiful garden filled with flower beds. The table is old, scarred wood, and Olivia places a red kettle onto an enormous cast iron stove.

"This place is amazing," I breathe. "It's like something out of a cozy story."

"Thank you, I love it here. I bought this place after—you know. And it's been the perfect place to get away from everything and heal. And now it's where Beatrix can heal, too."

Olivia makes tea and sets a teapot on the table with mugs, milk, sugar, and a tin containing a lemon cake. It looks homemade.

"How did you find me, Lilia? I've been searching for you everywhere," Olivia asks, slicing up the cake and passing it around.

I think quickly. "Private detective."

"Did you find any of the other women?"

"I found some of them online, but you're the only one I wanted to see." I turn to Beatrix, burning with curiosity.

"Olivia told me about you in the..." I glance at Olivia, wondering how to phrase it.

"Beatrix knows everything. You can talk about it freely."

I swallow. "In the cages in the cellar. She told me that you were missing."

Beatrix has both her hands wrapped around her mug and she tucks her hair behind her ear. "I was."

Olivia looks at her sister with a mixture of sadness and pride. "Beatrix had an even harder time than we did, but she fought so hard to get home."

Beatrix shakes her head. "I didn't do it by myself. I...never mind. You're here to see Olivia. You don't want to hear my story."

Beatrix has suffering etched on her face, and she's clearly still reeling from whatever has happened to her. "I'd love to hear it, if you want to tell me about it."

The sisters exchange glances, and Olivia nods encouragingly.

Beatrix takes a deep breath. "It started when I fell in love."

She tells us how she fell hard for a dangerous criminal, but she didn't care. I have to fight to keep a straight face and not stare guiltily into my own lap.

Girl, same. Times three.

Beatrix wanted to be with this man, and he adored her. He owned clubs. He sold guns and drugs. He had a glamorous lifestyle, and they flew in and out of Europe together, but the important thing to Beatrix was the way he made her laugh. How she could make him laugh. None of her friends and family knew what this man did for a living, but many sensed dangerous vibes from him and encouraged Beatrix to break things off with him.

But Beatrix had already given him her heart. She ran away with him, leaving her old life behind.

"I didn't even confide in Olivia. I was so reckless." Beatrix shakes her head at her own stupidity.

"Hey, don't beat yourself up about it. Later on, you would have called if you could."

My stomach sinks as I imagine the rest of the story. The man became controlling. Abusive. Frightening. She had no one to turn to when everything changed.

"Then he died."

I look up in surprise. "What?"

Tears spring into Beatrix's eyes. "I should have been there with him. He died all alone, bleeding out in the road. Killed by some of his rivals."

She grips her mug hard with one hand and wipes the tears from her cheeks.

"If you love someone and they love you, you have to cling to each other, protect each other. This world is cruel, and once they're gone, you'll never get them back." She lifts her eyes to mine. "Do you understand?"

I nod slowly. "I'm beginning to."

Beatrix goes on with her tale, telling us how the rivals took everything that belonged to her lover for themselves, including her. They kept her captive and forced her into sex work.

"There was no end in sight. I thought I was going to die in there." Her eyes are dark and hollow, and then they brighten. "And then they came. Two men, wearing masks and shouting in another language. It sounded like Russian. They had guns. My captors spoke the same language, and there was so much shouting, but I couldn't understand a thing. Then the two men started shooting. They were like machines. They killed every man in the place and got all the women out of there."

Beatrix shudders and takes a mouthful of her tea. The things she must have suffered, the things she must have seen. Unimaginable.

"I thought, *here we go again*. These two Russian assholes were going to force us into more sex work or something even worse. I couldn't believe it when they drove us to a women's shelter and dropped us off."

I sit back in surprise. Not criminals, but liberators? "Do you know who the men were?"

Beatrix and Olivia exchange glances.

"They were young. Mid-twenties. One was very tall and fair and the other had dark curly hair. I thought I heard the blond one call the dark one Kirill."

I sit up with a start and slosh tea over my wrist.

Olivia passes me a paper towel. "I know. That's what I've been thinking."

"Did the tall man have light blue eyes?" I ask Beatrix. "Did they both have tattooed fingers?"

Beatrix nods. "Yes, he did, and yes, I could only see their hands and throats, but they were tattooed. The blond man was very reserved and serious, but oddly reassuring as he got us out of that place. The darker-haired one didn't say much."

"When was this?" I ask.

"Six, seven weeks ago."

Right around the time that Konstantin, Elyah, and Kirill had started being secretive. If they did this, why didn't they tell me?

More importantly, why did they do this for Olivia and

Beatrix? Konstantin was so adamant that he wouldn't say sorry. The past was dead and done with.

Olivia leans forward. "It was them. Don't you think so, Lilia? I'm sure it was two of the men who held us prisoner at the pageant. The crazy one and your..." She trails off but I know what she was going to say.

Ex-lover.

Only he's my very current lover.

"But if it was them, I don't understand why, nearly a year after the pageant, those two men of all people would find my sister and send her back to me."

"Maybe...maybe they feel badly about what they did," I say slowly, trying to figure the answer out for myself. But if that were the case, why not tell me about it? If Konstantin was doing something good at last, I would have expected him to tell me about it.

Olivia gazes at me incredulously. "Those men? Feel bad about what they did? I don't believe it. Beatrix was probably being held by a rival gang and dropping her at a shelter was the quickest way to get rid of them."

There's so much bitterness on her face, and every drop of it is understandable.

"Olivia thinks it was just a coincidence, but I'm not so sure," Beatrix murmurs. "Maybe they do have a conscience about what they did at the pageant. Maybe you gave them one, Lilia, when you ruined everything."

Olivia shakes her head. "I don't want to think about them. I only want to think about my sister being back, and you being here, Lilia. I can't tell you how happy it makes me that we're all sitting here together."

I smile at her with genuine feeling. "So am I. It doesn't feel real."

"You need to tell us everything that's happened to you since the pageant."

My breasts are aching. Viktoria has a bottle of milk, but I need to pump or feed or I'm going to start leaking through my clothes. "Can I come back and see you again soon?"

Olivia's face falls. "You're leaving already? I thought you would at least stay for lunch."

Even Beatrix looks confused and hurt, and I feel a stab of guilt. "I..."

I should tell her about the baby.

I should get Viktoria and bring her in.

But Olivia will ask how old she is and realize she was fathered by one of the men. I can't bring that child in here with two traumatized women and watch their faces drain of color as they realize I'm with the men who caused Olivia unimaginable pain. It would be like a slap in the face of her suffering.

"I didn't know I was coming to see you. This was just as much a surprise to me."

As I babble my excuses, Olivia and Beatrix exchange glances. They don't understand what I mean, but they don't protest when I get to my feet.

We exchange numbers, and then Olivia walks with me to the front door and hugs me. My breasts ache against her chest when I'm trying to concentrate on saying goodbye.

"It's wonderful to see you. I'll see you again soon, I promise."

"I hope so, Lilia. Where..." She looks around outside the cottage for my car.

"I parked around the corner," I tell her, and confusion crosses her face again as she seems to wonder why I didn't park in front of the cottage when there's plenty of room. "I'll talk to you soon, I promise."

I walk away feeling sore, troubled, and guilty, wishing I was still full of all the happiness I felt when I first laid eyes on Olivia.

As I approach the car, I can hear Viktoria's cries of hunger, and suddenly all thoughts are wiped from my mind except to feed her. The urge is so strong it's like a switch being flipped.

"I hope she's been good," I say, unbuttoning my blouse at the same time that I reach for the baby.

Juliet was about to give her a bottle, but she puts the cap back on and stows it away. "She's been an angel, but she's happy to see you."

As Viktoria nurses, I rock her back and forth gently, smiling down at her. I can't help it. I was only gone for an hour, but I missed her so much.

Someone calls out behind me. "Lilia?"

My eyes go wide and I freeze.

Juliet is staring at someone standing over my shoulder. I turn around slowly, Viktoria in my arms.

It's Oliva, and she's standing just a few feet away and staring at me and the baby in naked shock. A smile washes over her face. "Why didn't you say you had a baby? You should have brought her in. Who's the father?"

"I..."

Olivia keeps smiling, despite the confusion in her eyes.

I don't deserve her smiles. I didn't deserve to set foot in her house.

Tears spill down my cheeks. "You're going to hate me so much."

The smile drains from Olivia's face as she stares between me and the child. Counting back the months. "Lilia. Is that...?"

I can tell from the dawning horror on her face that she already knows. One of the men who locked us up fathered this child.

"Oh, my gosh," Olivia whispers, staring at Viktoria. "Which one? Who's the father?"

"I don't know," I say truthfully. I haven't been trying too hard to figure it out, either. I just think of all of them as Viktoria's father.

Olivia barely seems aware of the fact that she's drawing closer to us. Viktoria has her eyes open as she feeds, and sunlight falls across her face.

"The scarred one," Olivia whispers, and a shudder passes through her. "It's his."

I stare down at Viktoria in surprise. I haven't seen her eyes in the sunlight in a little while, and I see they're not blue anymore. They're blue-gray.

My heart fills with love and excitement, and I can't wait to ask my men if they think—

And then I realize where I'm standing and with who.

Olivia looks up at me. "Of course I don't hate you, Lilia. You had to sleep with them in order to free us. It must have been such a shock when you found out you were pregnant. When did you realize you were going to have a baby?"

I remember how I sat and cried on the bathroom floor, holding on to the positive pregnancy test. It feels like decades ago.

A shock? That's putting it mildly. "In Trieste. My father tracked me down. He forced me to—"

Olivia raises up in alarm. "Forced you to what?"

I shake my head because I shouldn't put this all on her when she's been through so much and has her sister to care for. "There's so much you don't know about my past. So much I couldn't tell you when we were locked up together because I was trying to protect you. My father was not a good man, but he's dead now. That's probably all you should know."

Hurt flashes through her eyes, though she tries to hide it. "You can tell me. I mean, you're here. There's nothing I want you to hide from me, least of all a baby."

She reaches out to touch Viktoria's cheek.

I take a step back, holding Viktoria protectively to my chest.

Olivia's brow creases. "Lilia, what the hell? Do you think I'm going to hurt your baby?"

It's the other way around.

She's going to hurt you.

"You don't understand. I'm...with them." It hurts to say those words to her because I know she's going to hate me. I'm not just with them.

I love them.

The three men who put me in the car this morning with my baby, wanting me to see my friend again, and the sister that they rescued. I squeeze my eyes shut. I have to choose between my friend and the men I love, and it hurts so much.

But I choose them.

I'll always choose them.

"I'm sorry," I whisper through my tears. "I'll go. You don't have to look at me. You will never see me again, or them.

They'll never come here. You and your sister are safe. I'm so sorry for disturbing you."

Juliet has drawn away from us to give us some privacy, but she hurries forward to get the car door for me.

"Wait."

Olivia crunches over the gravel toward us and I turn slowly back to her.

There's so much pain in her eyes as she gazes at the child, but softness, too. Finally, she raises her eyes to mine. "I don't know how this happened, but I believe in what you did for us."

I squeeze my eyes shut and close my eyes briefly. It would have broken my heart to hear her say that she should never have believed in Number Eleven, after all.

"I can't say I'm not shocked. I don't understand how you could...how they could..." She trails off, staring at Viktoria. Then she lifts her gaze to mine. "But if anyone could, it's you. The scarred one..." She frowns, trying to think of his name.

"Konstantin."

"Konstantin. Is he being a father? Is he a good father?"

I recall finding him at his desk with Viktoria in his arms, typing one-handed as he talked softly to her. Kirill standing at the window with her and pointing out all the birds, giving her the Russian names. Elyah feeding her with a bottle and smiling as he told her she was going to grow up as strong as her papas and clever like her mother.

"He is. They all are."

Her eyes widen. "All? All three of them? Even the crazy one?"

"He needs this baby most of all. You can judge me. I would judge me."

Olivia shakes her head. "Please come back inside. Please stay. You're welcome in my house, and you always will be."

I glance at her cottage over her shoulder, longing to be in there with her. "I shouldn't. It would upset your sister."

"You really think that she would think any worse of you after what she just told you? Beatrix understands better than most that love is complicated. When she sees the baby, maybe it will make her smile."

I hesitate, glancing at Juliet. "Do I have time?"

Juliet smiles at me. "You have all the time in the world. Go on."

Beatrix's mouth drops open when she sees me step inside the cottage with Viktoria in my arms. "A baby? You have a baby?"

I gaze down at my daughter, the beautiful little miracle in the middle of all this. "Beatrix, the men who got you out of that place. This is their daughter."

There are so many questions flashing over Beatrix's face that she doesn't seem to know which one to ask first.

"I was worried that if you saw Viktoria it would upset you, so I left her with my driver."

"She's beautiful," Beatrix breathes. "Can I hold her?"

We sit down on the sofas in the living room and Beatrix rocks Viktoria in her lap. Tears drip down Beatrix's face.

"I wanted to have a baby. I wanted *his* baby. You're so lucky," she whispers fiercely. Then she shakes her head. "I'm sorry, that was insensitive. You didn't love the father of this child. You must have been so shocked when you found out you were pregnant."

I take a deep breath. "I was, but a lot has happened since

the pageant ended. The three men who held Olivia and I captive, I'm with them now."

I tell the two sisters my story as Viktoria sleeps on. When I finish, Olivia and Beatrix exchange glances.

"They helped me because they were going to be fathers," Beatrix says.

Olivia frowns, thinking about this for some time. "Actually, I think they did this for Lilia. At the pageant, they were all so taken with her. They thought they were in charge, and they thought they were going to vent whatever anger they had on us, but Lilia made them realize they didn't want that, after all."

They're probably both right. Elyah must have felt terrible for the women he'd hurt. Kirill wanted to unstick me from my past. Konstantin understood that deeds are more powerful than words.

"She's so beautiful, Lilia," Beatrix says, passing the baby over to her sister.

I nod, my throat feeling tight. "She's the most beautiful baby I've ever seen."

Olivia strokes Viktoria's cheek with the tip of her finger and glances up at me. "I need you in my life. Will they allow that?"

I lift my chin and say proudly, "Allow it? You think they can stop me?"

Olivia laughs with relief and wipes her eyes. "You really are the same Lilia. I can't tell you how happy that makes me."

~

All three of my men are waiting for me when I get out of the car that afternoon, Viktoria in my arms. Their expressions are more troubled, more hopeful than I've ever seen them before.

"Did you see her, Lilia? Did you all talk?" Elyah asks.

I stand in front of them, looking from one man to the next, shaking my head and glaring at them. "You... Why didn't you tell me about this weeks ago?"

Elyah smiles ruefully.

Kirill shrugs one shoulder and reaches for the baby. "Mama is in a temper," he murmurs, kissing the baby's head and flashing me a mischievous look.

Konstantin's expression is wary, and he waits.

"You couldn't just say *I'm sorry* like I asked you to do months ago? Two goddamn words, Konstantin? No, you had to make a great big secret out of it when I could have helped you."

"And if Number Ten's sister was dead? I was supposed to watch the mother of my child cry?"

I make a face at him. He's got an answer for everything. "Of the three of you, you had me the most worried. That you would want to be a *Pakhan* to this child, not a father."

Konstantin smiles slowly. "When have I ever behaved like a normal *Pakhan*? I share my woman. I let you tell me what to do. I let these assholes tell me what to do. I am at your feet, *malyshka*, and I always will be."

He reaches up to touch my cheek, his gray eyes softer than I have ever seen them before. "Lilia Aranova, you are my beloved, and you always will be."

"Thank you for what you did," I whisper fiercely. "You did it for me?"

He nods at Viktoria. "I did it for her, so she can love her fathers, not fear them."

I close my eyes, relief pouring through me and loosening my tense muscles. That's the answer I've been hoping for from him, and I didn't even realize it.

"That is even better than your love," I tell him.

"You have that, too," he tells me, and kisses my mouth.

Elyah comes forward and takes my face in his hands. "Once, this idiot told lie," he murmurs, nodding at Konstantin. "He told us that you are not bewitching goddess. That there was nothing special about Number Eleven, and we believed him. Then we watched you prove us all wrong." He kisses me softly. "I loved you from the moment I laid eyes on you, Lilia Aranova. This home will always be safety for you. I swear it."

Elyah has always seemed boyish to me, sometimes sweet, sometimes terrifying, but now he's looking at me as a man who knows what he wants and trusts in my heart as well as his own.

He presses his forehead against mine and closes his eyes.

"I love you, too," I whisper fiercely.

Kirill saunters toward me and jerks his chin in a way that tells me he wants me to turn my lips up to his, and I do.

As Elyah moves aside, Kirill says in a low voice, "Every time you and this baby are out of my sight for more than one second, I lose my fucking mind. If it were possible, I would tie you to me. Both of you." His jaw clenches and he swallows hard. "But that is not possible, so instead, every time you leave and come back to me, I will feel more joy than a piece of shit like me deserves to feel even once."

With his arms full of me and the baby, he kisses me hard.

"Always come back to me, *detka*."

I nod, my heart bleeding with the memory of all the blood that's been spilled in his past. The little boy who was beaten by his father. The baby who never got to live. The mother and grandparents who died brutal deaths. They're all ghosts, but the man who has endured it all is here.

If I run, what will he have?

"I promise," I whisper.

I turn to the house and walk up the steps, calling casually over my shoulder, "By the way, Olivia, Beatrix, and I figured out which of you is the father."

"Lilia! Is she mine? I know she is mine," Elyah says.

"Don't be stupid, Elyah. I was first."

"First doesn't mean anything," Konstantin reminds them.

I grin and walk across the threshold, grinning to myself as they continue arguing behind me. Maybe I'll tell them, or maybe I won't. They are all Viktoria's father in their hearts, and that's where it matters.

I step into the hall and turn back to look at the four of them. Here I am with all my beautiful men and my daughter. Full of love.

Finally home.

17

Lilia

The ruby sparkles in the sunshine, a lavish, scarlet stone brought back to life with a little care and cleaning. I lay the antique necklace on the table and gaze at it.

Beautiful.

And quite a find. I bought this piece from an estate sale, sensing there was something special about it. I was able to discover from the maker's mark that this piece was made in Germany in the nineteenth century, and with some cleaning up and a little repair work that's still to be done, it will be fit for a duchess once more.

Viktoria is nearly one year old, and ever since having her, I've been thinking about my bloodline. The female line in particular, and the strength that's been handed down to me from a long line of women stretching back into Russia's history. I recall how *Babulya* sold her mother's jewelry to keep us fed and warm when I was a child. With pain in my heart, I remember how I lost my mother's locket down a drain because of my school bully.

I won't have anything tangible to pass onto my daughter that belonged to the women of our family, but I can tell her about them when the time comes, and I can be a role model for her.

And so, I'm learning something new. I started reading about gems and the history of jewelry on a whim and found it fascinating how all the various precious stones in the world were made deep within the earth, lumps of colored rock that can be cut and polished into treasures. I bought more books and learned how to grade precious stones. I learned about the history of jewelry making, the types of metals and styles, what makes a piece valuable.

I started visiting antique stores and pawn shops with Viktoria in her stroller and discovered I have an affinity for antique jewelry. Pieces that remind me of Mom and *Babulya*. Beautiful pieces that I like to imagine once belonged to strong women. Every time I pick up a new piece, I wonder about its former owner and how she felt as she put on this pair of earrings or paired that necklace with her favorite dress. How much history she must have lived through. How much laughter. How many tears.

A few weeks ago, I remembered that I still possessed the locket that I purchased in Trieste when I was making the deal with the pawnshop owner to sell Konstantin's diamonds. I was pregnant with Viktoria at the time. So early in my pregnancy that I was still coming to terms with her existence. I held the necklace up to the light, examining it, and found it was actually quite a beautiful piece.

This was the locket that fooled Dad long enough to cover up what I was really doing in the jewelry store.

Mom's in this locket. So is *Babulya*, and so am I. It holds all our stories. This is a new family heirloom that I can pass onto my daughter. I cleaned it up and put photos of Viktoria inside, and now I wear it as often as I can.

Smiling, I gaze at the six antique pieces I've bought recently, cleaned up, and made minor repairs and changes to, all of which I will resell to high-end jewelry dealers for a profit.

There are four more broken pieces of jewelry that are waiting for me to fix them, but I don't have the skills yet. I'll need to learn silversmithing and goldsmithing first, and I'm already investigating courses I can take.

I've never had skills of my own before. I've never been allowed to be anything but a wife and a homemaker, but now I get to be anything I want. My men have been so supportive as well. Konstantin gave me a room on the second floor that I'm slowly turning into a workshop. Elyah loves to hear me tell him about what I've learned about precious stones and the history of jewelry. Kirill offered to steal some really beautiful pieces for me, and I burst out laughing before I realized he was serious. I made him promise not to do this because I want all my trades to be legitimate.

There's movement from the hall, and I see that Kirill is lounging in the doorway, dressed in ripped black jeans and a tight black tee, the ghost of a smile on his lips.

"Are you busy?"

I glance around at my desk, checking that I've finished

everything I wanted to do for the day. Viktoria will sleep for a little while longer. "I'm all done. Why?"

His smile widens. "Hide-and-seek."

Kirill's words send hot sparks through me. "Who's hiding and who's counting?"

"You're hiding. I'm counting. One…two…"

I jump up from my desk, hurry past him, and run down the corridor. When I glance over my shoulder, I see he's watching me go with his eyes wide open.

"No peeking, you cheater!" I call joyfully as I race up the stairs. My heart is pounding as I hunt along the next floor for a good place to hide. Kirill is way too good at sniffing me out, but I'm determined to outfox him one of these days.

What makes the chase even more delicious is the memory of the way he once hunted me down for real, covered in blood with a knife in his hand.

Maybe it's messed up, but we like it.

I haven't hidden in the walk-in closet in Konstantin's room yet. It's always seemed too obvious, but perhaps that might work in my favor today.

I hurry to the small room, lined with Konstantin's suits and rows of polished leather shoes, and hide among the winter coats. The man has more clothes than the rest of us put together.

The door opens a moment later, and I hold my breath and try not to move.

Not fair, he found me so quickly.

"*Solnyshko*, it is me," he whispers. "Are you playing with Kirill?"

I poke my head out and see Elyah standing there, dressed in a patterned shirt in soft colors, very much like the one he purchased with the intention of spilling coffee on as an excuse to be half naked in front of me. He looks mouthwateringly good in shirts like these, the fabric clinging to his muscles and bringing out the blue of his eyes.

Elyah sees me, then closes and locks the door behind him.

"We're not allowed to lock doors. That's a rule Kirill made."

He tugs me out from between the coats. "I am not playing with him. I am playing with you."

He makes an excellent point.

"Have you come today?" he murmurs, kissing my throat, and I shake my head. "Then get down on the floor so I can lick you."

I do as I'm told, wriggling out of my underwear, and pulling my dress up as I sink to the ground. Elyah moves between my thighs and gives me a kiss, before pushing me flat on the floor.

He takes his first lick and groans.

"Shh, Kirill is looking for me," I murmur, and then immediately give a soft cry of pleasure as Elyah slides one of his thick fingers deep into my pussy.

I'm panting with need by the time I hear someone trying to open the door.

"*Detka*. Are you breaking the rules?"

"No," I call out, sounding so close to coming that it's obvious what's happening in here.

"Elyah, you piece of shit. I was playing with her."

Elyah pretends like he hasn't heard his friend and slips another finger into my pussy. With two thick fingers pulsing into me and his tongue sliding so intensely against my clit, I lose all sense of everything and come with a loud cry.

While I'm still flat on my back and panting for breath, Elyah opens the door with a grin.

"Sorry, friend. Did not hear you out there."

Kirill pushes past him and glares down at me on the floor.

"Oh, no. You found me. Shall I hide again?"

Kirill's scowl softens as he stares at me with my knees spread and my dress rucked up around my waist. "I've got a better idea."

He hauls me to my feet and over his shoulder, and I'm laughing as he carries me to the next room and drops me onto Konstantin's bed.

"This was what I really wanted, anyway," he tells me, starting to undress.

He's got a new tattoo on his chest. Viktoria's name in Cyrillic. Elyah has the same one on his upper back. I cried when I saw that they had our daughter's name inked into their flesh. They got the tattoos done the day after I told them that Konstantin was her biological father.

She is our daughter, too, and we love her, Elyah told me.

A moment later, I'm pressed between Kirill's and Elyah's naked bodies with both their cocks bumping against my entrance.

They tussle with each other over who thrusts inside me first, Elyah grabbing Kirill's wrist and pulling his hand from my waist. Kirill pushes at Elyah's shoulder, trying to tip him off-balance. They're always careful with me when they do this, but the gleam in their eyes tells me how seriously they take this wrestling match. And they're not careful with each other.

"Ha. Beat you," Elyah groans, thrusting as deep as he can.

Kirill growls, filled with frustration. "You ruin my game. You take my woman from me yet again. *Detka*, I need to fuck you now. Hold still."

I was lost in the slow, languorous thrusts of Elyah's cock, and I open one eye. "What?"

Elyah has caught on already and he's angling my body into a better position. Kirill spits on his fingers and massages it onto his cock, and then I feel the head of him against my pussy. Trying to join Elyah inside me.

"Oh, shit—" I gasp, holding on to Kirill's shoulders and staring down at myself. They couldn't possibly both fit, but I forgot that no one's as determined as these two when they get an idea in their heads. I let myself go limp in their arms, my back supported against Elyah's chest behind me.

Elyah holds still, and we both groan as we feel Kirill slide into me along Elyah's length.

"Haven't you got your own beds to go to?" asks a voice from the doorway.

I smile breathlessly at Konstantin, my teeth sinking guiltily into my lower lip because we've just been caught. But not too guiltily because I'm having a wonderful time right now.

He stares at me and his head tilts slowly to one side as if he's surprised by what he's seeing. "Two cocks. Aren't you greedy?"

"Who, me?" I say, breaking off as his two enforcers thrust deep inside me.

Kirill points a finger at his *Pakhan*. "You? You can fuck off."

Konstantin laughs and comes toward us. "Why should I?"

"Because she's ovulating."

I lift my head in shock. "I'm what?"

Elyah gazes at me with a frown. He and Kirill have found a perfect rhythm together. "Do you not keep track of days, *solnyshko*?"

I told myself I would start once I finished breastfeeding Viktoria, but I never got in the habit.

"Maybe I want this next child, too. Let the best man win," says Konstantin.

Kirill shakes his head. "Sorry. There's no room. Not now, not for the rest of this month. Ask Lilia nicely for a blowjob if you want to come."

Elyah smirks at his friend. "Are you worried about your swimmers, Kirill?"

"No, I'm thinking about what a pain in the ass it will be to raise a whole pack of little Kostyas."

The smile drops from Elyah's face. "I did not think of that. *Solnyshko*, do not let him come in you until you are pregnant again."

"Oh, sure," I say, watching Konstantin push off his pants and underwear and take his hard length in his hand. "I'll keep track of where everyone's cocks and cum are while I'm in the midst of my orgasms."

I reach out for him as he steps closer, guiding him into my mouth. I love when it's all four of us together.

As I suck him slowly, I hold on to his bicep, my palm over the Viktoria tattoo he has there. It's on the inside of his left arm. Close to his heart, as he put it.

My eyes are closed, and someone's working his fingers against my clit. I have no idea who it is, and I don't care. All I'm thinking about it how delicious and heavy Konstantin feels in my mouth and how good the stretch is of both Elyah and Kirill filling my pussy.

"Are you close?" Kirill asks breathlessly, and I nod. The two of them working in unison is driving me crazy. He laughs. "I was talking to Elyah."

"Yes, I am fucking close," Elyah groans.

Konstantin grips the hair at the back of my head, his breathing growing harsh. He's so beautiful, standing over me. Muscular and strong. I'm caught between two more men who entrance me every time I look at them. Their strength, our love, our passion overwhelm me, and I come with a muffled cry.

Konstantin lets out a groan and his seed floods my mouth. Elyah and Kirill grip me tightly, their hands on my shoulders, my waist, my hips, and pound into me hard. I swallow Konstantin down and then my head tips back with a gasp of pleasure.

The three of us finish wrapped tightly around each other, one of my arms looped through Konstantin's thighs while we all struggle to get our breaths back.

"The two of us should fuck Lilia like this until she's pregnant again," Kirill says, a gleam in his eye as he and Elyah withdraw slowly.

"It is the only way to make sure it is fair," agrees Elyah, grinning at me.

Please. Like they won't both be sneaking into bed with me in the middle of the night to make sure the odds are in their favor.

From down the hall, the baby starts crying. Viktoria has woken up from her nap.

"I'll go," Konstantin says, getting up and reaching for the robe on the back of the bedroom door.

I wince as I hear that Viktoria is shrieking with particular indignation. "Are you sure? She might give you a migraine. I can go."

"Stay there, *malyshka*. Haven't you noticed? I haven't had a migraine in months."

I stare at him as he disappears out the door. Now that I think of it, I haven't seen him with bloodshot eyes and a sweaty brow in a very long time, and some days he has Viktoria screaming directly into his ear. She's very vocal when she's not happy about something.

"How the hell did that happen?" I wonder out loud.

Elyah is laying comfortably against the pillows with his arm around my waist and his eyes closed, and he murmurs, "He is happy, *solnyshko*."

"Being happy doesn't cure a bullet in the brain."

Kirill pushes his hands through his curls. "The bullet didn't even crack his skull. The migraines were...psycho-whatsit. I don't know the English word."

"Psychosomatic?"

"That's it."

I cuddle up in between my two men, thinking about it. It's an interesting theory, that Konstantin's headaches were a physical manifestation of all his unresolved hurt and anger about his past.

It's so warm and comfortable here between Elyah and Kirill. A moment later, Konstantin comes back with Viktoria in his arms, and she's miraculously smiling now that Daddy has come to get her. She's dressed in a onesie with elephants that bring out the gray tones in her eyes. Her hair has turned blonde, and I wonder if she'll take after me or if it will darken in time like her father's.

"I'm so happy about your migraines," I whisper, my cheek pillowed on Kirill's chest.

Konstantin sinks down on the bed next to us, and Kirill reaches out to Viktoria, who wraps her chubby hand around his forefinger.

"Have you decided what you want to do about what we all talked about?" Konstantin asks.

He means about the question they asked me a few weeks ago. Will I marry one of them? Officially. Legally. They all said that they wanted to be the man, but it's up to me.

Konstantin is very traditional, and I can tell he wants me to pick him. It's been his aim all along to marry.

Elyah pretends that he doesn't mind who I choose, but I can see the longing in his eyes.

Kirill is harder to read, and I can't tell if he's joking or serious about wanting to marry me.

"It's so hard to choose one of you. I don't want to disturb what we have when we..." I struggle for the right way to describe it. "Fit so well together."

"Don't we," murmurs Elyah, kissing my neck, and I can tell from the amusement in his voice that he's thinking about what we just did.

Konstantin's warm hand smooths my hair, and my mind drifts over my current jewelry designs as Viktoria babbles sweetly.

My eyes pop open. "I've got it."

But can I really do it? It's way beyond any of my skills. But someone could do it if I described what I wanted...

I sit up and extricate myself from the pile of warm bodies,

give them all a kiss, including Viktoria, and hurry out of the room.

Wrapped in a silk robe with my bed hair tumbling around my head, I run into my workshop and snatch the sketchbook off the desk, flipping to a fresh page.

It takes a week to get it right, ripping my drafts from the book and balling them up in frustration. I'm still learning to draw and design, but it has to be perfect because it's *us*.

Finally, I send them all a text and ask them to come to my workroom.

When they're all gathered by my desk, Elyah asks, "Have you made your decision?"

"I've decided." I smile at them all, breathless with anticipation. "I'm not going to marry any of you."

They stare at me blankly.

I hurry on. "Or rather, I'm going to marry all of you. In a way. Here, look at this."

I open my sketchbook and show them a design. A wedding band made up of three rings that fit together, which is exactly how I feel when I'm with them.

An ornate and decorative band with an emerald-cut diamond for Konstantin, very traditional and beautiful.

A circular-cut diamond for Elyah with small diamonds placed around it in the setting that looks like a radiating sun, because he's always called me his sunshine.

A square diamond for Kirill, sharp and to the point like he is, with a geometric pattern on the band.

The place settings overlap and complement each other, like my men do.

"All very pure, white diamonds, and the settings will be white gold. What do you all think?"

Elyah takes the sketchbook from me and studies it closely. "*Solnyshko*," he murmurs with a smile, understanding my design right away. My heart lightens as he passes the book to Konstantin. "I love it."

Konstantin examines the design and nods approvingly. "It's beautiful, *malyshka*."

Finally, Kirill peers hard at the page, his brows drawn together, and my heart is in my throat. What if he hates it?

He looks up at me. "Can you make each of us wedding bands that match this ring? What you have designed for my part of the ring, I want that for myself."

I blink in surprise. I hadn't thought of that, but a man's wedding ring with the same design on the band would suit him. It would suit the other two men to have bands with their designs, too. After all, each part of the ring is inspired by who they are.

"I can design it and we can have someone make all four rings. What do you all think?" I look carefully at each of them. "I know it's not marriage. Not legally. But this way, I don't have to choose just one of you. I'm choosing all of you."

They all exchange glances and nod.

"It probably wouldn't do our competitive natures much good if you chose one of us," Konstantin observes wryly. "Even if it's only legally."

Elyah is watching me carefully. "You seem different. Your color has changed. Your energy has changed."

"I must be excited about the rings being made," I say with a smile, closing my sketchbook. It will have to be a very experienced jewelry maker that we use, someone who can interpret my designs and bring them to life.

Elyah doesn't seem convinced and turns to Kirill. "What is the date?"

Kirill checks his phone. "Lilia. If you have not started your period, you are four days late."

I'm still deep in thought about the rings, and I finally look up. "Hm?"

Konstantin has Viktoria in his arms and he's smiling at me. "Are you pregnant, *malyshka*?"

I sit up in surprise. The possibility hadn't even occurred to me. Excitement starts to fizz through me, and I realize how much I do want another baby. "I could be," I say slowly.

"But whose is it?" Elyah wonders aloud.

"What if it's Kostya's again?" says Kirill, with a dark look at his *Pakhan*.

Konstantin shakes his head. "It's not mine. I haven't, as Kirill puts it, nut in our beloved since her last cycle."

I stare at him, thinking back through all my encounters with Konstantin this past month. He's right, he hasn't. And I think that's been on purpose.

"I could just be late, but I do have pregnancy tests," I whisper, unable to stop myself from smiling. "Shall I take one?"

"Do you even have to ask, *detka*?" Kirill says, already turning toward the door.

Upstairs, they all come into the bathroom, and I realize that three overeager men are going to watch me pee on a stick.

"We really have no boundaries, huh?" I say, opening up the pregnancy test.

Konstantin sits down on the edge of the tub. "None."

I hold the test between my legs and pee on it, looking

from one man to the next. "It's just so different to the last time I had to take one of these."

This time I'm happy.

This time I want it to be positive, and the men crowding around me in the bathroom? I love them all.

We all wait, not speaking, for the test to develop. Grinning at each other, but not too much because we don't want to be too disappointed if the test is negative. It will probably be negative because four days late is nothing.

"It's been two minutes," Kirill says, glancing at his phone.

I take a deep breath and glance at the test.

"Oh, wow," I breathe, staring at the two lines. It's really happening, and I'm filled with nothing but joy.

I hold the test up to them, smiling. The anticipation on their faces is the most beautiful thing I've ever seen. "Congratulations, daddies. We're having another baby."

EPILOGUE

Lilia

"Do you want to know if it's a boy or a girl?"

The obstetrician is holding the ultrasound scanner over my belly in her latex-gloved hands, and she pauses to smile at each of us. I'm laying in the chair with my bump exposed.

Konstantin has three-and-a-half-year-old Viktoria in his arms. Kirill has baby Mila in a pram. Mila has her father's dark eyes and curls, and where Viktoria is sweet and inquisitive, Mila is demanding and full of mischief.

Elyah is close by my side, holding my hand and shifting restlessly, his eyes glued to the screen.

We do this dance whenever I'm pregnant, and this third time is no different.

"Tell us. Do not tell us. No, wait, tell us." Elyah pushes his hands through his hair. "It should be surprise, but I want to know."

I watch Elyah with a smile on my face and my hands folded across my belly. When he runs out of steam and clenches his head in his hands in agony, I remind him, "Elyah. We never find out the sex of the baby. We always find out when they are born, remember?"

He takes my hand. "But it is not fair. Konstantin and Kirill already know that they have daughters. I need to know if I have son or daughter."

The baby is probably Elyah's. It's difficult to know, though. Things get messy among the four of us.

I burst out laughing. "That's because Viktoria and Mila are already here."

The obstetrician waits patiently for us to finish our discussion. After three pregnancies and all of us coming to her office for every checkup, she's used to our nonsense by now.

Elyah turns to her with a groan and says, "Thank you, but we will wait."

Konstantin tuts and shakes his head with a smile. "So impatient, Elyah."

"I am. Do you want to give Mommy a kiss?" Elyah asks Viktoria, and she holds out her arms to him as readily as if she were his daughter. Which, of course, she is.

"Who's Mommy's good girl?" I ask her, tweaking her nose and accepting a kiss on my lips from her and then Elyah.

The obstetrician has more things to tell me and we listen to her describe the baby's progress. Viktoria puts her head down on Elyah's shoulder and closes her eyes. He absent-mindedly rocks her back and forth in his arms.

Over his shoulder, Konstantin is watching me with a smile touching his lips. His scars have faded a little over the years, but they're still very visible on his face. He's never mentioned getting surgery to fix them and I doubt he would. Those scars remind him of how close he came to losing everything, and the things that made him the man he is today.

Besides, I think he likes the way they make him seem even more intimidating.

At the end of the appointment, Kirill helps me to my feet and settles my jersey dress back into place over my bump. Then he breathes in my ear, "You are so sexy like this, *detka*. It reminds me of Prague."

"With my bump?" I smile and brush my fingers over the nape of his neck. That little apartment in Prague feels like it belongs to another lifetime. So much has happened since then. I was a scared, pregnant woman in hiding, but that place will always be special to me because I fell for these men in that Prague apartment. And they for me.

As we walk out into the sunshine, I take a deep, happy breath. Our family is growing. There are six of us, with a seventh on the way. For all of us except Elyah, our family is dead to us, either literally or figuratively.

Except for *Babulya*. I must call *Babulya* when we get home, and update her on the baby and her two great-grandchildren. I miss her so much.

At home, Elyah makes pancakes for our daughters while he coaches me in Russian. It's a fair swap because my Russian is improving and so is Elyah's cooking.

Konstantin has a meeting with a real estate developer and Kirill is training some of the new men they've hired. Security.

Drivers. Financial advisors. No matter who they are, men or women, Kirill puts them through their paces because they have to be strong to work for my husbands.

I call them my husbands even though we are not legally married, and they call me their wife. We're a family, all of us.

"It is also how I tell if they are trustworthy or not," Kirill told me once. "If they cut corners doing laps or push-ups, they are out. I don't want them around you and my daughters."

Kirill has inflexible rules about who is allowed to cross the threshold of our home, and he enforces all of them.

When Mila was born, I've never seen such wonder on Kirill's face. It's like he almost couldn't believe she was real.

"Do you remember the day we killed your father?" he murmured one afternoon, gazing at his sleeping daughter.

My stomach lurched, because what a strange thing to bring up when you are holding your newborn. "Of course. I'll never forget that day."

"We made you think terrible things. That we were going to take your baby from you and hand you over to your father."

I think back to that moment. Most of the time, I remember Dad's hateful words and the triumph on his face when he thought he had won. But now, I remember something else. Kirill grabbing hold of my arm as I started panicking.

"You didn't want to do it," I said softly, realizing what that touch meant now. He was thinking of me and the baby. He was thinking of Katya too, and how she screamed for help and no one listened.

"It was what we had to do, *detka*. But I dream about it

sometimes, and Katya is there too, gazing at me like I am a monster."

I bent down, swept his curls aside and kissed his brow. "She forgives you. I forgive you."

I've been able to open up to Olivia and Beatrix just about everything in my life and they have never judged me. Olivia was already a kind person and Beatrix understands why someone would love dangerous men. Either I go to them or we meet somewhere for lunch, and though they haven't met my husbands, they always welcome my daughters.

What surprised me over our last lunch was that Olivia dropped hints about wanting to meet Konstantin, Elyah, and Kirill again, so perhaps one day we will all get together.

When I stopped breastfeeding Mila and we started trying for a third baby, Kirill constantly wound Elyah up with stories about sneaking into my room and trying to get me pregnant. Announcing that he was sure he had been the one to have sex with me during my fertile window. That the next baby would definitely be his. To his credit, Elyah didn't punch him in the face once.

The truth was, Kirill actually stepped aside every time for Elyah and would always finish on my belly or in his hand.

"Give Elyah a baby. The big fucking softie wants one so badly," he whispered once in the dark before going back to his own bed.

As if I had any say about it. My body would do as it pleased.

Baby Number Three is born on a stormy fall afternoon with rain lashing the windows. I have another home birth because I'm lucky to have uncomplicated births and swift labors.

We know right away that it's Elyah's. All of us but Elyah, apparently. He's the first to hold her, after me.

"I do not care if she is mine. I love her. Look at her, she is perfect."

Kirill takes one look at the baby in Elyah's arms and bursts out laughing. "How can you not know? Elyah, she looks exactly like you."

"Do you really think so?"

Konstantin moves to Elyah's side. "Oh, yes. Those are Morozov genes. Look her eyes. Look at her chin."

Elyah cradles our baby's head in his hand, the wedding ring I designed for him glinting on his finger.

"Little baby," he murmurs, gazing at her. "*Solnyshko*, did you have a name in mind for our daughter?"

"What were you thinking, Elyah?"

He thinks for a moment. "What about Kira? I think she looks like Kira."

I smile when I hear it. "Perfect. I think it suits her. Kira."

Konstantin stands at the end of the bed, folds his arms and raises an eyebrow at me. "Three daughters? You have given us three daughters? Now we are outnumbered. We will all be sent mad by their tricks and schemes." But he's smiling as he says it.

I smile back, exhausted but happy. "Oh, I hope so."

Having daughters makes me think about my mother and how I wish I still have her with me. I talk to *Babulya* several times a week on the phone and she tells me stories about Mom when she was small and how happy Mom was when I was born. It makes me feel connected to the parts of my family that I love.

But it's still not enough.

One morning when I've put Kira and Mila down for their naps and Viktoria is at kindergarten, I go in search of my men.

"It's *Babulya's* seventieth birthday today," I tell them, when I've found them in the lounge. "I will be calling her soon, but I wanted to ask you all something first."

My heart starts beating wildly.

Will they say no?

Or will they feel they have to say yes?

"I want to ask *Babulya* to come and live with us."

All three men stare at me in silence.

Then Kirill bursts out laughing. "That crafty witch? We will all be at her mercy."

"Even more women of your bloodline in the house? God help us all." But Konstantin is smiling as he says it.

I give him a half shrug and smile. "You love the women of my bloodline. We keep you on your toes. But seriously, if you hate the idea, I'll forget about it. It's just that there is that extra building connected to the rest of the house that would make a perfect self-contained annex, and it isn't being used."

"Whatever will make you happy, *solnyshko*," Elyah tells me. "And I am speaking for all of us."

I glance from one man to the next, and they seem relaxed and sincere. "If you're all sure? Well, I'll go and make the call."

I kiss all three of my husbands and practically dance down the corridor as I go in search of my phone. A moment later, I dial her number in America.

"*Babulya*, happy birthday!" I talk to her for a few minutes and promise to send her a video of the girls later with Viktoria saying happy birthday to her great-grandma. "I wanted to ask you something. What do you think about coming to London to live with us?"

"Me?" *Babulya* sounds baffled by the question.

"Yes, you."

A long silence stretches and I wince, waiting for her reply.

"I think it is a good idea. Someone has to keep an eye on those men in your life so that they behave."

"Oh, they've learned how to behave. Don't you worry about that."

"Hmmph. We will see."

I'm grinning as I put my phone down, and I text my men the news.

Lilia: *Babulya says she will come and live with us.*

Elyah: *I am so happy for you solnyshko.*

Kirill: *God help us all.*

Konstantin: *At least there is one decent relative the four of us can scrape together.*

Elyah: *That reminds me. I want to ask my sisters to come and visit. I have not seen them in so long.*

Lilia: *That's a wonderful idea. Look at us and our functional family relationships. Suddenly we have so many we can enjoy in this house.*

Elyah: *Haha. Maybe. You have not met my bossy sisters.*

I GET to work making the house ready for our guests and the annex ready for *Babulya*. Thankfully, it's a large house because Elyah's three sisters, two of their husbands, and all of their children are coming to stay for two weeks, which makes fourteen extra people under this roof.

The annex needs renovating as it's been used for storage for decades. There's enough room for a one-bedroom unit with a kitchen, living room, and ensuite bathroom. The builders install large windows in the living room and bedroom so that *Babulya* has plenty of natural light and can look out onto the beautiful garden. She's always loved flowers and watching the birds.

In the meantime, Elyah's sisters arrive with their families. They are all tiny compared to their brother and yet they ruffle his hair and talk to him with the affectionate bossiness of older sisters.

None of Elyah's family speaks much English, but my Russian is coming along well enough that I can make out most of what they are saying to me if they use simple words. Elyah is there to translate if I get lost.

All his sisters are delighted by our children, but they are particularly taken with Kira.

"She is adorable, like her papa," one of his sisters coos.

"Oh, what a cute little baby he was," another says, reaching out to pinch Elyah's cheek. He bats her hand away. "White-blond hair and big blue eyes. Always so serious, though he rarely cried."

"Spoiled," adds another sister with a grin.

"But so protective. Five years old and he threw himself in front of a dog that was barking at me. The dog was twice as big as he was."

They tell me all the stories I could hope for about Elyah as a child, many of them funny, and I get the sense that he was a handful as a little boy and a teenager.

"You are all worried about having daughters," I tell him with a grin. "Now I wonder how we will all cope when I start having sons."

Elyah passes on my comment about more children to Konstantin and Kirill, and they're all keen to get started on trying for another one. I tell them they'll have to wait until Kira is older, as I want to enjoy all the baby months with her that I can. They grow up so fast.

Viktoria and Mila love playing with their cousins as much as I enjoy getting to know my sisters-in-law and the house is alive with running, yelling, singing children. I never got to have this as a kid and it makes me so happy that my daughters get to experience it.

Elyah's family goes back to Russia, with promises to return soon, and *Babulya* arrives not long after that.

Babulya is stately as Konstantin helps her out of the car, glaring fiercely around at the house, my husbands. She has a fringed shawl draped around her bony shoulders and she's wearing a black dress, black stockings, and sturdy black shoes. The sense of the old country clings to her like strong perfume, and I wonder if she's done this on purpose to remind my husbands what they are dealing with.

I have Viktoria in my arms as we step forward to greet *Babulya*, and for a moment I'm worried that she's going to be terrified of this formidable woman and hide her face.

"I want to be just like *Babulya* when I grow up."

I laugh and kiss Viktoria's cheek. "And so you will, my love."

Once we're seated in the lounge, I serve tea in Russian tea glasses along with slightly wonky jam tarts that Viktoria and I baked together. *Babulya* is delighted by her great-grand-daughters and tells them what good and beautiful girls they are, and I remember with a lump in my throat that there was a time when the only smiles in my life were hers.

"What's news back home?" I ask *Babulya*, because I know she has friends there and she will be keeping up with them.

Konstantin, Elyah, and Kirill listen with interest to *Babulya's* stories about the Russian community in that part of America, especially Elyah because he knows some of the same people.

Elyah sits forward and offers the plate of jam tarts to *Babulya*, whose hands stay in her lap.

"You are too handsome," she accuses. Elyah freezes and looks confused. "I like you already and it is because you have a pretty face."

I purse my lips and try not to laugh. "*Babulya*, he can't help his face. I love his face. I love everything about him."

He sits back down, and says carefully, "I meant what I said in your house all those years ago. I would rather cut off my hands than hurt Lilia again."

Viktoria is unaware of what the adults are talking about. She gets up from her place next to *Babulya*, crosses to the other sofa, and clambers up beside Elyah.

"She is not your daughter, but she trusts you."

Elyah puts his arms around Viktoria and she settles her cheek against his shoulder. His gaze toward my grandmother has grown chilly. "She is my daughter. I love all my children. Please do not say that she is not."

Babulya watches him for a long moment, but he's not backing down or looking away. Then she nods slowly. "Of course. I apologize. You have very beautiful children. All of you."

Elyah nods. "Yes, we do."

"Thank you," Konstantin murmurs as the tension breaks. He flicks a glance at me as if wondering if I'm sweating.

Just a little bit.

Her talk of home has me wondering about something. "Whatever happened to Maxim Vavilov's father? I realize that we never heard from him again after he sent assassins to Prague." Surely he wouldn't have just given up on avenging his son.

Babulya makes a *tsk* noise and waves a dismissive hand. "He had an accident. It is no loss."

Kirill is smirking to himself. Konstantin takes a sip of his tea, his expression placid. I'm instantly suspicious.

"An accident, you say. What kind of accident?"

My husbands exchange glances but say nothing.

Babulya breaks the silence. "I will say it. He was drunk one morning and was run over by a garbage truck. His head exploded like a pumpkin." She eyes Kirill. "I was pleased to hear when it happened. It made an old woman happy to know the man who tried to kill my granddaughter and great-granddaughter had to be scraped off his driveway."

I wince at the mental image.

As usual, Kirill is untidily dressed and sitting with his knees spread. The pair of jeans he's wearing are artfully ripped. I wonder if *Babulya* is about to scold him.

She nods at his ripped jeans. "Give me those pants tonight. I will fix them for you."

Kirill laughs. "My jeans? I bought them this way."

"You bought pants that are already ruined?"

"How else will people know that I have stars tattooed on my knees?"

She shakes her head. "What a strange man. In my day, we would have been ashamed to wear torn clothes."

Kirill switches to Russian and stretches his arms over his head. "I have been poor, *Babulya*. I was treated like dirt in my hometown. Now I have decided to have no shame, and I am happier this way."

She gives him a shrewd look. Finally she says, "We are both a long way from home."

"And I am thankful every day for that fact." He reaches out and brushes a forefinger over Mila's cheek and murmurs to her.

I sneak a glance at *Babulya's* face and see how it has softened as she watches Kirill with the baby.

Finally, she turns to Konstantin. "This is your house. You have an old woman living here, *Pakhan*. Will it drive you crazy to have yet another woman under your roof?"

Konstantin places his tea glass on the coffee table and threads his fingers together. "Once upon a time we were sitting at your kitchen table and you slapped my face. I don't plan on giving you any reason to slap me a second time."

I feel my eyebrows shoot up. No one told me that part of the story.

"Will you make things hard for an old woman because she slapped you?"

Konstantin shakes his head. "You are under my protection. If anyone talks to you the way I talked to you that day in your own house, then you must tell me and I will deal with it." He glances at me, and his grim expression melts away. "You make our Lilia happy. You are welcome here as long as you like. You are more than welcome because you are family."

"How is your own family?" *Babulya* asks.

Konstantin smiles at her and rubs the scar on his temple. "A mess. Worse than a mess. So I love this one very much. It's the only one that matters to me anymore."

Babulya relaxes and sits back a little, and I feel relieved that the interrogation is finally over and everyone has passed.

Or perhaps it's not over just yet.

"You have one child each. Whose turn is it next?"

"Turn for what, *Babulya*?" I ask her.

"For a baby, of course. How does it work?" She glances at my men. "Do two of you have blue balls until my Lilia is pregnant again? Or do you let nature take its course?"

I choke on my tea and nearly spit it out.

Konstantin grins at her. "A little bit of both. And it's my turn next."

Kirill glares at Konstantin. "Who said it was your turn?"

"Maybe it is my turn again," Elyah murmurs, gazing at me speculatively in a way that makes heat flush through my body.

I listen to them arguing good-naturedly about who is next, and notice that *Babulya* is happily biting into a jam tart.

Finally, Konstantin turns to her. "Are you satisfied with Lilia's husbands, or do you still worry about how we are treating her?"

She examines each of them in turn. "My Lilia has the strength of heart to bring three stubborn Russian men to their knees. I am not worried about her. I am worried about all of you." *Babulya* lifts her chin proudly. "Her daughters will run rings around you. I hope you are ready."

Kirill grins at her. "Do not worry, we are ready. And able."

"And we have more love for these girls and our Lilia than you could imagine," Elyah adds, with a smile at me.

As I gaze around at my husbands and beautiful daughters, and *Babulya*, who is a mother and grandmother and friend, I can feel the past melting away. I'm happier than I've ever been in my life.

The road was long and bumpy, but we've made it.

ACKNOWLEDGMENTS

Thank you so much for reading the *Pageant* duet. These books were a wild ride for me to write and I hope you enjoyed coming on the journey with me.

I couldn't have written these books without my amazing betas. Huge hugs and kisses to my girls, Evva, Jesi, Darlene, Claris, and Arabella.

Thank you to my wonderful editor Heather Fox for your support and insight.

Thank you to my proofreader and all-round amazing person Rumi Khan.

And thank you to you for reading *Crowned*. If you enjoyed this book, please consider leaving a review on Amazon and Goodreads.

Keep reading for a look at what's next from Lilith Vincent...

BRUTAL INTENTIONS: A STANDALONE MAFIA ENEMIES TO LOVERS ROMANCE

He's devious. Corrupted. And his brutal heart wants me.

Lazzaro Rosetti just locked eyes with fresh prey: the virginal, high-school girl from a rival family. Me, Mia Bianchi. He's screwed his way through half the city's female population and he's running wild—until his family finds a way to curb his behavior by forcing him to wed.

When he speaks his vows at the altar, he's holding Mom's hands, but his menacing green eyes are staring right at me. From the moment he crosses our threshold, Lazzaro makes my life hell. I'm Mom's unprotected and despised youngest daughter, and Lazzaro inhales my vulnerability like it's the finest perfume.

Someone's going to pay dearly for his bachelor wings being clipped, and I'm his perfect victim.

Brutal Intentions is a standalone MF enemies to lovers romance with forbidden themes, breeding, an age gap, a possessive alphahole and a virgin. Laz is married, and not to the heroine. All characters are over eighteen. The story is dirty and delicious, so please read at your discretion.

Coming September 28 – pre-order now

BEAUTY SO GOLDEN: A REVERSE HAREM RAPUNZEL ROMANCE

You've made it to the Tower. Hope starts here.

These are the words we say to greet the scared, the injured, the hungry, when they finally reach the last safe haven. The Tower is the only refuge from the Blighted plague that has ravaged the land and turned the survivors into flesh-hungry animals.

We are the lucky ones, and everyone else is condemned to die. Mother tells us so.

Then one day comes a dangerous man with brutal brothers who tear these lies apart. Dexer, an adrenaline rush who leaves me breathless. Blaize, who makes my heart pound in crazy ways I never thought possible. Keenan, who fell from grace only to lift me up. They call me Beauty, and I am theirs in a brutal world.

But while the Tower still stands, we're doomed to fall. I've lost so much already, and I won't watch my men die.

This is no fairy tale. This is war.

Author's note: Beauty So Golden is a standalone reverse harem romance based on the fairy tale Rapunzel, in a post-apocalyptic zombie world. The story is dirty and delicious, the guys are dangerous and possessive, and the strong and sweet heroine never has to choose just one man.

Coming January 27 – pre-order now

ALSO BY LILITH VINCENT

Four ruthless men. A virgin mafia princess to unite them. But first, there will be blood.

On my seventeenth birthday, I learn a terrible secret about my family. My future is in the hands of four brutal men, and what awaits me at their hands is too terrible to imagine. Four men who desire me. Four men who vow to possess me. Four men who think they can destroy me.

As the only daughter of Coldlake's mayor, I should be kept far, far out of their reach. Instead, I'm being thrown to them as a sacrifice. My father insists only one of them can marry me, but all of them vow to secure my promise. A promise in blood.

They take. I bleed. Happy birthday to me.

Binge the series now

ABOUT THE AUTHOR

Lilith Vincent is a steamy mafia reverse harem author who believes in living on the wild side! Why choose one when you could choose them all.

Follow Lilith Vincent for news, teasers, and freebies:

TikTok

Instagram

Goodreads

Amazon

Newsletter

Printed in Great Britain
by Amazon